ISABELLE RONIN

 sourcebooks
casablanca

Published by Sourcebooks Casablanca, an imprint of Sourcebooks, Inc.
P.O. Box 4410, Naperville, Illinois 60567-4410
(630) 961-3900
Fax: (630) 961-2168
sourcebooks.com

The author is represented by Wattpad.

Library of Congress Cataloging-in-Publication Data

Names: Ronin, Isabelle, author.
Title: Always Red / Isabelle Ronin.
Description: Naperville, Illinois : Sourcebooks Casablanca, [2017]
Identifiers: LCCN 2017027747 | (softcover : acid-free
  paper)
Subjects: | GSAFD: Love stories.
Classification: LCC PR9199.4.R654 A79 2017 | DDC 813/.6--dc23 LC record
available at https://lccn.loc.gov/2017027747

Printed and bound in the United States of America.
WOZ 10 9 8 7 6 5 4 3 2 1

To Mama and Tatay. For everything.

CHAPTER

Veronica

THIS WAS IT. THIS WAS MY CHANCE TO MAKE THINGS RIGHT.
I just didn't know if I could take it.

Dread and anxiety chilled my spine as I stepped off the
bus. I stood in front of Caleb's apartment building with my
head bowed low, arguing with myself over whether or not
I should go in. It had been a few hours since the fight in
school, since I saw him drive away from the parking lot. It
had been less than twenty-four hours since I packed my bags
and left him.

This had been my home with him...before.

It wasn't anymore.

I knew good things didn't last. Every time something good
happened, something bad followed. Maybe, just maybe, this
time it would be good again.

Last time I entered this building, I had gotten a new phone

for myself and a present for Caleb. Had he seen it yet? Did he keep it or throw it away?

Heart racing, I clasped my hands together and tried not to wring them. Was he home? Would he let me in? What if he refused?

If Caleb rejected me, I didn't know if I could handle it...

You rejected him first. What gives you the right to ask him not to reject you?

Nothing.

Caleb's words burned in my mind. *I want you to fight for me just as I fought for you. But you wouldn't.*

I closed my eyes tightly. It hurt every time I heard his voice in my head. I hadn't been ready to hear everything he had to say before, but I was ready now. Beatrice-Rose said they had kissed and claimed they did more.

Caleb said they didn't sleep together. Now that anger wasn't clouding my thoughts, I realized that he had never lied to me before. If anything, he was too honest. Would he lie about something as serious as this? No, I realized, he wouldn't. And he...he was the only person who never gave up on me.

Don't ask me to let go of you. I can't, he had said.

But did he still want me? Had he let go of me after what I'd done?

My fears were nipping at my heels, waiting to pounce at my slightest weakness. I took a deep breath, pushing away my anxiety.

Gathering my courage, I stepped forward and entered the lobby. And froze. Beatrice-Rose was walking out of the elevator, her steps fast and determined. What was she doing here?

No one was allowed to go up unless the receptionist called

the tenant, and the tenant gave the go-ahead. So Caleb must have given her permission to go up. The thought made me take a step back to hide out of Beatrice-Rose's line of sight.

What if something was going on between them? What if Caleb had given up on me and realized I wasn't worth it?

No, no. Didn't you just say you believed him? You would fight for him?

Damn right I would fight for him.

Maybe Beatrice-Rose was trying to manipulate him again, pretending to be hurt and helpless to get what she wanted. If she tried anything with Caleb, she'd get more than a slap from me this time.

The kiss last night wasn't his fault. It was mine, she had said.

Did he really kiss her? I had to know, and the only person who could tell me was Caleb. I needed to talk to him.

I narrowed my eyes as I watched Beatrice-Rose get into a taxi. She had changed her clothes since I saw her a few hours ago. She wore a white baby-doll dress that ended above her knees. Her blond hair—now lengthened with expensive-looking extensions that bounced against her lower back—was swept off her beautiful face with a red headband. She had exchanged her heels in favor of white flats.

She looked as innocent as a dove. You'd never know that she was a snake behind that beautiful face.

Praying to God that Caleb hadn't removed me from the list of approved visitors who could go straight up, I casually strolled to the elevators, trying to avoid the concierge's hawk eyes. I froze when he spotted me, expecting him to call security to escort me out of the building, but he just smiled. I let out a relieved breath when the elevator doors closed.

As the elevator climbed up, my heart started to race. I felt nervous, my hands clammy and cold as I twisted them together. When the elevator stopped at Caleb's floor, I took a deep calming breath and walked out.

My steps were muffled by the carpet as I neared his door. It was so quiet in the hallway that I could hear my heartbeat in my ears.

Please don't hate me.

I stopped in front of his door, biting my lip. I had gotten used to going in without knocking, but I knew I had lost that privilege now.

Oh God. What if I lose him too?

Slowly, I raised my hand, forming a fist.

Just do it!

I closed my eyes tightly and knocked.

Nothing.

What if the concierge had called him and told him I was on my way, and Caleb didn't want to let me in? He *had* to let me in. He had to listen to me. He had to…

I knocked again. When there was no answer, I ignored the guilt I felt by invading his privacy and entered the code to unlock the door.

Oh God. What if he changed the code?

But the door opened easily.

Swallowing the lump in my throat, I stepped in. It was dark and quiet. I walked to the living room first, passing the couch where Caleb loved to sit and prop his feet on the coffee table. In my mind, I saw him turn his head to look at me.

"What's for dinner, Red?"

I blinked, and he was gone. The blanket he had covered me with the night I left him—which felt like years ago but was unbelievably just last night—was still on the floor where I had dropped it.

Had he not come home yet? Where was he?

I passed the kitchen, smiling sadly when I remembered how he had cooked dinner a long time ago. I had made him wear an apron, and he had pouted while frying potatoes.

"Fries are ready!" he'd declared. "I will call them the Amazing Chef Caleb's fries!"

I'd laughed. He had looked so proud. He'd burned the fries, and they were really salty, but I ate them all.

I miss him. God, I miss him.

Later that day, we'd gone out on the balcony and studied for exams, but Caleb had gotten bored quickly. He'd started playing with my hair, twirling it around his finger and tickling my cheek with it. When I ignored him, he pulled.

"Ouch. What the hell, Caleb!" It hadn't really hurt, but I'd glared at him.

He'd smiled at me cheekily, a naughty gleam in his eyes. Cupping my face, he'd turned me to face him and said, "If you blink, you want me."

"Wait, wait!"

I had laughed and tried to pull away, but he held on to my face. I couldn't help but blink.

"I knew it," he'd teased, grabbing my waist and pulling me onto his lap. "I always knew you had the hots for me, Red."

He'd held on to me so I wouldn't fall off his lap as he leaned forward to reach for my book. "Here, pretend I'm your favorite chair while you read your book."

I'd protested, but inside, I felt giddy. It was hard to concentrate on anything but Caleb when his strong arms were around me, his warmth and his scent filling my senses. He'd held me against him possessively, resting his chin on my shoulder and smelling my hair.

"I met an old friend the other day," he'd said, breaking the silence. "I mentioned that you're my girlfriend, and she said she wants to meet you."

All I could think about was *she*. He'd noticed that I had gotten quiet and changed the subject.

I blinked and pulled myself out of the memory. I realized now that the friend who wanted to meet me was Beatrice-Rose. That was weeks before I met her. So she had probably been scheming even then.

Even before I knocked on his bedroom door and there was no answer, I knew Caleb wasn't home. There was a charge in the air when he was in a room, and I always felt it. But this time, I didn't feel his presence. I felt nothing, just emptiness.

I left the apartment and entered the elevator, wishing for it to descend fast. A quick check on my phone told me the bus was due in ten minutes, the next one in two hours. It took at least twenty minutes to walk to the closest bus stop, and there was no way I could make it. Maybe if I ran really fast…

I stepped out of the elevator and was reminded of Beatrice-Rose doing the same thing a few minutes ago. Had Caleb gone out with her? I didn't see him with her in the lobby, but his car was in the garage basement and he would have taken the back exit. I saw her take the taxi, though, and if they were going out, Caleb would have given her a ride. I shook my head to clear my thoughts.

I need to find him.

I ran outside, almost tripping in my rush. I had to catch that bus.

I startled as a car behind me tooted its horn. I turned around and found Kara inside her car grinning at me. When she'd texted earlier, I'd told her I'd be at Caleb's. Grateful and surprised that she'd come to pick me up, I felt tears prick my eyes as I walked toward her.

"He's not home," I told her, feeling dejected as I climbed into the passenger seat.

Kara let out a loud sigh. "Well, hop in, girlfriend. Detective Kar has all the skills you need."

I grinned. I loved my best friend.

CHAPTER

Veronica

KARA STARTED THE CAR, REVERSING SO QUICKLY THAT I GRABBED on to my seat belt. "Did you call him?" she asked.

"I-I can't. What if he doesn't want to talk to me?"

She stepped on the brakes, turning to look at me like I just spilled my brains on the floor of her car. "What?"

"I can't."

"Pussy," she clucked. She held out her hand, palm up. "Give me your phone."

"Kar, no. I can't explain it, okay? I-I don't want to call him. I don't want to know."

"Know what?"

"That…that he doesn't want me. What if he doesn't answer? Or what if he does and then he hangs up? If there's a way that I can postpone it… It's ridiculous. I know. Don't you think I know that? I can't explain it." I was going to pull my hair out anytime now.

"You're fucking crazy, Ver, but you're lucky because I am too. All right. I'm sure Caleb's at Cameron's place. I mean, those two are practically married. No offense," she added.

I wanted to say "none taken," but I was a nervous wreck. Caleb.

What if he doesn't want to see me?

Oh God.

"You okay there, sweetie?" Kara asked after a moment.

My heart was beating madly in my chest, my hands shaking with trepidation. Without warning, a whimper escaped my throat.

Kara let out a sigh and grabbed my hand, squeezing it. "You can do this. You want him back, don't you?"

The fear and nerves were wreaking havoc in my stomach and climbing up my throat. I felt choked up. I nodded.

"How much?"

"I… Very much," I sobbed. "I want him back very much."

She gave an approving nod. "Good. Make sure you tell him that. I mean, it's Lockhart. The guy would probably cut off his balls for you if you asked."

But I knew that feelings changed in the blink of an eye. What if his had? I wasn't an easy person to care for, and I tended to push away the people who tried to get close. I guessed a big part of me had been waiting for Caleb to disappoint me. Everyone in my life had. A long habit of being distrustful was hard to break…but I would for Caleb.

"All right, we're here," Kara said as she parked across from Cameron's place.

Sweat trickled down the side of my face, and I quickly wiped it away.

"Are you sure you don't want to go back to the apartment and change? I can do your makeup for you."

I shook my head. "I'm okay, Kar. Thanks."

She shrugged. "All I'm saying is that the hotter you look, the more he can't refuse. Boys are visual creatures, okay? They think with their dicks. It's not their fault; it's just the way they're made," she babbled on. "I mean, the more ammunition, the better, right?"

Oh God.

"Ver? Ver." She was snapping her fingers in my face. "Geez. Are you sure you can do this?"

I nodded.

"I'd go with you, but you know." She shrugged. "The devil lives in that house."

I nodded again. She gave me a pat on the back and pushed me out of the car. My legs felt wobbly as I walked to the door, my hand trembling as I rang the doorbell.

Cameron opened the door, surprise on his handsome face. "Hello."

"H-hi. I'm—"

"Veronica. Yeah, Caleb told me who you are. I don't think we've been properly introduced." He gave me a kind smile and offered his hand. "Cameron."

I shook his hand. "I know. Kar's waiting for me in the car."

His eyes snapped behind me, searching for Kara. I knew that look; I'd seen it in Caleb's eyes too.

"How is..." He looked torn. "Would you like to come in?"

I shook my head. "Is Caleb here?"

He pressed his lips together. "He left a couple hours ago."

I swallowed my disappointment. "Oh. Did...did he say where he's going?"

"He went to his family's cabin. It's a five-hour drive out of the city." Cameron's ice-blue eyes were piercing as he studied my face. "He's staying there for a week."

"A...week?"

He nodded, crossing his arms as he leaned his side against the doorjamb. "Why did you come here?"

"I...came to get him back."

He smiled. "He cares for you more than he has for anyone. I've never seen him like this before."

My chest tightened.

"Listen," he started, his eyes narrowing, "he fell asleep and dreamed about you. When he woke up, Beatrice-Rose was on top of him, kissing him."

I gasped in horror. That was what Caleb was trying to tell me, and I had refused to listen to him because I was too stubborn, too afraid to trust.

"Caleb always sees the good in people; it's his weakness. And I've seen Beatrice-Rose take advantage of that." Cameron straightened and slipped his hands in his pockets. His eyes briefly darted behind me again.

"But when he tells you nothing happened, nothing happened. If you know Caleb, and I think you do, you know he's too honest for his own good."

"I need to apologize to him. I–I want him back."

"He thinks you don't. He thinks you hate him and that you'd left with Damon. Maybe you both need some time to cool off." He let out a sigh. "She was here too."

I frowned. "Who?"

"Beatrice-Rose. She was here looking for Caleb just an hour ago."

My eyes widened in alarm, and I looked at him questioningly.

"No, I didn't tell her where he is," Cameron said, smiling.

I gave him a watery smile in return.

"Will you"—he looked at Kara again, then back to me—"take care of her for me?"

I nodded, because he had taken care of Caleb for me. Because I could see how much he cared for Kara and how much he hurt.

I understood him. Even though I didn't know his reasons, I understood there were inner demons that prevented us from being with the person we wanted most.

I knew that very well.

When I got back in the car, I told Kara what Cameron had told me.

"Beatrice-Rose is like that evil spirit in *The Grudge*, you know? That ugly, scary mofo who follows people around? There was this one scene where she chased what's-her-name—that chick who played Buffy the vampire slayer? Have you seen that movie? Poor girl fell from the hospital building. Ugh. Beatch is exactly that evil spirit."

Do you like scary movies? We should watch scary movies together. I have a list… In my mind, I saw Caleb's handsome, smiling face asking me those questions as we sat in his car. I shook my head, trying to erase the memory.

"Do you want to go to the cabin? I'll drive you, but you have to get the address from Cameron."

My eyes welled up with tears. I was so emotional that I didn't recognize myself. I'd gone from having no constant in my life to having Kara.

I'd had Caleb too…but I was on the verge of losing him. He was changing me. He *had* changed me.

"Oh, Ver. Come here," Kara soothed, pulling me to her.

"He left. Caleb left me."

She rubbed my back. "Well, you hurt him pretty bad, sweetie. You were such a dick to him," she said after a moment. "You accused him of cheating, but cheating requires consent from both partners. Believe me, *I know*. He was a good friend who wanted to help Beatrice-Rose, but he was really stupid for lying in that bed with her. I mean, come on, Caleb—*really*? If you did that shit with another guy, he'd bust a nut."

I half choked and half laughed. Count on Kara to be blunt—and right.

Her tone turned serious. "You're my friend, Veronica, and I love you. I know you've got daddy issues and a whole buttload of other issues, but if you let them control you, you're going to lose Caleb.

"Do you want to hold on to your baggage or hold on to him? You know when they say 'If you love someone, let them go'—'or set them free' or whatever bullshit they cooked up to put on their damned meme? Fuck that. If I love someone, I'm going to hold on with both of my hands. My feet—hell, my teeth too. That ship ain't gonna sail without me."

She had a point, but I grew up in a family where I'd learned at a young age that staying with and fighting for a person could be toxic. Sometimes it was better to let go.

But Caleb was different. He had always been good to me. Losing him was what it took for me to realize that.

"He's a guy, Ver, and you kind of kicked his balls to the curb. So he just needs to feel like a man again. You know, clear his head, drink booze, not shower for days. Disgusting guy stuff. But if you want, we can still drive there."

I shook my head. "Not tonight, Kar. I don't think...I don't think he wants to see me. I'll wait till he comes back. He's coming back, right? He has to come back."

"Of course he will, stupid." She paused. "Know what? You need to get out of this funk you're in. I'm going to text Beth and see if she'll meet us at the coffee shop."

"Kar, I want to go home."

She patted my shoulder. "Well, that's too bad, isn't it?"

Ten minutes later, the aromatic smell of coffee and freshly baked bread greeted my nostrils as we entered the little coffee shop. My stomach rumbled, and I realized I hadn't eaten since morning. Kara's sandwich was still in my bag.

The coffee shop was only occupied by a few patrons, mostly college students since it was close to the school. An older lady with a big yellow Labrador was trying to sit in a booth, but her dress was caught on the side of the seat. She was wearing shades and holding a white cane to help balance herself.

"Hello," I said softly. "I'm just going to help you here a bit. Your dress is caught on the seat."

"Oh, thank you, young lady."

"You're welcome. You have a beautiful dog." I crouched in front of the dog, scratching her chin.

"Yes, she is. This is Catnip right here. My granddaughter named her."

I chuckled. "Hello, Catnip."

Catnip gave me a friendly grin and bumped her nose on my arm.

"Beth's not here yet. Let's sit here," Kara called out, choosing a seat near the window where there was a view of the airport.

It was getting dark, and the yellow and red runway lights flickered like a blazing fire.

"I'll get us some drinks," I said. "Chocolate milk shake?"

"Yup. With whipped cre—motherfucker."

I looked up in alarm and turned my head to where Kara was glaring.

"She's here," Kara snarled.

I looked over. Beatrice-Rose and Justin were seated at a table in the back of the café, talking quietly with their heads close together as if plotting something evil.

Beatrice-Rose was just everywhere today.

"Let's sit close to them. Come on."

"No. *Kar!*" But it was no use—she was already up and moving. "Kara! Come back here!" I hissed.

Kara sat at the table behind the older lady and Catnip, perfectly angled so Beatrice-Rose and Justin wouldn't spot us unless they turned their heads. I glared at Kara as I sat down across from her.

She grinned, and I grinned back because it was genius. I couldn't really hear what Beatrice-Rose and Justin were talking about, and I almost giggled because Kara was making gagging faces. But when I flicked my eyes toward Beatrice-Rose, my heart jumped into my throat.

There, around her forefinger, was the key chain I'd given Caleb as a present. She was twirling it.

My blood boiled. I wasn't even aware of what I was doing when I got up and marched toward her.

"Where the hell did you get that?" I demanded.

Beatrice-Rose's eyes widened in fear for a brief second before she hid the emotion and replaced it with disdain.

"Hi, Veronica," she said, smirking.

"Stop with the pretending. I'm getting sick of it." My eyes darted to Justin as he leaned back in his seat. He crossed his arms across his chest and grinned like he was ready for a show. His attitude made me sick to my stomach.

"Where did you get that key chain?" I asked again.

"This?" She raised her eyebrows in innocence. "Justin bought it for me."

Justin had a foul smile on his face. "Yep. I did. Cheapest shit I ever bought."

"You're lying."

"I don't know why you keep throwing these accusations at me," Beatrice-Rose said. "Frankly, I'm the one getting sick of you and your accusations. You're imagining things. I am trying to be patient and understanding with you, Veronica, but you make it so hard. And now you're accusing me of what? Stealing?"

"It's not any better than kissing a guy without his consent while he's asleep," I said coolly.

She paled.

"I saw you at Caleb's place a few hours ago," I added. "What were you doing there?"

I wasn't going to play her game. She was a professional liar and a great actress, but her face was getting splotchy and anger filled her eyes.

"Did you go up to his apartment and steal that?" I gestured at the key chain. "Did you force your way into someplace where you're obviously not wanted?"

"You bitch!" she shrilled. She stood up just as the server was delivering her coffee and cried out in anger as the coffee spilled on her white dress.

Kara laughed behind me.

"Fuck!" Beatrice-Rose screamed. Her eyes were wild as they zeroed in on me. When I saw her raise her hand, I took a step back, but she lunged at me.

"I'm the one he loves!" she spat out. "Me!"

I held her off as she threw her weight on me, trying to claw at my face. I would have fallen on the floor, but instinct made me step to the side, widening my stance for support, and I was able to push her past me instead and let gravity do the rest.

The low growling made me spin around. Beatrice-Rose was sprawled on the floor, her eyes wide with fear as she slowly got on all fours. Catnip was crouched low so that her eyes were level with Beatrice-Rose's, sharp canine teeth bared and ready to rip skin.

"If this dog attacks me, I will sue you, you blind hag. And this fucking coffee shop! Get it the hell away from me!" she shouted.

All bets were off now that Beatrice-Rose was showing her true self. So far from the sweet and vulnerable persona she had going the first time we met.

"You're so pathetic. I feel nothing but sorry for you," I said.

Kara came up beside me, placing her hand on my shoulder. She peered down at Beatrice-Rose. "Wow. You're really embarrassing yourself."

The older lady pulled Catnip back. The dog calmed down, but her eyes were trained on Beatrice-Rose, ready to attack if needed.

Beatrice-Rose got up, brushing away the hair that had fallen across her face, her extensions barely hanging on her hair. One plopped onto the floor. Her eyes widened in embarrassment as she kicked it away.

"I'm going to sue you!" she spat at me.

"For what? For attacking me?" I nodded at the small audience surrounding us. "We have at least five witnesses who saw everything."

Kara snorted beside me. Beatrice-Rose narrowed her eyes at her. I could almost see the wheels whirling in her devious mind.

"You're vulgar and cheap. I always wondered what Cameron saw in you."

"Oh my God, Beatrice-Rose!" Kara exclaimed, her eyes wide as she held her hands up. "Surprise me once in your life, will you? Say something intelligent. Oh wait, I forgot. Ask me if I give a flying fuck first." She raised an eyebrow. "That's right, I don't."

Beatrice-Rose sneered at Kara. Her head jerked toward

Justin, motioning with her chin. Justin sighed and got up. He took a threatening step toward Kara.

Before he could do anything, I got in his face. "Do you want me to beat you up again? Because this time I'll aim lower."

Justin turned red. I knew he was going to hit me even before he raised his fist, but he froze. I felt someone approach from behind me.

Theo. He positioned himself protectively in front of me. I turned my head and spotted Beth beside me, offering moral support. Her blue hair and mismatched eyes winking at me. I felt my heart expand as if it would burst with happiness. They were here for me, here to support me. Touched, I blinked back my tears.

Theo didn't say anything, just looked tall and intimidating and big enough to beat the hell out of Justin. He crossed his arms, his head turned down as he glared at Justin.

Justin backed away. "I wasn't doing anything, man."

"Leave," Theo whispered dangerously.

Justin held his hands up, grabbed his drink, and walked away. Beatrice-Rose looked from us to him, then back to us. She had a look of hate on her face.

"This isn't over," she warned before grabbing her purse from her seat and walking away.

"Bye, bitch. I hope your favorite dessert is disappointment because that's what you'll be having for a while," Kara singsonged.

When Beatrice-Rose was gone, Kara and Beth opened their arms to me. I swallowed a sob-hiccup and happily joined the group hug. Theo cleared his throat and awkwardly patted our backs.

I let out a contented sigh.

CHAPTER

three

Veronica

IT HAD BEEN A WEEK SINCE I LAST SAW CALEB. A WEEK OF TORTURE. A week of unsent texts and canceled phone calls. A week of mostly sleepless nights. The sleep I managed to get only lasted a few hours and was fitful and disrupted by nightmares. I'd wake up more exhausted than when I went to bed.

I often dreamed about Caleb asking me to fight for him, to run after him, but when I did, I never seemed to reach him. He always vanished whenever I got close.

I missed him.

People always say you never know how much a person means to you until they're gone. My mom had passed away, but I had always known what she meant to me. Caleb, though... I didn't know he was such a big part of my life until he was gone.

Almost every day after Caleb left, Beth, Theo, and sometimes even Damon came over to hang out at Kara's. I didn't know how

Damon had eased in, but he was now a part of the group. It touched me how supportive they were. I'd never had real friends before.

I worked almost every day at the garage that week and was surprised to find Damon working there one day.

I looked up when he approached my desk and handed me the keys to a truck he had finished working on. He didn't offer an explanation, just winked at me and swaggered away.

"Yeah, he comes and goes. He helps out when he's back in town to visit his mom," Kara explained when I asked her about it.

"I think I was ten when I met Damon. He was a few years older, this French boy who spoke English so perfectly. I mean, every word that came out of his mouth sounded so precise, like he had practiced saying every English word in the dictionary, you know? He was so damn cute. I had a crush on him then, of course. Everyone did.

"His dad passed away. His mom's Canadian, so she moved them here from France to live with her sister. Then his mom worked for my dad at the garage. She'd bring Damon along with her or he'd come here after school, so we grew up together. My dad just sort of adopted him. He's a drifter, though. I mean, he never stays in one place, but he always comes back here.

"By the way, Ver, Damon works at this bar downtown, and we both know the owner. I help them out now and then—waitressing and whatnot—and I'm supposed to cover a shift this week, but...something came up. Would you be able to cover for me?" She batted her eyelashes at me, pouting her lips like a duck.

"Um…"

"You don't have to mix drinks. You just have to take orders

from assholes, deliver their drinks, bus tables, maybe wash dishes.
That kind of thing. I'll give you my firstborn unicorn child as
payment. Plus, the tips are huge."

I agreed to do it.

The last time I was in a bar was when I first met Caleb. Now,
as I stood in this bustling nightclub, I remembered that night.
The way his eyes watched me intently, as if I were the only one
in the room. The confidence he exuded when he wrapped his
arms around my waist, and the almost comical look of shock on
his face when I rejected him.

I should stop thinking about him and concentrate on work.
I had served in a restaurant and a bar before, but this one was
busier, and Kara was right—the tips were huge. Maybe I could
apply for a casual position here, as long as it didn't clash with my
schedule at the garage and school.

Damon was on the stage, sitting on a stool with his guitar
propped on his knee. He seemed very comfortable up there, as
if he'd been performing his whole life. He looked the attractive
musician that he was with his black fedora, dark-blue plaid shirt,
jeans, and faded Converse shoes. His rings and silver crucifix
necklace winked in the light as he strummed his guitar.

A group of girls sat in front of him, giggling and whispering
to each other as they stared up at him. Damon winked at me,
and I rolled my eyes in humor.

Tapping his foot as he plucked his guitar, he started to sing
"Here without You" by 3 Doors Down.

I loved this song. Humming under my breath, I turned to take orders from the new group that had just come in. There were at least ten of them, and they were already seated.

My steps faltered, and for a split second, my heart stopped beating as I saw Caleb enter.

I drank in the sight of him: his beautiful face, the way he walked and held himself. His eyes looked dark and sad, his jaw unshaven. He wore a black shirt under a faded blue denim jacket with the sleeves rolled up, exposing the tight lines of his forearms. He had a backpack slung over his shoulder, and his long legs clad in dark jeans and black boots strode confidently through the club. He looked bored as he raked a hand through his hair.

Time stood still as I stared at him, my heart pounding, ringing in my ears as I waited...waited...

Please look at me.

And then he did.

My breath stopped as his eyes met mine, but whatever hope I had in my heart vanished like smoke as I realized his eyes held no recognition.

As if he didn't even know me.

As if I were a stranger to him.

He had written me off.

It felt like someone had ripped my heart right out of my chest. I heard my breathing, loud and shaky, and I realized that I was trembling. My legs felt like they were going to give out under me, so I held on to the table for support.

"You okay, luv?"

I nodded at Crystal, one of the nice servers at the club I had met earlier today.

"You sure? You've got a huge crowd at table six. Do you want me to take over?"

I watched as Caleb sat at table six with the big crowd that had just come in. I shook my head at her.

"I'm okay, Crys. Thanks."

"All right. Holler if you need anything."

I straightened up and pulled my shoulders back, even as tears pricked my eyes.

I'm strong. I've always been strong. I can do this.

"Hi. I'm Veronica, and I'll be your server tonight. Can I start you off with something to drink?"

I watched as one of the girls in the group got up and sashayed toward the guy sitting beside Caleb. She bent down and whispered something to the guy, flicking her blond hair over her shoulder as she eyed Caleb like a piece of candy. The guy grinned at her and stood up, offering her his seat. She winked at him in thanks and moved the chair closer to Caleb before sitting down.

I glanced at Caleb. He leaned back in his chair, his arms on the table as he stared at his watch. I noticed that his hands, clad in black motorcycle gloves, were formed into fists. His jaw was hard. I realized he was trying not to look at me.

"There you are, final—Hey, sweetheart, it's you!"

My head quickly turned at the familiar, obnoxious voice. It was Justin. I was so focused on Caleb that I hadn't noticed him.

"Yo, dude, Caleb! Your ex is here!" Justin hollered across the table.

I gasped as Caleb pushed the table with force, rising to his feet. "Shut the fuck up," he whispered, a warning in his tone.

The group fell silent.

And then Caleb turned and walked toward the exit.

"Excuse me," I choked out and fled the scene.

My hands shook as I took off my apron and went to the back. Relieved to find Crystal there, I told her I needed fresh air and asked if she could take care of table six for me. She looked at me with sympathy and told me to take fifteen.

I ran to the back exit off the kitchen, cupping my mouth with both my hands to keep my whimpers from escaping. I sat on the ground, burying my face in my arms as I cried. When I heard the door open, I didn't stop. I couldn't.

"Hey, Angel Face."

I sobbed.

"Hey, come on now. It's okay."

I felt Damon's arm around my shoulders, awkwardly patting my back. I let out a few breaths and calmed myself, wiping my cheeks with my hands.

"He was inside," I told him.

"I know. I saw."

"He looked at me like I was a stranger. He hates me. I…" My voice trailed off as I saw a figure walk in front of us.

The back door faced the bar's parking lot. And there in front of us stood Caleb. He looked at us for a moment, his gaze lingering on Damon's arm around my shoulders before he walked away.

I stood up, taking a few steps toward him. "Caleb."

He paused, standing in the dark as he waited for me to speak.

I opened my mouth, but nothing came out. I held my breath when, finally, he turned around to face me.

"Having fun?" he asked, his face devoid of any emotion.

Oh, Caleb.

"No."

I wanted to run to him, to beg him to take me back, but he was so cold now. He had never looked at me like that before.

It stopped me like a blow to the heart. And I just…froze. The words that I had practiced over and over melted on my tongue. Nothing came out.

"I'll see you around. Veronica."

I watched him get on his motorcycle. He revved the engine angrily, once, twice. He stayed there for a few moments, as if he was waiting for something. He rubbed his face with his hand, put on his helmet, and then drove away.

I broke down.

When the knock sounded on the door, I grabbed my blanket and covered myself, pretending to sleep. Just as I had expected, the door opened.

"I know you're still up."

It was Damon. He held two steaming mugs in his hands.

"I have hot chocolate. Kar said you have to drink it or she will pour it down my throat."

I sighed. I pushed off my covers and sat up, not meeting his eyes. He came into the room and handed a mug to me. "Here." He sat on the floor, leaning against my bed.

"Thanks." The mug was piping hot, but I took a sip of the scalding chocolate anyway.

"I don't know how you do that without blowing on it first. You just...drink it like that?"

I shrugged, then remembered he wasn't facing me. "Yes. I don't like it lukewarm," I answered. "I've always liked it really hot."

He shivered. "So you must like the feeling on your tongue when it gets burned. You know, that sort of dry, sore feeling, like a bunch of needles are pricking it?"

"Not really," I replied. "But the pain's worth it."

He nodded. Silence filled the room, but we were both comfortable with each other's company now.

"If something is really good, the pain is worth it, yes?" he asked.

I inhaled sharply. I knew where this was going. I had been forcing myself to not think about what happened tonight. If I did...

"Angel Face," he started, looking up at me with serious big, blue eyes. "I'm sorry for what happened tonight."

Every time I remembered the cold look in Caleb's eyes, I wanted to scream and cry.

"Don't blame yourself for everything. Look. I don't blame you for how you reacted that night when you left him. Lockhart had a friend who needed him that night, but he also had a girlfriend waiting for him at home. I know what you're thinking. If you can't trust him to do the right thing in a situation like that, then how can you trust him in worse situations?"

Damon let out a loud sigh and continued. "Are you supposed

to ignore your feelings, keep them inside just because you don't want to lose him? Girl, I tell you." He blew on his drink, then took a small sip. "If you do that, you're going to start resenting him, and it will destroy your relationship."

He bowed his head. When he spoke again, his voice was thicker. "Everyone has fears they keep tightly locked inside themselves." He turned to look at me now, searching my face. "But that doesn't make you weak. We judge ourselves too easily when we do something wrong, but you know what's the most important thing?"

I shook my head, and he gave me a soft smile. "It is how you get up after you've fallen. How you fix things and how you still find the courage to keep fighting, even after you have been hurt. How you face the wrong things you have done and make them right again. Yes?"

I nodded.

He stood up and tucked a strand of my hair behind my ear.

"Pretty Angel Face. You feel guilty for hurting him, and that's okay. But don't give up yet. Don't forget all the good things you shared together because someone has tried to break you apart. He's hurt. And he might have the wrong idea about you and me after tonight. I can talk to him if you like. But he needs you. Go to him."

I followed him with my eyes as he walked to my door. "Good night, Angel Face. Sweet dreams," he said softly. Then closed the door as he left.

CHAPTER

Veronica

I RESTED MY ARM ON MY FOREHEAD, COVERING MY EYES FROM THE sun. Thick white clouds floated in and out of my sight. I could smell the green grass, feel the coolness of the ground beneath my body.

Letting out a sigh, I closed my eyes. Perfect time to nap. I should feel content. It was a beautiful day, after all.

But my heart hurt.

I felt something beside me, but I didn't move.

"Hey, Red. Why so serious?"

My eyes snapped open. Heart beating madly, I turned my head. "Caleb?"

He was lying beside me on the grass. His eyes, clear and so green, gazed at me with that familiar naughty glint. His hair, bronze and thick, glinted in the sunlight. The wind picked up, and a lock of his hair fell, covering one of his eyes. He smiled.

"Hi, Red."

I held my breath, my hand slowly reaching out to smooth the hair from his face.

"You're here," I choked.

"I never left." He covered my hand with his, pressing it to his cheek. "I'm waiting for you."

He leaned his face closer to mine and licked my cheek. And then my nose. And the rest of my face.

What the hell?

"*Woof! Woof! Woof!*"

"Burp! Oh, come on! How many times are we going to have this discussion? You do not wake people up. Especially pretty girls you have never met before."

Damon?

I suddenly became aware of a heavy weight on top of me. When I opened my eyes, a goofy-looking white Lab blinked at me happily, pink tongue licking my face.

"*Woof!*"

"All right, that's it!" Damon scolded, sounding embarrassed.

The dog disappeared. Wiping the dog drool from my face, I sat up.

"I'm sorry. This is Burp, by the way. My mom's dog." Damon looked apologetic. He held the Lab at the foot of my bed, while the dog whined and gave me sad eyes. "He knows how to open doors and loves to wake people in the morning. It's kind of his thing." Damon shrugged apologetically. "He just woke up Kar."

Uh-oh.

I heard the clanging of pans and swearing in the kitchen. Apparently, Kara wasn't a morning person when woken up by a dog. Damon winced, looking a little scared.

"Well, I better go before Kar blows up." He pulled Burp to the door. "My mom baked croissants this morning and asked me to drop them off for you and Kar. I'm really sorry about Burp."

I raked my fingers through my hair, catching a knot. "Thanks, Damon. Nice meeting you, Burp. I can't believe you named him Burp."

Burp barked happily when he heard his name.

"I was going to name him Fart."

I chuckled. "Really? Why am I not surprised?"

He rubbed the tip of his nose with his thumb, grinning. "How are you?"

"I'm okay, Damon. Thank you. Really."

He nodded. "Let me know if you need anything. Let's go, Burp."

The dog plopped on the floor, refusing to move. I smiled as I watched Damon shake his head, nudging Burp through the door.

When they left, I dropped back on my bed, letting out a long sigh. I felt guilty dragging Damon into my mess when he was just being a good friend.

Another dream of Caleb. Another piercing stab in the chest.

Today. I will talk to him today.

Easier said than done, I reflected, my chest tightening at the memory of Caleb's cold eyes. Forcing myself to stop thinking about it, I climbed out of bed and followed the smell of coffee and the mouthwatering aroma of freshly baked bread to the kitchen. I usually woke up hungry, but this morning I had no appetite.

I found Kara in the kitchen, pouring coffee into a mug.

"Good morning," I greeted her, walking to the cupboard to grab a mug.

Kara was usually grumpy or quiet in the mornings, replying in snarls or grunts and monosyllables until she had a few hits of caffeine. After getting her fix, she'd be a flurry of energy.

She grunted, looking sleepy and irritated as she stood in front of the sink and stared out the window. She sipped her coffee quietly.

"I met Burp," I said.

"Uh."

I poured hot water in my mug, dumping a green tea bag into it. "How did those two get in?"

"Huh."

I waited. It usually took two cups of coffee for her to wake up. I smiled to myself as I watched her blink, the glaze of sleepiness and irritation in her eyes disappearing as the caffeine woke her system. This must have been her second cup. "Damon knows where I keep the key to the apartment," she replied.

"He does?"

"Uh-huh."

"Why?"

I probably shouldn't have asked. It was none of my business, but I wanted to focus on something else besides Caleb. I would go crazy if I didn't.

"Why? This"—she waved a croissant in my face—"this is one of the many reasons." She took a bite, moaning. "God. Antoinette's croissants give me a foodgasm every time. Have one."

I shook my head. "I'm not hungry."

She narrowed her eyes. "You're always hungry in the morning. Oh no, don't tell me you had a nightmare about Beatrice-Rose."

I wish. It would be better if my nightmares were about her. At least I wouldn't have this gaping hole in my chest every time I woke up.

I didn't answer.

"You know, Ver, I've been thinking. Beatrice-Rose kind of smells like a toilet," Kara mused. "A toilet that didn't completely flush."

I chuckled.

"You know, I'm all about you and Caleb making babies, but come on! Tonight is your exam, isn't it? Did you study?"

"I'll review more today."

"Professor Layton doesn't give extra credit or projects. You know that. You can't fail this exam. It's 50 percent of your grade," she lectured.

I watched as she swallowed the last of her croissant, pulled out Pop-Tarts from the cupboard, and tossed them in the microwave.

"Hey, maybe you can be a stripper if you quit school. That's not a bad idea. Strippers make loads of money. I can be your pimp. Sixty forty? That's not a bad deal. I'll help you come up with a name. Hmm...let's see."

When only two seconds remained on the microwave timer, Kara pulled it open. It drove her crazy to hear the beeps.

"How about Lolita? Strippers don't have last names, right? How's Felicia?" she continued.

When I didn't answer, she walked toward me and covered my hand with hers. "Ver," she said, her eyes full of sympathy.

I felt like crying again.

"If I decide to become a stripper, you can manage my schedule. I promise." I gave her a reassuring smile. "I have to study, so I'll see you later, okay?" I squeezed her hand and headed back to my room.

I forced myself to review for a couple hours, not really absorbing anything. I took a quick shower, blow-drying my hair and taking the time to apply makeup. Powder, mascara, and lip gloss—check. Red tank top and favorite jeans that made my butt look extra sexy—check.

I was going to Caleb's apartment, and assuming that since he was back in town, he would be attending his classes again. I'd wait for him there. Glancing at the clock, I noted that it was almost ten. I knew his class was usually over at twelve today. If I left now, I would get to his apartment before he did.

He might not feel the same way about me anymore, but I'd find a way to make it up to him. And if he still didn't want me back…I'd know at least I tried. At least I showed him how much I wanted him back in my life, that I was willing to fight for him. Even if I was too late.

Because he was worth it.

I was a mess when I got to his apartment. I knocked, and I wasn't surprised when there was no answer. I wouldn't dare go in after what happened last night. I had hurt him, enough that he wouldn't show an ounce of emotion toward me. Caleb was never one to keep his emotions inside, but last night he had.

Maybe he really doesn't feel anything for you anymore.

No, no. That wasn't true. He still felt something for me. I knew it. I had to believe that he still did.

I leaned against the wall outside his door, sliding down and sitting on the carpet. And waited.

One hour passed. Two, three, four.

He wasn't coming.

I felt the threat of tears. Pulling my legs against my chest, I pillowed my face on my folded arms.

Why didn't I just call him? Or text him? I was so stupid...but every time I dialed his number or started texting him, I couldn't follow through.

I wanted to talk to him in person. I wanted him to know how important he was to me. I wanted to see his face. I had seen my mom cry over the phone, begging my dad to come back so many times. So many damn times I had lost count.

Suddenly, I looked up and saw the blinking light on the elevator screen, indicating that it was moving up.

I held my breath. My heart pounded against my chest as my gaze focused on those doors. And then they opened.

Caleb was leaning against the wall of the elevator, looking up at the ceiling. He looked exhausted...defeated. My heart constricted in my chest. I wanted to run to him, to pull him against me and never let go.

And then he straightened and stepped out.

His steps faltered when he saw me.

I held my breath, waiting...waiting...

Please...

He stared at me, his eyes intense as he took a step forward.

And then he was walking fast toward me. I couldn't move. All I could do was wait for him. He stopped an arm's length away.

We stared at each other.

"Red," he whispered.

I cried. And then suddenly, he was shaking me.

"Miss, are you okay?"

I blinked up and saw Paul's kind face staring down at me.

Another dream.

This was hell.

"What are you doing in the hallway, miss?"

I swallowed my nerves. I couldn't tell him that I didn't live in the apartment anymore because he might kick me out. I was sure Caleb hadn't told them about the change in my living arrangements yet.

"Oh. I was just waiting for Caleb."

He looked at me like my head was leaking beer, but he didn't comment. I could hear him muttering as he walked back to the elevators. Before he disappeared, I heard the words *cuckoo* and *crazy pills*.

Feeling embarrassed, I pushed up from the floor. It was almost three o'clock, and if I didn't leave now, I would miss my exam. I would just have to come back to see Caleb.

Where was he?

I was huffing and puffing by the time I reached the floor where the exams were being held. I had less than five minutes before the doors to the exam room closed. I half walked and half ran, suddenly stopping in my tracks when I saw Caleb in front of me.

This wasn't a dream anymore, was it?

He saw me at the same time. He was wearing his red jersey. Even from a few feet away, I could see the sweat glistening on his face, on his sculpted arms. He stood in front of a drinking fountain, his arm on his mouth like he had been wiping it but froze at the sight of me.

I stared at him.

He stared at me.

Time stood still.

And then I saw it.

The hurt in his eyes.

Oh, Caleb. I'm so sorry.

"I'm going to close these doors in ten seconds, Ms. Strafford. Are you coming in or not?" Professor Layton's voice echoed in the hallway.

Caleb's arm fell to his side. He turned his gaze away and started walking toward me.

I stood frozen in my spot, holding my breath.

And then…he walked past me.

I felt light-headed as I exited the exam room. I had no idea if I'd passed, and I'd felt like crying during all three hours of it.

Was Caleb still here?

I had to check. Taking a deep, calming breath, I headed to the gym. The exam had been three hours, and it was dark outside now. The hallways were silent as a tomb, cold even, and it must have been colder outside. My steps echoed in the long, deserted hallway.

I was so lost in thought that I didn't notice the two guys walking close behind me. I inhaled sharply, feeling scared and angry. I stopped, looked behind me, and glared at them.

"What do you want?" I demanded.

They stopped, looking surprised—at my acknowledgment or hostility, I wasn't sure. One of them was tall, with a medium build, while the other was short but wide and heavily muscled. If I tried to run, they would just catch me. I reached for the knife in my pocket, gripping it just in case. The short guy smiled at me, handing me a piece of paper.

"How much? Call me tonight, babe."

And then they left.

What the hell?

I narrowed my eyes as I watched them suspiciously. When they disappeared, I opened the note and found a name and phone number scrawled on it. I crumpled it and threw it in the trash.

I felt discouraged when I saw the dark and empty gym. Maybe Caleb was back at the apartment now. It was past seven o'clock, but I knew he would still be up. He usually went to sleep late.

The wind picked up as I trudged to the bus stop. Three guys stood inside the bus shelter smoking, so I didn't go in. They should know better than to smoke inside it, let alone on school premises.

"Hey, babe. Heard you like it rough," I heard one say.

I frowned. Surely he wasn't talking to me.

"How much for a night? I love that picture of you, although it would have been better with you naked, wouldn't it?"

What?

Before I had a chance to turn around and make sure he wasn't talking to me, the bus arrived. I dismissed them and boarded the bus. It would take me an hour to get to Caleb's.

It doesn't matter. I can't stand Caleb feeling hurt anymore.

Any fear that he had no feelings for me had been erased when I saw the look of hurt in his eyes as he stood in the hallway. When I got to Caleb's building, Paul shook his head at me.

"He's not back yet, miss."

I swallowed my disappointment. "Thanks, Paul."

He nodded at me, looking at me with sympathy. Feeling dejected, I wondered if I should go up and wait for Caleb in his apartment. Or would he be angry that I had invaded his space after what I'd done?

When I reached his apartment door, I debated whether I should enter his access code or wait outside. It was probably better to wait outside. I slid against the wall and sat on the carpet.

Then the elevator doors opened. I froze. Just like my dream, I thought, my heart pounding. But this time, it wasn't a dream.

I turned my head, feeling disappointed as I watched a beautiful woman walk out of the elevator. She wore a peach-colored dress and an expensive coat. Her high heels didn't make a sound as she walked like a queen through the carpeted hallway. Her hair, bronze and shiny, was tucked in a chignon.

Could she be the tenant who lived across the hall from Caleb? But when she walked closer, I realized she looked familiar. Caleb had shown me a photo of her on his phone once.

Caleb's mom.

Oh my God.

I remembered Caleb mentioning he would take me out to dinner to meet his mom. But that wasn't happening anymore, and I doubted his mom would appreciate knowing that I was waiting outside his apartment like a stalker.

Swallowing my nerves, I pushed myself up off the floor, praying silently that she wouldn't stop and ask what I was doing in the hallway. I lowered my head and proceeded to the elevator.

Please ignore me.

She did. When the elevator doors closed, my shoulders sagged in relief. When my phone alerted me to a text message, I almost jumped.

> Damon: Your boyfriend is back at the club. Come
>   get him.

I called Kara right away.

"Kar? I need your help."

CHAPTER

Veronica

GETTING PRIMPED BY KARA WAS LIKE PREPARING FOR BATTLE. HER weapons were laid out tidily on the bathroom counter: a palette of eye shadow and different types of brushes were lined up like soldiers, and tubes of lipstick and powders stood like tanks.

"Now sit, Ver, and let the master take over," she said confidently, pulling up her sleeves and surveying my face. "Just close your eyes and let me make you more gorgeous than Cinde-fucking-rella at the ball. When I'm done, Lockhart will be on his knees, shoving that glass slipper on your dainty feet. Can you hear him begging yet?" She chuckled. "Cuz I sure can."

I trusted Kara. I really did, but when I felt the *pat, pat, pat* of her fingers on my cheeks, the different kinds of creams she slapped on my face, the soft whisper of brushes on my skin, and the creamy feel of lipstick on my lips, I was scared.

"Kar. Please. Just the red lipstick."

She scoffed and, to humor me, played Lady Gaga's "Telephone" on her iPhone. "Oh, puh-lease, I'm a black belt at this, Ver. You're going to worship the ground I walk on once you see yourself."

She started dancing, raising her arms and swaying them in tune with the music. "This is what I'm going to tell that asshole Cameron once he wakes up from his stupid Sleeping Beauty slumber and starts chasing me. Wait for the lyrics, wait for it…"

She belted out the rest of the lyrics, screaming at the top of her lungs how he won't stop calling and she's k-kinda busy. When she was done, she rested her hands on the back of my chair.

"Okay, ready? In three, two, one."

She whirled my chair around so I faced the mirror. I blinked at my reflection. I looked beautiful. I *felt* beautiful.

"Well?" she asked, eyebrow raised.

"You're a miracle worker," I whispered. "I'll build you an altar and worship you."

"I know, right? I'm Catwoman, and my whip is my cruelty-free makeup, baby. *Rawr.* Now squeeze your ass in that red dress, and let's go get your man back."

"Thank you." I hugged her.

"Now don't forget that trick I taught you. Bite your lip, blink slowly like in the movies, and flick your hair over your shoulder like an invitation, ya hear?"

"Yes, master."

"Good. Let's go."

The club was dark, with glowing lights and music that pulsated in my ears. The smell of spicy food and sweet drinks hung in the air. I was wearing the red bandage dress, high heels, and the red lipstick I had on that night I met Caleb. That night he saved me.

Tonight, I was going to save us both.

If he would let me.

My heart lurched when I spotted Caleb sitting with the same crowd from last night, except there were two girls sitting beside him now. One of them placed her hand on his shoulder.

Don't touch him!

He was wearing an open black leather jacket over a white V-neck shirt and dark jeans. A drink sat on the table in front of him, and he stared at it as if it held all the answers. He didn't look like he was having a good time or even paying attention to the people around him. Maybe he was planning on leaving soon.

Don't leave.

Not yet.

Not without me.

When the blond leaned toward him suggestively, jealousy coursed through my veins.

Caleb hadn't seen me yet.

My heart was pounding. I didn't like attention and usually hid or ran away when strangers paid attention to me, but one look at Caleb and I knew there was no way I would back out of this.

Memories came drifting back to me: the day he drove us to

the country and bought us soup, pizza, and ice cream, and we kissed under the moonlight. He told me how beautiful I was.

"I figured we'd be silly today, maybe pretend to be someone else."

"Who should we be?" I asked.

"Anyone," he had whispered. *"Mine if you want."*

Yours. I want to be yours, Caleb.

A new song came on. It was "Blind Heart" by Cazzette.

I strutted to the middle of the dance floor, raised my arms sensuously, and closed my eyes. I imagined Caleb's eyes on me.

I shut everything out and began to sway my hips. I took a breath and opened my eyes, looking directly—only—at him.

At the only boy who had ever really owned my heart.

My heart pounded against my chest as slowly…slowly… *slowly*…he lifted his eyes and found mine.

His eyes widened in surprise. He sat up straight, alert now, turning his seat to watch me closely.

I slid my hand down my neck, swinging my hair to one side as I moved my shoulders and hips to the rhythm of the music. I leaned back a little, running my fingers through my hair as I moved my body with all the sensuality I had.

The blond tried to catch Caleb's attention again.

I strutted toward him, our gaze still locked. I flipped my hair over my shoulder, giving him a sassy smile.

And just like the first time we met, I came up to him, hooking my arms around his neck. His eyes—so clear and green, just like in my dream—looked at me with intensity. He was so beautiful, it hurt my heart to look at him. He stood up, snaking his arm around my hips.

For one electrifying moment, we stared at each other. I could feel his hard body against mine, smell his masculine scent.

"Hey, baby." I said it softly, my heart thundering in my chest. "He's with me, aren't you?"

His eyes darkened as they studied me.

"Where have you been?" I asked, just like he had asked me when we first met.

Did he remember?

I leaned close to him, my lip almost brushing his ear. I felt him shiver. "I've been looking for you my whole life," I whispered, just like he had whispered to me a long time ago.

It was his turn to answer.

I held my breath. Whatever he said now would determine if he had forgiven me or not. If he still wanted me or not.

A small smile flitted on his lips as he whispered, "I've been waiting for you."

I felt like crying.

"Caleb…"

His palms cupped my face, his thumbs brushing away my tears. "I remember," he whispered, smiling down at me. "I asked you the same thing when we first met."

"Yes," I choked.

"Pancakes?" he murmured, his eyes filled with an emotion so intense and sincere, it filled my throat with longing.

"Pancakes," I answered.

CHAPTER

Veronica

We were back at the beach. It was past midnight, and the place was deserted, as if it had been waiting for us all day.

As if it had been waiting for this moment.

We lay on the sand, on the same blanket he'd brought when he took us here the very first time. It seemed like a long time ago. Before, he would have reached for my hand, threading his fingers through mine.

Not this time.

I turned onto my side so I could look at Caleb. His eyes were closed. The breeze blew a lock of his bronze hair against his forehead, and I wanted to brush it back so badly.

"I miss you, Caleb."

He didn't respond. His eyes remained closed, but I knew he heard me because I saw his breath catch in his chest.

I had hurt him badly, and he was probably still angry at

me. He must hate me, but I would rather have that than a cold shoulder.

I needed to explain. I needed to tell him what I really felt.

I took a deep breath, gathering courage. "All my life I had to work hard to get the things I wanted. To reach the places I needed to be. I had to be strong—stronger than most people. Because I had to be. I shut out everyone. And why not?"

I rolled onto my back and looked up to the dark velvet sky, at the bright half-moon and the stars glittering like diamonds. It was so beautiful, so peaceful with the sound of the lapping waves. But a storm was brewing inside me.

"People are selfish," I continued. "They always want something from you, and when they get it, they leave. So I never let anyone in. But then...I met you. You made me *feel*. You made me want things that I never allowed myself to want before. And it scared me. It scared me so much. So I didn't trust you. I didn't allow myself to. Every time I felt myself getting close to you, I pulled away."

"Why?" he asked, his voice low and quiet.

"Because...because it *hurts* to hope for the impossible. How can someone like you want to know someone like me? All I have is a suitcase of sad stories and a broken heart. My walls are high and impossible to break down, and I won't let anyone in. But I felt your warmth...seeping through the cracks. How did you know where to find me?" My voice broke. "No one else ever worked to find me, Caleb. No one else stayed long enough to even try"—I felt a tear slide down my cheek— "until you."

I sat up, pulling my legs close to my chest and burying my face in my arms. I felt him sit up and move closer to me.

"I didn't trust what you felt for me," I admitted. "I was scared. I kept waiting for you to disappoint me. Everyone else did. And I think that…that…somehow there's something wrong with me. Something missing. That I'm not enough to make you stay, that somehow, someday you're going to get bored with me and leave." I sobbed. "All my life, my dad told me it was my fault. That I was the reason for all the bad things…" I swallowed. I didn't want to talk about him. I didn't even know why I'd mentioned him.

"I wish he was in front of me so I could hurt him," Caleb said. "More than he hurt you."

I heard the anger in his voice. He paused for a moment, and I could hear him breathing slowly, trying to calm himself. When he spoke again, his voice had softened.

"Red," he whispered. "Do you know how I felt when you left me?"

I lifted my head and looked into his eyes. The emotion I saw in them—the intensity and the tenderness—filled my throat.

"I felt ruined. You ruined me. There is anger, but every time I see you, my anger fades away. And there is pain, but what is love without pain? Because, Red, every time you break me apart, you put me back together. And I always come out better than before. So." He cupped my face, stroking my cheek with his thumb. "Ruin me."

I sobbed, then bit my lip to stop more from getting out. When he opened his arms, I sank into them and let the tears fall.

He pulled me onto his lap, and I wrapped my arms around his neck. He held me so tightly, I could barely breathe.

"I'm sorry I hurt you," I said. "I didn't mean any of the hurtful things I said. I only said them to protect myself. I was being a selfish coward. I was afraid of getting hurt. But hurting you only hurt me—hurt *us*. I didn't trust you enough." I sobbed, soaking his shirt with tears. "I'm sorry, Caleb."

"It's all right, Red. If I could change what happened that night, I never would have left you. I'm sorry that I did."

"You were being a good friend, and she—"

"Shh. I want to explain."

I let out a sigh, my arms tightening around him. I felt him take a deep breath, stroking my back for comfort—for mine as much as his.

"I already told you what happened that night, but I let you go before I told you everything. And for that, I failed you and I'm sorry, Red. I fell asleep, and in my dreams, I was kissing you, but when I woke up"—he paused, his whole body tense— "Beatrice-Rose was on top of me. She'd taken off her top."

I took in a sharp breath.

"I pushed her away. She's only a friend, and I would never want anyone but you. Just you, Red."

He kissed my hair. I rested my cheek on his shoulder, silently urging him to go on.

"So I left her and came home to you. Trust is very important to me. My parents didn't have enough of it to make their relationship last. I didn't want that for us. So when I asked you if you trusted me, your answer meant a lot to me. And I knew you didn't."

"Caleb—"

"Shh. Listen, baby."

He waited until I relaxed before he continued. "I let my pain and my pride control me. I wasted so much time. I never should have left town. But I wanted you to realize how much I mean to you. I wanted you to fight for me. So I stayed away. You don't know how many times I desperately wanted to drive home and beg you to come back to me. I drove myself insane. I don't want scraps anymore. I want everything. All of you. You have to know. How can you not know? You are the most important person in my life. Look at me," he pleaded.

I gazed up at him and saw the desperation, longing, and pain in his green eyes.

"Red, when you left...I never felt so empty. Never felt so lost. It was like you cut out a piece of my heart and took it with you. I miss you so much, it hurts to breathe. I miss everything about you. I miss your body pressed against mine. I miss your soft sighs and the rapid beat of your heart when I touch you. I miss your hand in mine. I miss the vulnerability in your eyes that you hide from everyone but me. How can I not fall for you?"

I held my breath, waiting for him to continue. Afraid to hear more, but wanting—*desperately* wanting—to hear more.

"From the moment I saw you, you captured me. Body, mind, and soul. Take everything from me. It's all yours."

"Caleb."

"If I'm to choose my cage," he said, his voice thick with emotion, "I choose you. I'm a willing prisoner sentenced with a lifetime of loving you."

He cupped my face in his hands as his eyes, so sincere, looked into mine. "I love you," he whispered.

I felt something click into place, like the final piece of a puzzle.

"I love you, Caleb," I whispered before he claimed my lips and kissed me under the moonlight.

CHAPTER

seven

Caleb

WE STAYED UP ALL NIGHT.

I had her in my arms, and that was all I needed right now. That was all I was going to need for a long, long time. Her absence had left a gaping hole inside my chest. When she wrapped her arms around me, she filled that hole so quickly, so completely, it felt like it had never been there.

We sat on the beach and watched the sun rise. I wrapped her in my jacket and blanket. We left our shoes in the trunk of my car as we walked along the shore. I pulled her close to me as we walked, my arm around her shoulders, hers around my waist.

When she looked up at me, my heart thudded loudly against my chest.

God, how I'd missed her.

"Don't," she said, sounding embarrassed.

"Don't what?"

"Don't stare at me."

I grinned. "I can't help it."

She looked down at her feet and tucked her hair behind her ear as she blushed.

My blushing Red.

I knew she was still worried about what had happened between us, about the damage it had caused. I had forgiven her before she even asked. I was simply waiting for her.

I stopped, turned her toward me, and tipped her chin up to look at me. "I think I'm going to stare at you for a long time."

I dipped my head to kiss her lips. So soft, so warm. Her hands rested on my chest as I felt her sigh. I smiled against her lips.

"You missed me."

"I did. I do," she answered quietly, her eyes still apologetic, still a little sad.

I wanted to erase that sadness.

"Maybe you can give me another dance number," I teased.

She laughed and slapped my arm just as I wanted her to. "Maybe when you wear a dress."

"Ow." I rubbed the spot where she'd slapped me. She packed a strong one. "How about a G-string? Or better yet…"

She gave me a stern look, flipped her hair over her shoulder, and started walking again.

I grinned, staring at her back for a few moments before jogging to catch up to her. "Where did you learn to dance like that?" I asked.

"My mom worked in a dance studio for as long as I can remember, and I took free lessons there. I wanted to go to dance school, but we didn't have money for that. It's okay, though. I have new dreams now." She smiled, closing her eyes as she breathed in the fresh air. "My mom… She'd be really happy that I'm going to college."

I didn't think she noticed the sadness in her voice when she mentioned her mom.

"If we ever need cash, I can be a stripper, but you'd have to teach me that sexy move you did with your hips," I joked. "I can wear one of those outfits where everything comes off with just one pull."

She laughed, light and fun. And all was right again.

The sun was rising, the horizon exploding with colors of red, orange, and gold. A bird, huge and white, flew above the water and swooped down to catch its breakfast. The sound of lapping waves settled over us, comfortable and relaxing as we walked along the shore.

"Finals are in a couple of weeks, Caleb. Will you be okay?"

I knew she was worried that I'd missed a whole week of classes.

"It's fine. I know most of the material anyway. Besides, my grades are good enough for me to pass, even if I fail the finals. Which," I added, chuckling when she glared at me, "I won't."

"You're graduating this year, right?"

"Yes. Then I can start working. Save money for our wedding, a house, and then kids."

I waited a beat. She didn't say anything, but she didn't look shocked or horrified like the last time I mentioned marriage.

Progress.

And then she smiled. "I still have a year to go before I graduate."

"I'll wait."

Feeling happy, I lifted her hand and kissed it. "Will you come home now, Red?"

She bit her lip, looking like she wanted to cry again. "I thought you'd never call me that again."

"You will always be Red to me."

She squeezed my hand. "I went to your apartment yesterday."

Something inside me warmed. "You did?"

She nodded. "I saw your mom."

My heart flipped.

"I was hanging around in the hallway, waiting for you. In front of your door—"

"Like a stalker." I pulled her close and nuzzled her neck. "My stalker."

"Don't let it go to your head," she said, laughing. "She doesn't know who I am, obviously. But I don't think it's a good idea to go back to your place. I don't think she'd be too happy to learn we're living together."

She had a point. I knew my mom would love Red. Who wouldn't? But if my mom discovered Red and I were living together before they'd even been introduced, she would feel hurt. They were the two most important women in my life, and I wanted them to be friends. I had to do this right. I would rectify the situation as soon as possible. And then Red could come back to living with me.

Officially as my girlfriend.

I had more plans, but I didn't think she was ready yet.

"So have dinner with me and my mom," I offered.

Her eyes widened. "I…"

"I'll give her a call and set it up for this weekend, if you're available. Come on, Red. Do it for me. Please?" I smiled, flashing my dimples shamelessly. She had a weakness for my dimples.

"Okay."

I knew it. The dimples always worked.

"I phoned my mom when I was at the cabin. I told her about you, about us. Not everything, but enough to give her an idea."

Red squeezed my hand, looked up at me with worry in her eyes.

"I told her you're obsessed with me and that—"

"Caleb!"

"Kidding." When she slapped my arm again, I laughed. "I told her I'd found my girl, and she said she's looking forward to meeting you."

She rested her head on my shoulder.

"I love you," I whispered.

I saw her eyes darken, felt her body stiffen for a moment before she relaxed and leaned close to me. She laid her cheek against my chest, listening to my heartbeat as her arms wrapped around me. *Actions speak louder than words*, I realized with a smile.

And that, I thought happily as I closed my eyes and rested my chin on top of her head, was her answer. She had done this before—rested her cheek against my chest—but I hadn't recognized it for what it was.

I knew what it meant now.

CHAPTER

eight

Caleb

"Want to get breakfast?" I asked, opening the car door for her.

We stood facing each other. She was still wearing my jacket and wrapped in the blanket. She was so close that all I had to do was place my arm around her waist and pull her to me.

The wind blew her long, dark hair, the thick, shiny strands covering her beautiful face. Holding my breath, I gently tucked them behind her ear and stroked her cheek with the back of my hand. She closed her eyes, her body swaying closer to mine.

I want to eat you for breakfast, I wanted to say. *Breakfast, lunch, and dinner.*

I wisely kept my lips zipped. We had just gotten back together, and I didn't want to scare her.

When she opened her eyes and stared into mine, my strong desire for her knotted my stomach.

"What time is it?" she asked. But she whispered it, as if she felt the same way I did. Or maybe I was just desperate enough to imagine it.

Taking a deep, calming breath, I glanced at my watch. "It's time for Red to have breakfast with Caleb."

She bit her lip to stop herself from smiling. She failed miserably, and her lips split into a sweet smile. Her lips had been seductively stained with red lipstick last night, but they were bare now—and they looked more kissable than ever. How was that even possible?

"I have class today, a review for finals that I can't skip."

There was regret in her voice, and that made me happy. I knew she wanted to spend more time with me.

We'd been apart for over a week, but it felt like years.

She shivered when the wind picked up again.

"Get inside," I said, remembering my manners.

I closed the car door after her, then jogged around the car and scrambled inside.

"What time is your class?" I turned the heater on full blast.

She slid off my jacket and handed it to me. "Here. You wear this. It's cold." Then she pulled the blanket tighter around her body, rubbing and blowing on her hands for heat. "I don't start till ten."

I threw my jacket on the backseat. "We have time. Come here, Red."

The blanket fell from her shoulders as I pulled her close to me. I nuzzled her neck, blowing warm breath on her skin as I rubbed her back and shoulders.

"Better?"

"Don't stop yet," she murmured, bending her neck slightly to grant me more access.

"Are you still cold?" I murmured back, planting a soft kiss on her shoulder.

"Yes."

"Let me warm you up."

I moved my seat back. She gasped as I reached for her waist and lifted her, planting her on top of me so she straddled me, her legs on either side of my thighs.

Her eyes were wide with surprise—and something else.

Desire.

Her eyes were darkened, her pupils dilated. I stroked her shoulder with the back of my hand, light, teasing touches that fed the fire in her eyes.

"You're so beautiful."

I traced the shape of her lips with my finger. They parted, her warm breath fanning out, her eyes half closed.

"I want to bite you," I said. My voice sounded rough.

Her eyes opened, hooded with the same hunger I felt.

"I can't"—I kissed the side of her mouth, deliberately missing her lips—"get enough"—I kissed the other side, and she closed her eyes, shivering—"of you."

"Caleb."

When she pressed her body against mine, lifting her lips like an offering, I snapped.

I buried my hands in her hair, crushing my mouth against hers. Hungry and wild, I devoured, taking everything she gave.

I took more and more, until the sound of her moan filled my ears, making me burn.

I was too hungry for her, too starved for her taste, her touch, her smell to think about being gentle.

I needed her. Desperately.

All I could think was *more*.

She consumed me. Every thought, every feeling, every breath of my being belonged to her.

Her arms wrapped around my shoulders, her nails digging into my back. Her legs tightened around my hips as my mouth dragged along her neck, along the perfect skin above her breasts.

"Caleb."

My heart was thundering in my ears as she leaned back against the wheel. She closed her eyes as my hands worshipped her. I wanted to rip her clothes off.

She dragged my mouth back to hers again, reckless, wild, and hot. My hands ran up her exposed legs, squeezing, stroking, claiming. I wanted to touch her where I hadn't dared touch her before, but not here. Not here.

When she licked my neck, my eyes nearly crossed. We had to stop or…I would take her here. And that wasn't how I planned our first time.

I cupped the back of her head, touched my forehead to hers as our breathing slowed. Her eyes were closed, her shoulders rising in time with her chest.

Her chest…her…

Do not think about it. Do not even look.

"Pancakes?"

She opened her eyes, and I nearly groaned. She was still turned on; I could see the need burning in her eyes. She swallowed, nodding after a moment.

She smiled. "Pancakes."

CHAPTER

Caleb

"So." I BLEW OUT A BREATH, OPENING THE CAR WINDOW TO CLEAR my head. Red's intoxicating scent filled the car.

And I was drowning in it.

Think of something else.

"Have you been to Anna's?" I asked.

"The café and bakery?"

"Yes. That's the one."

Her face brightened. "I love it there."

If I'd known she loved that café, I would have taken her there a long time ago.

"Then we'll go there."

She smiled, and my heart thumped fast and loud against my chest.

"We have time to eat before I drive you to Kara's. My class isn't till one, so I'd have time to go home to shower. Unless"—I paused and waited until she looked at me—"you want to shower with me?"

I was only half joking.

I was expecting her to laugh or even roll her eyes like the last time I'd asked her this, but she didn't. She just looked out the window with a secret half smile on her kissable lips.

Does that mean she wants to…?

I cleared my throat and opened my mouth to say something funny, but I felt tongue-tied.

"Then we have time for breakfast," she said.

I really thought she was going to say something else.

Concentrate on the road.

"Want the radio on?" I asked.

I'm nervous, I realized. *What the hell?*

I noticed her eyeing my hands on the wheel. I waited a beat.

She took a deep breath, as if preparing herself, and then slowly reached for my hand. Laced her fingers with mine.

That was all it took.

For her to reach for my hand. And make me feel like the king of the world.

Jack Dawson had nothing on me.

I turned to look at Red. She was looking straight ahead, blushing, her fingers linked with mine.

And I knew, right at that moment, that I would die for this girl.

She was the one. She always had been.

"Caleb, I think we just went past Anna's."

Did she expect me to remember where Anna's was when my heart was about to burst?

I couldn't even remember my own name.

Was it Jack Dawson?

"Did you change your mind?" she asked.

"Never. I made up my mind a long time ago. I think I knew the first time I saw you."

I felt her eyes on me, felt her hand tighten against mine.

I made a U-turn at the light and whipped the car into a free parking spot behind the café. And just stared straight ahead.

"I remember the first time I saw you," she said. "It wasn't at the club. It was on campus."

I couldn't remember the time in my life before I knew her.

"What was I doing?"

She smirked. "Flirting with three girls."

I grinned. "Jealous?"

"No."

"Why are you frowning?"

She pulled her hand away and crossed her arms across her chest. "I'm not frowning."

"Yes, you definitely are."

"I am not."

"Yes, you—"

"Oh, this is so childish." She got out of the car and headed to the café's front entrance.

Grinning, I followed her inside like a puppy.

The café was small and cozy. It looked vintage, with antique mirrors and black-and-white pictures of Paris on the gray concrete walls. The brown tables and chairs looked old, but I knew they were new. A large blackboard hung above the bar, and the menu was written in different colors of chalk.

Red went straight to the glass display case where dainty and elegant-looking pastries and bread were displayed.

"These are so pretty." She beamed, her nose almost touching the glass as she gawked at the display. She looked adorable, like a kid in a candy store.

After we ordered, she chose a table near the window with a view of a charming street lined with tall, wide trees and blooming flowers. I sat across from her. She cupped her chin in her palms, her eyes shining with excitement. "Someday I'll have my own café. Just like this. But I'd want it in a small bookstore where people could read or hang out while having coffee."

Leaning forward, I propped my arms on the table, stroking her elbows, and caged her legs between mine.

She was sharing her dreams. She never did that.

"I'll be your first and most loyal customer," I promised. "Will you serve pancakes?"

"Especially," she whispered, smiling.

I smiled back, making small circles on the inside of her elbow.

She kept talking, but the sound of her voice was a siren's call to my ears. It felt like I hadn't heard it in so long. Her lips were moving, her dark eyes shining. She was so beautiful.

She kicked me under the table. "Caleb? Are you listening?"

"You said you love me."

She bit her lip, and I knew she was trying to hold in a laugh.

"I didn't know you liked croissants. I was sure you were going to get cinnamon buns," I commented after the waitress brought our order. I picked up my knife and slathered a glob of butter on my pancakes.

"Normally yes, but Damon has been bringing these amazing croissants to Kar's every other day. His mom bakes them. I think I might have to blackmail her to get the recipe."

I accidentally poured too much syrup on my pancakes. *Great.* I placed the bottle of syrup carefully on the table and looked down on my plate.

"Caleb?" She sounded alarmed. "What's wrong?"

What's wrong?

I raised my eyes. "What is he to you?"

She frowned. "Who?"

I gritted my teeth. "Damon."

Her eyes cleared in understanding. "Oh, Caleb." She shook her head, smiled teasingly. "Are you jealous?"

"Damn right I am." I heaved out a sigh. Jealousy was petty, but I couldn't help it.

"He's just a friend. That night when you saw us at the club, he was just comforting me. I…wasn't feeling good."

"I'm not going to tell you who you can be friends with—"

"Good."

"—but please understand that I feel murderously jealous when I see other guys touching you and that I am being completely reasonable when I break your friend's face if he's being more than friendly."

She rolled her eyes. "I told you—"

"Yes, you have, but is that all he wants? He just happens to be there every time you need a shoulder to cry on? What about me? I'm *more* than your friend. You can cry on my shoulder. My shoulder is always available for you. My shoulder is the property of Red. Do you want me to tattoo that on here?" I pointed to my shoulder. "Or do you want it—"

She dragged her chair around to sit beside me and rested her head on my shoulder.

Oh, this girl.

She had my heart. All of it.

"I know now," she said, "but at the time, I didn't. I thought you hated me."

"I could never hate you." I leaned my head against hers. "I love you," I said.

And waited.

"You're not used to hearing it. Okay. It's all good. But every time I say it, I want you to know that I mean it. I mean every word," I told her.

"I love you," she whispered after a moment.

Just like that. Yeah, just like that. She owned me.

I knew it. She knew it. She knew that I knew she knew it.

CHAPTER

Veronica

"How's living with Kar?" Caleb asked, maneuvering the car through morning rush-hour traffic.

"I love it."

"Not too much, I hope. I want you back home."

I pressed my lips together to keep from smiling.

God. This boy. I missed this. I missed him. I hadn't realized how much until he was gone. And now that I had his hand in mine again, I wanted to hold on and never let go. He stroked my palm absently with his thumb, unaware he was doing it.

Last night when we walked on the beach, he'd smell my hair or tug on it gently, or kiss my shoulder, or stroke my arm. Sweet little gestures that filled my heart and choked me up to the point of tears. I had taken those for granted before, but now they were everything to me.

I cherished every one of them.

I blew out a breath to relieve the pressure I felt inside.

"Caleb?"

"Yes, love?"

All these sweet names he was throwing at me made my heart flutter.

The window was halfway open, and the morning breeze blew his bronze hair back, framing his gorgeous face. His jaw was square, his cheekbones so sharp that I wanted to trace them with my fingers.

"What is it?"

I blinked. "What?"

He threw me a knowing smile. "You going to tell me what's on your mind, Red?" His voice was low. "Or are you just going to stare at me all day?"

Caught. Damn it.

I wanted to stay in the car with him, in this bubble where all that mattered was us. But reality was knocking—loudly.

I debated what to tell him. I definitely wanted to mention Beatrice-Rose possibly sneaking inside his apartment. It was an ugly invasion of his privacy, and he had a right to know. How much should I tell him, though? So many things had happened.

"What is it?" he asked after he'd parked his car in front of Kara's apartment. "I can keep secrets," he added teasingly.

He lifted my hand, folding all my fingers but my pointer, and slowly traced an X on his chest with it. His eyes were so green, so deep and intense as they looked into mine. "Cross my heart," he whispered and brought my finger to his lips. Kissed it. "Hope to die."

I was on the brink of hyperventilating.

"Red? Wanna share your secret now?"

What secret? My mind had turned into mush.

He looked out the window. "I don't want to repeat what happened between us." When he looked back at me, his eyes were serious. "It was hell without you."

My breath caught. "It was hell for me too."

"So tell me what's bothering you."

I wasn't used to telling anyone my fears or problems. I wasn't used to telling anyone *anything*. But this was Caleb. The time we were apart made me realize how much of my life he had claimed. Before, I had been afraid of giving him too much of myself. I'd resisted giving him more because I was afraid he would destroy what I gave him and I'd end up with nothing—like my mother.

What I learned from Caleb is that I didn't want anything back.

It was his to keep—all of me.

"Does anyone besides me and your mom know the code to get into your apartment?"

"No," he answered. "Just you and Mom. Why?"

"That night I came over to your place, I saw Beatrice-Rose walking out of the elevator."

Caleb let out a low expletive. "She knows it. I gave it to her a long time ago. I actually forgot until you brought it up. *Damn it*. I'll change it as soon as I get home. She's also friendly with the guards, and they know who she is. I'll have to talk to them too." Frustrated, he raked his hand through his hair, and then his eyes darkened. "Did she harass you again?"

I bit my lip.

How much should I tell him?

I had been taking care of myself for so long. I had kept everything inside and fought everything alone for so long that I still found it hard to talk about my problems.

Besides, I didn't want to sound whiny. But this was Caleb.

Baby steps, Veronica. Baby steps.

"Not at the time. But have you been back to your place since you got back from the cabin?"

"Yes."

"Was anything missing?"

"Not that I know of." He narrowed his eyes. "What are you not telling me?"

He knew me so well.

I opened the car door. "Let's go inside."

"Can I see your bedroom?" he asked as soon as we entered Kara's house, toeing off his shoes beside the door.

My heart started to beat wildly. I swallowed. "Sure."

I walked ahead of him, taking a deep breath before opening my bedroom door. I stepped inside without looking behind me and headed to my closet to get a change of clothes for my shower.

"I miss seeing your things. I miss the smell of the place when you're baking or cooking. I miss the peanut butter in the fridge. It's not the same when you're not there. It feels empty."

I turned around. He was lying in my bed, his arms behind his head, his ankles crossed as he watched me.

"Lie down with me?"

I wanted to. So badly, but… "I have to get ready, Caleb."

"We have time. Don't worry, I won't do anything. I just want to hold you. And ask you a few questions," he added.

"What questions?"

He turned onto his side. "All right, let's do it my way, shall we, Red?"

"What do you mean?"

"I know you've got something you want to tell me. Let's do Twenty Confessions."

"What?"

"It's a game. Twenty Confessions. Instead of questions, they'll be confessions."

I narrowed my eyes at him. He just grinned.

"What if I have nothing to confess?" I asked.

He just raised his brows.

"How about confessions *or* questions?" I suggested.

"All right then. Lie down with me, Red," he cajoled, patting the spot beside him. "I promise I won't bite. Please?" He smiled, dimples winking at me.

"Fine."

I stretched out beside him, my back to him. His arm wrapped around my stomach as he tucked my head under his chin.

"You feel right. So right." He smelled my hair, then kissed it. "Ladies first."

"No, you go first."

He didn't hesitate. "That night at the club—behind the club, when I saw you with Damon—I thought you'd moved on and forgotten about me." His voice had become quiet and soft.

"No, Caleb."

"I thought you and him were together. I waited for you to come to me, to let me know that it was still me. It was still me you wanted."

"It's still you. It's only you."

I felt him relax behind me. "I thought maybe you wanted to come to me, but he was stopping you. I was seriously debating whether I should run him over."

A strangled laugh escape my throat. "No, Caleb. That's not how it is with him at all. Last night, Damon was the one who texted me and told me you were at the club. He said, 'Come get your boyfriend.'"

"Really? Well, maybe I'll just run over his toe. Your turn," he murmured in my ear.

"I…" I cleared my throat. "When you called me by my name…it hurt."

His arm tightened around me.

"It's ridiculous. It's my name, but you always call me Red. You had never once called me by my name until that day. And it hurt." I blew out a breath. "Your turn."

"Don't be sad, baby."

"I'm not anymore."

"You'll always be Red to me." He paused. "I have a question. How many times did you come over to my apartment?"

I shook my head. "Nuh-uh. Not telling you that."

"Admit it. You're crazy about me, Red."

"You sound so sure, hotshot."

"I am. You've probably made an altar to me already, haven't you? You probably have naked pictures of me or something."

I laughed. "In your dreams."

"Was it more than once?"

I nodded.

"I knew it. I can give you a lock of my hair, if you like. To add to your collection."

When I didn't respond, he gently tugged my shoulder and turned me around so we faced each other.

"What is it, Red? I know something is still bothering you."

"I bought you a present."

The worry in his eyes disappeared as his face broke into a grin. It made me feel angrier about what Beatrice-Rose had done. "I bought it that night after you drove Beatrice-Rose home. And I put it on your bedside table."

He frowned. "I didn't see anything there."

"I know."

"I don't understand."

"Do you remember when I told you I saw Beatrice-Rose come out of the elevator at your place?"

He nodded.

"The other day, Kara and I were meeting some friends at a café. I saw her and Justin there. She had the same thing I bought for you in her hand—the exact same thing."

His eyes turned hard and cold.

"Caleb, forget about it. It wasn't expensive. It was just a token. I'll get you another one."

"No." His tone was firm, final. "It's one thing to invade my privacy, but for her to steal from me—especially a present from my girl—is unforgivable. Don't ask me to let this go. I won't."

"Caleb."

"Red. You've never given me a gift before. Do you really think I would let this go?"

"This is what she wants. Don't you see? She wants you to confront her so she can keep in contact with you. It doesn't matter if you're angry or happy or hateful. She just wants a connection with you. She's obsessed. Caleb, please don't."

He gritted his teeth. "I can't promise anything."

"Just promise me that you'll think about it. This is important to me."

His nod was imperceptible.

Was this what would happen if I opened up to him? If he was angry about this, he would be spitting mad if I told him what had happened at the café.

I held his face in my hands, felt the rough texture of his unshaven jaw, kissed his lips lightly. "Don't be mad."

"I'm not mad at you."

"I know. But don't be mad at all." I kissed him again.

He didn't respond. He was still in a funk over the gift. So I kept kissing his lips, his cheeks, his nose until his body relaxed and he was kissing me back.

I slapped his arm playfully. "Okay. I need to shower now. If you want coffee, there should be some in the kitchen."

"You can't go yet." He grabbed me by the waist and pulled me back in the bed. On top of him. "Did anyone ever tell you to finish what you started?"

"Caleb," I warned.

"Red."

Laughter danced in his eyes. I recognized the glint, and I quickly scooted off the bed before he started piling on the charm and kisses. I really couldn't be late to class today.

Avoiding his gaze, I grabbed my change of clothes and hurried to the bedroom door. I could feel his eyes on me, could imagine the naughty smile on his beautiful face. As I closed the door behind me, I thought I heard him say *chicken*.

I showered in haste, brushing my teeth at the same time. Even after blow-drying my hair for ten minutes, it still wasn't dry, so I just tied it in a knot on top of my head. I slipped into my jeans and a white top with lace on the collar and hem and slapped on some powder and lip gloss.

I still felt tired from the all-nighter, but the shower refreshed me. When I walked into my bedroom, I found Caleb asleep on my bed.

He was lying on his stomach, his arms folded under his cheek. His hair covered his eyes, and I brushed it back gently so as not to wake him. He looked so peaceful, his boundless energy absent in sleep. Dark circles hung under his eyes from lack of sleep, but it didn't take away from the perfect handsomeness of his face.

I kissed his forehead, stroked his face tenderly. I grabbed my alarm from my bedside table and set it, making sure he would have enough time to go back to his place and get ready for his class at one. I wrote a short note for him, then boarded the bus and went to school.

I let out a deep breath as I left the theater hall. My wrist ached from writing review notes from all three of my classes, but I felt in control and confident for finals.

What was Caleb doing now?

I was smiling as I searched my bag for my phone, wondering if he had texted me. I couldn't wait to see him again.

I was about to check my messages when I heard a commotion near the multipurpose room. When I heard someone shout Caleb's name, adrenaline and fear flooded my veins and I ran.

I watched in horror as Caleb wrapped a hand around Justin's throat and shoved him against the wall. The loud bang echoed in the hallway.

Caleb's face was livid, his green eyes dark with anger. He lifted Justin a few inches off the floor. I could see Justin's face turning blue as he tried to gasp for air but couldn't. And then Caleb spoke quietly, dangerously.

"If I even hear you say her name, you're dead, motherfucker."

CHAPTER
eleven

Caleb

"Make me forget, Caleb." Red closed her eyes, her seductive lips slightly parted. "I want you to rip my—"

The shrieking ring of the alarm snapped my eyes open. Disoriented, I instinctively slapped it off.

A dream, I realized, as I fell back on the bed and covered my eyes with my arm. A very, very good dream.

A wide grin stretched across my face. It didn't have to be a dream. I could find Red and...kiss her right now.

Where was she? I remembered she told me she was going to have a shower.

Wait. How long was I out?

I sat up, looking around her small tidy room and spotting piles of books neatly stacked on her table, on the floor, and even on the windowsill. I knew it wouldn't be her room without books. When I built our house, I'd make sure there was a library for her and a big kitchen with all the state-of-the-art appliances, since she loved to cook and bake.

I glanced up at the quick, sharp knock on the door.

"Red?"

"Keep dreaming, big boy. It's Kara."

"Oh, hey, Kar."

The door opened a fraction. "You naked?"

I laughed. "Only in my dreams," I muttered under my breath.

"Huh?"

"Nope. Got all my clothes on. You're safe to come in."

"Well." She pushed the door wide open. "So I guess that means no makeup sex for you."

I shook my head.

She gave me a pitying look. "Really? And here I thought you were a master."

I laughed again. "Where is she?"

"School. Guess you conked out. She texted me and said to feed you. Come on." She walked off.

Rising, I spotted a note from Red beside the alarm clock and smiled goofily as I read it. Folding it neatly, I tucked it in my wallet for safekeeping and followed Kara to the kitchen.

She was just placing a box of Lucky Charms and a box of Cheerios beside the milk carton on the table when I walked in. "Here you go. She said healthy breakfast. Cereal is healthy. It has fiber."

Did she really believe that? But then I saw her smirk.

"I love Lucky Charms," I said. "Thanks."

"Take a seat. I hate cooking, so this is as good as it gets. Want a croissant?"

"Hell no," I growled.

"Whoa. Chill, buster."

"Sorry." I shook cereal into the bowl and then poured milk. "I really don't like croissants."

"Yeah, I think I got that. Make sure to tell her I fed you."

"You bet." Then, as nonchalantly as possible, I asked, "So what's the deal with Damon?"

She took the seat across from me and smirked. "What do you mean?"

She knew what I meant. She just loved to torture people. "Kar," I warned.

"Oh, calm down." I hadn't taken a bite of my *healthy* breakfast yet, and she pulled the bowl in front of her and started eating. "They're just friends."

I frowned. "Has he made a move on my girl?"

She raised an eyebrow. "*Your* girl? So I take it you guys are okay now?"

I nodded, grinning. "As if she hasn't told you. I know you girls talk."

She rolled her eyes. "We girls haven't talked yet. I'm going to get the dirty deets later."

"You do that." It didn't bother me for one second. I loved it when Red talked about me. I tried to turn on the charm. "So…I know you tell each other everything…"

"Uh-huh."

"I thought this was *my* breakfast?" I grabbed the bowl back. "As I was saying—"

"You want me to spill the dirt on her?"

I guess I was that transparent. "You look really pretty today, Kar. That top looks phenomenal on you." In my experience, compliments would get you anywhere with girls.

Usually.

"I know, right? In fact, I could use another one. In fuchsia, I think."

I didn't even bother smirking. "If you tell me more, I'll buy you two."

"Deal! What do you want to know?"

"How many times did she go to my apartment after I left?"

When Kara called it quits, I had most of the information I wanted and had promised to get her a Stella McCartney gift card on top of the two blouses she wanted.

"One last thing," I added. "Does Damon know that she's mine?"

Kara rolled her eyes. "What do you think?" She grabbed the bowl back. "Did you have to eat all the marshmallows?"

"Tell him I'll kill him if he so much as touches her again. If he plans on making another move on her—"

"Hold up. He never did. Damon's not like that."

"Just tell him."

"Why are you so hung up about Damon?"

"Red doesn't hang out with any guys." Except for *me*. "But she hangs out with *him*."

Kara bit the side of her lip.

I scowled. "What?"

"I guess you didn't know about Theo."

I straightened in my seat. "Theo?" I asked quietly.

She waved her hand dismissively. "Just a friend. He belongs to Beth anyway, so stop being all alpha male. She told you about Beatchy-Rose sneaking in your apartment and stealing your key chain?"

I wanted to ask more about this Theo, but the key chain distracted me. "So that's what Red got me? A key chain? I want it back."

"Well, Beatch's got it now. Whatcha gonna do about it?"

I felt a muscle tick in my jaw. "Red doesn't want me to do anything about it."

"You gonna do everything she tells you?"

I half snorted and half laughed.

"She told you about Justin too?"

I grabbed the bowl back and shook more cereal into it. "Just that he was with Beatrice-Rose at the café."

Her face turned grim.

"What is it, Kar?"

"That prick was going to hit her, Caleb."

I put the spoon down slowly. "What did you say?"

"Justin was going to fucking punch her."

I really hated it when I let my anger control me. In my experience, nothing good ever came from letting it take over. But someone threatening to hurt Red, especially when I wasn't there to protect her—and someone I considered a *friend*? Unforgivable.

By the time I arrived at school, I was ready to beat Justin's face to a pulp.

"Hey, man!" Amos came up beside me. "Slow down, will you? I've got something important to tell you, bro."

Not now, I wanted to tell him. But I refused to speak. I was afraid that if I opened my mouth, I would start yelling like a madman.

"Caleb, listen. It's about your girlfriend."

That stopped me short. I glared at him. "What about my girlfriend?"

He handed me a crumpled piece of paper. "I found this in the locker room after practice last night."

It was a picture of her dancing at the club that night I first saw her. Her hair down her back, her red dress hugging every inch of her body. Below the picture was a list of…sexual services with prices beside them. Then a message that said *Find me in E Building*, signed *Veronica Strafford*.

My ears rang as I felt blood rush to my head. "What. The. Fuck. Is this the only copy?"

Amos shrugged. "I don't know, Caleb. I doubt it."

I took a deep breath, trying to calm myself. It didn't work. "Where the fuck is Justin?"

"Justin? Whoa, dude, hold on. I don't know if Justin did this."

I grabbed Amos's collar. "Where. The. Fuck. Is. He?" I knew in my gut Justin had something to do with it. I just knew.

"Caleb." I heard Cameron's voice behind me, his tone serious. I turned to look at him. His eyes were questioning, but he didn't ask what was wrong.

Amos put his hands up. "If you do this now, you might get suspended. We're graduating, Caleb."

I glared back at him. "I don't care. No one hurts her." I crumpled the paper in my fist. "Tell me where the fuck Justin is."

"Justin's in the multipurpose room," Cameron said. "Let's go."

I don't even know how I got to the multipurpose room. When I spotted Justin, I headed straight for the fucker. Nothing could have stopped me.

Justin's eyes widened in fear when he saw me. He backed away slowly, as if he was being careful not to anger me further. But it was too late. I was way beyond angry.

I was going to kill him.

He looked behind him, searching for an escape, but there was only the wall. "Dude, she came on to me—"

There was a satisfying crunch as my fist connected with his face. He stumbled back, tripping over his feet. I was on him before he could recover. I heard shouts around me, but I didn't care.

He had hurt my girl. He was going to pay.

He was on the floor, his nose bleeding, his eye nearly closed. But I wasn't finished. I pulled him up by his shirt collar and shoved him against the wall. My hand wrapped around his throat, squeezing. It would be so easy to crush his windpipe. So easy.

"If I even hear you say her name, you're dead, mother-fucker." I heard voices around me, but I ignored all of them. I shook him. "Do you fucking understand me?"

I stiffened when I felt a hand on my back.

"Caleb."

It was her. It was my Red.

She was safe.

My hold loosened a fraction, but not entirely. The asshole began wheezing and coughing.

"Please. Let go of him." This time, she stood beside me, placing her hand on my arm. "Caleb."

There was no one who could make me do things I didn't want to do. Except her.

I would do anything for her.

I let go.

"You're bleeding!" Red cried out in alarm.

She was sitting beside me in my car. I should have felt calm and relieved, but I couldn't get us the hell away from this place fast enough.

Someone had alerted Coach while I was beating the crap out of Justin. Coach had sent us to the dean of our department, where I would have stayed longer if not for my mom phoning him.

I tried to pull my hand away from Red's. She held on. "Hold still."

I felt a soft cloth on my knuckles.

"Caleb?"

I took a deep breath, calmer now that she was within my reach. Where I could protect her.

"I'm okay, Red."

"What happened?" she asked.

I desperately wished there was a way to protect her from this, to stop her from knowing what happened, but hiding it from her would only make things worse.

She was one of the toughest people I knew, but I was also aware of how vulnerable she was. And this was a huge violation of her privacy. It made me angry that I hadn't stopped it from happening.

"Red. Listen. I'll do everything to protect you. I'll make sure there are no traces of that poster. You have to trust me."

"I don't understand. What poster?"

I ground my teeth. "Someone saw Justin putting up a poster in the locker room. It was a picture of you at the club where we met." My hands fisted. "It had some writing on it."

"Tell me."

I looked down and shook my head slightly, grinding my teeth to dust.

"Tell me, Caleb." I looked up at her tone. Her eyes were hard.

"It had a list of...fucking ugly things that you'd do for a fee. *Fuck.*"

When I saw the shock in her eyes, I wanted to yell like a madman. And when the shock turned into hurt, I wanted to beat Justin's face to a pulp all over again. I reached to gather her in my arms, but she pushed me away.

"Don't." She balled her hands into fists on her lap to stop them from shaking.

"No." I reached for her shoulders, turning her to me. "Don't shut me out. Stay with me. Right here." I held her face in my hands and kissed her lips. "I'm sorry this happened. I'm sorry, baby."

She nodded.

"Listen," I said. "There was only one poster in the locker room. As far as I know, only a few people on the team saw it."

She shook her head. "There were...there were guys following me, and one of them gave me his phone number. It makes sense now why they were asking me about...those things."

"Asking you what? Who are they?" It was a struggle for me to keep the anger at bay. "Did they hurt you?"

"No. *No*," she said. "They didn't hurt me. Just said a few things. I don't remember who they were, Caleb. It doesn't matter. Justin can't get away with this." She took a deep breath, and when she moved away, there was fire in her eyes.

That's my girl.

"What should I do?" she asked. "I need to file a complaint with the department—" Suddenly, her eyes widened. "Caleb! What did the dean say? Did you...get suspended?" I could hear the worry in her voice. She was more worried about me than what had happened to her.

"No." I probably would have if my mom hadn't called the dean. She was a member of the school's board. I hated using my name to get out of sticky situations, especially with my mom's help. But I would fight dirty for Red.

"But the bastard got suspended and kicked off the team," I added. Personally, I thought he should be kicked off the planet. But I knew how important it was to Justin to be on the basketball team. It elevated his status, made him feel superior. He still had a year before he graduated, and being suspended and spending the year off the team would not be easy for him. "This wasn't the first time he did something like this."

"What do you mean?"

"He emailed everyone a naked picture of his ex-girlfriend after she broke up with him."

"Are you serious? How can he get away with doing that?"

"He denied it. They couldn't trace the email, but everyone knew it was from him. This time, though, one of the freshmen from the basketball team saw him put up that poster in the locker room."

She was silent.

"Don't worry, Red. This won't happen again. I promise."

She shook her head. "It's not that. I don't want you to feel like you have to protect me all the time."

"It's my job to protect you."

"Caleb—"

I parked in front of Kara's and turned to face her. "I want you to sleep at my place tonight." When she opened her mouth— probably to argue—I cut her off. "Please. I need to feel that you're safe. Just tonight. Please, Red."

She nodded. "Okay."

"I'll be back in two hours. I told Matthew to text the team to meet at his place. I need to make sure there are no more posters around."

"It's over now. Do you have to do this tonight?"

I held her face in my hands, rubbing her soft cheek with my thumb. "Yes. He won't hurt you again. I'll make sure of it."

Veronica

"The truth is…" I hesitated, closing my eyes. "It scared me to see Caleb…like that."

Kara frowned, sitting next to me on the couch where she'd placed a bowl of popcorn mixed with M&M's on my lap. She grabbed the remote and absentmindedly channel surfed.

I glanced at the clock again. Caleb had left hours ago. What was taking him so long?

"Like what?"

"I didn't recognize him. It was like he was a different person. He was so angry. It just…reminded me."

"Reminded you?" Kara huffed. "Why don't you explain all this to me so I don't sound like a damn parrot?"

"My dad," I answered after a moment.

"Oh." Kara reached for my hand, her eyes apologetic. I squeezed her hand, let go, and wrapped my arms around my middle. I suddenly felt cold.

"But I realized that he was protecting me. Caleb would never hurt me."

"Ver." She turned off the TV. "Lockhart would cut off his hands before he hurt you."

I nodded. "It's just—"

Kara's phone rang. When she glanced at the screen, her eyes widened in incredulity. "Who is it?" I asked.

"It's Cameron."

I raised my brows when she just stared at the screen. "Are you going to answer it?"

"No." But she pressed the answer button and lifted the phone to her ear. "Hello?"

A voice spoke on the other end of the line, but I couldn't make out the words. Kara listened with a stoic expression. A moment later, her face paled.

Alerted, I straightened in my seat.

Kara got up from the couch, whispering into the phone. I stayed where I was to give her privacy. She would tell me if she wanted me to know.

A few minutes later, she came back. Her hazel eyes were wide and full of worry.

"Ver," she said cautiously.

"Kar. You're scaring me. What is it?"

She took a deep breath. "Caleb's in jail."

CHAPTER

twelve

Veronica

Four hours earlier…

"I'LL BE BACK IN TWO HOURS," CALEB SAID. HIS GAZE WAS APOLO-getic, as if he didn't want to leave but had to. "I told Matthew to text the team and meet at his place. I need to make sure there are no more posters around."

I tamped down the trepidation I was feeling. I didn't feel good about this. "It's over now. Do you have to do this tonight?"

"Yes. He won't hurt you again. I'll make sure of it," Caleb promised, his eyes dark and intense as he held my face in his hands.

I closed my eyes. I was torn between flinching away from his touch and wanting more of it. The memory of Caleb mad with anger, almost blinded with it, wouldn't leave my mind.

I nodded and slipped out of the car. I paused when I reached the front door of Kara's apartment, then turned around. Caleb was still parked, waiting for me to get inside before leaving. His car windows were tinted so I couldn't see inside, but I knew he was watching me.

I waved goodbye and entered the apartment. As soon as I got inside, exhaustion overtook me. I hadn't slept in more than twenty-four hours. Maybe I'd just take a nap.

The apartment was empty. I glanced at the clock and noted that Kara's class would be done in an hour and that I needed to make us dinner. I'd just close my eyes for half an hour...

I always hated the dark.

The dark brought bad things. It carried the promise of pain. Especially if you were a bad, bad girl.

I tried to be good, to follow the rules, because if I didn't, the monster would come back. The monster who looked so much like my daddy.

But the monster had been gone a long time. That meant that I could play in the forest again. Maybe I could even have friends now. One of Daddy's rules was never to talk to prying adults or damned social workers or tell any-fucking-body what happens in our house. Be a good girl or else. That was his warning.

But the monster was gone. So today I went to the forest and met a boy with green eyes. He even gave me a peanut butter sandwich. Eating it made me scared and excited at the same time, because I knew the monster hated peanut butter. But the monster was gone, and I could eat whatever I wanted.

We made mud by mixing dirt and water, and we painted

our faces with it. I looked like Batgirl and he looked like Batman, and we played all day. When it got dark, I had to say goodbye. He said he would come back tomorrow and we could play again.

I ran home, feeling excited to tell Mommy about my day. Maybe we could pick flowers from the garden again tomorrow. She had such pretty vases we could put them in. I pushed the screen door open, clutching my half-eaten sandwich. I didn't want to eat it all. I wanted to save it. Because if I ate it all, then how could I be sure the boy with the green eyes was real and wasn't just a dream? I finally had a friend, and I was happy. Very happy.

"Hello, Veronica."

My body filled with dread, and the sandwich fell from my hand.

The monster was back. It looked like Daddy, but I knew it wasn't. Daddy didn't have those eyes that looked at you like he wanted to hurt you. Daddy was good and never hurt me or Mommy.

"What is this?" The monster picked up the half-eaten sandwich from the floor. He sniffed it, his eyes widening in disbelief. "Where the fuck did you get this?"

The monster grabbed my arm, and I cried out in pain. It hurt so much. Tears pricked my eyes, but I refused to let them fall. The monster hated tears. If I cried, it would only hurt me more.

"You've been a bad girl. Do you know what happens to bad girls?"

I stared at him, frozen with terror. I wanted to run, but my body wouldn't move.

"Dom! Leave her alone!"

It was Mommy. The monster shoved me away and lunged at her. I watched helplessly as he dragged her to the kitchen by her hair.

"Please don't!" Mommy cried out.

With a quick swipe of his arm, he sent the vase flying off the table, and it shattered on the floor. The flowers that Mommy and I had picked from our garden were broken now.

The monster was still holding Mommy by the hair as he opened cupboards, grabbing everything that Mommy and I had carefully arranged and throwing it everywhere.

"Where the fuck is it? I told you not to buy it. Simple rules, Tanya, but you can't even do them right, can you? You useless piece of shit."

"How could you talk about rules? I saw you with your woman yesterday."

That made the monster angrier, and it threw Mommy on the floor. Right where the broken glass was. Mommy cried out in pain. And then she looked at me with frightened eyes and mouthed, *Hide!*

I ran to the laundry room, hiding under the sink and pushing my palms against my ears so I didn't hear anything.

But I heard Mommy screaming, and inside my head, I was doing the same.

No, no, no. Please don't. I won't ever eat peanut butter again. I won't ever...

And then Mommy stopped screaming.

I won't eat it again. I promise. Don't hurt Mommy.

My eyes were wide with terror as I watched the cupboard door open. The monster's face was wild with madness as it grinned at me. "There you are."

"Veronica! Wake up!"

I opened my eyes, panting. Kara knelt beside me, her face pinched with worry as she shook me awake.

"Jesus. What were you dreaming about?"

Bile rose in my throat, and I scrambled up and ran to the bathroom. I knelt in front of the toilet and threw up. I shut my eyes.

No. I don't want to remember. I can't remember...

I went to the sink and washed my mouth and face, willing myself to forget it. The nightmare was already fading away.

"If I didn't know you guys haven't had sex, I'd say you're preggers."

I sent Kara a grateful look as she tried to lighten the mood. Her eyes lingered on my face, searching. I turned my gaze from hers, hoping she wouldn't probe for answers I wasn't ready to give.

"I wasn't sure if you were coming home tonight, so I picked up chow mein and veggie spring rolls. There's enough to share," she said. I could still feel her eyes on me. "I'll be in the kitchen."

I nodded. I waited until she was gone before I closed the bathroom door. I leaned my back against the door and slid to the floor, pulling my knees to my chest and burrowing my face in my hands.

The nightmares were back.

I didn't want to be the scared, helpless little girl who was afraid of the dark. I wasn't that girl anymore.

I let myself relax, taking deep breaths. I knew the scene I'd witnessed on campus today triggered the nightmare. The scene where Caleb let violence consume him. It had scared me to see him beat Justin that savagely. I had seen Caleb fight before, with Damon, but it was nothing like the rage he'd released when he had Justin by the throat…

Don't worry, Red. I'm going to protect you.

Oh, Caleb.

He made me feel safe, cherished…loved. Even when I pushed him away, he never stopped loving me.

That moment in the multipurpose room, when I thought he was going to kill Justin, I'd called out his name. And he came back. He came back for me. He didn't cause pain just because he could or because he got off on it… He did it to protect me. Because…because he loved me. He wasn't like the monster in my childhood. He wasn't like my dad.

I got up from the floor and stared at my reflection in the mirror. My face was pale, and dark circles hung under my eyes. I brushed my teeth quickly and washed my face again.

I was going to eat a goddamn peanut butter sandwich.

CHAPTER

Caleb

PATIENCE HAS NEVER BEEN ONE OF MY BEST TRAITS.

I stood by the window, my hands in my pocket, jiggling my car keys. I wanted to go home to Red. Preferably now.

I'd just arrived at Matthew's place. Cameron and some of the team had helped me go back to the campus to find and destroy those damned posters. There weren't any more. Thank God.

Justin needed to start praying and offer a couple sacrifices to save his neck if he tried hurting my Red again. I was sure I would do more than choke him if he did.

I glanced at my watch and noted that it was almost two hours since I'd left Red.

"I gotta go," I said.

Levi tried to raise his chin from his chest to look at me. He was clearly drunk. He had stayed behind with a couple other guys at Matthew's place to make sure there weren't any of those damned posters online. After all was clear, he and the other guys had decided to make it their life mission to finish two bottles of scotch from Matthew's father's liquor cabinet. Empty beer bottles and boxes of pizza littered the floor.

The other guys had already left before I arrived. I found Levi slumped in one of the chairs. Matthew was sprawled on the couch, his eyes zoned in on the TV screen. He was watching *The Avengers*.

"Do me a favor, dude. Bring this sack of limp biscuit with you," Matthew pleaded, throwing Levi a disgusted look.

I tamped down my impatience. I wanted to go straight to Kara's place to pick up Red.

Before Red had slipped out of my car, some emotion had flashed in her eyes that I couldn't decipher. It made me uneasy. I wanted to make sure everything was all right.

We'd just gotten back together. I didn't want to lose her again. If I lost her again, I would… I didn't know what I would do.

My eyes narrowed as I spotted a yellow truck pass by Matthew's place. It looked like Justin's truck.

"Does Justin know we were meeting at your place?" I asked.

"Hell no," Matthew answered. "What makes you say that?"

I grunted as I watched the yellow truck disappear and forced myself to relax. "All right. Let's go, Levi."

"What? Did you say *boner*?" He hiccupped.

Matthew choked. "Yeah, dude. Something you wouldn't know about."

I shook my head as I hauled Levi up from the couch. He was hammered.

"If you throw up in my car, I'm going to leave you on the side of the road," I warned.

"That sounds uh-mazing," he slurred. "Why you carryin' me? D'we get married or sumthin'?" He puckered his lips and swung his head dangerously close to mine.

I pushed him away, laughing. "Just stay away so nobody gets hurt. Got it?"

"Hurt me, master. Whip me. You know I like it."

I heard Matthew's roaring laughter before I closed the door and stepped outside.

"Get in the car, dude. Seriously, I need to pick up my girl."

I opened the passenger door and shoved him inside, slamming the door closed. Just as I was putting on my seat belt, a police car slid into the spot behind me, red and blue lights flashing. I waited until both policemen had approached my side, then rolled down the window.

"Good afternoon, Officers."

They both nodded. One officer looked like Popeye, while the other one looked as skinny as a pole. Popeye eyed Levi suspiciously.

"Is this your house?" Officer Pole inquired, his face friendly and open.

"No, sir. A friend's."

"What were you doing here?" Popeye asked. If Pole was the good cop, Popeye was definitely the bad cop. His eyes narrowed as he studied my face.

"Just visiting," I replied.

"Hey, say what, you guys got some doughnuts on you?" Levi piped up.

I groaned.

"Seems like your friend is drunk."

"I'm driving him home."

"*Are* you?" There was a challenge in Popeye's tone.

I gave him a nod.

"I need to see your license and registration."

What the hell?

"What the fuck for?" Levi interrupted.

"Levi, shut up. Let me handle this."

"I'd buy you ten thousand boxes of doughnuts if you guys leave us the fuck alone," Levi slurred.

I gave him a warning glare, shaking my head slightly. When I was sure he'd gotten the message, I turned back to the officers.

"Sorry about that. Is there a reason for this?" I asked.

Pole answered, "We received a peace disturbance report about this residence."

"And that someone is dealing drugs," Popeye added.

I gritted my teeth. *Justin.*

Levi let out a loud snort. "I could use some dope right now."

I closed my eyes tightly. Damned Levi.

Popeye stepped back, his eyes hard. "We need to search the car. Please step out of your vehicle, sir."

I didn't need this right now.

"I have the right to refuse," I said.

"You do," Popeye replied, smirking. "Sounds like you have something to hide."

I took a deep breath. "Go ahead and search then," I told him as I slid out of the car.

It took a while, but Levi managed to get out of the car. They asked us to step away from the vehicle and wait a few minutes. Levi slumped on the ground. I had a heavy feeling in my stomach as I watched them search my car.

I knew the moment they found something. And I knew in the pit of my stomach that it was bad.

It was really bad.

Officer Popeye walked up to me. "Want to explain what this is?"

He dangled a small bag filled with white powder in front of me.

Fuck.

CHAPTER
fourteen

Veronica

A FEW MINUTES AFTER CAMERON PHONED KARA, HE ARRIVED TO pick us up. I was thankful. We asked him what happened, but all he would say was that Caleb was unhurt, safe, and would explain everything later.

Kara hounded him nonstop for more information, but he wouldn't budge. He never gave in to her insults. In fact, he was smiling. I would have appreciated and paid more attention to their banter if I hadn't been worried to death about what could have happened to Caleb.

I wrung my hands during the trip to the station. Kara noticed and tried to lighten the mood.

"By the way," she chirped, "Caleb might take you to an exotic restaurant and feed you fried alfalfa sprouts."

"What?" I asked, distracted.

"I gave him false information this morning when he asked me

to spill the dirt on you. Just pretend everything I told him was legit until he gives me my payment, okay?"

I nodded absently and heard Cameron's quiet laugh.

"Was it a Stella McCourtney gift card?" he muttered, chuckling.

"Stella McCartney. You never get anything right, do you?" Kara glared, crossing her arms and turning to look out the window.

"I did *one* thing right," he replied after a moment, his voice solemn. I saw him glance at Kara longer than necessary.

I blocked their conversation after that. It took forever, but we finally arrived at the station. Stomach rolling, I went inside with Kara and Cameron. Her hand squeezed mine as we saw the police officer standing behind a messy desk.

"Are you sure you don't want to wait in the car? I can bail him out by myself," Cameron offered.

Kara shot him a glare. "Are you saying that because we're girls, we can't handle something like this? That we're weak?"

I heard Cameron sigh. "Not at all. Come if you want."

"I'll do whatever the fuck I want."

"Careful, Sunshine. Your words could draw blood," Cameron warned.

"Then I hope you bleed to death."

Cameron fell silent. I gave him an apologetic look.

We approached the police officer's desk. "We'd like to post bond for Caleb Lockhart," I said, my voice shaky.

"Can I see some ID?"

"Oh. Of course." My hands were shaking so badly that I nearly dropped my wallet as I searched for my ID.

"Veronica, I'll get the bail," Cameron said. "Caleb won't like it if you paid for it."

"Let him," Kara added, touching my shoulder.

I was distressed and exhausted enough not to argue. I nodded before turning to the officer. "I'd like to see him, please. Is he okay?"

"Why don't you wait in the lounge?"

A few minutes later, the officer appeared again. "He's in the interview room now, waiting for you. Follow me."

He led me through a door to the left, then to a narrow hallway with three rooms. He opened the door to his right and stepped back to let me in. There was a single table in the middle of the room and two chairs. Caleb was sitting on one, his elbows on his knees as he cupped his face in his hands. When I saw his wrist cuffed to a bolt, I nearly fell to my knees.

Oh, Caleb, what have you done?

Images of him hunting Justin with his teammates—or, worse, murdering him—flitted through my mind.

"Caleb."

He looked up, his eyes wide with fatigue and worry. "Red."

My legs trembled as I approached him. "Are you okay?"

"Yes. God." He reached for me with his free hand, gathering me against him. "You're all right. Thank God."

"What happened?" I turned to the officer. "Please, can we have some privacy?"

"I'll be outside." The officer left us alone.

"Did Cameron come with you?"

"Yes, and Kar. Caleb, you're scaring me." I searched his face for any sign that he was hurt. Other than looking exhausted, he appeared uninjured. "What happened?"

His face turned hard, cold. "They found drugs in my car."

Of all the reasons I would expect him to be in jail, drugs wasn't one of them. My heart dropped to my stomach.

"I was about to leave Matthew's and give Levi a ride home. He'd been drinking. Two police officers arrived and said they had gotten a report about drug dealing at Matthew's house. Then they asked to search my car. I let them because I had nothing to hide. But they found drugs." His face mirrored his anger and frustration. "I don't deal with drugs, Red. I would never do that. Someone planted them."

A woman's voice spoke from behind me. "Caleb?"

Caleb looked over my shoulder. "Mom?"

I had only seen Caleb's mom once in person—when I waited for Caleb outside his door. She was more beautiful than I remembered, dressed elegantly in a conservative blue dress. Her worried eyes studied her son's face as she walked to him, a police officer trailing behind her. She looked like Caleb, with bronze hair and stunning green eyes.

"I had to hear about this from Beatrice-Rose. Why didn't you call me?"

Beatrice-Rose? How did she know that Caleb was in jail?

"I didn't want to worry you. Mom, this is Red. Red, this is my mom, Miranda. This isn't how I planned for you to meet my future wife, Mom."

I pressed my lips tightly together to keep from groaning. I should have been used to Caleb's bombshells by now…

She ignored me. "Is this why you've been getting into fistfights? Missing a week in school right before your finals? You're graduating. And now you're in jail?"

Her eyes turned to me briefly, and I caught the warning in them. I felt sick.

Caleb observed the exchange between his mom and me. His green eyes were anxious as they studied me. I willed my face to look blank, empty, but inside, I felt nauseated.

She turned to the officer. "Release my son."

The officer obliged her. The rattle of the metal handcuff grated in my ears. I could feel the pulse in my temple begin to throb.

"I've spoken with the chief of police," she announced, reprimand and disappointment in her voice. "There will be no record of this. Caleb, how could you let this happen?" Her voice cracked and she paused. "I already told your friends to go home, so I will expect to see you in your apartment with a reasonable explanation in half an hour."

Although her face was stoic, her hand shook as she reached out to touch her son's face. "You've frightened me. When will you ever learn, Cal?" I could feel the worry and fear in her voice, and the strong love she had for Caleb.

Caleb stood and wrapped her in his arms, murmuring in her ear. I stepped aside to give them more room. He was talking too softly for me to hear, but his mom nodded. I felt like a trespasser. She kissed him on the cheek and then turned and left with the officer—without glancing at me.

"I'm sorry, Red. Don't worry about my mom. I'll talk to her."

I shook my head. "She's right."

His eyes filled with fear as he cupped my face in his hands. "You're not thinking of leaving me again." It wasn't a question.

"N-no."

His hands fell to my shoulders, pulling me close to him. "Do you trust me?"

He had asked me this before. This time, I didn't hesitate. "Yes. I trust you, Caleb."

"Good." He kissed my forehead. "Come home with me, baby."

I wanted to be with him, especially after what had happened today. But I couldn't. "No. Caleb, your mom just asked you to come home."

He pulled back, staring at me intently. "You promised you'd stay with me tonight."

"Don't be unreasonable." *Don't make her hate me more than she already does*, I thought, but I didn't say that. "Your mom's upset, Caleb. You've got to take care of that. I'll see you tomorrow. Please."

He nodded tightly. "Don't go anywhere, Red."

"I won't," I promised. And this time, I meant it.

CHAPTER

Veronica

I WAS SO EXHAUSTED THAT I HAD TROUBLE SLEEPING. THE LAST time I'd had more than five hours of sleep was the night before I went *hunting*, as Kara eloquently put it, at the club to get Caleb back.

It didn't make sense. Shouldn't I be able to sleep as soon as my head hit the pillow? My body might be depleted of energy, but my mind wouldn't stop worrying.

Caleb had beaten up Justin because of me. He went to jail because Justin or Beatrice-Rose had set him up. Again, because of me.

And now his mom was upset with him because of me. I knew how much Caleb loved his mom, and the thought of her disliking me was depressing.

She was right, though. All the bad things that had happened to Caleb were because of me.

You bring nothing but bad luck. I should have picked the other kid to adopt. Tanya and I would still be together if not for you.

My dad's voice echoed in my mind. Of all the hurtful things he had said to me, this one hurt the most. This one I could never forget. Maybe because deep down, I knew he was right.

I love you, Red.

Caleb's voice drowned out my dad's. I hugged my pillow tighter, wishing he were here. But even when he wasn't, the thought of him made me smile. He was always taking care of me. But most of all, he loved me. I believed that now. No matter how many demons chased me in the dark, he was the light at the end of the tunnel.

I nearly jumped when I heard a noise near my window. I grabbed the copy of *Harry Potter and the Philosopher's Stone* that was lying on my bedside table, intending to use it as a weapon if necessary. When I heard the noise again, I quietly tiptoed over to the window.

Rocks. Someone was throwing rocks at my bedroom window.

I opened the window and stared down, mouth slightly agape.

He was here.

"Caleb?"

"Hi, Red," he whispered, a sheepish grin on his handsome face.

Butterflies exploded in my stomach.

He had changed his clothes and looked incredible in a simple, white V-neck T-shirt that showed off his arm muscles, ripped jeans, and Nikes. He wore a dark beanie that pushed his bronze hair back from his face.

He stood below my window, his feet planted apart, gazing up at me with one arm up as if he was about to throw another rock.

"What are you doing here?" I hissed, trying my best to stuff down the delight I was feeling.

"I miss you."

I had to hold on to the wall to keep myself from jumping out the window into his arms. Yeah, a little overdramatic, but that was how he made me feel.

This was insane.

"What are you wearing?" he asked.

I choked on a laugh.

"Can I come in?"

"Were you throwing rocks at my window?"

He nodded, still grinning.

"Ever heard of calling on the phone?" I teased.

"Yeah, but I want to charm you," he replied. "Isn't it sweeter if I throw rocks at your bedroom window? Besides, you never answer my texts."

"I…" I looked behind me to search for my phone. Where did I put it?

"Can I climb up to your bedroom window now?" There was a naughty gleam in his eyes.

"How about I let you in through the front door like a normal human being?"

He winked. "That works too, but how about you meet me in the backyard? I brought you something."

I bit my lip to keep from giggling. This was ridiculous. "Okay."

I looked down at my exposed legs, wondering if I should change. I wore a tank top and really, really tiny red shorts. Caleb would certainly love this outfit. Before I could stop myself, I rushed outside as quickly and quietly as I could.

When I opened the door, Caleb was standing in the yard. The soft light from the porch illuminated his frame. My breath caught as I spotted a huge bouquet of lavender lilacs in his hands that nearly hid his whole torso.

"These are for you, my Red."

In a daze, I stepped out. His green eyes were so focused on me that I felt my heart trip. And I fell a little deeper in love.

He must have seen it on my face. His eyes widened slightly, and he opened his arms for me. I stepped into them, wrapping my arms around him, burying my face in his chest and inhaling his familiar scent.

"I miss you," I said softly.

He rested his chin on top of my head, his arms tightening around me. "Say it again," he requested.

"I miss you, Caleb."

I felt him sigh. His shoulders relaxed as if a heavy weight had fallen from them.

"You make me happy when you say that," he said.

"I'm sorry I don't say it often."

"It's okay. We'll work on it." He moved away briefly and placed the flowers on a bench. His body swayed as he held me again, as if we were dancing. "Practice makes perfect. Now say, 'I love you, Caleb.'"

I laughed quietly. "I love you, Caleb."

I felt him nod in approval. "Good. You get an A. Now say 'Caleb is the best'—*ow*!"

I bit his chest.

"What'd you do that for? Now you get a B minus."

I was smiling. I couldn't seem to stop. He was the best. I rubbed the spot where I'd bitten him. We danced for a moment, the sweet fragrance of the lilacs surrounding us.

"I got you lilacs because of what they represent," he murmured in my ear.

I shivered when I felt the warmth of his breath. "What do they mean?"

"First love."

I felt my heart stutter.

"You're my first love, Red. And my last."

My heart felt full, like it was about to burst. Like it was too big for my body. I wanted to find the right words to express what I was feeling, just like he always found the perfect way to express himself to me.

But I couldn't.

So I just rested my cheek on his chest, right over his heart, and squeezed my arms tighter around him.

I sighed, feeling safe, content, and loved—for the first time in my life.

"I love you, Caleb," I murmured, meaning every word.

CHAPTER
sixteen

Veronica

CALEB MADE A SMALL FIRE USING THE FIRE PIT IN KARA'S BACKYARD. The sharp scent of burning firewood filled my nostrils. I wasn't sure what kind of wood he used, but it smelled sweet.

Mesmerized, I stared at the fire, enjoying the pleasant heat on my face. It crackled and hissed, sparks dancing around it like fireflies.

Caleb sat on the grass and rested his back against the wooden bench. He had tugged me down so I sat between his legs, my back against him and my head resting on his shoulder.

I could count on two hands how many times I'd felt happy before Caleb came in my life. After Caleb? I had lost count.

He pulled me closer, his arms wrapping around my stomach. He couldn't stop touching me, and I didn't want him to. I felt him kiss my hair, rubbing his cheek against it. Then he started kissing my shoulder, little nibbles that sent electricity down my arm.

If this continued, I wouldn't be able to talk to him about the important things that had happened today. And I needed to know why...why... Wait, what was it that I needed to know again? He was distracting me, making my brain foggy.

"Caleb, I need to talk to you about—"

He nuzzled the side of my neck with his nose, rubbing up and down, up and down. I heard him take a deep breath and sigh leisurely, like a big cat, as if he was savoring the scent of my skin.

"Hmm. You smell so good. About what?"

He licked my skin, and my head fell back.

"Huh?" I asked absently.

I felt him smile against my neck before he ran his lips and tongue over that sensitive part just below my ear.

"About what, Red?" he murmured seductively.

"Um..." I bit my lip, stopping any embarrassing sound from escaping. I had to take a few moments to gather my thoughts. I cleared my throat.

"Caleb?"

"Hmm?"

His fingertips traced small circles on my arm, and his lips brushed my ear again.

"Y-your mom...hates me."

He paused for a moment, and I nearly wanted to take back what I said. I wanted him to keep kissing me.

"No, she doesn't. She just didn't understand what was happening. Don't worry. I went to see her and I talked to her about us." He started kissing me below my jaw.

"What...did she say?" I insisted.

He pulled back and sighed loudly. "She wants to have us over for dinner."

I bit my lip.

He rubbed my arms for comfort. "Please?"

This time, I sighed. "All right."

"Don't worry. She doesn't bite." And then he pressed his lips to my neck again. "But I do."

He bit me softly. I let out a shaky laugh. "Caleb?"

"Hmm?"

I closed my eyes, my breath catching as he took the strap of my tank top between his teeth and nudged it off my shoulder. He placed a chaste kiss there, and the sensation of his soft lips on that newly exposed skin felt so erotic, I shivered.

This was getting out of hand. I really needed to talk to him about what had happened, and if we didn't stop now, I wouldn't remember anything but his kisses.

"C-Caleb." *Breathe.* "Who do you think…" *Inhale.* "Set you up?" *Exhale.*

He growled, pulling back. That stopped him from kissing me, and I took advantage of that by dragging in deep breaths, hoping it would calm my wild heart.

He raked a hand through his hair, looking frustrated. "Justin."

"Maybe it was Beatrice-Rose."

He froze.

"Remember at the station when your mom said she had to hear it from Beatrice-Rose? How did she know you were in jail?"

His eyes turned cold as his whole body tensed.

"Where are your spare car keys?" I asked.

"I—" He paused for a moment. "I remember looking for them one time, and they weren't in the last place where I put them, so I just didn't bother looking for them." He clenched his jaw.

"Does Justin know the code to your flat?"

"He doesn't."

"Remember that night when I told you I saw her leaving your building? And you said she knows the code to get into your flat. What if…she stole your spare keys and planted the drugs in your car?"

His eyes flashed. "She wouldn't dare."

I let him digest what I'd said for a moment.

"Son of a bitch," he growled after a moment. "Son of a bitch!"

The energy around him vibrated. I could tell from the way his eyes sparked with anger that he was starting to realize Beatrice-Rose's potential role in this fiasco. I knew he still couldn't believe his childhood friend could be so deceiving, so manipulative.

I could be wrong—maybe she didn't have anything to do with the drugs in Caleb's car—but I wasn't going to eliminate the possibility. Caleb might think she wouldn't dare cross a line that could cause him real harm, but I knew better. I knew she was capable of anything.

"Is Justin pressing charges against you?" I asked.

"Why the hell would he press charges against me?"

"Because you nearly killed him?"

"No." He blew out a frustrated breath. "My lawyer has taken care of it. Look," he started, his tone softening. "I don't want you to worry. Leave it alone, okay? Trust me to take care of it."

"Don't tell me you'll take care of it." I felt a flash of anger. *Good*, I thought. I was coming back.

I had been feeling disconnected from myself since I had that nightmare, exhausted from trying to push back bad memories from my childhood. Feeling anger was good.

"I don't need your caveman, 'me man, take care of business; you woman, no-worry' bullshit right now."

I narrowed my eyes when he started laughing.

"I'm serious—"

"Baby," he said softly, turning me around and cupping my face in his hands. "Look at me," he pleaded. "I will do everything in my power to protect you. There is nothing he can do to you as long as I'm here. And it's not because I don't trust you to take care of yourself. I need you to believe in me."

His green eyes were tender as they looked into mine. "You are the strongest and most independent person I know. But you don't have to be strong by yourself anymore because…" He brushed his thumb against my cheek. Helpless, I leaned in to his touch. "Because now you have me."

My throat felt thick with emotion. No one had ever made me feel this way.

I reached up for his hand, pulling it from my face. I kissed his palm, then his lips. "Caleb," I said. "When you know that someone in this world is thinking about you…when you know someone wants to be with you, that they think the world of you…when they make you fall in love with them over and over again…it makes you feel like the world is a better place after all. Even when everyone is against you, it's okay. Because you know that one person will never leave your side. For me, that person is you."

He looked down for a moment, and I saw him swallow. When his eyes turned up to meet mine, the look of tenderness in them made me feel loved. But I didn't like the guilt I was feeling. It didn't belong between us. I felt the need to apologize.

"I'm sorry for everything. The fight, you going to jail, your mom getting upset with you. These things wouldn't have happened to you if it wasn't for me—"

"No." His voice was firm. He pulled back. "Listen, Red. My mom was wrong. Whatever she said to you at the station was based on what Beatrice-Rose told her. You didn't cause that fight with Justin—I did. That bastard did. He was asking for it." His upper lip curled into a snarl. "It's not your fault he's a sick, perverted, *hateful* asshole. Why are you blaming yourself for other people's mistakes?"

I froze. My body felt numb, but I could feel my heart beating against my chest. When his eyes met mine, they widened slightly. As if he saw what I was thinking, knew what I was feeling.

He held my face in his hands, silently begging me to look at him. But I couldn't. Finally, he said it. "Look at me, love."

I blew out a shaky breath and raised my eyes to his. Hot tears threatened to spill, but I blinked them away.

"I know what you're thinking. There's only one person who can put that look in your eyes. And I wish I could hurt him right now."

He knew, I realized. Without a word from me, he knew what I was thinking.

"People who love to hurt others to make themselves feel better, who break your heart and deliberately make you lose your self-respect and self-worth over and over again…"

I felt my throat close up.

"Your dad didn't deserve your love. He wasn't worthy of it. It wasn't your fault."

I closed my eyes tightly.

"But you gave him your love anyway. Doesn't that tell you a lot about yourself? You told me before that you blamed yourself for what happened to your parents. That your spineless dad blamed you. But I know you know better than that, Red. You know better. It wasn't your fault," he repeated. "And what happened earlier today was not your fault either."

I wasn't aware the tears had already fallen until he wiped them with his thumbs. I'd rarely cried before I met Caleb, because I thought tears were a sign of weakness, a sign that something bad had happened. But now I knew that tears could mean good things too.

"Baby," he whispered, sounding pained. I knew he didn't like seeing me cry. He hated it. "People can't give something they don't have in themselves. Your dad chose not to love, or maybe he doesn't know how. But you do. And you have so much to give. So much." He kissed my lips softly, to comfort, to soothe. "And I want it all. I want all your love, Red."

Undone, I threw my arms around him, burying my face in his neck. "They could all hate me right now. I don't care. As long as you're with me, Caleb. As long as you're with me, I can endure anything."

It was a moment before he spoke again. "Red." His voice was rough, but his hands were gentle as they stroked my back, his arms wrapped protectively around me. "You can't make me love you any more than this."

CHAPTER
seventeen

Veronica

CALEB SPREAD A BLANKET ON THE GRASS BESIDE THE FIRE. HE sprawled in the middle of it, folding his arms behind his head and crossing his ankles. The picture of a pampered, gorgeous rich boy.

He closed his eyes, humming. I stood beside him, raising my eyebrows. "Did you need anything else, master? Some refreshments, perhaps?"

He opened one eye and grinned. "I thought you'd never ask."

I snorted. He was hopeless. Earlier, his sweet declarations had made me cry, and now he made me want to laugh and slap the silly insolence off his handsome face at the same time.

I turned around to grab something to throw at him. "I'll show you refreshm—aah!"

He sat up quickly, reaching his arms out to grab my waist and pull me to his lap.

"Caleb!"

He maneuvered our bodies, grasping my waist in his strong hands so I was lying underneath him.

His bronze hair fell over one eye. The other stared at me challengingly. "Who's the master now?"

I pressed my palms to my mouth, trying desperately not to dissolve into laughter. And then he started tickling me mercilessly. I made inhuman noises, trying to slap away his hands and cover my mouth at the same time. It was late at night, and I really didn't want to wake up the neighbors.

"Who's the master now, Red?"

"Me!"

"Wrong answer." He tsked. "Try again."

"Caleb, don't!"

He grabbed my wrists, pulling them above my head. He held them in place with one hand—he was so strong—so he could continue to torture me with his fingers.

"Don't what? Unless you give me the answer I want—"

My sides hurt from laughing. "Caleb, no!"

"I'm going to keep doing—"

I kissed him. There was no other way to stop him unless I gave in and told him he was the master. But I was in a playful and defiant mood, and I didn't want to give in.

"You play dirty," he breathed.

"Who's the master now?" I fired back.

His shoulders shook as he laughed quietly. His eyes were shining and happy. Wrapping his arms around my waist, he rolled on his back and took me with him so I was lying on top of him.

"You are," he answered softly. "Now what would you like me to do for you? I have many talents, master. For example, my tongue can—"

I covered his mouth to keep him from finishing his sentence. I knew it was going to be something dirty.

His eyes danced with laughter as I shook my head at him. And then he opened his mouth and bit my palm. I pulled my hand back, a strong current of electricity zinging up my arm.

He chuckled, lifting his head to kiss me again. His lips were soft, smooth, and warm as he caught my bottom lip and sucked.

I felt that kiss all the way to my toes.

When I pulled away, his eyes were glinting naughtily as if to say *We both know who the real master is.*

I was still tingling, so I didn't say anything. I just rested my head on his chest, my arm going around his torso. He wrapped one arm around me, while the other stroked my back gently. We stayed like that for a few minutes. Peaceful. Relaxed. Happy.

He stretched a hand up above us, making a cup shape with his palm. I looked up to see him closing one eye and staring at the sky with the other.

"What are you doing?" I asked.

"Holding the moon in the palm of my hand," he answered quietly.

I moved until I could see what he was seeing—exactly that, the moon in the palm of his hand. I relaxed against him, smiling. But he wasn't. There was a somber expression on his handsome face and a hint of sadness in his eyes.

"You're like the moon, Red," he murmured. "I can only pretend that I'm holding you in my hands."

"What do you mean?" I asked. My voice was hoarse.

His eyes were serious. "I feel like you're going to slip away again."

My chest tightened. "I won't."

I reached for his hand, intertwining his fingers with mine. And then I kissed his palm, placing it on my cheek.

"What am I going to do with you?" he asked, a small frown marring his forehead.

Love me. Just love me.

As if he saw the pleading in my eyes, he nodded. "If you are the moon, I am the stars. There are millions across the sky. I surround you." He smiled.

Oh, Caleb.

I let out a deep breath, trying to relieve the heaviness in my chest. My heart felt full.

I pillowed my cheek on his chest again, closing my eyes as I listened to his heartbeat.

"I'm glad," I admitted.

There was comfort in silence and contentment in his touch. I was just drifting off to sleep, lulled by the rise and fall of his chest, when he cleared his throat.

"Don't get mad," he muttered apprehensively.

My body tensed. I looked up at him. He looked nervous.

"I got you something else."

I couldn't blame him being nervous, because every time he tried to give me something, I threw it back at him. But something had changed in me, something he had opened up or fixed, because I didn't feel defensive or suspicious anymore.

Because I knew he loved me. And it was real.

"Okay."

"Sit here and wait for me. I won't be long."

My heart beating wildly, I got up and sat on the wooden bench to wait for him. When Caleb came back, his green eyes were wide, the pupils dilated. He was raking his fingers in his hair, a sure sign that he was anxious.

I expected him to be holding a gift box or a fancy paper bag, but he wasn't holding anything. I stared up at him, but he only sat beside me.

He tapped his long foot against the edge of my slipper, teasing.

I tapped him back. "Did you forget the gift at your place?" I asked.

He reached behind himself and presented a long, thin box.

"I wanted to give you something to remember me every day," he started, still sounding nervous. "I had this designed for you. Weeks ago."

I stared at the box he held before me, unable to move.

"Open it, Red." He smiled adorably, dimples appearing on his cheeks. "For me," he added softly, his eyes beseeching.

Slowly, I reached for it. Opened it.

It was an elegant necklace with a butterfly pendant. The butterfly was silver, the size of a penny, with delicate scroll-like filigree inside the wings. Tiny diamonds encrusted the wings, glinting in the moonlight. A pear-shaped, blood-red ruby connected the wings.

It was breathtaking. Mesmerizing.

I didn't miss the symbolism of it. A shaky breath shuddered out of me, tears pricking my eyes.

"Do you like it?"

Like it? I love it.

But I could only nod. I was afraid that if I opened my mouth, I would start crying.

"Do you remember the story I told you about the green caterpillar and the butterfly?"

I nodded again. He smiled gently, as if he knew what I was feeling. Maybe he did. Caleb knew me like no one else did.

"I'd like to see it on you." He lifted it out of the case. "Please?"

I had my hair up, so I turned around and let him place it around my neck. After he locked the clasp, he touched my shoulders and turned me to face him. His eyes were tender as he gazed at me.

"You make everything beautiful, Red."

I cupped the pendant in my palm. "Caleb, this is terribly expensive."

His eyes turned dark and intense. "I would sell everything I own for you."

My breath caught, my hand falling limply to my lap.

How could I respond to that? But even if I knew what to say, my throat had closed up. He reached out and rubbed my lower lip with his thumb, back and forth, back and forth. I held my breath, waiting for his kiss. Wishing for it. But then he leaned back against the bench, his gaze returning to the fire like he was contemplating something.

His mood had changed.

Unsure, I waited for him to say something. Anything.

After a moment, he spoke. "Want to hear a story?"

I scooted next to him, our sides touching. I waited for him to reach for my hand, but he didn't. "Of course."

He took a deep breath. "Once upon a time, there was a boy who had everything," he began, his voice becoming deeper and warmer. "Or so he thought. One night, he decided to walk in the forest. He was bored, restless. There was something missing in his life, and he couldn't figure out what it was. And then he saw a tiny, beautiful bird on the ground. Her wing was broken.

"He picked her up very, very gently and took her home. He nursed her until her wing healed. He put her in a cage to prevent her from flying away and hurting herself more. And to prevent others from hurting her. You see, the cage was like a shield, a form of protection.

"They were together every day after that. She sang for him, and it made him happy. After a few days, she was healed. Still, he kept her in the cage, worried that she'd be hurt again. But then she stopped singing.

"The boy knew what he was doing was wrong. He was keeping her for himself. He was being selfish. She made him happy, filled those missing parts of himself, and made him feel content. He wanted to keep her, to own her.

"But he found that he couldn't endure it when she was sad, when she was lonely. He realized that all he wanted was to give her happiness, even at the expense of his own. So he opened the cage." He paused, raking his hand through his hair. "And he let her go."

His eyes looked so sad, and they pulled me to him. I wanted to touch him, give him comfort, but I was scared that I would ruin the moment.

I would forever regret that I didn't trust him and had left him before.

He took another deep breath. "She flew away and left him."

Now I reached for his hand, lacing our fingers together. "Did she come back?" I managed to ask.

A small smile flitted on his lips. "Yes," he replied, the sadness in his eyes disappearing. "She did."

I smiled back.

"Sometimes I want to put you in a cage," he confessed. His eyes were intense, passionate. "But you were the one who captured me. And I would gladly stay there and belong to you."

Something powerful was forming inside me. And it was drowning me deeper and deeper. But I didn't want to come up for air.

"I know I'm not exactly a prize. I'm stubborn and impulsive. Immature. I say and do stupid things all the time. But…"

I looked at him, waiting for him to continue.

"But please stay with me," he said softly. "Stay."

My heart melted. I knew this time I wouldn't be able to stop the tears. He got up suddenly, and before I could say anything, he was kneeling in front of me.

I could hear the blood pounding in my ears as I watched him.

My eyes widened as he presented me with a small jeweler's box, like an offering. I noticed that he didn't look nervous anymore. He looked, I realized, like a man who had been looking for something his whole life but had now found his answer. He looked as if peace had settled in him, calm and purposeful.

My breath caught as I saw a ring lying in a bed of velvet.

White diamonds surrounded a tear-shaped ruby in almost the same design as the necklace. Two tiny butterflies encrusted in diamonds flanked the dazzling red stone.

"Red, will you be my wife?"

Speechless, overwhelmed, I stared at him. I saw him swallow. Suddenly, his eyes filled with alarm.

"I was going to wait for the perfect time after you graduated, but…I just needed to… I need…" He shut his eyes. He looked like he was in pain. "Red, will you marry me? Will you spend the rest of your life with me? Have kids with me? I'll build you a house, buy you a dog…anything you want. Just say—"

I fell into his arms, clasping his neck. He caught me easily, wrapping his strong arms around me.

"Yes! Yes, Caleb. I'll be your wife."

His hold tightened around me, and when he spoke again, his voice was gruff. "I love you, Red. You're the only girl, the only one, who took my heart. Please don't give it back."

"I won't. I won't," I sobbed. "It's mine."

"It's yours. It's always been yours."

CHAPTER

eighteen

Veronica

"RED, COME HOME WITH ME TONIGHT?" CALEB ASKED. "I MISS waking up with you close to me."

I was no match against the power of his adorable dimples and insistent green eyes.

So I told Caleb to wait for me in his car while I packed a change of clothes and some books for my class tomorrow. I moved as fast as I could, taking care to be quiet so as not to wake Kara.

I was just placing a note for her on the fridge when my eyes landed on the engagement ring on my finger.

God. I'm engaged to Caleb Lockhart.

I pressed my hand to my stomach, feeling a flutter there.

We hadn't known each other long, but it felt like we had been through so much already. It felt like I had known him for a long time.

It felt...*so* right.

I grabbed my bag and stepped outside.

"Hi," he whispered.

The sight of Caleb leaning against the car caught my breath. The light from the lamppost illuminated him: the way his eyes flickered with pleasure at the sight of me, the way his lips stretched into a gorgeous smile, and the way his long and lean body moved as he grabbed me by the waist and kissed me long and hard.

It didn't matter if everyone was against us. Caleb mattered. He was all that mattered.

"Hi, yourself," I said breathlessly, my lips tingling from his kiss.

"Ready?" He released me, opening the car door for me like the gentleman that he was.

I watched as he walked around the car, admiring the confident way he moved, the way his eyes flicked to me through the windshield. He opened the door and slid into the car, a huge grin on his face as he turned to face me.

"Hi again, my Red."

We just sat there for a moment, looking at each other with goofy smiles on our faces.

"Finally," he murmured.

I knew what he meant. We were together—finally. We had just gotten back together, and everything around us seemed to be trying to pull us apart. But when Caleb was beside me and his eyes looked at me like I was his everything, nothing else mattered. It was overwhelming to feel this way about someone. But it felt really good.

He reached for my hand and intertwined our fingers before

he stepped on the gas. The roads were empty as we drove to Caleb's apartment. I pushed the button to open the window, closing my eyes as the air teased my hair and skin. It felt good.

"Red, about this dinner with my mom…"

I tensed. His hand tightened against mine as he threw me a worried look.

"It's actually a dinner party. It's my birthday."

His birthday?

I groaned, covering my face with my hands.

How did I not even know his birthday?

I'd never asked, and he'd never told me. Birthdays just didn't hold good memories for me.

"She throws a party for me now and then at our house. My mom still lives there. You'll be able to see where I grew up. There's a lake in the backyard," he continued excitedly. "I can take you to see my cottage on the property. It's a small one. Ben, my…dad, and I built it."

Now I was the one who squeezed his hand to offer comfort.

"When is your birthday?" I asked quietly, ashamed.

His face fell. "You don't know when my birthday is?" He pouted.

I worried my bottom lip, but then I saw his lips twitch from trying to suppress his laughter.

"Caleb!"

He laughed. "I was born June 25. A big, healthy, handsome baby boy. I know when your birthday is. It's September 15, isn't it?"

I felt my shoulders tense.

"I asked Kar," he clarified. "What's wrong?"

"I'm sorry I didn't ask about your birthday before. I'll remember it from now on."

He threw me a quick look, his eyes searching my face, checking if something was wrong.

"It's okay, Red," he said after a moment.

"When is the party?"

"I don't know the exact date yet, but it's after finals. So it's perfect. You have time to get me a gift."

I pursed my lips to keep from grinning again. "Who's going to be there?"

"Vampires and werewolves," he teased. "Just people, Red. I'll be there beside you as long as you want me to."

"Will you chew my food and spoon-feed me too?" I fluttered my lashes at him.

He looked blank for a few seconds before he threw his head back and laughed.

Caleb parked his car in the underground garage of his building, got out, and opened my door for me. He reached for my bag before he grabbed my hand and led me to the elevators.

When we entered his apartment, his hand tightened around mine, and I looked up at him.

He was grinning.

I knew how he felt. I was home. *We* were home.

"I'm just going to get something to drink."

"Okay. I'll meet you in the kitchen—be right back."

"Okay."

I opened the fridge, looking for something to nibble on. Had he eaten yet? Maybe I could prepare something for him.

Suddenly, I heard "Storm" by Lifehouse playing through the speakers. Caleb only played Lifehouse when he was in a sentimental mood. I smiled and hummed to myself.

Not even a minute had passed when I heard him enter the kitchen. I was bent over, looking in the fridge, searching for the eggs and ham so I could make him an omelet.

"I guess you haven't gotten groceries yet," I commented absently, frowning at the contents—or lack thereof—in the fridge.

"Caleb?" I asked when there was no response.

"Yeah?" The huskiness in his tone made me straighten and turn to look at him.

My breath caught. Caleb was leaning against the kitchen island, facing me, his hands resting on the counter, watching me with hooded eyes. That lingering, intense, and measuring look caused my pulse to quicken.

He raised an eyebrow.

"Um…" I had to search my brain for my thoughts. Oh right. Dinner. "Did you have dinner yet?"

His pink tongue darted out to lick his bottom lip. "Yeah." He paused, then said, "But I feel like eating."

I held on to the fridge door for support. My knees suddenly felt weak. "I-I'll make you something to eat. What would you like?"

He shook his head no, but his eyes told me everything he wanted. And then…

"I would really like," he said, his voice low, "to eat you."

My eyes widened, breaths coming in pants as my heart thudded against my chest. He made a mesmerizing picture, standing there watching my every move.

"Did you wear those for me?" he asked.

What?

His eyes swept from my face down to my legs, lingering there before moving back up to meet my gaze. "Sexy."

Oh. The shorts.

"Come here, Red."

Mesmerized, I walked to him, letting the fridge door slap shut behind me. I stopped a few feet away, close but not *too* close.

He angled his head as he watched me. Then he grinned.

There was something powerfully irresistible about him when he was in this mood. Playful, teasing…in charge.

As if he wouldn't take no for an answer.

As if he would just take what he wanted, whenever he wanted. It was magnetic.

I felt the charge in the air, felt something momentous was about to happen. My steps faltered, and I averted my gaze. I knew if I took another step toward him now, it would change everything.

A million thoughts crossed my mind. Doubts, insecurities, hesitations, paralyzing me for a moment.

"Red."

I looked up. The look of love and tenderness in his green eyes was all the answer I needed. This was Caleb. The boy who had taught me how to trust.

The same boy—the only one—who had shown me what it was to desire. To want to be touched, be kissed, be savored, and to make him feel the same.

The same boy who had shown me how it was to love and be loved in return.

It was like having a secret I'd held in my fist for so long, but now I wanted to let it go. I wanted to reveal it, but only to him. Only to him.

All of the things that I had gone through—all the suffering and heartbreak—had led me here. To him. To my Caleb. To this moment.

I stepped forward.

I felt the heat of his gaze on my skin as he watched me close the distance between us. I stopped a few inches from him.

"Close enough?" I croaked.

A triumphant smile spread on his full lips before his hands banded around my waist, dragging down to cup my ass as he turned us around and lifted me onto the counter.

"Yeah, and you know what?" he purred, spreading my legs.

I parted them willingly, and he stepped in between them. My head fell back, and I flattened my palms against the counter to keep my balance—and give him better access.

Caleb pressed his lips to that sensitive part below my ear, licking and sucking, sending goose bumps dancing along my arms and legs. His hands slid down my thighs, up and down, up and down, fingers digging into my skin. He pulled me closer, fitting snugly between my legs.

"I'm really, really hungry. In fact," he growled, "I'm starving."

I swallowed a moan and unconsciously arched my hips up against him. The tone of his voice, so low and deep, made me feel a hot longing in my stomach.

"There are so many things I want to do to you." He hooked my legs around his waist and ground his hips against me, pressing his arousal against that part of my body where every sensation seemed to be magnified a hundredfold.

This time, a moan of pleasure escaped my lips. Feeling bold, I asked, "Like what?"

He pulled back a little, and I could tell he hadn't expected me to ask that. But he recovered quickly, smiling in a way that said *Challenge accepted*.

He touched the tip of his tongue to his top lip before he leaned closer and murmured in my ear, "I want to bury my face between your legs."

I gasped loudly.

Hot. I felt hot. All over.

"Does that scare you?" he asked.

I swallowed. Hard. Suddenly, I wanted to close my legs, wanting to rub them together. The way his green eyes lit up made me think he knew exactly what I was feeling.

Something very warm was sliding through my veins, making my skin feel tight. I had this unexplainable urge to be closer to him—closer than this. I wanted to feel him skin on skin. I shook my head.

He chuckled, low and deep. "I've been without you for so long. So long. I barely sleep without you, Red. So I think about you instead. I think about you all the time."

His lips grazed my ear, and an involuntary shiver raced up my spine. "Do you know what I think about?" he asked.

His big, warm hands moved down to caress my thighs, squeezing them possessively.

"Tell me," I gasped, unable to stop myself from arching into his touch.

"I think of your taste…in my mouth," he rasped. "I think about what you'll look like when I suck you. Lick you. Eat you up."

His words drove me wild. If this was madness, I would blindly jump into it if it meant I could keep listening to his words, feeling his touch, tasting his kiss.

"Would you let me?" His eyes searched my face. "Red?"

Instead of answering, I looked into his green eyes and flattened my palms on his chest, startled by the static between us. The warmth of him under his shirt made me yearn to touch his bare skin. Gingerly, I reached for the hem of his shirt and slowly lifted it, revealing his defined stomach. His eyes widened a fraction as he understood what I wanted.

He was quiet as he watched me lift his shirt up and off him, letting it fall to the floor.

He was beautiful, his tan skin looking smooth and healthy in the dim light. My fingertips softly brushed the light trail of hair below his navel, and I heard him suck in a breath. I stopped, unsure, and looked up at him.

The skin around his mouth was tight, his eyes a darker shade of green. "It's okay," he said hoarsely. "You can keep going."

He closed his eyes, a deep groan escaping his lips as I slowly traced a line over the planes of his torso. His skin was hot to the touch, his muscles hardened like iron.

"Red," he said softly, opening his eyes and lightly brushing my inner thighs with his thumbs as he pressed a soft kiss to my lips. "Let me worship you."

"Yes," I murmured against his lips. "Yes, Caleb."

His tongue traced the seam of my lips, coaxing me to open them. He pulled my bottom lip between his, tugging and sucking gently.

Everything felt so intense: the burning touch of his skin, the warmth and peppermint scent of his breath, the hungry sounds he made at the back of his throat.

I opened for his kiss, and his tongue dipped inside to taste, exploring my mouth. His lips slid against mine eagerly, impatiently, as if he couldn't get enough.

When I touched my tongue to his, a low growl erupted from his chest. He buried his hands in my hair, gripping tightly as he angled my head to deepen the kiss. For one staggering moment, the kiss became hot, hungry, and *wild*.

I felt on fire. There was something building inside me that I had no name for. I was in this cocoon of pleasure that Caleb had built around us, and I wanted more.

"I've never wanted anyone this desperately," he rasped. "Never." He pulled back to frame my face in his hands.

He held my gaze as his hands slid down to caress the exposed skin underneath my top. He tugged on the hem, raising his eyebrows in question. I reached down and helped him pull my top off. He reached behind me to unhook my bra with an expert flick of his fingers. With trembling hands, I pulled the straps down my arms, discarding my bra on the counter.

His lips parted as his eyes drank me in. My arms itched to cover myself, but the look of hunger and appreciation in his green eyes made me feel wanted. *Craved*.

"You're so beautiful," he said, his voice rough. His fingertip traced a line down my throat, his eyes lighting up when he saw the necklace he'd given me. He continued until he lightly brushed my nipple, sending a bolt of electricity traveling down my spine and between my legs. I moaned, arching into his touch. He bit his bottom lip as he watched my face.

"Caleb…please." I strained toward him, wanting more.

I closed my eyes and moaned as he bent his head and took my breast in his mouth, sucking lightly, then sucking hard, then lightly again. The contrast in pressure from his mouth drove me wild with longing.

I plunged my hands into his hair, gripping firmly as his mouth continued to torture me with pleasure.

He straightened to kiss me with wet, openmouthed kisses that robbed me of breath. "Lie back for me, love," he whispered.

I leaned back and let his warm hands help lower me onto my back. My hands gripped the sides of the counter as I watched him continue kissing me, working his way down my body, drinking and nipping my skin until he reached the edge of my shorts. His eyes flicked up to look at me, full of heat and promise.

"Red, do you want this?"

The look in his eyes—the hunger, the need, but most especially the *love*—took my breath away. What I saw mirrored my own feelings—my hunger, my need, and my love for him. In this moment, I realized I really wanted this with him. He was everything to me, and I would give everything to him.

"Yes," I choked out. "Yes."

His eyes filled with fervent satisfaction before he pulled my shorts and panties down my legs. He grabbed my hips and jerked me closer to him so that I was on the edge of the counter, and he was flush between my legs. Grinding his hardness against me, he leaned forward and firmly held my wrists to my sides so I couldn't move them to touch him.

"I want you. I want you so bad, it hurts," he growled and buried his face between my legs.

"Caleb!" I cried out, shocked at the feel of his hot, wet lips there—against the most intimate part of my body. I almost jumped off the counter, but his strong hands released my wrists to caress my thighs soothingly. He kissed me there like he would my lips—small, openmouthed hungry kisses that made me strain against him.

"I knew it," he whispered. "You're intoxicating here too." His nose nuzzled me *there*.

I thought I couldn't have been more scandalized than I already was, but when I felt his nose nuzzle me there and heard him inhale—

"Caleb, no!" I covered my face with my hands. I wanted to hide in embarrassment.

"Red," he murmured softly. "It's okay, baby. I love your taste. I love your smell. I love everything about you. Look at me," he coaxed.

I couldn't. How could he expect me to? I was beyond embarrassed. No one had ever...

I heard him straighten. I let out a sharp breath when I felt his hands close around my wrists gently.

"Baby," he cajoled, pulling my hands away to expose my face to him. But I couldn't look...

His lips drifted to my shoulders, my neck, my cheeks, all the while murmuring sweet things to me.

"You're so damned beautiful. You taste like a dream, like a drug."

I was panting. I was lost, so lost in him.

Slowly, I opened my eyes. He was gazing at me, leaning forward, his hands flat on the counter on either side of my hips. He had a small smile on his lips.

"Hi, beautiful."

"Caleb." I hitched up on my elbows, feeling hot, needy, and scared. "I've never done something like this before," I admitted shakily.

"It's okay." He ran his hands up and down my thighs, soothing. "Do you want to stop?"

He stared at me with eyes filled with such tenderness and longing that my breath caught in my throat. Caleb's hair was mussed from my hands, his lips red and swollen and wet from kissing me. He was so beautiful. I swallowed my anxiety—and felt a jolt of heat and need all the way to my core.

"No. Don't stop," I whispered, meaning it.

A wolfish grin lit up his face. "I'm going to take care of you, baby," he promised. Then he started all over again—greedy kisses and slow licks and bites that started on my lips and moved down my body. He took his time, caressing, savoring, and worshipping my body until I was feverish with need.

"Caleb, please…"

He hooked my legs over his shoulders as he once again pleasured me in the most intimate part of my body.

"So fucking good," he groaned.

The sight of his broad shoulders and his dark head between my legs and the feel of his warm tongue eagerly pleasuring me sent bolts of electricity through my body.

A series of moans escaped my throat as I gripped his hair. I couldn't seem to decide whether I wanted to pull him closer or push him away. I wanted him to stop. I wanted him to keep going. I wanted more. I wanted to find relief from this agonizing pleasure that was building in me.

"Yeah, just like that. Just like that," he coaxed, working me with his lips and tongue until I was thrashing against him.

My mind went blank as pleasure tore through me, shooting throughout my body and finally sliding silvery over my limbs until I collapsed, crying out his name.

So that's how it felt...

I was floating, my mind completely detached from everything else. It took a moment for me to realize he had carried me to his room and gently placed me on his bed. When he reclined beside me, he placed his arm underneath my head and I curled up into him, burying my face against his neck. He pulled my leg between his as he caressed my back soothingly with his other arm. I was still trembling.

"Red? Was that your first orgasm?" he asked softly.

I nodded, burying my face in his neck. Vaguely, I became aware that Lifehouse was now crooning "Everything" through the speakers.

"You don't know how that makes me feel," he whispered hoarsely. "I..."

The tone of his voice alerted my senses. He sounded like he was in pain. Suddenly, I grew aware of the hardness between his thighs, the uncomfortable tightness of his legs and shoulders.

"Caleb?"

"It's okay, love."

But it wasn't. He had shown me what it was like to come apart, but why did I still feel incomplete?

I wanted—*needed* to make him feel what he'd made me feel. I wanted to give that to him.

My heart belonged to him, but I wanted us to belong to each other *completely*.

I kissed his neck, inhaling his scent. So addicting, so *male*.

"Make love to me," I said.

He pulled me back, gazing down at me with a question in his eyes.

I placed a gentle kiss on his neck, reassuring him. "Please."

His nostrils flared, his eyes turning a darker green. "God. You're going to fucking ruin me," he groaned.

I framed his face with my palms, marveling at the beauty of his features before pressing my lips to his. Tentatively, I caressed his lips with my tongue, and a groan escaped his mouth as he positioned himself on top of me, taking control.

He was in charge, and we both knew it.

His hands palmed my breasts, stroking and caressing while his mouth feasted on my lips, my neck, the skin above my breasts. His hand slid down my ribs, my stomach, my hips, and between my legs, but he never stopped kissing me.

And then his finger was there, petting and making circles. I pulled my mouth away from his as I let out a loud moan, my head falling back against the pillow.

"So beautiful. Come for me, baby. Come all over my hand."

My fingers dug into his skin as I bowed off the bed, pleading with him to give me relief. His mouth swallowed my cries as I came apart.

Dimly, I was aware of him getting up. I heard the snap of a drawer, the rustle of clothes, and the crinkling of plastic before he was back.

I blinked up at him, still floating in the haze of pleasure he had put me in. I noticed the tight skin around his mouth, the way he gritted his teeth, the lust and love in his eyes as he gazed down at me, and his arousal that pressed against my thigh.

"Caleb?"

"Yeah, baby?"

I heard his sharp intake of breath as I reached to unbutton his pants. He stopped my movements with his hand.

"Are you sure?" he asked hoarsely.

I nodded. "I want to belong to you completely, Caleb."

He kissed me hungrily, his arousal pressing between my legs. He took off his pants and boxers, and I felt heat flood my cheeks as I noticed how big he was, how aroused as he rolled the condom on. Suddenly, he was back on top of me, his arms on either side of my head as he gazed down at me with hunger. I felt him press himself between my legs, rubbing himself against my center. He was hot, hard, and unyielding. I closed my eyes, preparing myself.

Then nothing. When I opened them, I found him smiling at me tenderly.

"Here. Stay with me. Right here. Just right here, my Red."

His hand trembled as he stroked my face. He bent his head and drank from my lips, all the while murmuring about the love he felt for me.

"I'm scared. I've never done this before and"—I drew in a shaky breath—"and I don't want to disappoint you. I know you have a lot of experience and you have expectations, and I'm scared that I won't be able to—"

"Red." His voice was low and rough. "Nothing could even come close to how you make me feel just by being here. How could you even think you'd disappoint me?" He smiled, lovingly stroking my cheek. "What you've given me is more than I could hope for, and if you decide you don't want to continue, we'll stop. I want to make this perfect for you. This night is all about you."

At that, all my fears melted. I reached for him, pulling him down to me for a soul-searing kiss. His hands reverently touched my thighs, my hips, circling around my waist until he gently caressed my breasts, his thumbs flicking my nipples before he bent his head and sucked my nipple in his mouth. I moaned, wild with pleasure.

The love he spoke of was in his touch, in the hungry movement of his lips, his tongue, his teeth as he kissed me. I was soaked with it, drowning in it, and I wanted more.

He searched my eyes as if looking for some hesitation—but there was nothing. My mind and my heart were made up. It was scary and overwhelming, and there was no turning back for me after this. As I looked into his green eyes, I knew—I didn't want to turn back. I was at the edge of the cliff, hanging by my fingertips. And I realized I was ready to fall forever. He was the one. He always had been. There would be no one else for me.

I loved him. It had always been him. I didn't want to fight it anymore. "Caleb," I murmured, sliding my fingers into his hair and pulling him to me for a kiss. "I love you. Make me yours."

He closed his eyes for a moment, breathing hard. When he opened them, I felt lost, so lost in him.

"I love you. I will love no one but you," he whispered before he entered me.

My breath hitched as I felt unwelcome pain pierce my pleasure-hazed world. I closed my eyes tightly, fighting the urge to push him off me. I felt full, ripped apart. Above me, Caleb froze.

"Baby, are you okay? I'm so sorry, love. Do you want me to stop?"

The fear in his tone made me open my eyes. His hand caressed the side of my face as he gazed at me with worry, and I melted.

"Talk to me, love," he murmured, kissing my lips, my cheeks, my nose.

He started licking my bottom lip, sucking it in his mouth. His hand slid between my legs, stroking small circles in my center and causing a now-familiar sensation. The feel of him inside me, so hard and full, and the slow motions of his fingers made my moan turn into a sob.

My fingers tightened in his hair, pulling him close for a demanding, almost desperate kiss. He groaned deep in his chest, turning demanding into carnal as his tongue plunged in my mouth, swallowing my moans.

I moved my hips experimentally and discovered that the pain was fading, replaced by an inexplicable pleasure that spread between my legs and shot up my spine. I bit my lip, closing my eyes tightly as I moaned. He abruptly pulled back from me, his face a mask of hunger and pain.

"Red, damn. I can't… Please don't move, baby."

Caleb placed his hand on my hip when I tried to move, commanding me to stay still.

"It's okay, Caleb. It feels…good."

"Yeah?"

I nodded, sliding my hips against him. The pleasure was building, spreading to my spine, my legs, my arms, and between my legs.

"Caleb, please… I need…"

He kissed me roughly, his hands reaching for my wrists, then dragging them up over my head. "I got you, baby."

And then he was moving—slowly, languorously, his green eyes watching my face. I was panting, my breath loud and fast as he plunged inside me, in and out, taking his time, driving me wild.

"Take everything—my body, my heart, my soul. Take them. They're yours," he rasped. He began to move faster, harder, wilder.

Everything felt tight, my body bowing as I pumped my hips in time with his thrusts. Pleasure was sharp and demanding as it built and spread inside my body. My whimpers turned into sobs, desperate to find relief.

"Let go, baby. Let go," he said softly, kissing his words into my mouth.

All I could do was wrap my legs tighter around him, my finger-nails digging into his back as his thrusts became wild and frenzied.

"Oh Jesus. Oh *fuck*."

Caleb's mouth latched onto my neck, sucking hard as he palmed my ass, grinding inside me so hard and so deep that I came apart with a scream.

"I love you. God, I love you so much. I love you so fucking much," he said roughly. He groaned out his pleasure, mouth parted, eyes half closed, head thrown back in abandon. I felt him drive deep one last time before he cried out my name and released.

CHAPTER
nineteen

Veronica

THE SIGHT OF CALEB'S HANDSOME FACE GREETED ME IN THE morning as I opened my eyes. He was lying on his stomach, his pink lips slightly parted as he slept peacefully, his arm wrapped around my hip.

He needed a haircut, I thought, noting that his hair was long enough now to cover his eyes. It was sticking up everywhere… like someone had buried their hands in it and pulled…

Oh God.

I did that to his hair last night when…

I think about your taste…in my mouth.

I shut my eyes, my breath hitching. The sound must have woken him up because I felt him move.

"Good morning, my Red," he said quietly. Huskily.

I knew it. You're intoxicating here too…

When I felt his lips on my neck, felt his arm pull me closer,

I jumped off the bed, snatched the blanket, and hastily wrapped it around me.

I let out a horrified squeak, covering my face with my hands. *Naked.*

Caleb was naked!

Oh God.

My eyes shifted from below his torso to his eyes. He was watching me, unperturbed, completely unselfconscious as he sprawled naked on the bed. He took in my reaction, biting his lip as he tried unsuccessfully to keep from laughing.

I grabbed the pillow and threw it right at his groin. I heard his *oof!* before I ran—no, more like waddled like a panicked penguin—into the bathroom.

I vaguely registered Caleb's laughter and nearly tripped over the clothes lying on the floor. *Were those his boxers?*

Closing the door with a thud, I turned the lock and sat on the floor.

Oh God.

I covered my face with my hands, shaking my head.

"Red?"

I froze.

"You okay there, love?" There was laughter in his voice, and that made my face feel hotter.

No. Definitely not okay. "I'm fine! I need a minute."

"Please open the door."

Open the door? No way. "I need to shower, Caleb."

My eyes widened as I heard him jiggling the doorknob. I scooted across the floor so I was leaning against the door. Just in case.

"Well, then open the door. I want in."

In? My hands went limp, and I barely caught the blanket before it fell from my body. "What?"

"I want to shower with you."

"No," I said weakly. "Just…no."

There was no reply on the other side of the door. Maybe he'd already left.

"I love you, Red."

My heart stuttered. It did every time he said those words.

It was a quiet declaration, but I heard it nonetheless. His voice felt so close that I only had to close my eyes and imagine he was behind me, without the door between us.

"Want pancakes?"

I nodded before realizing he couldn't see me. "Pancakes. Great. Sounds great."

"Okay."

When I heard the door close, I got up from the floor, turned on the water, and stepped into the shower, wincing at the unwelcome soreness between my legs. I closed my eyes, sighing at the delicious feel of warm water on my face.

I felt…different. Somehow I was more aware of my own body, of the places that I never thought were sensitive and that had never made me feel almost-desperate longing until last night. A picture of Caleb above me, green eyes intense as he watched my face, lips slightly parted as he touched my breasts…

I shook my head, reaching for the soap.

Caleb had been very considerate, sweet, and…thorough last night.

And I…I hadn't done anything but lie there.

A groan escaped my throat as I replayed everything I had—or had *not*—done last night.

Caleb had slept with a lot of girls before me.

The thought of him doing the things he had done to me to other girls made my heart hurt. Made me feel jealous. And insecure.

I knew the girls who came before me didn't mean anything to him, that I was his first love, but he had shared his body with them. They had, I was sure, satisfied him because they knew how to please a guy, and I…didn't.

Why didn't I do anything to please him last night? I glared at his shampoo as I squeezed some into my palm and massaged my hair with it.

I hated being a cliché about this, but I couldn't help thinking: *How was it for him last night? Was he…satisfied? Did I please him?*

I hated these thoughts.

What was I supposed to do? Ask him?

Hey, Caleb, did you have fun last night? Even though you did all the work?

Hey, Caleb. I know this is awkward, but…if you could rate last night, would that be excellent, good, average, or poor?

No. Just *no*.

I was driving myself nuts.

Even if I didn't satisfy him, I was sure he wouldn't admit it to me. He'd be worried about what I would think and feel.

What if I didn't please him at all?

Would he…would he find someone else to satisfy those needs?

I almost pulled my hair out as I rinsed. I let those thoughts swirl in my head as I finished my shower. And was still thinking about them when I stepped out.

Maybe I could ask him to rate it on a scale of one to ten. Correction—*zero* to ten.

No? No.

How about grading it with stars?

Just shut up! Zip it. Put a sock in it.

Fog covered the mirror, and I scrubbed it with my ringless hand. I reached for the ring, stroking the round shape of it. I had removed it and looped it around the necklace Caleb gave me last night before we left Kara's. Now all I needed was my bag so I could get ready. My bag. The one I'd left in the kitchen.

Damn it.

Carefully, I opened the door. And my heart melted for the second time this morning when I spotted my bag beside the door.

Caleb must have placed it there.

I remembered the time at Kara's when I'd asked Caleb to leave my things on the counter and I'd found him standing there waiting for me while I was in a towel.

I grabbed my bag and didn't waste time in pulling on jeans and a fitted, white gypsy tube top that ended just below my navel. There were red flowers stitched along the borders and white lace trim. The top showed off my shoulders. It was something that I usually didn't wear, but Kara had bought it for me and I really liked it. I wished I could see my reflection in the mirror, but it was still foggy.

Huffing in frustration, I realized I had forgotten to bring my blow-dryer with me last night since I was in a hurry. I had no choice but to put my hair up in a bun on top of my head. I hated tying my hair when it was still wet.

I quickly made the bed, nearly groaning when I spotted Caleb's boxers and jeans on the floor.

Oh God.

Caleb had a habit of leaving a trail of clothes on the floor, and he never picked them up, no matter how much I reminded him.

And—oh God. My clothes would be... Last night... The kitchen floor...

Had he picked them up?

Stop procrastinating. It's time to face the music!

I blew out a breath and stepped out of Caleb's bedroom. I smelled the pancakes right away.

I paused when I saw him in the kitchen. His back was to me, his head down as he busied himself over the stove. He was shirtless, the muscles in his arms and back rippling as he moved to grab the butter on the counter.

Déjà vu.

I felt transported to that first time I'd seen Caleb in his apartment. I could picture him in my mind. He had turned around, and as he'd spotted me standing exactly where I was standing now, a piece of bread had fallen out of his mouth.

I laughed quietly. Caleb turned at the sound, his handsome face softening as he smiled at me. His green eyes tracked my movement as I walked to him.

My heart did a long, slow jump in my chest.

I felt him draw a deep breath as I wrapped my arms around

him, burrowing my nose in his neck. His arms automatically embraced me.

"I love you, Caleb."

He rested his chin on top of my head.

"Again, Red," he coaxed. "You almost got it. Keep saying it."

"I love you."

He let out a mock frustrated sigh, shaking his head. "You need to do that a million times more before I'll feel satisfied."

I stiffened at the word *satisfied*.

Was he?

"Hmm... You smell like my shampoo and my soap." He nuzzled my cheek. "I like that."

Smelling the pancakes, I stepped away from his embrace so I could finish cooking them.

"What time is your class?" he asked, twirling a loose strand of my hair with his finger.

"Not till three."

"Good. We have time to... What's wrong?"

"Nothing. Take a shower. I'll finish making the pancakes."

But he turned the stove off, then held my face between his hands.

"I know that face. Tell me what's on your mind, Red."

"I said 'nothing.'"

"Was I too rough last night?"

I could feel the blush flushing my cheeks. "No."

"Then what is it?" he demanded.

I let out a frustrated breath and tried to step away from him again, but he wouldn't budge.

"I don't know. I've never had sex before. And you...you haven't said anything. Let me go."

I shook his hands off and stepped back.

"You have no idea what last night meant to me, do you?" he asked.

I raised my eyes to his, challenging.

"Everything," he whispered, kissing me softly. "It meant everything."

It wasn't what he said but the way he said it. The way his eyes looked at me, the way his hands held me to him.

He meant it, I realized.

And just like that, my insecurities vanished.

"It was perfect." He looked at me with suddenly hooded eyes, which were turning a darker green. "I can't stop thinking about last night. I want you again. It was wildly erotic. The sounds you made, how good you felt when I was inside—"

I shrieked and covered his mouth, blushing furiously. "Okay." I blew out a breath. "Okay."

I felt foolish now for letting my insecurities get the better of me.

His eyes glittered wickedly as he pulled my hand down and placed it on his chest. "Did you enjoy last night?" He blinked slowly, his lashes casting shadows on his cheeks. "Did I make you feel good?"

I didn't know I could blush harder than I was already. When his hand slowly slid behind my waist, his fingers seeking the skin on my lower back, I swallowed a moan.

"Can I—"

I didn't give him a chance to finish as I moved away from him, but the vulnerability in his eyes stopped me from walking away. It had never crossed my mind that he would feel the same insecurities I felt. He wanted to know if last night was good for me too.

"It was," I said breathlessly. "Really good."

I groaned inside.

It was really good?

What kind of response was that? But when I looked up at him again, his eyes were smiling and I knew he understood what I meant.

He was right. It was perfect.

"Why don't you take a seat?" he suggested, pulling out a chair for me. "And let me cook breakfast for my queen."

As he busied himself again at the stove, I quietly grabbed Mr. Clean and a rag and vigorously cleaned the counter, hoping to block last night's memories from my mind.

Keep cool and clean.

I kept my back to him, biting my lip and knowing my face was crab red while I scrubbed. I searched the floor for any of my clothing but didn't see them anywhere.

Where had he put them? I decided not to ask him and to look for them later.

Breakfast was a stack of distorted pancakes—Caleb had gotten better at making them, since there were no eggshells—charred bacon, and fruit cut into bite-size pieces.

I told him I was giving him an A for effort. He seemed pleased.

I had insisted that we eat on the balcony, not at the counter. He flashed me a meaningful smile but thankfully didn't say anything.

Since we had a few more hours before my classes started—his wasn't till four—we grabbed our textbooks and started studying.

I stared at the same page for fifteen minutes, absorbing nothing.

Caleb sat across from me. He was wearing a black muscle shirt, his toned arms exposed. My eyes followed the line of his neck, the strong, sharp curve of his jaw. His eyes were focused on the book in front of him, a little furrow in his brow marring his smooth forehead. I'd noticed he had a habit of biting the end of his pen, as he was doing now. My gaze shifted to admire the shape of his lips, the way they parted slightly so the end of the pen was just inside his mouth. His mouth…

His eyes suddenly slid up to mine.

And my breath caught.

His grin was slow. And knowing. Naughty.

I averted my gaze and reached for the orange juice. Drank deeply.

"Hey, Red?"

I placed the glass back on the coaster with a loud clunk.

"What?" I injected irritation into my voice, flipping to the next page in my book. Pretending to read.

I didn't need to look to know he still had that mischievous grin on his lips.

"Want a kiss?"

I bit my lip, which desperately wanted to form a smile. "No."

He leaned closer. "I do." He pouted his lips for a kiss.

I let out a strangled laugh. "Caleb, move over."

"Sure thing." He moved his chair closer so our arms touched. "Close enough?"

His phone started vibrating, and since it was on the table, my eyes automatically glanced at the screen.

It was Beatrice-Rose calling him. He ignored it.

"My kiss, Red, where—"

It rang again.

I sighed. "Aren't you going to answer that?"

"No." He shrugged. "I have nothing to say to her." He grabbed his phone and turned it off.

What did it say about me that I felt thrilled that he'd turned his phone off so he could concentrate on me? Just me.

He reached for my hand, interlacing our fingers.

"Is it okay with you if we don't make an announcement yet?" I asked him carefully. "I'll tell Kar and Beth when I see them, but besides them, let's just keep it to ourselves for now."

He leaned away from me, but not before I saw the hurt look in his eyes. "Why?"

"Caleb, it's not what you're thinking. I…" I paused, gathering my thoughts. I knew I had to find the right words to make him understand. I hated seeing him hurt.

I turned to face him. He was sprawled on his seat, his head bowed low so I wouldn't see his eyes.

"This. Us. It's too important to me," I began, willing him to understand. "I'm too selfish to share this with the world yet. I'm not ready. I want—"

He cut me off with a gentle, tender kiss.

"Okay, Red," he said softly, smiling. "Okay."

It was hard not to smile back. "Thank you."

"But I'm telling everyone at my party."

I sighed. "All right."

"But you still won't move in with me."

"Can we talk about this after finals?"

"Let's talk about it now." There was just enough authority and demand in his voice to raise my hackles.

"Why are you being testy?" I asked, frustrated.

"Testy? I'm not the one who is refusing to live together."

"You know why."

"I don't know why, because you won't even discuss it."

"It's different now," I said simply.

He waited for me to continue.

"It's not like before when you were just helping me. We're... engaged now, Caleb."

There was a flutter in my stomach at the word *engaged*. It was still so new, so overwhelming, so...wonderful.

"Exactly. All the more reason for you to be living with me."

"Caleb..."

"What's the real reason? Why won't you tell me?"

He would push and push until he was satisfied. Or until he had me convinced that what he wanted was what I wanted too. It was just the way he was.

"Your mother," I admitted finally.

"What?"

"Your mother doesn't like me. I can't imagine she'd approve of our engagement. And if we moved in together, she will dislike me more. I"—I raised my hands in frustration—"I want her to like me," I confessed quietly. "I know how important she is to you, Caleb. And I want her to like me because it's important to you."

"Red," he murmured, reaching for me. "I love you. It makes me happy that you want to make me happy. Baby, look at me."

He tipped my chin up so I was looking straight into his green eyes.

"*You're* what's important to me. You matter to me more than anyone in this world. More than anyone," he repeated. "And I can't wait to start our lives together. Nothing else matters. Move in with me." He pulled me closer. "Please?"

I'd known this was going to happen. "Okay." I let out a soft sigh. "But I want to give your mom some time to get used to the idea first."

"She will love you. How can she not? We'll get your stuff from Kar's—"

"Caleb!"

I stepped away from him and let out a frustrated sound, tears threatening to spill. I didn't know how I could explain what was really bothering me. I told him I wanted his mom to like me because it was important to him—and that was totally true. But deep down, it wasn't the only reason.

His parents were getting divorced, but he still had both of them. They were still alive. He grew up with the support of his mother, his brother. When my mom died, I had…no one. Some nights I would wake up, unbearably sad and lonely, wishing for my mom. And I knew, just as sure as the sun would rise, that she would never be back. I would never hear her voice again or see her face. A heavy pain in my chest always came at the thought of her.

How could he possibly understand what it was like to be an orphan?

I knew it was irrational of me to want his mother's love, but I did. And I just couldn't explain it to him right now.

"Baby, what's wrong? Please don't cry. We'll give her some time if that's what you want. Whatever you need, Red. I'm sorry, baby. I'm sorry."

He opened his arms to me, waiting. I blew out a breath and stepped into them. He embraced me readily, kissing the top of my head.

"I just…miss you," he said quietly. "So much. I can't sleep when you're not here…beside me. I think of the time when I almost lost you, and I know that pushes me to be unreasonable."

I knew his techniques now—the way he charmed and cajoled—but what always got me was his sincerity. I sighed deeply, wrapping my arms around him.

"And demanding," I said to his neck, trying not to be obvious that I was inhaling his scent.

He chuckled. "And demanding. I'm sorry, Red. Forgive me?"

I nodded, pressing a soft kiss to the base of his throat. "I really need you to drop me off at Kar's after class."

I knew he was frowning but felt him nod his assent.

"Caleb. I know you want me to stay the night, but you're distracting me. I can't concentrate on anything but you when you're around me." I pulled back and glared at him. "Happy now?"

His smile was wide. "Yes. You make me very happy, Red."

It was half past two by the time we were ready to leave for class. Caleb grabbed my hand before I stepped out the door.

"Hold on." The look he was giving me made it clear what he wanted. "You look really sexy in that top."

"Caleb—"

"But I think you might want to put a sweater on. Or a jacket."

I raised an eyebrow. "And why is that?"

He was *not* telling me what I should and should not wear. He hadn't before, and it wasn't starting now. Just because we slept together didn't give him the right to.

I frowned when he pointed at his neck, then his shoulder.

"What are you doing?" I asked.

"Last night was the best night of my life." And then his mouth twitched. Right before he bit his lip.

I narrowed my eyes at him. Humor danced in those green eyes of his. "Uh-huh."

"I think I sort of…lost control and…"

My eyes widened in horror as I realized what he was trying to tell me. I ran to the powder room off the kitchen and stared at myself in the mirror.

Hickey.

No. Hickey*s*.

There was one on the side of my neck and one near my ear. One—correction, two—on my shoulders. And those were only the ones I could see.

What the hell.

"CALEB!"

"I'm surprised Lockhart didn't bind and gag you when you told him you weren't going back to his place," Kara mumbled after taking a big bite of her mushroom burger. We were camped in her kitchen with textbooks, pens, highlighters, papers, and food competing for space on the small dining table. "He looked like he was going to set up a tent outside my apartment when he dropped you off."

I watched in fascination as Kara took another big bite of her four-patty bean burger, chased it down with Diet Coke, then wolfed down a bucket of fries.

Where does she put all of it?

"Well, if you ask me," she continued, pointing at me with a fry, "I wish it would go to my tits and/or ass, but no, I think I expel all of it."

I didn't realize I'd asked out loud.

"I never seem to gain a pound. Anyway, spill it. The dean interrogated you?"

I nodded, still watching her. She started another burger.

"Tell me, does he still have that stupid mustache? The one that makes his face look like a vagina?"

I choked on my drink. "Kar. Geez." I laughed. She was right about the mustache, though.

She raised an eyebrow. "Well? I haven't got all day. Start talking."

"I went to the dean's office after my last class. It wasn't an interrogation. He was really nice about it. He just wanted to know if Justin had harassed me and if I've seen the poster—"

"Which you didn't, since Caleb has forbidden you to."

"Not really. I know he would show it to me if I really wanted him to. I don't."

"Why not?"

"Why would I? It would just stress me out. I don't need that kind of trouble in my head, Kar. If I saw it, it would just make me angrier. I don't want to give that creep any more attention than I already have."

She nodded. "I feel ya." Leaning against the chair, she rubbed her stomach and covered her mouth before letting out a quiet, dainty burp.

"It's being addressed. Believe me when I say Justin is in trouble. This wasn't the first time he's done something like this. He's suspended from college, and there was talk of expulsion."

"Good." Kara snorted. "Anyone with half a brain would know he and that bitch Beatrice-Rose planted those drugs in Caleb's car."

"Yeah. Caleb said the detective assigned to the case is a family friend so he gets inside information about the investigation. I think he mentioned he also hired a private investigator."

"It helps to be filthy rich and able to do all that. Are you going to eat your fries?"

It didn't surprise me that Kara wanted them. "No, you can have them."

"Thanks! Sssssssooooo…" she said.

I looked up from my textbook to see her wiggling her eyebrows up and down.

"Why the hell are you wearing Lockhart's jacket?" she asked.

I could feel myself blushing. "H-how'd you know it's his jacket?"

She rolled her eyes. "You think I'm stupid? His name is written on the back."

Oh. "It was cold this morning."

"It was sweltering this morning. If I had balls, they'd be scrambled and fried from the heat by now." She narrowed her eyes. "You're sweating."

"It's just…water…from earlier when I washed the dishes. I washed them earlier. The dishes."

Kara leaned back, crossing her arms over her chest and grinning like the cat that ate the canary. "You did a good job. Feel free to scrub the tub later too. So." She knew something was up and that she was going to find out what it was very, very soon. "What did you guys do last night?"

I knew from how hot I felt that I was red as a ripe tomato.

She suddenly stood up from her seat and leaned across the table, her hand reaching for the jacket. She grabbed the zipper at my neck and pulled it down.

And just stared in silence.

I didn't dare look to see her reaction.

"Wow. Lockhart sure sucks like a vacuum."

I couldn't help the laughter that bubbled out of my throat. "Kar!"

"Why are you still blushing? Holy motherfucking shit. You had hot jungle sex with Lockhart, didn't you? Didn't you?" She slumped back into her seat.

And then in a reverent tone, she asked, "Was it rough, I'm-going-to-swing-from-the-chandelier sex, or was it gentle, even-my-soul-orgasmed sex? You're not leaving until you tell me everything!"

I worried my lip—and then thought, *What the heck?*

"He asked me to marry him."

She blinked once. Twice. Opened her mouth, but nothing came out.

Grinning, I pulled out my necklace from beneath my shirt. The ruby glittered in the light.

"I said yes, Kar." My breath hitched. "I said yes to Caleb."

CHAPTER

twenty

Caleb

I caught myself grinning again.

Like a creep.

I couldn't help it, I realized as I grabbed a pillow and smashed it against my face.

It had been a week since the best night of my life happened right here in my bedroom. Red was so...

My seven o'clock alarm blared, half an hour after I woke up. I pushed up from the bed, and a pillow landed somewhere on the floor.

What a miracle, I thought, scratching my chest as I headed to my bathroom. It always took a few hits of the snooze button before I got up. Maybe because I'd rather be awake and thinking of her than asleep.

Did I go too fast with her? Too slow?

Was I too gentle, too rough?

Not enough? Or was it too much?

Damn. I'd been torturing myself with these thoughts all week. What the hell was happening to me?

I'd never had these doubts before, but with Red, it was a different story. It was very important to me that she enjoyed that night. I could only hope it meant to her even half of what it meant to me.

Up until that night, I'd never realized how it was to give and take from someone who owned your body and heart.

There was no doubt she owned both of mine.

I knew how great a step it was to finally give herself to me. What it meant. Just thinking about it was tightening my throat, making my chest ache.

She loved me.

Red. Loved. Me.

I grinned again.

I grabbed my toothbrush, squeezed toothpaste on it, and jammed it in my mouth. *Ouch!* I should have been grimacing in pain, but when I looked in the mirror, I was still smiling.

I'm a freaking psycho.

All my exams were done yesterday, but Red still had two days to go. This week passed in a blur—sometimes too fast because of exams, and sometimes turtle-ass slow when I thought about when I could see her again.

She had banned me from seeing her all week, complaining that I was a distraction and I'd better not even try or else. I wondered what *or else* meant. I promised to find out. And I did when I dropped by to see her at Kara's. She booted me out not even ten minutes later.

When Red was studying, nothing could take her away from it. Unless it was me.

And how could that not make me grin like an idiot?

I thought I could never want her more than I had before, but after that night in my bed, the want had only gotten worse. I wanted—needed—her so badly, I ached.

I knew she felt the same. I could feel her desire when I broke her rules and dropped by to see her. The way her eyes lingered on me just a little longer, the way her lips parted at my slightest touch.

There was something different between us after that night. And I loved it. I couldn't wait to explore more of it. More of her.

But I wasn't going to do anything again until she was ready. The next move would be up to her. Even if it killed me, this time, I'd wait.

I stepped in the shower, fantasized having her under the spray of warm water with me. How wet and soft she'd be. How responsive, making those erotic sounds at the back of her throat. Feeling her fingers digging into my back. Her hips rising to meet mine…

It took me longer to shower this time.

I was padding to my closet to get dressed when my phone burped a text. Rubbing the towel on my hair, I headed back to my bed to check my phone, nearly stepping on the pillow. Thinking of Red and how she always told me to pick up my stuff, I grabbed the pillow from the floor and threw it on the bed.

She should be here with me right now.

Sighing, I picked up my phone, barked out a laugh as I read Ben's text, and sent him a reply. It had been a while since I'd seen him. I missed my older brother. His text said something about a woman he was dating. She'd accused him of being the most unromantic guy on earth.

Romantic. I certainly wasn't before Red. It took the right girl—my girl—before I'd realized I had a lot to give. I'd been wanting—no, *needing*—to do something romantic for Red. I wanted to make her feel special, to let her know how much that night meant to me. How much she meant to me.

When she was done with her exams, I could take her to a swanky restaurant and pile gifts on her. Problem was, she didn't like either of those things, I thought as I pulled on some jeans and headed to the kitchen.

I wasn't sure what to do.

So much for my romantic side. I did a quick search on the internet on how to create a perfect date for your girlfriend. Correction, fiancée.

I grinned again.

According to the internet, the most-voted-for dream date for women was having a special dinner cooked for her (*Click here for recipes that will blow her mind!*) with the mood set by hanging fairy lights (*What the hell are fairy lights?*), arranging an elaborate table, and don't forget to fold the napkins! It's sooo important, and she will appreciate it! (*Click here for instructions on how to fold a napkin!*) Slow music, candles, and flowers will definitely make her swoon. It's the thought that counts! Good luck and hope you get lucky tonight!

Right.

I took a glass from the cupboard, grabbed the orange juice

from the fridge, poured, and drank deeply. I was definitely better at cooking. Maybe this wasn't a bad idea after all. But what if I screwed up? I should practice cooking the meal before our real date. I'd ask her out in two days.

I got dressed, hopped in my car, and dragged Cameron with me to the store. I wasn't brave enough to go there by myself, and Cameron was done with his exams too.

"If you had a brain, you'd haul Levi here instead of me. You know I don't cook worth a damn," Cameron complained from behind me.

We were outside the Superstore, and I noted only five cars—including mine—in the parking lot. It was still too early for people to be shopping, and, like me, Cameron wasn't a morning person.

Well, I wasn't until Red.

I inserted a dollar coin in the slot and pulled out a cart. "I brought you here for moral support. Now shut the hell up and push the cart," I said.

Cameron's ice-blue eyes narrowed. "Why do I have to push the cart?"

"I'll buy you beer." The door opened automatically, and we stepped inside the store. "Why don't you grab some?" I suggested.

"You know they don't sell beer at Superstore, don't you?" he said in a dry tone.

I scowled. "Why wouldn't they?"

He just shook his head and walked ahead of me, pushing the cart expertly.

I pulled out my phone and opened the website where I'd bookmarked the recipe, scanning the ingredients I had to buy.

"Let's get your stuff, Mary, and get the hell out of here. Don't forget your apron while you're at it," Cameron drawled, pushing the cart to the meat section.

"At least I'll look hot doing it."

Last time I was here was with Red. The memory made me smile. She'd hated me back then—didn't want to hang around me and seemed to enjoy biting my head off. We'd come a long way.

"So what are you making?" Cameron asked. He stood beside me at the counter, looking at big globs of packaged raw meat. I didn't know it would be this complicated. They all looked different.

"Definitely lasagna. It's her favorite."

He snorted. "Sounds dangerous. Call me if you set your apartment on fire."

"Oh ye of little faith!"

"Oh ye of little faith here knows the real score. Why don't you just order something and say it's your own?"

I scowled at him and then at the meat. Maybe I should just make pork chops. It'd be easier. I shook my head. *I can do this.* "It's the thought that counts," I told him, repeating what I'd read in the article.

He shrugged.

"What kind of meat should I get?" I asked, scratching my head.

"How the hell would I know? Grab that one. It's calling your name."

I reached for a solid package of meat as big as my bicep. "This?"

"Why not?"

"Maybe I should get two in case I screw this one up."

"In that case," he said, smirking, "grab three."

I thought about it for a second. "You're right."

It took an hour and a half to find everything on my list, and Cameron bitched all the way back to my apartment. By the time I found all the pots and pans I needed, Cameron had set out the meat in the sink and was sucking on a beer.

"Dude, it's supposed to look like this." I showed him a picture of the lasagna. "How come the meat looks different in the picture?"

He leaned against the counter. "Maybe you should put it in a blender."

"You think so?" I asked.

He gestured with his beer. "How else are you going to make it look like that?"

"Maybe you're right."

"Do you have a blender?"

"Do I look like I own a blender?"

"Yeah," he replied. "Totally."

"Let's go to the store and buy one."

"You're on your own, bud." He placed the empty beer in the recycling. "Gotta go." He walked to the door.

"Pussy."

He turned around and gave me the finger before disappearing through the door.

Maybe I should cut it into small pieces.

What in the hell was I thinking? I should call in and order.

But then an image of Red's lips curving into that beautiful

smile pushed me on. I searched for a recipe on the internet and got to work.

An hour later, I'd lost count of how many times I had cut my fingers. Great clouds of smoke billowed from the oven. I shut it off quickly and turned on the exhaust system. I'd possibly burned my hair, and the damned smoke detector was shrieking. Coughing my lungs out, I ran a towel under cold water, dragged a chair to the smoke detector, and covered the damned thing with the towel until it shut up.

This was an epic fail. Time for plan B.

I called Kara.

Today was the last day of Red's finals. *Finally*.

It made me so happy when she called me as soon as she stepped out of her last exam, excitedly telling me how well she did. Then apologizing that she couldn't see me tonight because she was working. I grinned and kept my mouth shut because she had no idea what was coming.

It had taken a lot of planning to make sure everything was in order. I needed to make tonight perfect for my girl.

The Nuit Étoilée Tree House was located outside the city. It was far, but I kept thinking about Red's dreams of having a bookstore/café someday. I'd love to take her everywhere, show her everything, help her in any way I could. Maybe visiting a few bookstores and cafés would give her ideas for her own. I could even talk to the owner, and maybe Red could apprentice here if she wished.

Nuit Étoilée Tree House was tucked in the middle of a small forest, surrounded by a circle of ancient trees that were as tall and thick as buildings. Inside the circle were smaller trees that housed in their branches charming huts connected by wooden bridges so that people could walk from one hut to the next.

There was something magical about the place. Fog covered the ground, and the stone steps that led up to the tree house barely peeked through the fog. In-ground lighting—in the shape of moons and stars—provided a whimsical cast to the path. Strings of ice-blue lights were looped in the trees, on the roofs, and across the wooden bridges. *Fairy lights.* It clicked. I chuckled.

In the background, Pachelbel's *Canon in D* was softly playing.

I wondered what Red would think of it. What she would feel. She had no idea I was waiting for her. She thought she was covering for Kara's work shift tonight at a party. I gave Kara my credit card so she could buy Red a dress and asked her to tell Red it was the uniform she was supposed to wear.

I knew Red hadn't been sleeping well this week, staying up all night to study and still going to work at the garage. Her willingness to pick up a shift upset me a little—although it made me admire her more since it was to help a friend. She obviously needed to relax. Tonight, I was hoping I could give her that.

It was nearing dusk, and she'd be here soon. Anticipation was making me nervous. What if this was too much? The place looked beautiful, but what did I know? It was just a place. It didn't mean anything until she was here.

I walked back and forth across the bridge, holding an armful of red roses. Was wearing this tux too much? I ran my hand through my hair. Would she feel uncomfortable here like she had on our first date when I took her to that fancy restaurant?

I loosened my tie, jiggled the keys in my pocket.

Blowing out a breath, I leaned my elbows against the railing of the wooden bridge and lowered my head. I had sent a limo to pick her up and told Kara to say it was complimentary from the employer.

Where is she?

I was about to phone the limo company when suddenly, my skin prickled. She didn't make a sound, but I knew it was her.

Slowly, I turned. And the sight of her knocked the breath out of me as she stood on the other side of the bridge.

Something tickled my memory.

My love.

And then she stepped forward.

As I watched her approach, I saw our lives flash by. Growing old together, laughing, crying, making love, our kids surrounding us. This was the woman I wanted to be with for the rest of my life. I needed her with a sweet, desperate longing I'd never felt before.

She glided toward me—a dream in red lace with dark hair, red lips. She stopped just an arm's length away, looking at me through the dark cat eyes I'd come to remember even in sleep.

I just looked at her, taking my fill.

I was afraid to touch her for fear she might disappear. "I'm wondering if you could tell me," I whispered, my voice hoarse, "what I've done in this life to deserve you."

She blinked up at me, a small smile softly curving her lips.

I touched her cheek. "Tell me you're not a dream, Red."

"If I am," she whispered back, leaning into my touch, "then so are you. Let's not wake up anytime soon."

"That sounds good to me." I lifted the roses. "For you."

Her eyes lit up as she took the flowers and inhaled their scent. "I love them. Thank you."

I placed my hands on her lower back, pulling her closer to me. I'd been waiting a long time for the shape of her, the feel of her in my arms. "You're so beautiful. How can you be real?"

Her blush was endearing. "You and Kar planned this." She frowned at me, but her eyes glowed with pleasure.

I smiled at her sheepishly. "I wanted it to be a surprise. Do you like it?" I asked eagerly.

"How can I not? It's beautiful here." Her dark eyes filled with wonder as she looked around. The glow from the lights reflected in her eyes, and I could see myself in them. I wondered if she could see herself reflected in mine.

I laced her fingers with mine and led her inside the hut to the pretty round table set in the middle of it. The silverware sparkled, the light soft; the smell of roses and fragrant candles mixed in the air. But all I wanted to see, wanted to steep myself in, was her.

I pulled out her chair, making sure she was comfortable, and couldn't resist kissing the top of her head before I took the seat across from her. The waiter appeared, greeting us, filling our glasses with champagne, and whisked away her roses for safekeeping.

"I hope you're hungry," I said. I took a sip, watching her over the rim of my glass. It was hard to keep my eyes off her.

"Starving." She looked around the room at the built-in

shelves that were brimming with books. "How?" she asked curiously, clearly impressed.

I knew what she was asking. The tree house was the talk of the town, and it wouldn't be open to the public for another month. Apart from a handful of staff, the place was empty.

"I have my ways." Like having a big brother who had connections to a number of influential circles. "Would you like to look at the books? It's quite a collection."

"Maybe after we eat. I heard the owner used to live here before he transformed it into a library and café. I didn't know they planned to serve meals here. I thought it was going to be just coffee and pastries."

"You're right, but I hired a chef. She's prepared a menu just for us. I made sure she knew your favorites."

Her eyes warmed; she was clearly taken by surprise. "Caleb…"

"You might know of her. She's extremely popular, and she just opened her fifth restaurant."

Her eyes widened. She knew who I was talking about. She had excitedly mentioned the chef to me a time or two.

"This is…"

"Too much?"

She shook her head, and a lock of hair fell to the side of her face. I leaned forward and tucked it behind her ear.

"It's incredible. Thank you, Caleb. I feel so special."

The waiter materialized with our food, and the delight on Red's face made me decide that I'd do this for her often. She twirled her pasta with her fork, slid it between her lips, and moaned. I felt my insides tighten.

I cleared my throat. "So now finals are over, got any plans?" I shoveled noodles into my mouth and was pleasantly surprised by the burst of flavor. The food was incredible.

She put down her fork and dabbed the side of her mouth with her napkin. The way she did it was so feminine, it made me smile. "I'm planning on working a lot this summer, getting a second job so I'll have more hours. I know I still have a year to go, but I feel like I'm so close to the finish line. My future doesn't seem unclear anymore. And I'm...I'm really excited for what's to come."

She blushed again. I had no idea she could be even more irresistible than she already was. I'd been so wrong. I bit my lip and tightened the grip on my fork to keep from pulling her to me.

"What about you?" she continued. "You're officially done with school. Congratulations, Caleb." She grinned.

I grinned back. "Thanks, baby. There's one thing. You can look for a second job...or if you'd like to apprentice under your favorite chef, just say the word. I told her about you, and she wants to meet you after dinner."

I saw the struggle on her face whenever I offered her something. Last time, when I offered to pay for her loans, I thought she was going to slap me. I knew she was thrilled at the idea of meeting her favorite chef, and I also knew she wouldn't accept my help with an apprenticeship. But I had to try.

"Or you can come with me to Regina," I added.

Her eyes narrowed. "What's in Regina?"

"I made a deal with my mother. I agreed to help with our hotels and real estate business as soon as I finished my economics degree. I've wanted to help out; I just didn't want to do it while I was in school."

Her eyes flashed with surprise and then distress for a second.

"My mom manages our hotels abroad, and Ben manages the ones here in Canada. I told her I'd help Ben and learn the ropes, so I need to fly to Regina on Friday to discuss."

"In two days?"

I nodded.

"Will you…live in Regina then? For a while?"

I shook my head. "I'm just staying a few days. I'll try to be home the night before my birthday to see you. Nothing can keep me away from you."

When I saw her breathe a sigh of relief, my insides warmed. She hated the idea of being apart too.

When the chef served the peanut butter caramel cake for dessert, I saw Red fangirl for the first time. It made me laugh, watching her chat with the chef so enthusiastically and with her face shining with pleasure. They clearly liked each other. When the chef left, Red slid out of her seat.

My heart jumped when her arms wrapped around my neck. "Thank you, Caleb. This is the best night ever."

I pulled her onto my lap. "It's not over yet." But I could tell the excitement and the sleepless nights had taken a toll on her. She looked beautiful but sleepy. "Are you tired, baby?"

"Just a little, but I don't care. I don't want this night to end. Let's stay here for a while." She rested her head on my shoulder. "The stars are so pretty. Will you dance with me?"

One of Chopin's nocturnes played softly in the background.

"You only need to ask."

I sat her on the chair, her eyes lighting up in surprise as I knelt in front of her, gently removing her high heels. I didn't want her feet to hurt. And so we danced. I pulled her close so she could lean against me, her body soft and warm against mine, the side of her face resting on my chest.

"I love you, Caleb."

"I love you more."

She rose on her toes and kissed my neck. My breath hitched. God, I wanted her. My hands tightened around her waist, pulling her just a little closer. Her scent was driving me crazy. But I would not have her tonight, no matter how much I wanted her. She was tired, and I planned on pampering her. Making this night all about her was my mission.

"Remember that house I told you about?"

"What house?" she asked sleepily.

"The house that we're going to get. I'm buying or building you a house, whatever you want. I'll make it happen."

Now she was awake. She pulled back a little, her dark eyes wide.

Before she could say anything, I plowed on. "I asked Ben to give me a list of prime real estate near the campus so you don't have to commute far. You can have your dream kitchen, with a big stove that spits out real fire when you turn it on—where you can bake and cook whatever you like. And a big library to store all your books. And I can have my man cave."

"Caleb—"

I knew she was going to protest. I expected it. I framed her face with my hands, looking into her eyes. "You're still going to nag me when I don't put the toilet seat down and get mad at me when I eat that last piece of cake you've been hiding from me in the fridge, and I'm going to complain when I don't have enough space in the closet because you have too many clothes—"

"Caleb, this is too fast—"

"Let me ask you this," I continued, stroking her arms. "Do you want to be with me?"

"That's not fair—"

"Do you want to be with me, Red?"

"You fight dirty."

"Answer the question."

She didn't answer right away. I just looked at her patiently. Waiting.

"Yes, damn it. I do. You know I do."

I released the breath I was holding and grinned. "Then let's get a house. Be with me, Red. I'll make you happy."

To me, it was as simple as that.

"Let's make a family, Red."

At that, her eyes teared up. "I..."

"Ah, baby. Don't cry. Wouldn't you do everything in your power to take care of the one you love? To give them everything you can offer?" I kissed her cheeks, her lips. "The things I want to give you don't come with a price. I don't expect anything in return. That's what love is. Or haven't you figured that out yet?"

She looked down for a moment, struggling with words. And then she glanced up. "Caleb," she began, her voice shaky. "I've never had anything like this before. Never thought I *would* have it. It seemed like an impossible dream. A dream that was too good to be true. But with you, I know it's real, and I'll embrace it with open arms and protect it with everything I have."

I was done for. This girl would be my ruin.

I scooped her in my arms and carried her across the bridge to the other hut where I had already placed blankets and pillows on the floor. I gently placed her there and sat beside her. She turned on her side to face me.

"This is the best night ever."

"Stay still like that." I reached for the notepad and charcoal I had placed beside her pillow when I was setting up earlier.

"What are you doing?"

"Drawing you."

Her eyes lit up. "I had no idea you can draw."

When I was reading up online about the perfect date, one of the tips was to sketch her face.

When I was done, I showed it to her. "What do you think?"

She burst out laughing. Her eyes were half closed, her body limp on the blanket. She pillowed the side of her face with her hands as she looked up at me, sleepily.

"Better stick with economics, Caleb."

I grinned at her. The picture wasn't bad. I thought I drew her cat eyes pretty well.

"Tell me a story," she said sluggishly.

I put the notepad down and lay down beside her, pulling her into my arms so that her head rested on my chest. I stroked her hair for a moment, gathering the thick and soft strands in my fingers.

"Once upon a time," I whispered gently, kissing her hair. "There was a boy who met a girl on a bridge…"

But when I glanced at her, she had already fallen asleep.

How beautiful she is, how perfect.

I closed my eyes and pulled her closer.

I was born to love this girl.

Veronica

Caleb was leaving today.

It had been two days since that incredibly romantic night at the tree house. It had been so sweetly unexpected. He'd put so much effort into making it perfect for me that even now the memory of it made me smile.

Sun poured cheerfully through the hallway windows as I made my way to my locker, intending to empty it for the summer. I glanced at my watch and noted that we had a few hours before Caleb left for his flight. He was supposed to pick me up in ten minutes. We'd both been busy with work, and I was really looking forward to spending time with him. I grabbed my books and was hurriedly pushing them in my bag when a piece of paper fell out.

I laughed when I saw a picture of a house. Caleb had been leaving pictures of ridiculously beautiful houses—near the lake, in the city, out of the city—and I knew they each had to cost more than a million. "Take your pick, and we'll see them next week," he had said.

For a girl who'd lived her life struggling to pay her way, it was hard to let him take the reins.

I knew when I was being stupid, but I wasn't comfortable with him paying for everything. And I was still in school. I had a decent-paying job, but most of my income went to paying my debts. Caleb had offered to pay them off, but there was no way in hell I would let him do that. He wouldn't budge about the house, though.

"If you want to make me happy, let me make you happy, Red."

So I let it go.

Because I did want to make him happy.

And then we could make our plans.

Our plans.

I knew I was grinning like a loon, but I couldn't help it. I couldn't wait to start our life together.

A house, I thought, overwhelmed by the idea. A house where I would live with Caleb as his fiancée. Where we would make memories and build our life together.

It didn't feel temporary, and it didn't feel like we were playing house anymore.

It felt permanent. Real. Very real.

A home. A family. With Caleb.

"Hello, Veronica."

I stopped in my tracks and turned around. Beatrice-Rose's gaze locked with mine. My good mood plummeted instantly.

She strutted toward me in a tight red dress, her lips painted the same bold color. The dress was undoubtedly designer, her makeup immaculately applied, but the red looked garish on her. It reminded me of a little kid playing dress-up.

"Caleb's party is next week," she said. "I assume you're attending. I hope it won't be too uncomfortable for you."

When I didn't say anything, she continued, "You're more used to being the help than one of the guests, aren't you?"

"Just like you're used to *being* helped?" I took in her garish outfit. "Unlike you, I've never needed to depend on Mommy or Daddy to give me my allowance. I work hard to earn an honest living. But you wouldn't know what that is, would you?"

Her eyes glinted with anger. "That just shows you're not part of Caleb's world. Men like Caleb marry debutantes like me. It's what our world approves of and expects. Everyone will be there at his party—Miranda, their business associates, investors. Caleb needs someone beside him who will help him become successful."

She looked me up and down, smirking. "What makes you think that's you? Miranda will never approve of you. You have no class, no breeding."

My stomach felt jittery. If anything, she knew how to strike where it hurt. Too bad for her I knew how to fight back.

"And you do?"

Her smile was smug. "Of course."

"I think you've got a couple of loose screws in your head, Beatrice-Rose. You should have someone tighten those things. Last time I checked, desperately throwing yourself at a guy who doesn't want you isn't classy or a strong indicator of breeding."

Her smile disappeared. "You bitch."

"I can be if I have to. You had to send your dog to do your dirty work for you, didn't you?" I continued, thinking of Justin. "Afraid to get your hands dirty?"

"I don't know what you're talking about."

"Sure you do. I'm warning you." I took a threatening step toward her. All I could picture was Caleb sitting in that interrogation room, his hand cuffed to a bolt. That was enough for me to lose any pity I might have felt for her. "Leave Caleb alone."

Beatrice-Rose stepped back, her eyes flashing with spite. "Do you think I'm scared of you?"

"You should be. Keep doing what you've been doing, and you'll find out."

And with that, I turned and walked away.

"Veronica!" she called out, just loud enough for me to hear. "I'd watch your back if I were you. See you at the party."

This time, I glanced back, flashing a bold smile that said *Bitch, bring it*. "You bet."

CHAPTER
twenty-one

Caleb

RED HAD BEEN QUIET SINCE I'D PICKED HER UP FROM CAMPUS.
There was a tiny furrow between her eyebrows. You'd miss it
if you weren't looking hard enough.

I always looked.

It wasn't difficult to figure out Red's emotions. I'd studied
her face and her moods for a long time, and I could almost
always tell what she was feeling.

She didn't wear her emotions on her face around other
people, but around me, she'd started to. There were times when
she didn't, but she could never hide them for long.

Now, her face was a blank canvas, devoid of emotion. You'd
never think something was wrong unless you looked, unless
you knew her facial expressions and their corresponding moods.
And I knew that very tiny furrow meant she was annoyed. On
impulse, I made a sharp U-turn and drove through a deserted

park, sliding my car in a parking lot that was hidden between densely packed trees.

"What's wrong, baby?" I asked, but she was looking outside through the window.

I wanted her eyes on me. Just on me.

"If I did something wrong, I'm sorry. I'm an idiot, and I will do anything—grovel at your feet, buy you diamonds, a car—no?" I grinned when she looked up at me dryly. "Okay, how about if I buy you a big jar of peanut butter?"

That teased a small smile out of her.

"Now why don't you tell me what I did wrong so I can start making it up to you? Right," I added, backtracking quickly when she narrowed her eyes at me. "I should know what I did, but I'm—" I stopped myself before I said *I'm drawing a blank.* She'd just skin me alive. "Let's see…" I sucked my bottom lip.

"I picked my clothes up on the floor this week, every day. Just like you told me. Ask Maia." Maia was the wonderful older lady I'd hired years ago to do household chores for me three times a week.

Red flicked her hair over her shoulder. Okay, it wasn't the clothes then.

I sniffed at my armpits. "I showered."

A twitch on her lips. Those pink lips…I knew how soft, how giving, how delicious they were when she…

When she caught me staring at her lips, I grinned.

"Do you have your period?" I asked.

Now she laughed reluctantly, looking at me with exasperation and fondness.

"I saw Beatrice-Rose today," she said finally.

My smile disappeared. "Did she say anything to you?"

"I didn't know she's coming to your party."

I straightened in my seat. "If I had a choice, I wouldn't have her invited to my party. Actually, I wouldn't even *have* a party. It'd just be you and me."

I sighed when she didn't say anything. "My mom arranges these things," I explained. "I have no say on the guest list. And I really don't care. She says it's a birthday party for me, but it's never just a birthday party."

"What do you mean?"

I picked up her hand, traced circles on her palm.

"My mom is a businesswoman. That party is mostly an excuse for me to meet our business partners' investors and to get more investors. Think of it this way: My mom is a T. rex. She needs food to feed herself and her babies. So she sets up a place where all the animals with the most body fat gather. And then she starts picking out the fattest of them all."

She laughed, rolled her eyes, then grinned at me. "Only *you* would make an analogy like that."

"That's why you like me." I kissed her fingers.

When her breathing picked up and those tempting lips parted, it was all I could do not to pull her out of her seat and into my lap—and kiss the hell out of her.

"Baby…"

I leaned closer so I could feel her breath on my face. Her eyes glazed in yearning, and I noticed the rise and fall of her chest, the creaminess of her skin. I wanted to lick it. "Let's—"

And then she pulled away, clearing her throat. "What color should I wear? Is there a dress or color code?"

Her hand shook as she tucked her hair behind her ear. I closed my eyes for a moment, gathering control. Took a deep, deep breath. Let it out real slow. When I opened my eyes, she was staring down, biting her bottom lip.

Damn.

"Yeah."

When I didn't continue, she looked up at me, waiting.

"Let's see. What color should you wear? How about transparent?"

When she didn't react, I knew she hadn't recovered from that moment we just shared. I didn't think she even heard me.

"Oh, you mean for the party. Red. Wear red for me."

She nodded.

"Hey, Red?"

"Hmm?" She smiled and reached out to push my hair away from my face. "You need a haircut."

"I want to spend more time with you and would postpone my trip if I could. I want to get our house right away. I have appointments lined up for us. We'll do those next week—"

"Caleb."

She covered my mouth with her hand to shut me up. I licked it.

When she slapped my arm and laughed, I felt better. I knew then it was okay. She leaned closer and shyly kissed my lips.

I knew she only wanted a brief kiss, but I had been going

crazy dreaming about her lips, her hands on me, the sounds she made when I touched her. I had been going insane replaying that night when we made love. Going insane from craving the feel of her nails biting in my back, her legs tightening around me, and her eyes glazing over when she reached what I was desperately trying to give her.

So when her soft, soft lips grazed mine, I lost control. I gripped her hair in my hands and pulled her to me. Into me. And I devoured her.

This was a hunger only she could satiate.

I couldn't think of anything but the feel of her body as I claimed what I had been dreaming about for days.

"Oh God, *Caleb*."

I bit her bottom lip lightly, sucked on it. "Come here."

I lifted her on top of me.

"Just a little more. Give me a little more, Red."

I adjusted her so she was sitting where I wanted her. I gripped her hips, urging her to move where it felt good.

Her eyes were clouded with desire as they met mine. I thrust my hips upward, mesmerized when she placed her hands on my shoulders and leaned her head back, exposing her neck to me. I licked at it hungrily.

She let out a sexy moan and started to rock her hips faster.

"Yeah, that's the way, Red. Damn. Keep going."

I watched as she took what she needed, as she let herself get lost in the incredible sensation of our bodies sliding and rubbing against each other.

I would have given her anything she asked of me. She was

so fucking beautiful I couldn't help but watch as she took and took and took.

I kissed her hungrily before she shattered in my arms.

It was a moment before I could finally speak. She was draped on me, her lips on my neck as her breathing finally slowed down.

"You just dry humped me in the parking lot," I murmured.

And then her shoulders started to shake before her loud peals of laughter filled the car.

"I love it," I added.

"Oh my God, Caleb. You drive me crazy."

I pulled her to me, kissing her again. I couldn't get enough. "I can drive you crazier. Just wait until I—"

She growled and covered my mouth with her hand. When she was sure I wouldn't say anything, she rested her chin on my shoulder and I stroked her hair gently.

"I'll come home to you as soon as I can," I promised.

"I'll be waiting."

"I miss you already."

"I know," she whispered. "I miss you already too."

CHAPTER
twenty-two

Caleb

"RED, WAIT."

I should have let her go. I was parked in front of Kara's home to drop her off. I needed to rush to the airport before my plane left, but I grabbed her hand before she could slide out of the car.

"I want to walk you to the door."

When her eyes softened, I drew her in to me and just held her close.

Would I ever get used to this?

Would I ever get used to the way my heart pounded every time she let me wrap my arms around her, the way she let her walls down for me, the way she let herself trust and allowed herself to…just love me?

"I don't want to go," I said.

Her arms came around my back. "I know," she said quietly. "But you'll be back soon."

"Think of me."

"I think it's impossible not to."

I. Couldn't. Stop. Grinning.

I pulled away and looked at her. Taking my fill, memorizing her face. "Hold on."

I pulled out my phone and quickly took a picture of her.

"Caleb!"

"There. All set." I hid my phone before she could grab it and look at my photos. I think there were five pictures in my photo gallery that *weren't* of her. Okay, maybe four. I loved taking candid snapshots of her—especially when she wasn't expecting it. When she was studying at her desk. Standing at the stove cooking pancakes, holding up her hand to block the camera but grinning. Glaring at me as she picked up my clothes from the floor. There was one I took as she napped that I really cherished. I felt a little guilty, but not too guilty.

Yep. I'm a creep.

Her creep.

"Where's your phone?" I asked.

She frowned. "Why?"

"Just give it to me. No arguing." And then I added, "I'm leaving tonight. Please be nice to me."

I batted my lashes at her, and she laughed. She gave me her phone reluctantly.

"What's your pass code?" I asked.

"Just give it to me. I'll do it," she said.

"What is it?"

I looked up from the screen to see her blushing. I raised my brows, waiting.

"It's your birthday," she admitted.

Damn it. *Damn it.* Again, I couldn't stop grinning.

"Why you so obsessed with me, Red? *Ow!*"

I rubbed my arm where she'd pinched me. She was still glaring at me, so I just leaned beside her so our faces were touching and took a picture. I sent the photo to my number, made that her wallpaper, and returned her phone.

She shook her head and gave me an exasperated look, but she was smiling.

"Are you nervous? About going to work, I mean," she asked.

"A little bit," I answered. She tucked a loose hair that had come out of her bun behind her ear.

I remembered her ponytail coming loose earlier when I kissed the hell out of her in the parking lot. I remembered plunging my hands into the dark thickness. I'd watched her struggle to gather herself together, and it was a treat to see. I would have enjoyed it more if I hadn't had a raging hard-on at the time.

I loved how I could make her lose control like that. I really wanted to see it again and maybe do…other things. When I felt my pants start to tighten, I nearly cursed out loud.

I blushed when I saw her watching me, and I had the terrifying thought that she could read my mind. But then I realized she was still waiting for me to explain.

What the hell were we talking about?

"I guess you'd have a lot of responsibilities," she prompted.

Right. Work.

I nodded, releasing that lock of hair she had tucked behind her ear and twirling it around my finger.

I found that I had to touch her whenever she was near me. I couldn't help myself.

"I don't mind. I'm more excited than nervous, and I'm looking forward to it. Although I wish you'd go with me."

"I can't." *But I want to* was what I heard in her voice. Of course she didn't say it, but I knew anyway. "I have to work, Caleb."

Telling her I didn't want her to work was on the tip of my tongue. Luckily, I shut my mouth before it came out. But there had to be some way.

"If I offered you a job, what would you say?"

She let out an annoyed sigh. "I'd say you can kiss my butt."

I knew it.

"Okay." Then I widened my eyes. "What? Right now? You're so insatiable. I thought that parking lot session was enough, but I guess it left you wanting more. Now I have to satisfy you in…other ways."

Her mouth fell open. I just had to laugh.

Although…I was serious. I was really serious. In fact I was thinking that—

"Like what?" she asked.

I froze. Her eyes had darkened. Damn. My pants felt tight.

Then she shook her head as if to clear her thoughts. "I'm serious, Caleb. Don't."

Huh?

"Don't what? Satisfy you in other ways?"

She was blushing so hard that even the tips of her ears were red. I realized she hadn't meant to have that unguarded moment when she asked, in that sexy, make-love-to-me voice, *Like what?*

She had fried my brain with that simple question and the look in her eyes.

I couldn't keep up with her. She drove me wild.

"No," she replied quietly. "Let's stop talking about sex for a minute, please?"

Why?

But I nodded. I didn't want to push her on this. But damn. I wanted her so damn bad.

And I really needed to adjust my pants. When she looked out the car window, I quickly did.

"I have my own job. I don't want you to give me work. I want to make it on my own."

We were back to this. Okay then. I let out a defeated sigh. There was no arguing with her when she was in this mood. I knew when to push something and when to let it go. The set of her jaw and the warning in her eyes told me this was nonnegotiable.

"Okay, then I didn't say anything. It was your imagination. Can I hold your hand now?"

Her lips stretched into a pretty smile, and I reached for her hand, played with her fingers.

"You said you had a deal with your mom. I'm trying to understand why."

"Why what?" But I knew what she meant. And it embarrassed me to talk about it.

"Why wouldn't you want to work for your company while you were in college? It would have been a big help to you, wouldn't it? In school and for your position in the company now, if you had more training."

Embarrassed, I rubbed the back of my knuckle on the tip of my nose. "I did actually work for Ben before. You know I wasn't always this responsible and respectable."

She raised her eyebrow. *I know that very well,* her expression said.

I let out an uncomfortable laugh. "Even before my parents' marriage completely fell apart, my dad had already moved out."

My embarrassment was replaced by resentment so quickly that I didn't realize my hands had turned into tight fists until she pried them open gently. With her sweet, silent coaxing, she laced her fingers with mine.

"I just switched off, I guess. I didn't want to care that much. My dad wanted me to be one of the best hoteliers, so I worked my ass off. And when he left when I was in high school, I rebelled. Didn't want to make him proud, didn't want to do anything with him."

I looked down at our joined hands, swallowed the bitterness climbing up my throat, and took comfort in Red's touch. She calmed me down.

"But I realized that the more I resented him, the more I told myself I didn't care, that he was not a part of my life, had no say in my life… It just meant I was letting him influence my decisions."

I looked up into her eyes. Dark cat eyes that always visited my dreams at night.

"I was letting him control me. Giving him more power over me. And it had to stop. You know when I realized that?"

She shook her head.

"When I met you," I confessed quietly. "You woke me up. I saw how hard you were working, how independent and dedicated and stubborn you are, and I felt...ashamed. But most of all, you inspired me. Still do. And you make me want to be a better version of myself."

I heard her draw a sharp breath, felt her fingers tighten around mine.

"Sometimes I wonder what my life would be like if I hadn't met you that night. I have very, very bad thoughts about that."

"Caleb," she said tenderly and leaned forward to lay her soft lips on mine. "I need to tell you something."

"Okay."

"I know in your line of work you need...someone who can help you."

I straightened in my seat, alert now. Was she going to say that she wanted to work for me? Quit her job and just be with me?

"Someone to make your personal and business life easier. A wife who has connections that will open doors for you. Who goes to club luncheons and charities. Someone in your social circle—"

"Whoa, whoa, Red. Where the hell is this coming from?"

And then I realized: Beatrice-Rose.

Damn it!

Frustrated, I raked my fingers through my hair, barely containing my anger. Beatrice-Rose was really testing what little patience I had left for her.

"Listen to me," Red ordered. "I'm not finished."

The quick flash of temper and sharpness in her voice shifted my eyes back to her face. Her eyes were dark and blazing with anger.

Damn, I loved my girl when she was furious. I had to be sick.

"Yes, master." I couldn't help it. I had to say it.

She narrowed her eyes. "I know all that. And it might make your life easier if you marry someone with social standing like Beatrice-Rose."

"Now, wait a minute—"

"I said I'm *not finished*."

I felt like a student getting a lecture. Except that I really, really wanted the lecture because the teacher was hot. Blazing hot. I realized I was grinning when she narrowed her eyes into slits again. I had to work hard to keep a straight face.

"I didn't grow up in your world, but that doesn't mean I don't know these things. I'm not stupid. I know it would be more beneficial for you to marry someone from a family with a prestigious name. Someone who could play the piano and eat caviar and goat cheese and snails and disgusting rich-people food—"

"Snails give me indigestion, Red."

"—and someone who has a degree in art history or philosophy. Who wears Louboutin shoes and expensive dresses."

She was getting angrier by the second. And I was mesmerized.

"Someone who manages your household and has her own business but still has energy when she comes home to you and knows all these wonderful tricks in bed."

"Wait, what tricks?"

"Caleb."

Now her voice hitched, and when she looked at me, her eyes were vulnerable. My heart squeezed painfully.

"I don't care," she said quietly. "I have nothing to offer you but myself. But that's everything I have. That's all I have. And it's yours."

My chest filled with so much love for her that I forgot to breathe. If I'd been standing, my knees would have given out on me.

Oh, this girl. This girl owned me. Body and soul. I had never loved anyone like this.

"Red."

She looked down at her lap.

How could one girl consume me like this? But I knew. I knew. She wasn't just any girl. She was the one meant for me.

"It's all I need," I whispered.

I waited for her to look at me before continuing. A tear fell onto her lap, and I felt...destroyed. I was nothing—*nothing* without her.

"You're all I need," I said. "You're all there is. Nothing else matters."

I held her hand and placed it where my heart was beating against my chest. "Sometimes when I look at you, this feels like it's going to burst. I feel so much. So much for you. I never wanted anyone the way I want you, *need* you. I want it more than breathing. I don't want anything or anyone else. Just this, just you, right here. Give me this, give me yourself, and I'm the happiest man on earth."

She wrapped her arms around me, and I felt her tears on my neck.

I wanted her laughter again, her smiles.

"I'm not very fond of those Louboutin shoes anyway," I said. "Do you know how much those heels hurt? One girl stepped on me, and I swear my soul cried out in pain."

Her shoulders shook, but this time, I knew it was with mirth.

"So…what kind of tricks *were* you talking about?" I asked.

When she realized what I was talking about, she laughed, pulled away, and lightly smacked my arm. I looked at her face, and the sadness was gone.

"I love you, Red."

"I love you, Caleb."

She took a deep breath and smiled at me so beautifully that my brain stopped functioning for a minute.

I blinked. "Sorry?"

"I said you're going to be late for your flight. You better go."

I slipped out of the car to open her door, but as usual, she beat me to it.

I held her hand as we walked to the door. She was just opening it when I stopped her.

"Can I come in?" I asked.

"Don't you have to be there a couple hours before your flight?"

"I'll make it. I won't stay long. Maybe ten minutes."

She tightened her hold on my hand and smiled. "Okay. Come in, Caleb."

As soon as I entered, I froze.

Damon was sprawled on the couch, a big bowl of popcorn

on his lap as he watched a hockey game on TV. He looked over when he heard us come in.

What the hell was he doing here?

CHAPTER
twenty-three

Caleb

I INSTINCTIVELY PULLED RED CLOSE, POSSESSIVELY PLASTERING HER to my side.

"Hi, Damon," she said. "What are you doing here?"

My gaze whipped from his face to hers. She was smiling. I gritted my teeth.

"Oh, hey, Angel Face."

Angel Face? Who the hell does he think he is? Who the hell gave him permission to call her that?

"My DVD player broke," he explained. "I'm just watching reruns. I miss hockey."

No one asked you.

But I wisely kept my mouth shut. I knew Red would just get annoyed.

What the hell could I do? I was possessive when it came to Red. I wasn't going to hide that.

When Damon's eyes turned to me, he nodded. I was sorely tempted not to return the nod, but I was raised to be polite. And I remembered Red telling me that Damon was the one who had texted her that I was at the club where he was working that night. For that, I nodded back.

Still.

I narrowed my eyes and studied him. I guessed some girls would think he's handsome. With that tame-me, I'm-a-drifter look about him. But Red wasn't some girl. She wouldn't even consider Damon handsome…would she?

And what was up with that guitar he carted around with him? He was probably using it as a chick magnet. Like a dirty old man carting around a cute dog so girls would flock around him.

So what if he played guitar?

So what if I had no musical talent whatsoever? If I decided to play something, it would be video games. Not a pansy-ass guitar.

Wait. Did Red like it?

Maybe I should start learning…

I realized I was so absorbed in my thoughts that I'd missed some of their conversation.

"That sounds good," Red was saying. "Let me know what other jobs you can get for me. I'm free this summer."

What? She would accept a job from him but not from me?

How the hell did that make sense?

I was starting to feel frustrated on top of my jealousy. I was starting to feel aggressive. I didn't care for it.

"I have a gig tonight and tomorrow, and on Sunday, I'm serving drinks at a swank party. And standing around looking good," he added, winking. "I can probably get you in if you're available."

"Oh. Not this weekend. I have a shift at the shop tomorrow, and I have a special day on Sunday. By the way, where's Kar?"

"In the kitchen," he answered. "Want some popcorn?"

Enough.

"No, she doesn't." I glared at him and took Red's arm, pulling her toward the bedroom. "I need to talk to you, Red. Hi, Kar," I added as we passed a surprised Kara, who just raised her eyebrows and gave me two thumbs up.

"Wait," Red protested, but we were already at the bedroom door. "What's going on?"

As soon as I pulled her in and closed the door behind us, I locked it. Without warning, I pushed her against it. Her dark eyes widened with shock at my behavior, but beneath the shock was desire.

"Tell me you love me, Red."

"Caleb, what's—"

I closed the distance between us, fitting my body to hers— soft, generous curves and that scent that was exclusively hers. Hip to hip, she'd feel how much I wanted her.

I closed my eyes tightly, fighting for control. The need to take her against the door like an animal was overtaking reason, but I didn't want to scare her. I was sliding off the edge, and I desperately wanted to take her with me. But I had to be gentle.

"Caleb." Her voice was quiet and soothing, as if she knew what I was battling inside me. Perhaps she did.

I felt her brush my cheek with her fingers, stroke my jaw in comfort.

"I love you," she whispered.

When I opened my eyes, her face swam in my vision. Beautiful, dark cat eyes I wanted to drown in.

With a kiss, I softened the rough way I handled her. Cupping her face with my hands, I fit her mouth against mine, exploring her taste with my tongue. She moaned, gripping my hair with her hands.

When I pulled back, we were both breathing hard.

"Kar and Damon are outside," she gasped. "They're going to know what we're doing in here."

Good. I wanted him to know that Red was mine.

"I don't care."

Just like that, the need was back.

"But…we just…we just…in the car…"

"I still want you."

She bit her lip. "Oh. I…"

God. She was so fucking sweet and innocent. And I just wanted to—

She jumped suddenly when there was a loud knock on the door, followed by voices behind it.

"Whatever you guys are doing, keep doing it. We're leaving!" Kara yelled.

I cleared my throat. "Thanks, Kar!" I called out.

"You owe me, pal!"

When I looked back at Red, her eyes were shining with humor and embarrassment.

"Do you want to…" I began. My heart was racing. Why did I suddenly feel nervous?

Only Red. Only Red could make me feel this way.

"Do you want to touch me?" I murmured. "Red?"

Her eyes were half-closed as she stared at my lips, but she didn't say anything.

"I'm sorry. I don't want you to think that you have to… I just…I just. Right now. I want to feel…" I let out a loud breath, scrubbing my face with my hand. "*Fuck.* You tie me in knots. I don't even know what the hell I'm saying."

"I do." She lifted her eyes to mine, and my breath caught. She was so beautiful. "Let me."

"I need you to."

"You're going to miss your flight," she rasped.

I watched the rapid rise and fall of her chest, and I wanted—

"I'll catch another one."

I held my breath as her hands slowly reached for the bottom of my shirt. Tugged it up, then off. She let it fall to the floor.

When she placed her palms on my naked skin, I hissed.

Her eyes quickly shifted up and looked at me. Those eyes— they were dark, vulnerable, and full of questions.

"Did I do something wrong?" she asked.

"No, love. It feels so damn good."

I closed my eyes, breathing through my mouth. I didn't want to come early, but…*fuck*… she made me *feel*.

"Tell me what you like, Caleb. I want to…please you."

"This." I placed her palm on my stomach. "You can't possibly know how good your touch feels. Everything you do to me pleases me. Just do whatever you want with me, Red. Whatever you want."

"Caleb…"

Her touch was hesitant, and I realized she hadn't done this before. And I felt so damn good that I was the first one she would touch this way, and that no one else knew her this way—or would know her this way.

She was mine.

"Here." I dragged her palm back where my heart was beating fast. "Feel that? You do this to me. Make my heart race, and you've just started. You have the power to make me feel whatever you want me to feel. Touch me."

Her eyes filled with understanding, gleaming with womanly knowledge that excited me.

Her hands were soft, smooth, and curious as they traveled down my body. When she removed my belt and tugged my pants down, I swallowed hard.

Slowly, leisurely, she placed her lips on my neck and kissed and licked her way down, down, down until…

"Jesus."

Her mouth was hot, soft, and wet.

Another second and I would push. Another second and I would beg. Another second and I would explode.

I pulled her up and kissed her mouth savagely as I dragged her to the bed. Climbed on top of her. Filled my hands and my mouth with her taste, her scent.

Our hands shook as we frantically pulled at each other's clothes. I was blind with the need to possess her.

"Caleb."

"Here. I'm here. I got you, baby."

Pure satisfaction penetrated the haze of craving when I heard her stunned gasp as I ripped off her panties.

Blood pounded in my head, and my heart drummed madly against my chest. I gripped her leg, hooked it behind my hip. Looking into her eyes, I asked breathlessly, "Do you want me, Red? Like I want you?"

Dark eyes clouded with lust and love, she nodded.

She closed her eyes and bit her lip as I plunged into her, calling out her name.

Her breath stuttered out and her eyes opened, shimmering with the need for release.

I was captivated. Every move she made, every hitch in her breathing… I was so tuned in. The world could burn around us, and I wouldn't notice it. She was everything there was. Everything.

"Caleb." She whispered my name with a wonder that seized my heart.

Her nails dug into my back, and the pain and pleasure urged me to go faster, harder, deeper.

I claimed her mouth as I drove into her, muffling her choked cries. The need was vicious and painful as it took over every instinct. When her body went taut with release and her eyes clouded with ecstasy, I pounded myself into her.

My last thought before I let myself fall was *I love you.*

CHAPTER
twenty-four

Caleb

I was grinning when I boarded my flight. Everything was going great because:

(a) Red and I had made love.

(b) I was able to snag another flight just an hour after my original flight was scheduled to leave.

(c) Red and I had made love.

(d) Red and I had made love.

Of course, it's *because* of a, c, and d that I missed my flight, but I'd miss ten thousand flights if it meant I could have her again.

I texted her as soon as I landed.

Regina International Airport was small but sleek and modern, with its steel beams, high, impressive skylights, and glass windows that welcomed the rich sunlight.

I hated huge airports because I always got lost in them. They seemed to have too many entrances and exits, and too many people. If I wanted to sign up for a tour of the Matrix, I'd go find Neo and the Key Maker.

Strolling through the crowd, I spotted a Subway, a Tim Hortons, and a kiosk with a tiny white bear wearing a red Royal Canadian Mounted Police uniform on display.

I thought of Red right away. She liked cute things like that. So I bought it.

As soon as I stepped outside, the heat and humidity hit me like a punch in the face. Red had booked a limo for me in advance, and I was more than happy to get into the air-conditioned vehicle.

"Miranda Inn, please," I informed the driver.

I was just settling in, taking in the sights, when my phone burped a text. It was Ben telling me to meet him in the hotel lounge so we could have drinks and catch up before we talked business.

Miranda Inn's success was due to my grandfather's inherent knack for business—and luck. He had won the first hotel in a poker game, acquired all the rights and filed all legalities, changed the hotel name to his daughter's, and in less than five years had expanded it into a chain countrywide. When he passed away, my mother inherited the business and took it international.

I got out of the cab and entered the hotel. I observed its muted colors and tasteful modern furnishings as I wandered inside, silently approving of the classy marble fountain in the middle of the lobby—though wouldn't it be cool to have a life-size T. Rex skeleton instead?

My mom would probably sell me before she'd put dead dinosaur bones in her hotel. She had a spare son anyway.

I found myself grinning when I spotted Ben in the

lounge, sitting on the window seat overlooking the beautiful manicured gardens.

Almost a year had passed since Ben and I had seen each other. He'd been more than a brother to me as a child; he'd also been a best friend and a father to me when ours left.

Dressed in a charcoal suit, he looked very sophisticated—if you didn't count the dark blond hair that fell loose just above his shoulders, giving an impression of wildness. Even as a kid, he'd always been both a little proper and a little wild.

People always remarked how we didn't look like brothers. He had our dad's strong, masculine looks, while I'd inherited our mom's softer features. He had a rakish face. Confident and intelligent gray eyes that could charm a woman or silence a grown man with just one look. A strong nose, a square jaw.

I had punched that jaw many times when we were kids, about as many times as he'd punched mine. He was the one who'd taught me how to fight.

He must have felt my presence because his eyes abruptly shifted to mine. And then he grinned.

"Look at that face," he greeted, rising from his seat and wrapping me in a fierce hug. "Still butt-ugly."

"Goddamn. I missed you."

"Don't cry now. People will think I broke up with you," he said, but he only hugged me tighter. "Sit your ass down and tell me what you've been up to." He signaled for service as we took our seats.

"What's with the hippie hair?" I teased.

"Ah. Gives me an exotic look." He smoothed his dark-blue tie. "Women love it."

I scoffed. "Women just like you for your money."

He chuckled, then smiled at the girl who placed a cup of coffee in front of him and a glass of orange juice in front of me. He thanked her, and she blushed. "We'll have dinner in fifteen minutes."

"Yes, Mr. Lockhart," she said.

"I ordered for us already," Ben explained as the server walked away. "So, a college graduate." I watched as he poured cream in his coffee, stirring it with a silver spoon. "You're all grown up and ready to take over the world."

"Let's start with one hotel. I heard you have a job for me."

"If you want it. Mom wants you to supervise this hotel. It needs a lot more attention than the others." He paused, sipped his coffee. "But you'd have to relocate here."

"I'd rather stick to home," I replied instantly.

I wasn't budging. Red needed to finish one more year of school. Ben raised his brows.

"For a year or two. At least," I added.

He straightened in his seat, crossing his legs. "Mom won't be pleased."

I shrugged. I hated disappointing my mom, but this was nonnegotiable for me. "I'll tell her myself."

"You got a girl?"

"Yeah." I grinned. "Yeah, I've got a girl."

"There are two types of women in a man's life," he started, his gray eyes twinkling. "First type: Damn, she's hot. I want to bang her."

"And the second?" I asked.

"Damn, she's hot. I want to bang her."

I laughed and then thought of Red's dark eyes, the way they laughed in delight or blazed in anger or determination. I felt my heart trip. "Nah. She's more the 'Damn, she's perfect. I want to marry her' type."

He nodded, picked up his coffee cup, and drank again.

"I already proposed," I blurted out.

Ben choked, placing his cup back on the saucer as he cleared his throat. "What?"

I grinned at him. "Several days ago."

"Goddamn, you horny bastard. Is she pregnant?"

I thought about that heated, wild moment with Red when I didn't use a condom. Had it just been a few hours ago?

I'd never been so careless. I'd never *not* worn one when I needed it.

"Today she might be. But I hope not, because she's going to be absolutely pissed at me. Although I wouldn't mind if she is... pregnant, I mean."

A picture of a little girl with dark hair and gleaming cat eyes flitted into my mind. And then a little boy with the same features. No, I thought, I wouldn't mind at all.

"What did you do to my brother, and where did you put his carcass?" Ben asked, looking confused and shocked.

I laughed. I couldn't blame him. I was a very different person before Red came into my life.

"You'll meet Red—Veronica," I corrected, "on Sunday. I'm surprised Mom hasn't told you."

"I've been busy. I took over Mom's meetings in Europe this

month. I came back from Paris a week ago, actually. The last time I spoke with Mom, she told me Beatrice-Rose had come to visit her at home to speak about you."

I let out an expletive. "You mean she bad-mouthed my fiancée to Mom."

I could feel the anger trapped in my hands as they turned into fists. I had never hit a girl in my entire life, and I wasn't about to start now, but the thought of Beatrice-Rose spreading lies about Red made me want to hit *something*.

Why wouldn't she leave Red alone? I could put up with Beatrice-Rose making trouble for me, but I would not tolerate her making trouble for my girl.

Ben narrowed his eyes. "Why would she bad-mouth your fiancée?"

A dull ache started to throb at the base of my neck—the threat of a headache coming on. I cupped my neck with my palm and tried to massage it out.

"Is your fiancée a terrorist, a dog thief, or a stripper?" Ben teased.

It was supposed to be a joke, but it only fueled my anger, reminding me of the poster Justin had put up in the basketball team's locker room. Lucky for him, we hadn't found one anywhere else.

The dull ache climbed up to my temples.

"I was joking, Cal. Calm the hell down."

I realized I was gripping my glass hard enough to crack it. I loosened my grip and took a deep, calming breath. "Sorry. It's not you. Beatrice-Rose has fucked with my life in more ways than I care to count."

"Explain it to me."

Usually he would have known this by now because I always told him everything, but all these things had happened so fast and we'd both been busy. So I told Ben everything. He listened without interrupting, but I noted that his gray eyes flashed with incredulity when I spoke about what had happened in Beatrice-Rose's house and why Red had left me. They darkened with anger when I told him about Justin putting up that infuriating poster of Red in the basketball team's locker room. And finally, they conveyed cool, deadly calm when I told him about the drugs that were planted in my car.

Out of the corner of my eye, I saw the server walk toward us, but Ben held his finger up, signaling her not to interrupt. She nodded and left.

When I finished, I reached for my drink. Even though Red and I were back together, recalling the time we were separated brought an ache to my chest.

"So you hired a PI?"

I nodded. I knew Ben was going to ask about that first. He had protected me since we were kids.

"Is the PI any good?" he asked.

"Uncle Harry recommended him."

Ben nodded, satisfied. Uncle Harry was a retired private investigator and an old friend of our grandfather.

"Keep me updated," Ben said.

"I will. What is it?" I asked.

Ben had propped his elbows on the table, lacing his fingers

together and resting them on his lips. His sharp gray eyes narrowed in thought.

"If you'd told me Beatrice-Rose was capable of this three weeks ago, I would have been skeptical and very likely stunned."

"What do you mean?"

Ben took a deep breath, his eyes looking solemn. "I know how much she loves you. Remember, I watched the two of you grow up. I'm not defending her," he hurried to say before I could interrupt and say I didn't give a rat's ass.

Beatrice-Rose's love was poison. If you could even call it love.

"I'm just trying to make sense of the situation," Ben explained.

I nodded. Ben always analyzed a situation from all angles. That was what made him an astute businessman and a good brother. When I was an angry teenager, he'd told me that when you were too close to the situation, it was hard to see the big picture, and that had always stayed with me.

"I told you I was in Paris for business—about three weeks ago. I ran into Beatrice-Rose outside the restaurant I was just leaving after my meeting."

I frowned. Beatrice-Rose was in Paris? Three weeks ago...

"When I saw her that day, I could tell she wasn't well. She was walking by herself, looking lost."

Three weeks ago, so were Red and I. "I don't care—"

"Cal, listen to me." The grim tone in his voice caught my attention. "She looked ill, like she'd been suffering from a cold for a month. She was pale, withdrawn, and thinner than I've ever seen her. So I took her to dinner. It was...disturbing."

Ben leaned back in his seat, his eyes bleak. "There was a

manic quality to her. She'd be perfectly polite and calm for ten minutes, and then she'd scratch her arms until they bled. She kept muttering about her dad and her bunny rabbit. Then out of the blue, she'd be calm again. So I told her I'd take her to the hospital. She must have realized I wasn't going to let her go because she told me she was already staying in a clinic."

"A clinic?" I asked, perplexed.

Ben turned his head to look outside for a moment, as if contemplating something, before he shifted his serious gray eyes back to mine.

"It was a mental facility, Cal."

"What?" I could only stare at him, shocked.

"I couldn't believe it either. She told me she's been getting therapy there for years. It started when her dad got sick. She had been doing better, but when she went back this time, she'd gotten worse."

God. I had no idea.

That was around the time Red and I broke up, and that was also when I had scorned Beatrice-Rose. She must have checked herself into the clinic after that.

Guilt churned in my stomach, making me feel sick. I knew Beatrice-Rose wasn't dealing well with her dad's condition, but had I pushed her to the brink?

"That was when…Red and I broke up. I talked to Beatrice-Rose and told her to stay away from me. I was really angry. I said a lot of harsh words to her."

Ben studied me for a moment. "It's not your fault."

Maybe not. But I had added to it.

I stared at my hands, balling them into fists. "Maybe she wasn't faking her panic attacks."

"Maybe she was, maybe she wasn't," he said. I looked up into his gray eyes and saw sympathy there. "You can't blame yourself for reacting that way after the stunt she pulled. Were you supposed to just let it go? You're not stupid, Brother. If a person tried to stab you, would you just stand there and take it? There's something wrong with her," he continued. "But it doesn't exempt her from the consequences of her actions. She needs to be back at the clinic."

"She's home now," I informed him.

"I know. Sometimes it's best to step back and let other people help her. She's not your responsibility."

"She was my friend," I said.

Ben nodded. "Yeah. All we can do is be there for her when she's ready to accept help. But you need to learn to step back when she's out to destroy her life and wants to take you down with her. Let the doctors and professionals who are more equipped to deal with her condition help her. That's who she needs now." He raised his brows. "We good?"

I let out a relieved breath. "Yeah, good."

The server arrived with our food. I wasn't hungry, but since it was there, I picked up my burger and took a bite, eyeing Ben's steak. "You're such a cheap date. How come you just got me a burger and fries?"

"You always get a burger and fries," he reasoned.

"Yeah, but I want a steak this time."

"You want a steak because I have a steak."

He was right. It was out of principle, really. When we were kids, if he had a new toy, I had to have the same thing. If he wore a Batman shirt, I wore a Batman shirt too.

"Switch," I demanded.

"What are you, seven?"

"Twenty-three in less than two days."

I rose to swap our plates, but he grabbed his plate before I could reach for it.

"It's my birthday," I reminded him.

He gave me a bored look. "You exhausted your birthday excuses a long time ago."

In the spirit of brotherhood, Ben pulled a coin from his pocket. "Flip you for it. Heads, I get the big slab of dead cow. Tails, you choke down your burger and fries. And you're paying for beer later," he added.

"You got it."

He flipped it, and our gazes remained fixed on the coin. It landed on the table between us. When Ben looked up at me, his smile was smug.

I sneered. "Ass."

He shrugged, still sporting a cocky grin. "Where's my beer?"

CHAPTER
twenty-five

Caleb

IT WAS ALMOST MIDNIGHT BY THE TIME I GOT BACK TO MY ROOM. I was exhausted, dying for a shower and an aspirin for my headache.

Scientists were always coming up with new things. Why not a pill to stamp out headaches in a matter of seconds? Or a shower room where all you needed to do was step inside, and three seconds later—bada bing, bada boom—you were all scrubbed and clean. Without moving a muscle.

Wouldn't that be cool?

I wanted all of that. But most of all, I wanted my Red.

Walking right past the bathroom, I tugged off my shirt, discarding it on the floor as I made my way to the bed. Jeans and socks came off next, and finally—*finally*—I stumbled facedown in bed.

Red had lectured me so much about leaving my clothes on the floor that I felt a little guilty. I briefly thought of getting up and picking them up off the floor.

But the bed felt so good, and there was no way she'd find out. And…

I could still smell her faintly on me. I could close my eyes and imagine her.

Maybe I'd postpone that shower till tomorrow.

She'd probably be asleep by now. She liked to sleep early.

But sometimes she'd forget to silence her phone and my texts would wake her up. She was such a light sleeper.

What was I supposed to do? I missed her. She wouldn't move in with me yet, but I'd put an end to that soon. As soon as I got home, I'd drag her to see the three houses I'd lined up with the real estate agent.

When my cell rang, I was tempted to let it go to voicemail. But maybe Red was calling. I hit the button without looking at the screen.

"Hello?"

"Hi, Caleb."

A huge smile split my face. It almost hurt.

"Who is this?" I asked seriously.

"It's me."

"Who?" I flipped on my back, settling against the pillows as I imagined her lying in her bed with her hair spread nicely on the pillow. She was probably wearing those tiny red shorts, and her legs would be bare and…

"Caleb?"

I cleared my throat. "Are you the girl who left underwear under my pillow? Because…you know, that's not normal."

"What the hell are you talking about?" Pause. "What girl?"

I almost laughed. Almost.

"Wait a minute," I teased, still in a very serious tone. "You sound like the girl who's obsessed with me. The one who climbed through my bedroom window the other night."

"Wait. That was *you* trying to climb through *my* bedroom window!"

When I heard her soft laughter, I closed my eyes and imagined her face: dark eyes shining with humor, red lips stretched into a beautiful smile.

"Yeah, I'm the obsessed girl who climbed through your window—and ripped off your eyebrows," she finished.

"Huh?"

"*Paper Towns*. John Green?"

"Who the hell is John Green, and why would he rip off someone's eyebrows? That's…cruel."

"No." She snickered. "The one who wrote *The Fault…* Oh, never mind."

Ah. Had to be one of the million books she read.

"Hi, Red," I whispered after a moment.

"Hi, Caleb."

I knew we were both smiling, feeling happy to hear each other's voice on the phone.

"Tell me about your day," she said.

I thought about the situation with Beatrice-Rose, and my good mood plummeted. But then I remembered my day had started really good—with Red. Really, really good.

"Ben showed me around the hotel, introduced me to the staff. After the tour, we went up to the office to start my training. He works like a maniac, and he expects everyone else to do the same. We went through accounts, brainstormed proposals on how to acquire more investors. Then we came up with new ideas for promotional offers and packages for the coming summer and fall, to attract more guests to our hotel. And now I have my girl on the phone. Pretty good deal, all in all."

"Sounds like a productive day." I heard the smile in her voice.

"I kept thinking about what happened in your bedroom," I said, my voice hoarse. "Are you sore?"

There was a pause on the other end, and I imagined her face blushing.

"A little," she whispered.

And then I remembered…shit. Condom. Or, more accurately, *lack of* condom.

"Red?"

"Hmm?"

"I'm sorry I didn't use a condom."

Another pause. Soft, fast breathing. "It's okay."

What did she mean, it's okay?

"I'm taking birth control," she explained. "I went to see my doctor weeks ago."

"Oh. Good."

I frowned. I didn't know what to think when I felt a flicker of disappointment. I guessed I was hoping she might be pregnant.

"Did you finally get to catch up with your brother?" she asked.

She was still uncomfortable and shy discussing things like us making love. I wanted her to be comfortable enough to tell me what she yearned for when we were in bed. I wanted to satisfy and fulfill all her desires. I wanted her to—

"Caleb?"

"Yeah, baby?"

"Did you spend time catching up with your brother?" she repeated.

Oh. Right.

"Yeah, I did. But he's a workaholic. I have my work cut out for me."

"You're good at the things you love to do. I know you'll do great."

Oh, my girl. She was so sweet.

"I love that you think of me that way," I said. "I felt like a kid again. Ben and I used to tag along with our grandfather when he went to work. I grew up visiting and learning about hotels from him. Even as a kid, the work, the adventure, even the drama inside the hotel fascinated me."

I heard her moving around, then the rustle of pillows and blankets as she lay on top of them.

"Tell me a story about it."

"Hmm, let's see. I remember when I worked there as a bellman—"

"You did?"

I didn't know whether I should be insulted or amused at the shock in her voice. "Yep. I told you I'd worked at the hotel. What, did you think I was just a spoiled, gorgeous rich boy who drove around in fancy cars and picked up women?"

When she didn't answer, I realized she *did* think of me that way. I scowled. "Ouch."

She chuckled. "That was so accurate, it wasn't even funny."

Way to rub it in, Red.

"But that was then. I didn't know you before," she whispered. "Now I do."

"And now you're so in love with me, it's not even funny," I concluded. "All right, let me tell you a story. This one happened at our hotel in Vegas. You have to promise not to tell anyone. It's top secret," I warned.

"I'd spit in my palm and give you a high five right now, Caleb, but you're too far away." She uttered it so sincerely and so sweetly that it took a moment for me to realize she was joking.

"Feisty." I chuckled. "There was this very famous actress. VIP status."

"Which actress?"

"Ah. That I cannot disclose. See, we may be hotel employees, but we're basically like priests. Or doctors. Or lawyers. We can't possibly disclose the names of clients," I whispered.

"Like CIA," she whispered back, absolutely on to the game.

"Yes," I murmured. "Like those guys. But since you're my fiancée, I'm allowed to tell you." I told her the name of the actress, and she was impressed. "This A-list actress books the entire floor. For herself. Her manager and assistant were on a different floor."

"Okay. So maybe the girl loves her privacy. There's nothing wrong with that."

"No, there isn't," I confirmed. "But we were still curious."

"Uh-huh."

"No one was allowed on that floor, except for maids and room service. And since she was VIP, well, you know, we try our best to give them everything they ask for."

"Of course."

"So it was only natural for me and Ben to sneak in. We dressed up as room service."

"Naturally," she replied, deadpan. "So, what'd you find out?"

"We thought she was making a porno or…murdering someone, but we found out she was cheating on her boyfriend."

"Oh. That's why they broke up."

"Yeah," I replied. Paused. "She was cheating on him with another woman."

"Really? I had no idea."

"But then the boyfriend, a very famous singer, came for a surprise visit. He was holding this enormous bouquet of roses in front of him and had a small band trailing behind him, carting around their equipment—guitars, violins, you name it. He was going to propose."

I heard her quietly gasp. "Aw. Poor guy."

"I know. He also decided to…um…take off all his clothes before knocking on her door. He probably figured, hey, might as well go all the way. Door opens, he sees them. Both naked as a bird. Two minutes later, a flat-screen TV came flying out the window."

"Oh God."

"Nearly killed a bellman."

By now, Red was in fits of laughter. "I'm sorry. I shouldn't laugh, but…"

"Go ahead. It was kind of funny, considering he ran out of the room naked and mad as a bull. All the way down to the lobby."

"*What?*"

"I swear it's true. You didn't hear that on the news?"

"I don't really watch the news."

"Come on, everyone was talking about it. I remember my grandfather was happy. It was free advertising for the hotel. Good or bad, it was still advertising, he said. Anyway, a week later, the singer was already dating a different actress."

She sighed. "I guess it wasn't real."

"I guess it wasn't. Red?"

I wanted to keep the good mood going—I loved hearing her laugh—but I knew I had to tell her what I'd found out today.

"Hmm?"

"I need to talk to you about something."

I heard the sharp intake of her breath, as if she was bracing herself. "All right, Caleb. I'm here."

I smiled. *I'm here.* It was a simple sentence, really. But it held a lot of promise.

"Ben told me he saw Beatrice-Rose in Paris a few weeks ago. She's sick, Red."

"You're worried about her," she observed.

"No... Yeah. I don't know," I replied, frustrated. I sat up in bed, rubbing my face with my hand.

"It's okay to be worried about her, Caleb."

"I don't want to worry about her," I said a little sharply.

Sliding out of bed, I started toward the kitchen. "What I *do* know is that I'm not ready to forgive her or let her back in my life. She hurt you." I made it to the fridge and grabbed a bottle of water, twisting off the cap harder than I intended. "And going by what you told me about when you saw her today, she doesn't plan on stopping soon."

I took a sip and walked to the small eating area.

"I can handle her, Caleb. She can't say anything that will change how I feel about you," she said softly, and I heard the apology in her voice. "She's a manipulative liar. Nothing gives her the right to hurt and abuse people. You don't have to subject yourself to that kind of abuse. No one deserves to be abused. Not even her," she finished.

"I know."

"My dad… He was the same. He nearly…killed my mom," she choked out. "And me. He didn't care as long as he got what he wanted. Tell me if that's right. Tell me if you want to be around people like that. Tell me if you deserve to just take their abuse."

She took a deep breath. "Beatrice-Rose needs help, Caleb. I feel bad for her, I really do, but it doesn't mean I'll stand by and do nothing when she decides to harm the people who are important to me. What she's doing now… It's a cry for help."

"I know."

I had asked for a bottle of aspirin from the front desk earlier, and when I found it sitting on the dining table, I sighed in relief. I shook two pills into my palm, swallowed them, and chased them down with water.

"The PI phoned me earlier," I said. "He found something."

"Did he find out who planted the drugs in your car?"

"Yeah," I replied. "It was Justin."

I heard her sharp intake of breath.

"There's a warrant for his arrest now. They found footage of him in the underground parking lot of my building. He had keys to my car. That's why the alarm didn't go off."

"How did he get your keys?"

"I'm not sure. Before you lived with me, I'd invite the guys to my place for a beer. But only a couple of times. Justin might have stolen them then. I'd never needed my spare keys before. I just kept them in my room, but when I checked, they were gone."

"Someone had been in your room. Are you missing anything else?"

"Yeah," I said, swallowing the anger rising inside me. I still couldn't believe I'd been robbed by someone I considered a friend.

"A Piaget watch I inherited from my grandfather is missing, some cash. I don't know what else. Clooney, the PI I hired, is checking the security footage of the building. There are no cameras in the hallways. I refused to let them put one in, but there are cameras in the elevators and lobby."

I stumbled back into bed, hugging my pillow. I wished it was her.

"I don't want to talk about this anymore. I'm so tired, Red. I wish you were here."

"Me too. I miss you," she said. "I-I was hoping to spend more time with you today. Watch movies, make you dinner. I don't know. Something."

My eyes felt heavy, but I managed a smile.

I reached sluggishly for the lamp and turned it off. Better to hear her voice and imagine her beside me in the dark.

"I would have loved that," I murmured. "Hey, Red?"

"Yes?"

"What are you thinking about?"

"Um…"

"Are you thinking about me? And what happened in your bedroom?" I whispered.

Soft, fast breathing was her reply.

"Because," I continued, "I can't stop thinking about it."

"Yes," she said breathlessly. "Me too."

"Good."

"You sound so tired, Caleb. Get some sleep. I'll call you tomorrow."

"Okay," I murmured. "I have this picture of you in my head when I close my eyes. Just you," I whispered. "Just you."

I settled into my pillows, feeling sleepy and lethargic, wishing she was curled up beside me.

I want to make love with you again.

Today.

Tonight.

Tomorrow.

Every day.

For the rest of our lives.

"Come home soon, Caleb."

"Soon, my Red."

I hung up the phone and closed my eyes, imagining her beside me as I drifted off to sleep.

CHAPTER

twenty-six

Veronica

"I KNOW EXACTLY WHERE WE CAN GET PRETTY DRESSES FOR cheap," Kara chirped, hooking her hand around my arm. "If we're lucky, we'll find one that looks like a million bucks. But first, let's get milk shakes."

I could hear the excitement in her voice as she steered us to the nearest coffee shop, then spent hours dragging me into thrift stores and consignment shops. She loved finding a good deal, but when we couldn't find anything, she gave up and drove us to the mall.

"So, you got your lover a present yet?"

I nodded. "I knitted him a beanie."

"In the middle of fucking *summer*?"

She looked at me like I was some kind of alien. "You're giving him that thing for his birthday?"

What's wrong with it? She made it sound like a crime.

"Well, yeah. He can use it during the winter. He loves wearing beanies. Plus, I made it myself," I argued defensively. I'd worked hard making *that thing*. "Do you know how hard it is, knitting a beanie during exam week? I barely had time to finish it!"

She shot me a pitiful look. "Look, you're my friend, so I have to be honest with you or this won't work." I scowled at her before she pulled me inside a nearby store. "Your gift-giving skills suck."

I let out an exasperated noise. "I'm giving him the beanie," I insisted stubbornly.

She sighed, defeated. "I guess you're lucky Lockhart has everything already. And I guess..." She pulled a green dress off the rack and turned to me, narrowing her eyes as she plastered the dress to my front. After a brief contemplation, she shook her head and put the dress back. "Lockhart's so addicted to you, he'd just think it's charming that you blow at giving gifts."

"There's nothing wrong with it," I persisted. "Besides, if he doesn't want it, I'll use it myself."

I was giving him the beanie, and that was that.

"All right. I give up. We can't all be perfect, I guess." She flicked her hair behind her shoulder like the diva she was.

I shot her a sour look. "Geez, Kar. You're so perfect that you should have a statue erected in your honor. And a flag with your face on it."

She winked at me. "I know, right?"

When she pulled out another green dress—what was with her and green today?—I shook my head and told her it needed to be red. She rolled her eyes, and we walked to another section.

"So," she said casually, plucking another dress from the rack and tossing it to me. She proceeded to another rack and I followed. "How big is Lockhart's pickle?"

If I'd had a drink, I would have choked. "Kar!"

She rolled her eyes again. "Don't think I didn't know you guys were playing hide-the-salami in your bedroom yesterday."

"Ohmygod." I let out a strangled laugh, looking around to make sure no one had heard her. I felt my face heat up in embarrassment when I spotted the clerk trying not to laugh. "Kar, shut the hell up."

She wiggled her eyebrows. "Try that on," she ordered, shooing me inside the dressing room.

I locked the door behind me, goggling dubiously at the little piece of spandex I was holding.

"Give me one detail then." She paused. "Is it true he can go all night?"

I bit my lip, blushing again—but for different reasons.

"You're killing me here," she whined.

"Yes," I murmured after a moment.

"Yes, what?"

"Yes." I cleared my throat. "He can go all night."

Silence.

"I'll start praying for your poor but totally satisfied va—"

I cut her off. "Kar!"

"Soul. I was going to say soul."

I sighed.

"How about his tongue? Can he do the helicopter—"

"Kar!"

"Ugh."

I knew Kara. She wouldn't stop until she got what she was fishing for.

"Maybe we can talk about this at home. Not here," I suggested.

I could practically hear her eyes rolling into the back of her head.

"Fine! Oh, hi, do you have that dress in red? No, not that one, the one beside it, with the high slit going up her neck—yup, that. Is that skirt vegan leather? It's cruelty-free?" Her voice flitted away as she chatted with the clerk.

I glanced at my reflection in the mirror, frowning at the tight dress. Although it was a long-sleeved dress and covered half of my neck modestly, it was shorter than I would have liked.

I almost jumped when there was a sharp knock on the door. "Well, come out and let me see you," Kara ordered.

She curled her top lip as I opened the door.

"I hate you," she pouted. "If I had that ass and those tits, oh *Lord*. I'd save money on clothes because I wouldn't wear any."

I snorted. "I don't think this is what I'm looking for, Kar."

She nodded. "You're right. You need something classier. You look like a conservative hooker. Let's go to another store, bestie."

"Nowhere expensive."

"It's all good. I've got Lockhart's credit card."

My mouth fell open. "Y-you what?"

"I'm kidding!" She burst into giggles. "You should have seen your face."

I grabbed a hanger and threw it at her. "I'm thinking of making custom tea bags for Caleb's mom," I said, to change the subject. "I could buy her a book—"

Kara opened her mouth and acted like she was going to vomit.

I ignored her. "I could buy her flowers or—"

"Why don't you knit her a beanie?"

I grabbed a lock of her hair and pulled.

"Ow. All right. Fine. She'd probably appreciate diamonds more."

"Kar," I said, finally letting my panic slip in my voice. "I want to make a good impression on Caleb's mom. It's important to me because…it's important to Caleb. Please, I need your help. I'm really bad at this. What do you think?"

She blew out a breath. "Well…I don't know his mom. I hope she isn't a bitch, for your sake. But custom-made tea bags? Really?"

I bit my lip. "I thought… Well, it's more personal and thoughtful. Isn't it? Caleb said she loves tea…"

"Oh, she does? Well, okay, I see. No, you're right. I thought it was one of your incredible pull-it-out-of-my-ass gift ideas, but if she loves tea, give'r."

"I will. I bought a blend of herbs the other day, and I think they'll help her relax after a long day. I just need to find a pretty wooden box or tin to put the bags in."

"Sweet. Maybe add a teapot and a cup too, for good measure."

"Good idea. Thanks, Kar."

She gave me a smile and patted my back. "What are friends for?"

When we reached the next store, both of us stopped and stared at the mannequin dressed in a red gown.

The dress had delicate straps and a sweetheart neckline. It fit every inch of the mannequin like a second skin and ended a couple of inches above the knees. A sheer overlay of chiffon flowed over the skirt and spilled to the floor, while a slit up the front showcased the mannequin's legs.

"Do you feel it? This is your dress, Ver. It's speaking to us. It's saying, 'Buy me, and I'll make you feel like you have J. Lo's ass.'"

I chuckled nervously. She was right. But how much was it? It looked really expensive.

I wanted to buy it so badly. I wanted to look good for Caleb on his birthday. I also wanted to impress his mom and look presentable on Caleb's arm when he was introduced to his new coworkers and clients.

We entered the store and I circled the mannequin, discovering that the back of the dress was scooped low. It exposed a considerable amount of skin. I reached for the price tag and caught my breath when I saw the cost.

"It's expensive, Kar."

She glanced at the price tag. "Not for this dress. You have to get it."

My face fell.

"I'll lend you money," she offered cautiously. She knew how sensitive I was about the topic. "You can pay it back after you graduate and find a job. How's that?"

I let out a defeated sigh. I couldn't possibly take her money. There must be some way... I did a mental calculation in my head of bills that were due this month—my rent, groceries, and now my phone bill too. I was short. Really short.

"I can't, Kar."

"Hi there." A store clerk bounced in front of us, smiling brightly. "How are you ladies today?"

"Good," Kara answered, still looking at me in exasperation.

"I noticed you were looking at this dress. We're in the process of clearing out our old stock, and this one in particular is on sale for—"

"Holy shit. It's on sale! That's it. You're getting it."

"Kar, calm down."

The clerk laughed. "It's from last season's designs, if you don't mind that. It's 60 percent off right now. All dresses with the red tag."

It was still slightly over my budget, but for Caleb, I would take it. It'd be worth the monthlong peanut-butter-sandwich diet I'd have to endure to pay for it.

I was in the dressing room trying it on when I heard Kara drag a chair outside the door.

"So where's Lockhart now?"

"He's in Saskatchewan," I replied. "They built a hotel there a few months ago, and Caleb said it needs a lot of attention since it's new. His brother is training him."

"Benjamin Lockhart?" Kara sounded impressed. "Have you met him?"

"Not yet. Caleb mentioned he'll be at the party. You know him?"

"Not really. I heard rumors around campus about him. I saw him, though. Damn. The Lockhart brothers are insanely gorgeous, but...get ready. Benjamin Lockhart is deadly. You know those types who give you one look—just one look—and you're ready to drop your panties? That's him. Yup."

I snorted.

"Hold on. Will Caleb be staying in Saskatchewan?"

Oh.

"I-I'm not sure. We haven't talked about it."

"What if he is?" she asked quietly. "Will you be moving there with him?"

Would I?

"My life is here."

"I know." She sighed. "But that was before you met Caleb."

My knees felt weak, so I sat down on the bench inside the dressing room. I hadn't thought about relocating.

"I don't know, Kar. Caleb wants us to buy a house here so I just assumed…"

"He wants to buy a house?"

"Yes."

"Wow. He's thinking long-term commitment. Like the have-my-babies kind."

I took a deep breath, forcing myself to calm down and cut off my disturbing thoughts. I refocused on the conversation.

"No." I laughed, but it was strained. Yet I felt a flutter in my stomach at the thought of carrying Caleb's child someday. I shook my head. "Every time I give Caleb an inch, he takes a mile."

"Don't they all?" Kara said wryly. "Listen, I've watched you and Lockhart this past week. You look at each other like you want to rip each other's clothes off. It's pretty sick, really."

"Jealous?" I teased.

"Bitch. Of course I'm jealous."

I laughed when she rapped the door loudly.

"I also know you well enough to say that if you don't want to give him that mile, you won't," Kara continued. "You're really stubborn. But you do give it, so that means you want it too. There's no point in denying it.

"That's why you're perfect for each other, you know? You think too much, worry too much. He looks like he doesn't, but I've got Lockhart's number now. You think he's just another dumb, handsome face, but he's pretty smart. And sneaky. That bastard."

I giggled.

"He knows what you need, what you want, even though *you* haven't realized it yet," Kara continued.

"You're too careful to take risks; he isn't. And he makes you see how simple it is, because you never do. Sometimes it *is* that simple. You don't need to make it complicated."

I thought about Caleb's mom. "But sometimes it *is* complicated."

"Shut the hell up. He loves you; you love him. He wants to marry you; you want to marry him. You want to be together. So be together. Simple. There will always be problems. It's just how the world works. You'll figure it out. If you keep waiting until you're ready, well, you'll be waiting forever. No one's ever really ready." She paused. I heard her draw a deep breath before continuing in a pained, quiet voice. "It's a different story if he doesn't want to fight for you."

"Kar…"

"Gah." I imagined her waving her hand in front of her face, dismissing her thoughts. "Are you impressed with all these amazing quotes I'm spouting at you? Damn, I even impress myself sometimes." She laughed, but it sounded feigned.

It was Cameron again, but I knew if she wanted to discuss it, she would. So I let it go.

"What the hell are you doing in there?" she demanded. "Knitting another beanie? Come out and let me see the dress!"

"You need to zip me up."

"Yeah, yeah. Just get your ass out here." I opened the door, and Kara whistled. "Damn, you look hot." She stared at me wide-eyed, giving me two thumbs up. "If I were a guy, I would totally do you," she added, zipping me up.

"Well, well, well. That's quite a dress, Veronica."

I froze, my gaze whipping to the source of that familiar mocking voice.

"Can you afford it?" Beatrice-Rose derided.

She stood near the dress racks in front of us, a clerk beside her. I noticed that even in her expensive clothes and makeup, she looked pale and gaunt, as if she had lost weight.

I knew from what Caleb had told me that she wasn't well. I took a deep breath, trying hard to conjure up patience and sympathy for her.

Before I could think of something to say, Kara interjected. "I think we need an exorcist, Ver. I'm feeling an evil spirit in the vicinity."

"Don't be crass, Kara," Beatrice-Rose sneered.

Kara cupped her ear. "Did you hear something?"

Beatrice-Rose ignored her and turned to me. "Make sure you don't embarrass Caleb at the party. There will be a lot of important people in attendance. Or maybe just don't show up. You know you'll look cheap in whatever you wear anyway."

Patience and sympathy could go to hell.

Maybe I was a bad person for this, because no matter how hard I tried to understand her, I couldn't help the retort that came out.

"Why would I do that," I said calmly, "when Caleb told me I'm the only one he wants to show up at his party?"

Her eyes flashed with anger. "You must be really good in bed if Caleb's willing to introduce you at his party. You know he's going to leave you sooner or later. He gets bored pretty quickly."

There was a gleam of malevolence in her eyes as she smiled.

"Did you know," she started, "that Caleb loves it when I kiss his stomach?"

I suddenly felt sick.

"Or," she continued, smiling widely, "when I lick down—"

"Hey, bitch. How are the hair extensions? You have to buy the good ones, girl, or your bald spot will show," Kara interrupted.

There was a horrified expression on Beatrice-Rose's face as she shifted her eyes to Kara.

"I don't have a fucking bald spot!" Beatrice-Rose shrieked, loud enough that the clerk inched away from us and a few of the customers glanced warily in our direction.

"It's all right. There's nothing wrong with that," Kara continued in a comforting tone, like she was speaking to a small child. "The first step to getting over your hang-up is acceptance."

"You fucking bitch!"

Beatrice-Rose's face had turned red, her hands balled into fists. She was breathing hard, her eyes glowing with hatred. It reminded me of a rabid dog about to attack. I took a step forward to protect Kara.

And then, as if a switch had been flipped, her face transformed into a calm mask.

"You're nothing but bad luck," she taunted, sneering at Kara. "Bad luck to the people around you. No wonder your ex-boyfriend is destitute now. You've infected him. You've *ruined* him."

Kara paled. "What do you mean?"

Beatrice-Rose cocked her head, a nasty, self-satisfied smirk on her lips.

Before she could say anything, I walked up to her threateningly.

"One more word," I warned her quietly. Dangerously. My palm was tingling. "One more word, and you'll find your face on the floor."

Beatrice-Rose's mouth curled with contempt, and we stared at each other for a moment. I could feel the hatred pouring out of her.

I noticed she placed her hand in her pocket. Then she took a step forward.

"Is everything all right here, ladies?"

The malice on Beatrice-Rose's face suddenly disappeared as she threw the manager and the clerk a polite, gratifying smile, so completely at odds with her smirk just a minute ago. I wasn't surprised. She'd appeared to be an innocent dove when I met her the first time.

"Oh, just catching up with some friends. I'll see you at the party, darlings," she cooed, waving her fingers. "Ciao."

With my dress packed in a pretty paper bag and thrown in the backseat, I watched as Kara absently started the car. She stared through the windshield, her eyes filled with anxiety.

"Are you all right, Kar?"

She leaned back against the headrest. "What did the bitch mean by that? My ex is destitute? Cameron is fucking loaded." She took a deep breath, running a hand through her hair. Turned her head to look at me. "What does she know that I don't?"

"She's probably just talking bullshit."

She stared out the windshield again. "Yeah."

"If you're really worried, I can ask Caleb."

Kara was quiet for a moment, lost in her thoughts. "Nah. It's fine. You're right. Bitch was probably high. What was she doing there anyway? Not her usual scene." She curled her lip. "Doesn't she shop at Bitches-R-Us or something?"

She eased out of the parking lot, tooting her horn at a bunch of teenagers who'd decided to make the road their skateboard park. There was litter around them—McDonald's wrappers, cigarette butts, empty soda cans.

"Fuck you, lady!" one of them yelled, slapping the side of the car.

Kara rolled her window down, grabbed what was left of her milk shake, and threw it at them.

My jaw dropped. Kara didn't say anything, just rolled her window back up and stepped on the gas. When we were three blocks away, she glanced at the rearview mirror. I turned and looked behind us to check if they were following us. Thank God they weren't.

"I'm having a bad hair day," she announced, giving me a lopsided smile. "Anyone stupid enough to piss me off when I'm having a bad hair day gets mutilated." She sniffed, and I wondered if she was going to cry. "Now I'm more pissed off. Fuckers took my milk shake away."

"You're lactose intolerant anyway," I reminded her, hoping she'd get angry instead of sad. "You don't need it."

She glared at me. "Just for that, I'm getting another one."

I hid my smile as she pulled into a Tim Hortons and ordered an Iced Capp with extra whipped cream, glaring at me the whole time.

"Beatrice-Rose is sick, Kar."

"She's sick, all right. Sick in the head."

She couldn't have been closer to the truth if she tried. So I told her what Caleb had told me last night.

"I don't feel good about this. Just stay away from her, Ver."

"I'm not planning on having any sleepovers with her, that's for sure," I replied dryly.

Kara snorted. "Bitch'd probably cook you for breakfast if you did."

She parked the car at the farthest end of the lot.

"Too bad she's not sick enough to be committed involuntarily. Maybe she's just faking it to get sympathy. Everyone goes to therapy now, so what? I don't feel bad for her at all. Everyone's life has shit in it. Sometimes some people have more shit than others, but having more shit doesn't give you the right to throw shit on other people. You know what? Let's forget about her. Give me that Iced Capp."

"Don't start farting at work," I reminded her, pulling it from the cup holder and handing it to her.

She gave me the finger and snatched the Iced Capp.

"Are you sure you want to work tomorrow?" Kara asked. "You can take the day off. It's your fiancé's birthday."

I shook my head no. Weekends were very busy at the shop. I couldn't do that to Kara. Besides, Caleb wouldn't be back until later that day. He'd wanted to pick me up, but I told him I'd drive there with Kara.

"Okay, then take a half day," she insisted.

"No. Besides, we'll go to the party together. We have enough time to get ready and be there on time."

"Yeah. I got your back, sister."

I was counting on it.

I woke up the next day excited and anxious. Today was Caleb's birthday party.

At work, I glanced at the clock again—for the hundredth time. Why does time move so slowly when you're waiting for something?

I was excited to see him, very anxious about meeting his mom again, his brother, and all of his guests. There would be a lot of affluent people attending.

That shouldn't intimidate me, but it did.

Grabbing my phone, I pressed the home button and stared at the background picture of Caleb kissing me in the car. And I suddenly felt better.

He would be there. That was the important thing. I remembered our phone call from this morning.

"Today's my birthday," Caleb had said excitedly.

I laughed. "Happy birthday, Caleb."

"It's not that happy until I see you. Are you sure you don't want me to pick you up later?"

"I'm sure. Kar's driving me, and it's all planned out. I'll see you at your party."

"Don't forget my gift."

"What makes you think you're getting a gift?"

"What?"

The shock in his voice made me laugh.

"Are you sexting Lockhart?"

I blinked and realized I had been grinning stupidly at my phone while replaying the memories from this morning.

"You have that creepy smile on your face," Kara pointed out.

I rolled my eyes at her and glanced at the clock again. We had half an hour left, but Kara was already pulling the cash out of the till.

"Want to balance now? There are only two more cars waiting to be picked up, so we can probably balance everything now."

"Yes, please."

"Lockhart must be itchy to see you. He's texted you every five minutes—"

Kara froze as we heard angry shouts from the back of the shop. We stared at each other in alarm and started to race to the back to see what was going on.

"What the fu—"

Before we even made it to the door, the walls shook. I had a second to witness the horror in Kara's eyes before I heard the explosion.

CHAPTER

twenty-seven

Caleb

"You could've told me you were hiding your sorry ass up here."

I looked over my shoulder and spotted Cameron in his black tux, holding two cans of beer. He tossed one to me before joining me on the balcony, propping his elbows on the stone railing, and looking out at the city lights in the distance.

"Needed some air," I replied, delighted and amused that he had found beer. Mom would never serve beer at parties. Unless the prime minister had requested it. Or Mick Jagger. "Where'd you get the beer?"

Cameron eyed me mockingly as if to say, *Oh please.*

I nodded, acknowledging his genius before taking a sip. "Seems like I can't blink without someone making a business proposition to me down there." I gestured with my own beer at the party below.

Among the sea of soft lights and lavish gardens, women paraded in elegant gowns and glittering jewels, and men in stylish penguin suits. It looked like a dazzling play.

"Guess you've got a lot to learn," Cameron commented, curling his lip as he watched the people. "Better have an excellent poker face, because you're going to deal with a hell of a lot more than business propositions."

I shrugged. He was right. I really didn't mind it. In fact, I liked people, parties, and socializing. Usually.

But Red wasn't here yet.

Everything felt wrong.

"How the hell would you know?" I asked, just because I was irritated.

He tapped his beer against his temple. "Because I have a brain."

"Oh? That's news to me."

He sniggered.

"You know what they say about a man with a gorgeous face?" I asked nonchalantly.

"He has a little dick?"

I took a sip of my beer and looked at him smugly. "I don't even need to talk. I just stand around and get what I want." I paused. "I'm holding a beer, aren't I?"

He laughed. "Nah. Mostly, I feel sorry for you. Guess she's not here yet."

I glanced at my watch for the hundredth time. "She's not answering her phone."

I reached for mine in my pocket. No text, no calls.

Where is she?

"You phoned...Kara?" Cameron asked.

"Yeah," I replied. "Phoned at the shop too, but no one's answering."

"It takes them each a week to get ready. And there are two of them." Cameron shuddered. "Besides, the shop is open on weekends during the summer. They get really busy at this time."

Raking my hands through my hair, I leaned against the balustrade. "I'm leaving in half an hour to get my girl."

He was just taking another sip of beer when he stilled, stared at me with his brows raised. "Your mom will kill you."

I just eyed him silently.

"Fine," Cameron replied with a self-deprecating sigh. "But I'm driving."

I grinned at him knowingly. "See? Didn't even say a word. I'm just standing here."

He laughed. "Fuck you."

"Cal?"

We both turned at the voice. Beatrice-Rose was standing at the door in a red gown, eyes soft and pleading as they watched me.

I felt a mix of emotions at the sight of her. Pity, guilt, anger. Somewhere beneath all that was affection for someone I had grown up with—and bewilderment at the thought of a childhood friend being hateful enough to hurt the only girl I loved.

She approached us slowly and warily. Beside me, I noticed Cameron change his stance. He looked relaxed, but I knew it was only a facade. Like me, he was braced for a confrontation.

"Hi, Cameron," Beatrice-Rose said.

"Beatrice-Rose."

"How are you?"

"Good."

Cameron was a man of few words when the mood struck him. He used his intense too-blue eyes to let you know what he was thinking. But I had to admit that it only made the air more tense and awkward.

"How's your dad?" Beatrice-Rose asked softly.

She didn't seem to get the hint that Cameron didn't want to talk to her. Or that *I* didn't. I had been avoiding her throughout the party, but she'd found me this time.

"Still in jail, I'm presuming," Cameron answered coldly.

Beatrice-Rose's mouth dropped open in shock. "Oh…I…"

Cameron cut her off. He had no patience for empty words, but his voice was less harsh when he asked, "How's yours?"

"H-he's not doing very well. I… Can I have a moment to talk to Caleb?"

Cameron just leaned against the balustrade, pointing his beer at me. "That's up to him."

I nodded at him. He threw me a pitiful look before he left, shaking his head.

Uncomfortable silence lingered as I waited for Beatrice-Rose to speak. She had her eyes down, her hands clasped in front of her.

"Happy birthday, Cal."

I nodded, but since she wasn't looking at me, I decided to finally open my mouth and speak. "Thanks."

She bit her lip, tucking her hair behind her ear.

She's sick, Cal.

I shut my eyes tightly, blowing out a breath. She needed help, and I'd be a major douchebag if I didn't at least try.

"How are you?" I asked.

She glanced at me, her eyes tearing up.

She has a penchant for faking her panic attacks to get what she wants...

I felt like an ass for thinking this when she needed a friend, but I couldn't help it.

"I'm fine." She paused, her lip trembling. "Actually...I'm not doing well."

"I'm sorry," I said uselessly.

When she started to scratch her arm, I held her hand to stop her. Ben had told me she would keep scratching until she bled.

As soon as I touched her, I regretted it.

She took it as a sign that everything was back to normal between us. Tears started to pour down her face as she stepped forward and wrapped her arms around me.

"Oh, Cal! I feel so alone. I can't do this alone."

"Beatrice-Rose..."

"Please," she sobbed, burying her face in my chest.

I raised my arms awkwardly. I knew the right moves when a girl cried on my shoulder, but I couldn't seem to wrap my arms around her in comfort. I patted her back instead.

"Are...are you"—she hiccupped—"still mad at me? Cal?" When I didn't answer, her arms wrapped more tightly around me. "Please don't be, Cal. Please. I don't think I can take more heartache. I'm going through a lot with my dad, and if you're mad at me too, then..."

"I'm sorry for what you're going through right now. I really am."

"Oh, Cal! I missed you so much! I knew you wouldn't stay mad at me for long."

"Beatrice-Rose—"

"Veronica was just a distraction, yes? Miranda says you're going to live in Saskatchewan and manage your new hotel there. Once you're there, Veronica won't be around to amuse you anymore. I can go there with you—"

"Stop."

"—and help you with anything you need. Anything, Cal. I'll give everything—"

"Listen to me."

My eyes shifted to the door as I heard someone clearing their throat. I spotted Ben first, and then my heart jumped into my throat as I saw Red beside him, staring at us.

Through the guilt and pity I was feeling for Beatrice-Rose, relief and pleasure flooded me as I realized Red was finally here. Then pleasure turned into horror as I realized how this might seem to Red. Beatrice-Rose was still holding on to me, crying. And I had my arms around her.

Fuck.

Reluctantly, I returned my gaze to Beatrice-Rose. "I'm sorry. I appreciate the help, but I'm not relocating to Saskatchewan." I gently removed her arms from around me. "My fiancée's here, and I go where she goes."

"F-fiancée?"

I froze when I saw how pale she was. "Beatrice-Rose? Are you all right?"

She stepped away from me, covering her mouth with her hands as tears continued to stream down her face.

"Beatrice-Rose…"

But she wasn't listening to me. Her eyes darted toward Red, and what I saw in them chilled me to the bone. But whatever was in her eyes disappeared in a flash, and I wondered if I'd just imagined it.

Beatrice-Rose turned on her heel and rushed through the door toward Red.

For a moment, I had the strongest urge to stop her before she reached Red. But she only went past Red and headed for the stairs.

I sent Ben a grateful look as he nodded at me and went to soothe Beatrice-Rose.

Everything faded as I looked at Red again.

She looked so alluring, so captivating standing there in her red gown. Her dark hair cascaded down her back. Red lips, dark eyes. Just the way I liked it.

Grabbing her hand, I laced our fingers together and pulled her with me.

I walked fast, past the guest rooms and the library to the west wing where my old room was. As soon as I'd closed the door behind me, I held her face in my hands. Leaned my forehead against hers.

"You're here," I whispered. "God, I missed you."

Her smile was warm as she wrapped her arms around my waist. We held on to each other a little longer than usual. A little tighter. "Happy birthday, Caleb."

"Now it is."

I kissed her. Slowly, tenderly, savoring her taste. Her lips were soft and tasted like chocolate. Like love. Like everything.

"You look like a dream."

"I love the all-black suit. And the red tie. Very debonair." She rested her head on my chest. "We match."

"Perfect," I murmured, kissing her hair. "You're not mad at me?"

She pulled back a little to look at me, one dark eyebrow raised. "Should I be?"

I angled my head to study her face. She didn't look pissed or even irritated, but her face told me something was wrong. "Was that a trick question?"

"Caleb." She whispered my name in a way that squeezed my heart. "I trust you."

"And I love you." I kissed her again. "Is that my present?"

"Here. They wanted me to leave it downstairs with all the other presents, but I wanted to give it to you in person." She bit her lip.

"Good. I want to open it now." I looked inside the huge paper bag and found two boxed presents. "Did you get me two presents?"

"No. The pink box is for your mom."

How sweet was that?

"She'll love that. She loves presents."

I eagerly pulled out my present. I tore off the paper, opened the box, and saw a red beanie inside. I knew instinctively that she made it for me. Something warm wrapped around my heart. "You made this."

"Yes," she answered, breathless. I shifted my eyes back to hers and found that she had her bottom lip tucked between her teeth. "Do you like it?"

Did she even have to ask?

"I love it. Thanks, baby. I'm wearing it."

"No." She laughed. "You can't."

"Of course I can."

"Caleb," she warned, snatching the beanie before I could place it on my head.

I narrowed my eyes at her. She must have caught the gleam in them because she started backing away, holding my beanie behind her.

"Where do you think you're going?" I drawled with a hint of a challenge in my tone as I stalked her.

But she only smiled that secret smile of hers and kept walking backward until she hit the wall. I grinned as I closed the distance between us, placing my hands on her waist. Slowly and deliberately, I ran my hands over the hourglass shape of her torso, her ribs, and the sides of her breasts.

Her breathing became erratic, loud and fast in my ear.

I leaned close to her ear and whispered, "I caught you."

I grazed my nose over her cheek and down to her jaw while my hands cupped her breasts, molded her through her dress.

"This dress is sex. Tell me, Red. Did you wear it for me?"

I heard her swallow audibly before she nodded.

"You have to wear it again. I have…plans for you and this dress."

She let out a hot, sexy moan and I turned rock hard.

"I've never brought a girl into my old bedroom before," I said, enjoying the arousal I saw in her eyes, the fast pulse in her neck that told me how much she wanted me.

"T-this." She cleared her throat. "This was your bedroom?"

"Yeah," I replied, tracing the shape of her earlobe with my lips. "I had…fantasies of bringing a girl here before." Sucked. Licked. Sucked. "Want to hear them? Or better yet, why don't I show you?"

"Caleb, please…"

"Please what?"

"Kiss me."

"Where?"

"Caleb."

The longing in her voice as she moaned my name made me feel so fucking good.

"Where should I start?" I teased, sweeping my fingertips down her bare arm. "There are so many places to choose from," I continued, skimming at the tops of her breasts now. "It's so hard to decide. Need a little help."

I bit my bottom lip to keep from smiling as I heard her make a frustrated sound.

She was staring at my lips, licking hers. At that point, I knew it was either kiss her or die.

Need punched into my stomach as I pushed my fingers into her hair and leaned down to claim her lips. It was powerful, this yearning I had for her. And I surrendered willingly.

I slipped my tongue inside her mouth, exulting at the feel of her, at the taste of her.

"I need you. *Now*," I growled.

Before she could answer, there was a knock on the door.

CHAPTER

twenty-eight

Caleb

I snarled. "Who is it?"

"Yo mama."

Red's eyes widened in horror as she started wiping her lipstick from my mouth. Although from the look of her still-red lips, the lipstick hadn't faded from hers.

I needed to calm the hell down.

Deep, calming breaths. I stepped away from her. Away from her luscious body and the tempting-as-sin scent of her skin.

I had to think of something else. Didn't want big brother to see I had a raging hard-on when I opened that door. *Think!*

There are billions of people starving on earth.

People barfing.

Smell of the locker room just after a game.

Gross!

I was feeling better—not entirely calm, but it was a start.

I blew out a breath. "It's all right. It's just Ben," I reassured her. "You still have your lipstick on, by the way. How is that even possible?"

"Kar used this magic, chocolate-flavored Harry Potter lipstick she got. Caleb, hold still!" she hissed, rubbing my bottom lip hard enough to hurt.

"Ow. Red."

"All right. There. It's gone. How's my hair?"

"Gorgeous."

She glared at me. "Caleb. Be serious."

"I am serious." I grinned, grabbing her hips and pulling her toward me.

The knock sounded again. Red's eyes were filled with panic. I kissed her on the mouth before yanking the door open.

Ben stood at the door, his hand raised to knock again. His eyes shifted from my face to Red's. Then he smiled charmingly. I narrowed my eyes at him.

"Don't stare at her," I barked.

He ignored me.

"I'm sorry I didn't introduce myself earlier. You must be Veronica. I'm Ben, Caleb's older brother."

"Yes. *Older*. He's *old*," I inserted.

She ignored me too.

"Nice to meet you, Ben. Thanks for helping me find Caleb."

"Pleasure is all mine."

When he reached for her hand—and I knew from seeing his smooth moves with women that he would kiss it—I grabbed her hand and laced her fingers with mine.

"He's scared you'll fall in love with me. I'm the better brother, after all," Ben said, winking.

I snorted.

Red let out a soft laugh and turned to me as she explained, "I was wandering around, looking for you. This place is too big, and I got lost. Ben found me." Then she turned to Ben, frowning. "Is Beatrice-Rose…?"

"She's fine," Ben replied. "Don't let it ruin your evening."

"Thanks," I said.

Ben turned to me. "You. I'm done covering for you. Time to face the music, little brother."

I nodded, smiling as I glanced at Red. "I'm good now."

She's here.

Ben shook his head in surprised amusement. He hadn't seen me act like this before. Ever.

"I'll see you both downstairs," he said, heading to the stairs.

Red stuffed the beanie into the huge paper bag and hid it behind her, out of my reach. I winked at her and lifted her hand to my lips, kissing the back of it as I led her down the stairs, then to the garden where the party was happening.

"Caleb, wait."

She pulled at my hand, stopping me in my tracks. When I looked at her, her eyes were downcast.

"Red?"

She raised her eyes, and her voice was barely a whisper when she said, "I love you."

The way she said it—like a whisper, like a promise—clutched at my chest.

I swallowed the lump in my throat as I gathered her in my arms, kissing her hair. "I love you, Red."

She burrowed her face in my neck, gripping me to her. There was something in the urgency and possessiveness of her grip that told me something was wrong. I pulled back a little, studying her lovely face.

"Baby, what is it?"

She shook her head. "I just… Can you wrap your arms around me for a moment? Please, Caleb."

"Of course, love."

"Don't let me go."

Whatever was hurting her, I would destroy it.

"Never. Tell me what's wrong."

"Tonight, I won't let anything be wrong. I don't want anything to be wrong," she said. "It's your birthday, and you're here with me. That's what's important."

"I wish you would tell me so I can fix it."

"You already did." Now she smiled. Her hand reached up to stroke my jaw. She rose up on her toes, kissing my lips tenderly.

There was something in her eyes, the way they lingered over my face just a little bit longer, as if she was afraid I would disappear in front of her.

"Will you tell me later?" I asked.

"Yes. Tomorrow. First thing."

I blew out a breath. I knew she didn't want to tell me because it was my birthday and she was afraid it would ruin my day. But not knowing what it was, not being able to fix it, was doing just that. If she wanted to forget about it tonight, so be it. Tomorrow would be a different story.

"I'm glad you're wearing your ring and necklace tonight."

She smiled up at me. "I promised you I would."

"The ring is a symbol. It lets everyone know that you're mine when Ben makes the announcement."

"Announcement?"

"Of our engagement, love."

Her eyes widened, her lips parted in surprise.

"I want to spend the rest of my life with you, and I want everyone to know."

I watched as her eyes warmed with affection, her lips stretching into a tender smile.

"All right."

A set of stone steps led us to the garden path under arched trellises thick with vines and roses so lush and fragrant that the scent was intoxicating. The shrubs lining the path were green and fresh. A white bench sat conveniently on the side if anyone wanted to relax and enjoy the blooms. At the end of the path was the gazebo, highlighted by soft lighting.

Red's eyes twinkled with pleasure at the grand display of blooming flowers.

"This is stunning. I can't believe you grew up here. And the house… It's incredible—and huge."

I chuckled. "I used to play hide-and-seek with Ben and my… dad here. They could never find me. I had all the good hiding places. We can hide from everyone now, if you want. They'll never see us. Wanna?"

"If only." She sighed softly. "I always knew you were rich. But I was wrong. You are extremely rich. No, scratch that—you're *wealthy*."

I winced. "My mother is. Not me."

"Same thing. I was very intimidated when the butler ushered me inside your house. It's ridiculous to call it a house. It's a castle."

"I'll give you one if that's what you want."

She let out a soft laugh. "What would I do with a castle? Besides, it'd just give you more floor space to litter with your clothes. I'd be exhausted every day picking them up."

"I'll pick them up."

She rolled her eyes, but I only grinned, bent down to pluck a red flower from the garden, and tucked it behind her ear.

She smiled up at me sweetly. "I don't want a castle, Caleb. I never did. I just want a home. A simple one. With you."

My heart somersaulted. How could she still do this to me? I didn't want it to ever stop.

"Then I'll give you one," I said, lacing our fingers together again while we strolled. "I have a couple houses lined up for us to look at. Make time for me this week, love?"

"All right. Let me know when, and I'll ask Kar for a day off."

I frowned. "Where *is* Kar, by the way?"

She was quiet for a moment. "She's sorry she couldn't come tonight."

"Oh. How come?"

She just shook her head and murmured, "Later."

So that was part of the later too. All right then.

I could see the throng of people and hear the faint sound of music and muted conversation floating in the air. I heard Red take a deep breath, felt her anxiety in the way her hand gripped mine as we walked through the crowd.

"Are you hungry? Let's get you something to eat before you say hi to my mom. She's looking forward to seeing you tonight."

That was supposed to make Red feel better, but when I turned to look at her, worry lines creased her forehead, and she bit nervously at her bottom lip.

"What do you think about snails?" I teased, slowly leading her to the empty dance floor.

That earned a laugh. "I'd rather eat broken glass. I'm not hungry."

Her eyes suddenly dropped to my mouth. I couldn't help it; I licked my bottom lip.

When her eyes shifted up to mine, I said quietly, "I am."

She blushed.

People were looking at us, staring at *her*, and who could blame them? She was the most beautiful woman at the party. On earth. In the whole wide fucking universe.

It wasn't just her beauty, although that alone could make anyone stop and stare. But a lot of people possessed beauty on the outside, God-given or man-made. The vulnerability in Red's eyes made you want to come closer; the secrets in them made you want to know more. And if you were lucky enough, she'd let you have a glimpse.

"Dance with me, Red."

She looked up at me, her eyes wide and nervous. I just smiled reassuringly, took her small purse and the paper bag from her hands, placed them on a nearby table, and returned to her.

The lights dimmed and softened as she placed a hand on my shoulder. Watching her lovely face, I offered her my hand, palm up. She smiled warmly and took it. I smiled back before curling my other hand around her waist and pulling her closer.

"You're so beautiful. It almost hurts to look at you," I murmured, wishing that we were alone.

A breeze blew gently around us, carrying the scent of roses. It mixed with the alluring scent of her skin. I heard her sigh softly as she rested her cheek on my chest. Music drifted around us. Janacek, I realized. Ben must have chosen the band's playlist tonight. I closed my eyes, slowly swaying her body with mine.

"I thought you weren't going to come," I whispered in her hair.

Gently, I stroked my fingertips along the exposed skin of her back. It felt so smooth, so warm. When I felt her shiver, I smiled knowingly. I wanted to be alone with her.

"I wouldn't miss your birthday for the world."

"Half an hour more without you, and I'd have been out of here to pick you up. You weren't even answering your phone."

"I'm sorry, Caleb."

The sadness was back in her eyes. I wanted to make it disappear.

"I'd ask them to put on your song so you can do that magic thing with your hips—"

She laughed. I would forever remind her of this, even tell this tale to our kids once they were old enough.

"—but that dance is exclusively mine."

When she looked at me, the sadness in her eyes was replaced with amusement. "What did you say to Beatrice-Rose? She looked really angry," she said.

"I told her you're my fiancée."

"Ah."

"I don't want to talk about her."

"She has the same dress."

"What?"

"She has the same dress as me."

I pulled back to look at Red's face. "Really?"

"Caleb. You didn't even notice?"

"I wasn't paying attention to her. I know what *your* dress looks like."

"And you didn't notice that she's wearing the same dress as mine?"

"Um…"

She rolled her eyes, laughing softly. "Caleb."

"I'm sorry. It's not my fault."

I only had eyes for her. Was that a sin?

"Ladies and gentlemen, may I have your attention, please?"

The band stopped playing. I looked up to see Ben on the stage in front of the band, holding a glass of champagne, ready to make a toast.

"I have a very joyous announcement to make."

And suddenly, I was grinning. A very, very wide grin that hurt my face. I looked down at the face of the only girl I'd ever loved, the girl I wanted to spend the rest of my life with. And I knew, as I knew every time I looked at her, that she was the one. Even after I died, even in the next life and all the lives after, she was the only one.

She stared back at me, her eyes shining with the same

excitement as in mine as we listened to Ben say, "I am overjoyed to announce the engagement of my only brother, Caleb Nathanael Lockhart, to Veronica Strafford..."

A round of applause broke out around us, and I blocked out everything else after that. Ben was still talking, and as soon as he finished, the band started to play another song, but all I could think about was my girl in my arms.

Her eyes were shimmering, her cheeks flushed, and she was the most beautiful thing I could possibly dream of.

But the most unbelievable thing was that she belonged with me.

This girl belonged with me.

There were congratulations after that, invites to several parties and dinners, pats on the back, women asking to see her ring. And all I could think about was when I could get her alone again. When at last the commotion died down, I led her back to a table, snagged two champagne glasses from the server, and handed one to her.

"Thirsty, love? I could get you water if you like."

"Mr. Lockhart? I'm sorry to disturb you, but you have a phone call from a Mr. Darcy. He said it's urgent."

Damn it.

I nodded at Ben's assistant. "Thank you. I'll be there in a moment. Red? I need to find Ben and deal with this. This particular deal is time sensitive. Come with me?"

She shook her head and smiled at me reassuringly. "I'm okay here, Caleb."

"Cameron is around. Find him for me, will you? Stay with him until I get back. Mom is probably busy socializing right now." My gaze roamed around us, looking for my mom, but she was nowhere in sight. "When I get back, we'll find her."

"Sounds good."

I pulled her into a close embrace and kissed her hair.

"I'll be right back, Red. Don't go anywhere."

"I won't."

CHAPTER
twenty-nine

Caleb

"Of all days to finally come out of his cave, he picks today?" I griped.

Ben leaned back in his chair, propping his feet on top of the desk. We had just finished making our offer to Darcy's people and were waiting to hear back from them. "Maybe he wants to give this to you as a birthday present," he replied, toying with a Rubik's Cube. "Shut up and sit your fat ass down. Darcy's people are playing the game."

Ben's gray eyes gleamed with challenge. He loved this.

Mr. Darcy was a millionaire hermit who owned a big slice of land very close to the city. The land was prime real estate, and if we acquired it, it would be a huge investment for our company.

Everyone wanted a piece of it, but Mr. Darcy had made it very clear that he wasn't selling. Lady Luck had her generous eye on Ben when Mr. Darcy stayed in one of our hotels. Ben opened the door to the possibility of Darcy selling property to us and initiated negotiations. Ben could be very convincing if he really wanted something. He was a shark in negotiations.

"You know," Ben began, "I'm pretty good at getting a handle on people."

I threw him a glance. He was looking at me with amusement as he placed the completed Rubik's Cube on the desk. What a nerd. He rose and shrugged out of his gray tuxedo jacket before neatly placing it on a chair.

I briefly thought that he was going to get along well with Red. They were very similar in the tidiness department.

Since he mostly lived in hotels, Ben kept an office at my mother's house at her insistence. It was spacious and luxurious with books lining the walls and a fireplace beneath a Van Gogh painting. The desk was antique, and two high-backed chairs were situated in front of it.

Ben sauntered to the bar to fix a drink. "Your Veronica strikes me as someone who can handle herself. Unless I'm wrong."

He strolled toward me and handed me a glass. I took a sip and went back to gazing out the window. My heartbeat accelerated at the sight of my mom and Red talking.

"You're not wrong," I answered. "She's the strongest person I know."

"Then why are you standing there watching like someone's going to abduct her?"

I snorted. "I'm not…" I paused, realizing that, yeah, I was. Reluctantly, I pushed away from the window and leaned against the wall to look at Ben. "I just don't want Beatrice-Rose to upset her."

"You're worried about Beatrice-Rose, but what about Mom? You know Mom'll eat Veronica alive if she doesn't like her."

I frowned. "She'll like Red. How can anyone *not* like her?"

Because he'd put the thought in my head, I went back to watching through the window again.

"Mom likes *me*, and she still scares the crap out of me," Ben argued.

This was not helping.

"That's true," I conceded, taking a sip from the glass. "Still, I'm 100 percent sure Mom will like Red."

I turned away from the window, confident in my girl's feisty side. She could handle anything. I was sure of it.

It didn't take long for Mr. Darcy's people to phone back and accept our deal. Ben and I had made sure that they couldn't refuse our offer.

Good. Now I could get back to my girl. I looked out the window again to where I'd last seen her, but she wasn't there anymore. I scanned the garden and couldn't find her. She must have come inside the house. I was in good spirits by the time I made it downstairs and more than looking forward to dancing with Red again. Maybe after that, we could sneak out of the party.

But she wasn't inside the house. I went outside to the party, to the gardens, even back to my bedroom and balcony, but she was nowhere to be found. She wasn't even answering her phone.

Where was she?

Maybe my mom would know. I was going back to the garden to ask her when I heard a familiar voice. "Caleb, Son."

My heart flipped in my chest before dropping into my stomach. My dad stood in front of me.

I hadn't seen him in months. He looked familiar and strange at the same time. More lines were etched around his eyes and mouth as he smiled at me. On his arm was his latest mistress. She was probably younger than I was.

Resentment and love warred inside me as I gazed at my dad. What the hell was he doing here?

"Happy birthday, Son."

He stepped forward, looking like he was going to hug me. I stepped back before he could get any closer. His smile disappeared.

"Thanks," I said coldly. "Enjoy the evening with your"—*child*—"date."

I turned to walk away.

"Caleb."

I stopped, gritting my teeth.

"Can I have a moment with you? Please?"

I faced him, my hands balling into fists. I kept my expression stoic as I waited for him to speak. How dare he show up here with his mistress? Was he rubbing it in my mom's face? Did he know how hurt or humiliated Mom would be by him bringing her here?

"Son?" he pressed.

I tried really hard not to sneer. "You're overusing that word." I let out a sigh at his puzzled expression. "You stopped being a father a long time ago."

His face hardened. My eyes shifted to the girl beside him as she pulled at his arm. She gazed at me with an unmistakable look of invitation in her eyes.

I nearly curled my lip in disgust, but my mom had taught me to be nice to children.

"I don't want to be rude," I said patiently, returning my gaze to my dad. "But who invited you?"

"Your mom did."

I just stared at him, shocked.

"I asked her to send me an invitation for your birthday, Caleb. I wanted to see you."

Anger rose up in my throat. "Did Mom tell you to bring her here?"

Guilt marred his face. "No, but—"

"It wasn't enough that you divorced Mom? You want to humiliate her by bringing this...*girl* here?" I looked up at the dark sky and blew out a breath. "Let's be honest and stop wasting each other's time. What do you need?"

"Nothing, Son. I'm here for you."

"Bullshit. What do you really want? Wait, you know what? I'm not interested. See you around. Or not."

With that, I turned and left. My heart pounded in my chest, and my face felt hot as I nearly ran to get away from him.

He was here *for me*? What a load of crap.

He was a liar, and a selfish man who used people. He only remembered his family when he needed something. I had accepted that a long time ago...but acceptance didn't mean it couldn't hurt me anymore.

"Cal." Beatrice-Rose stepped in front of me, blocking my way. What the hell did she want now?

"I don't have time for you right now, Beatrice-Rose."

"Are you looking for Veronica?"

I narrowed my eyes at her. Her face was a picture of innocence, but I knew better. Underneath it, she was anything but. Red said they had the same dress, but all I could remember was that Beatrice-Rose had also worn red. She must have changed, because now she had on a white gown.

"She's in the gazebo. I just saw her there."

"Thanks." I turned to leave.

"Wait! Caleb, I-I don't think you want to see what she's doing right now."

"What do you mean?"

"She's with this...guy."

If she was here to make trouble for me and Red again, I swear... I took a deep breath to calm myself, pinching the bridge of my nose.

"They look really cozy together," Beatrice-Rose continued, looking worried. "It's the guy you had a fight with on campus. He's got his arm around her—"

I walked away before she could finish. I felt my blood boiling. My temper, already aggravated by my dad's appearance, reached its boiling point.

"Caleb?" It was Cameron this time. "Where the hell have you—"

I ignored Cameron and kept walking. Faster. Faster until I started running.

CHAPTER

thirty

Veronica

I KNEW SEVERAL PAIRS OF EYES WERE WATCHING ME. CURIOUS, baffled, judging eyes. Because of this, my spine was straighter, my walk sassier, my face devoid of any emotion.

Inside, I was anything but.

I could hear the whispers.

Who is she?

Look at that ring Caleb gave her! And that necklace! Fabulous.

Strafford? Is her family in the same hotel business as the Lockharts? Real estate? Which company do they own?

Look at her dress. Her shoes. I don't think her family owns anything worthwhile. This one was followed by mocking, condescending giggles that two women tried to stifle when I passed.

I ignored them. The champagne they were sipping cost more than my whole outfit. So what? If I let that bother me,

I'd be running from here with my tail between my legs. My mother had taught me better than that.

Caleb deserved more than that.

I deserved more than that.

So I made sure to wear an I-dare-you smile on my lips.

"I hope you're having a lovely evening so far."

Caleb's mom practically glided over in a conservative and gorgeous royal-blue dress, hair and makeup perfect, polite smile in place.

"Mrs. Lockhart." My voice cracked.

She was still Mrs. Lockhart, right? I knew Caleb said his parents were divorced...but was it final yet? He didn't like talking about it so I'd never asked.

Why didn't I ask? Oh God.

I cleared my throat. "Yes, I am. Good evening, ma'am. I'm Veronica."

"I remember."

Her tone was courteous, but I sensed that it was loaded with meaning. Was she thinking about that first time we met in jail?

With growing horror, I wondered if she remembered that time when I was sitting outside her son's flat, waiting for him like a stalker.

Suddenly, I remembered the gift I had carefully wrapped in a pretty box. I pulled it out of the paper bag and held it out to her. "Th-this is for you. You have a very beautiful home."

Mrs. Lockhart hesitated just slightly before she accepted the gift. "Thank you."

"Thank you for inviting me."

"Of course. It would be in bad taste if I didn't invite my son's fiancée, wouldn't it?"

My stomach dropped.

Her eyes bored into me as she continued without pause. "Interesting choice of dress."

What should I say? Thank you? It didn't sound like a compliment the way she said it. It sounded like a challenge.

She could probably tell it wasn't designer and was trying to be polite. Or maybe…I narrowed my eyes as I saw Beatrice-Rose coming down from the steps. She had changed into a white gown.

"Beatrice-Rose mentioned you were at the store yesterday when she was trying on the same dress you're wearing now." I drew in a sharp breath, and Mrs. Lockhart continued. "That dress must have made quite an impression on you if you'd risk wearing the same dress she's wearing at my son's party."

I blinked slowly, taking a deep breath. Then a second one. *Fuck it.*

"I know you don't know me, ma'am, and we didn't meet under the best of circumstances, but I can tell you I love your son very much. I would not humiliate him or *myself* with something as petty as deliberately wearing the same dress as Beatrice-Rose. Or anyone, for that matter."

She must not have expected that I would defend myself because her eyes widened in surprise.

"Beatrice-Rose has it backward," I continued. Adrenaline drove me now. "I was trying on this dress yesterday when she came into the shop. It looks like she changed now."

Mrs. Lockhart looked me directly in the eye for a few seconds before she responded. "Yes. She asked me if she could borrow one of my dresses."

"Well, it's a good thing she didn't pick the same dress that you're wearing then."

Oh God. Did I just really say that?

"President Miranda."

I tried to gather my composure as Mrs. Lockhart's secretary approached and whispered something in her ear.

"Will you excuse me for a moment, Veronica?" Mrs. Lockhart asked.

I nodded. I couldn't be sure, but I thought I saw a gleam of respect in her eyes before she walked away. My knees felt weak as I watched her.

God. I needed a drink.

"Hello, Veronica."

I shut my eyes tightly for a second before turning.

Why the hell didn't I go with Caleb when he offered?

Because I wanted to prove to him that I could handle his world. I wanted to make him proud. I wanted to make *myself* proud.

Beatrice-Rose looked at me with a smirk on her face. A short and stocky older man with bifocals was holding her arm.

"I don't believe you've met Joe yet. Joe, this is Veronica, Caleb's…girlfriend."

"Fiancée," I corrected.

Her lips curled into a hateful sneer before turning into a delighted smile as she looked at Joe, laying her hand on his arm.

"Joe is one of the biggest investors in Miranda Inn. I really don't think the chain could have run as smoothly without you behind it, Joe."

"Come now, Beatrice-Rose. You flatter me too much."

"Nonsense." She batted her lashes at him before shifting her gaze back to me. "I was just telling him I should have pursued a career in ballet. I do have the legs for it. Don't you think so, Joe?" She shifted her dress to show off a bit of her leg.

"Sure, sweetheart."

Beatrice-Rose let out a soft giggle. "Such a sweet talker. Joe also owns several lucrative restaurants around the country. Veronica is a professional when it comes to restaurants. Isn't that right, Veronica?"

"Oh, is that right?" Joe looked at me with polite interest.

There was a glint of mischief in Beatrice-Rose's eyes as she continued, "She has considerable experience as a waitress, I've heard. Isn't that true?"

Joe frowned at Beatrice-Rose.

"As a matter of fact, it is," I answered coolly.

Beatrice-Rose's smile was haughty. "We're somewhat short on help right now. Be a sweetheart and bring my glass back to the kitchen, won't you?" she asked sweetly, offering me her half-empty glass.

My hot temper simmered under my skin as I narrowed my eyes at her. I nearly grabbed the glass and threw the contents in her face. But I kept my arms at my sides.

Then I smiled, baring my teeth.

"I'm sure you're more than capable of doing it yourself,

Beatrice-Rose. Why don't you use those *ballerina* legs and take your glass back to the kitchen?" I suggested just as sweetly.

Joe choked on his drink. Beatrice-Rose's face was quickly turning an ugly shade of red.

I didn't care. I was seeing red. If she thought I would take her insults lying down, she had another think coming.

"Oh, and, Beatrice-Rose?" I said, batting my eyelashes at her. "Try not to copy anyone's dress while you're on your way to the kitchen."

A movement behind her caught my eye, and I nearly cried at the sight of Caleb's mother staring at me. Watching.

Damn Beatrice-Rose. Damn them all to hell.

This wasn't my world. I would never fit in. I'd never wanted to. I turned to leave.

"Veronica, wait!" Beatrice-Rose exclaimed. She grabbed my hand, and my clutch fell to the ground, almost like she had pulled on it. Its contents spilled.

What happened next was reflex. I jerked back, hitting Beatrice-Rose accidentally and spilling her drink on her dress.

I heard her outraged gasp before I snarled at her. I looked to the ground and was sorely tempted to leave my things there, to just get away from her and her drama.

But my phone was lighting up, vibrating. Caleb's message popped on the screen.

Almost done, Red. Can't wait to dance with you again.

Sighing in frustration, I tamped down my anger and crouched

to pick up my things. I froze when I spotted a clear plastic bag, barely hidden under my purse. It had white powder in it.

Blood pounded in my ears, and I felt my face pale. My brain shut off and I stared into space, not seeing, not hearing, not conscious of my surroundings. The next thing I knew, someone was tugging at my arm.

"Let's get you the hell out of here, Angel Face."

Damon's kind blue eyes looked at me with sympathy. What was he doing here?

When I didn't respond, he tugged on my arm again. "Come on. Are you going to let these assholes win?" he whispered in my ear.

His words spurred me on. I stood up straight, remembering to raise my chin and walk steadily. But all the while, I was gripping Damon's arm very, very hard.

I only realized this when we stopped and he groaned in pain.

"I know I have mouthwatering biceps, but could you loosen your grip?"

I blinked, mumbling an apology as I did just that. I looked around and realized he had taken us to the gazebo.

Still shaken, I leaned against a post and stared at the darkness surrounding us where the flowers around the gazebo weren't illuminated by lights. I wished the darkness could hide me too.

"Oh God," I whimpered, covering my face with my hands.

Damon sighed. He gently tugged my hands away from my face. "It's okay, Angel Face."

He was leaning in front of me, his face level with mine.

"It was really cool to watch you spill that drink on the blond.

She looked very, very mad." Damon laughed, tapping my chin playfully with his thumb. "Tell me, did you do it on purpose?"

He straightened up, lacing his fingers together and raising his arms upward in a long stretch. I noticed he was wearing the standard black-and-white server uniform. He looked striking, with his longish dark hair and a silver earring winking from his earlobe.

He let out a lazy groan of satisfaction as he completed his stretch and looked down at me with a big smile. When I didn't return the smile, he leaned beside me against the post, bumping his shoulder against mine teasingly.

"Hey, smile. You probably just got me fired."

I frowned.

He laughed. "This gig sucks. I'd rather be serving drinks at a bar or playing my guitar. If I'm being honest, I was looking for a way out. So really, you saved me." He winked. "They're not very nice people here."

I bit my lip, shutting my eyes as I remembered the scene with the not-very-nice people.

"Gum?"

When I opened my eyes, he was waving a stick of gum in front of my face. I shook my head at him.

"Are you sure? It's cupcake flavored."

When I whimpered, he unwrapped it and popped it in his mouth.

"Whoa. Okay, no gum." He fished something out of his apron pocket and brandished my clutch in front of me. "I got it here. See? Don't cry. Please."

"Damon! Oh God. Thanks." I grabbed it from him, sending him a grateful look. I opened it and saw that he had picked up all my stuff. When I saw the plastic bag filled with white powder, my vision turned red again.

"Yes, don't mention it. I've always wondered why women bring these tiny bags with them. I mean, do they like it that they're always holding something at a party?" He scratched his head. "It's so small. What could you possibly fit in there? But now I know."

I knew he was trying to cheer me up, but everything was coming back to me now.

Especially the anger.

"Caleb's mom probably thinks I'm a cokehead."

Probably thinks I was the one who planted the drugs in Caleb's car. Oh God.

"I don't think she saw it, whatever that thing is. Is it really coke? Geez, Angel Face. I didn't know you were into that."

"No, no! God. This day is officially shot to hell." A strangled laugh escaped me. "It's not mine, Damon. I don't know why it's there. I… Beatrice-Rose probably planted it there. I'm going to kill her!"

I was breathing hard. My eyes filled, tears threatening to spill.

"Okay, let's think about this for a second," Damon interjected. "Do you have proof?"

"I don't need proof. Didn't you see what happened? She planted the drugs in Caleb's car, wore the same dress, knocked my purse out of my hand deliberately… My *God*, I'm going to tear off those demon's hairs one by—"

Damon raised both his hands, palms up. "Listen, I share your feelings. But there are many witnesses at the moment...so why don't we just breathe in and out, okay? That's good. Breathe in. Breathe out."

I did just that for a few moments. He was right. When I was feeling slightly calmer, I looked up at him gratefully.

"You're very good at this," I commented.

He shrugged. "I have experience with Kar. Do you know how many times I had to keep her from killing someone when we were kids?"

"Kar! Oh my God. I have to call her and check in."

I rummaged for my phone in my clutch.

"I thought she came here with you."

"Damon..." I started cautiously. "I guess you didn't hear about it yet. There was a fire at the garage."

"What?" Fear leapt into his eyes, and his voice shook.

My stomach clenched as I remembered the wreck in the garage.

"Tell me everyone is okay."

I nodded. "Don't worry. Everyone is safe."

Relief washed over his face. "What happened?"

"According to the police, a group of kids set fire to the shop. You know there are chemicals and equipment there. It burned half of the shop and—"

I gasped as I felt a strong hand grip my arm from behind, whipping me around. Cameron's intense blue eyes drilled into mine with urgency and pain.

"Kara? Is she okay?" Cameron asked.

"She's okay. Everyone is okay."

He swallowed in relief, releasing me from his hold. "I have to go," he said, looking at something over my shoulder.

I turned around and spotted Caleb standing there. His jaw was hard, his eyes cold with anger. And he was looking right at me.

CHAPTER
thirty-one

Veronica

CALEB'S GREEN EYES WERE LIKE BURNING DAGGERS AS THEY GLARED at Damon. They turned hot and accusing as they shifted to me.

He looked beautiful and dangerous as he stalked toward us. His eyes never left mine as he grabbed my wrist, then turned and dragged me behind him.

I heard Damon move, and I looked back at him, giving him a shake of my head in warning. I let out a relieved breath when Damon stayed where he was.

Caleb's legs were long. For every step he made, I had to take two.

In high heels.

"Caleb?"

He kept walking.

"Caleb, wait!"

"Don't even—" he snapped.

He was so angry, he couldn't finish his sentence.

As I stumbled after him, it all sunk in. He was mad? At me? What the hell for? Did he think I was doing something with Damon at the gazebo? The way he kept glaring over his shoulder told me he did. My temper soared viciously.

I tried to jerk my wrist from his hold, but he must have been expecting that. His grip tightened, and his steps quickened.

"Let go of me," I warned.

Did he know what I'd just gone through with that mental case who was obsessed with him?

Did he know how much effort and patience it took for me to smile and talk to these people who looked at me like I was beneath them?

Did he know what kind of *hell* I'd gone through today to get to him?

"If you don't let go of me right now, Caleb, I swear to God—"

"Shut up," he growled.

For a moment, I wondered if I'd heard him correctly. Did he just tell me to shut up?

It shocked me that he could be like this. He was always playful, always gentle with me, even when he was angry. I wasn't sure how to process the way he was acting now.

"What the hell did you just say to me? Who the hell do you think you—"

My words caught in my throat as he suddenly stopped and faced me, keeping hold of my wrist. His handsome face was a tight mask of fury as his eyes, hot and hurt, searched my face. Next thing I knew, he'd thrown me over his shoulder.

"Put me down. *Now.*"

He started walking faster. I could feel the strong muscles in his back and shoulders bunch as he carried me like I was weightless. I lifted my head and saw that he was heading for a small cottage on the property.

"Oh, is that what the princess wants?"

For the second time in the space of a few minutes, my mouth fell open.

Where does he get off talking to me like that?

Indignation boiled in my blood. It pulsed in my temple.

"You bastard! Put me down!"

I flailed furiously in his arms, hitting his back, his shoulders, his arms. Everything about him was rock hard, and my struggle didn't seem to affect him. It only made me angrier.

"Now is not the time to argue with me, Red."

I heard the loud bang of a door opening and hitting the wall with force. A few seconds later, I lost my breath as he dropped me unceremoniously on a bed.

"What the hell!" I fumed.

I fully expected him to grab me again, but when I sat up, he wasn't anywhere near me. I watched, shocked, as he strode to the door.

Was he going to leave me here?

Livid, I scrambled off the bed.

"Who do you think you are!" I screamed. "Get back here!"

I caught him before he reached the door, snarling as I grabbed his jacket and yanked.

He turned around so fast that my breath caught, and I took a step back.

His face was beautiful even in anger, half in shadow. The unmistakable fury in his eyes reminded me of a wild panther.

His big hands clamped around my arms and jerked me to him so our faces were only inches apart. I could feel and smell his hot, minty breath, and his intense green eyes bored into mine.

"I'm trying so damn hard right now. Don't test me," he whispered.

Like a warning.

A threat.

A promise.

I felt my eye twitch.

I slammed his back against the wall and heard his surprised grunt at the impact. My eyes roamed his face, and I saw the hurt and naked vulnerability in his eyes.

I couldn't believe this was all about Damon. Did Caleb really think I'd cheated on him? It hurt that after everything we'd gone through, he would think this of me.

He was breathing hard, his cheeks flushed. The beauty in his face and the strength in his body that he controlled so thoughtfully always affected me, but it was the way he let me see what no one else saw, the way he exposed his weakness and his real emotions to me that pulled at my heartstrings.

But since he'd seen me with Damon at the gazebo, he'd hidden himself from me, only allowing his anger to show. Until now. His green eyes had always been expressive, and they were looking at me with pain and sadness.

I was furious with him, taken aback by his whiplash anger and the uncharacteristic carelessness of his actions. But as I looked at him now, my anger subsided. We had been apart for only a couple of days but it felt like a long time. I had missed him, and after what happened today at the shop, the threat to life that suddenly shocked my system, it made me realize we were only on borrowed time. Caleb could be taken from me any moment.

Still, it hurt. I needed to know why he was acting this way. I knew he was hurting too, and I felt helpless and frustrated that we were both too stubborn and proud and angry to stop fighting.

"What's wrong, Caleb?"

He remained silent, gritting his teeth. Suddenly, his eyes blazed with heat and accusation again, wiping away all vulnerability. He had closed up, and he wouldn't allow me in. All the understanding and sympathy I felt a few seconds ago left me, and I knew there was no way my anger would subside now. It had to spill out.

He loosened his tie, narrowing his eyes at me. The muscles in his arms strained against his dinner jacket. His jaw was hard, which made him appear more masculine, more alluring. It made me more furious that I still wanted him even now.

Lust and anger sang in my blood as I grabbed his jacket and pulled it off him, tossing it carelessly to the floor. I moved in to him, grabbing the back of his neck and pulling him down for a punishing kiss.

It was like being swallowed by a tornado. If his hunger didn't match mine, it would have scared me in its intensity.

My breath caught in my throat as he spun me around and shoved me against the wall. My palms slapped against it as he pressed his solid body against my back. I felt his hardness pushing against me.

Without warning, he gathered my hair in his fist, coiling it around his hand like a rope as he pulled it to the side.

"You drive me fucking crazy," he murmured dangerously in my ear.

His lips hovered near my mouth, a silent demand for a kiss thickening the air.

He shut his eyes for a moment, almost as if he was in pain. When he opened them, they were filled with an impatient hunger.

"You do this to me, Red. Every fucking time. I'm losing my mind because of you. You have no idea…"

He gripped my hair tightly as he ran his other hand down to caress my neck and shoulders, and then further down to squeeze my breast.

"I won't be gentle with you tonight," he said before he crushed his mouth against mine.

He bunched the material of my dress that hindered him from touching what was underneath.

And ripped.

"Oh God," I panted.

I was so unbelievably turned on as his fingers tweaked and teased. I strained against him, needing him to give me more.

"Stop me now if you don't want this, Red. Otherwise"—he breathed heavily, using his other hand to remove his belt and open his zipper—"I'll take you right here."

"No."

I felt him stiffen, and I smiled in victory as his hard hold slackened.

"No, I don't want you to be gentle," I told him.

I whipped around, reached for his tie, and yanked him down to me, fusing his mouth to mine.

Need was a furious demand in my stomach as we sank to the floor. I straddled him, biting his bottom lip. He let out a low moan before I felt his tongue slip inside my mouth.

He raised his hips, shoving his pants and boxers down. I grabbed his shirt and pulled. Buttons snapped and flew. That only urged me to take more.

He clutched at my dress and pushed it up to my waist. He stroked his fingers in my center until I was gasping for breath.

I bit my lip to keep from making a sound as he gripped my hips and pulled me right where he was rock hard between his legs. It felt so good.

I had to place my palms on his naked chest to steady myself. His skin was burning hot and lightly covered with sweat. It shocked me that I wanted to lick it.

I was breathing hard. My skin felt tight and sensitive everywhere.

"Lift your hips for me, Red."

I was still so angry, and I wanted to punish him for what he said to me earlier—for his stupid assumptions about Damon, and for everything else that happened tonight. So I ignored him, continuing to rub myself against him instead.

"Red…" he moaned. "I need you."

His strong hands slid over my hips to cup me from behind, squeezing and increasing the friction. My body suddenly flooded with hot need. I finally looked him in the eyes and raised my hips.

"Yes," I gasped. "Yes, Caleb."

His fingers found the tiny scrap of lace that covered me from him and pushed it aside.

I cried out as he slammed into me. He was so hard, so huge that I felt so full inside.

"Ride me, Red. Yeah, just like that."

Biting my lip, I rocked my hips against him.

Up and down.

Back and forth.

Up and down.

"Put your arms up, hold your hair. Fuck, you're so beautiful. Fuck, yeah. Like that."

His hands gripped my hips as I let my head fall back, lifting my arms as I held my hair up for him.

And rode him.

The love and need and longing I felt for him overwhelmed me as I watched the haze of pleasure play over his handsome face. His eyes darkened as he watched me on top of him, his face a tight mask of control as he gritted his teeth.

Then his hands were cupping my breasts, squeezing, his thumbs circling.

My eyes shot to his.

Take me.

Suddenly, I wanted him to come. Desperation pushed me to go faster. I could hear the slap of skin on skin, feel the slippery wet slide of our bodies, smell the intoxicating scent of his sweat.

His hands curled around my neck as he pulled me down for a desperate, rough kiss.

"Just like that, Red. Go slow. Fuuuuck."

He pressed his lips to my ear and whispered dirty secrets about what he'd always wanted to do to me.

It drove me mad.

I pushed away from him, keeping my hands on his chest. My nails dug into his skin as he grabbed my hips and hammered into me.

Fast and shallow, slow and deep.

Faster.

Until my head was spinning and my lungs felt tight and everything around me exploded in a burst of light as I climaxed. I slumped on top of him, boneless.

"I'm not done with you yet," he whispered in warning.

I gasped and swallowed hard as he shifted us until he was on top of me.

"Hold on to me," he said before he drove me to the brink once again.

And again.

And again.

CHAPTER
thirty-two

Veronica

CALEB STROKED MY BACK GENTLY, THE TIPS OF HIS FINGERS LIGHTLY trailing from the small of my back to the top of my spine. I felt his chest rise as he took a deep breath before he kissed my hair.

My muscles and bones felt liquefied, but my heart refused to slow down as it continued to knock sharply against my chest.

The *tap, tap, tap* of the rain against the roof and the soft whooshing of the wind should have relaxed me, but they didn't. Our argument had planted a persistent ache in the pit of my stomach.

"Red," Caleb whispered softly. Achingly. "I'm so sorry."

The pain and sincerity I heard in his voice grabbed at my heart, but hurt and anger still had their claws in me. I rolled away from him, pulling the blanket to cover myself.

What the hell was I thinking? Ending up in bed with him because I couldn't separate the anger and longing I felt for him.

I had never done anything so…shocking in my life.

Especially after he'd acted like an asshole. It was a little overwhelming to realize how much power he had over me, but then again, in the back of my mind, I'd always known he did.

My throat tightened as he looked at me with tortured eyes, but I refused to let him see my emotions. I kept my face blank.

He rubbed a hand over his face, exhaling a short, sharp breath as he rose and sat on the edge of the bed, his back to me.

"Fuck me," he said quietly.

The muscles on his back and shoulders stood out as he leaned forward, propping his elbows on his knees and lowering his head into his hands. He looked miserable, and I wanted to reach out to him, comfort him, but remembering the way he'd let his jealousy control his actions earlier held me back.

Oh, so now you're holding back, my subconscious lashed. *You definitely weren't holding back when you were on top of him. Or when he was on top of you.*

I closed my eyes, ashamed of my actions. I had let myself succumb to my desire for him. And look how we both felt now: still heartbroken. The sex had taken out some of the aggression we had both felt a few hours ago, but it didn't solve anything.

Maybe if I were the old me, I would have run away the second he grabbed my hand and dragged me away from that gazebo, but I had learned a lot since Caleb came in my life.

I had learned that there was no perfect relationship. It was up to you to make it work, to keep fighting for that one person and never give up because that person was worth your effort and love.

Everyone possessed darkness and lightness inside them. Caleb had always shown me his light, but I'd only seen glimpses of his darkness. Tonight, he had revealed it. I wasn't going to run away from it.

Loving a person was never easy. I knew that from the start. Caleb had shown me that loving the right person was worth the pain. And he was definitely worth it.

That didn't mean I would let him step all over me. It just meant I was willing to stay and work things out.

I would fight and argue with him, even drive us both insane until we'd cleared up the heaviness we both felt inside. This time, I wouldn't walk away without a fight.

"When I saw you with him—"

"Choose your words very carefully," I warned him. "If you think I'm cheating on you—"

He turned to look at me. "Never," he said strongly.

"—you better think again because… What?"

"I never thought you were cheating on me," he continued. His jaw was tight, his mouth a straight line of displeasure.

"Then what the hell, Caleb?"

"I know you, Red. I know you'll never cheat on me. I'm sorry I acted like an asshole. You deserved to be treated better. And I…"

The helplessness and pain in his green eyes pulled at me, the way his mouth curled down in remorse.

I closed my eyes, blowing out a breath to help relieve the ache in my chest. It felt a little lighter now that I knew he didn't think I was cheating on him, but the ache was still there.

His eyes were still on me, and I could sense him waiting for me to answer.

When I felt him move, I finally opened my eyes. Naked and completely unselfconscious, he stalked to the window and looked outside. His back was to me, but I could tell he was angry by the unyielding set of his shoulders, the way he bunched his hands into tight fists.

"Did I hurt you?" he asked, his voice hoarse. "I was too rough again, wasn't I? I can't seem to help it with you."

He raked his hands through his hair, dragging his hand down his neck as he lowered his head in shame.

"I…want you too damn much, even when I'm so mad. Mad at you. Mad about you. You drive me fucking insane. Why in the hell would you tell him and not me?"

I could feel the hurt and anger in his tone. Most of mine had subsided when I realized why he was angry. It wasn't because he thought I was cheating on him with Damon, but because I'd told Damon about the fire.

Caleb had been insistent earlier, trying to find out what was bothering me, but I had refused to tell him. When he heard me tell Damon about it, that's probably when he lost his temper.

If I switched our roles and I'd heard him talking to another girl about what had been bothering him all night, I would have been hurt and angry too.

But still…he had no right to act the way he did, dragging me like a child, ordering me around like I was his property.

He turned around. My eyes lowered, and I felt the blush creeping in my cheeks as I took in his nakedness. He was completely at ease with his body, and why wouldn't he be? He was hard and lean all over.

Memories of what we'd shared a few minutes ago flitted through my mind. I bit my lip to keep from groaning out loud when I felt the soreness between my legs.

"Does this bother you?" He gestured. "Does this make you feel uncomfortable?"

"Just…" I cleared my throat. "Put some pants on, Caleb."

He watched my face for a moment. "No," he said.

I looked up at him, noticed the narrowing of his eyes. He was still angry.

"You're being childish," I accused.

"Am I? You're the one who keeps blowing off my questions."

"I'm not…"

Frustrated, I dragged my fingers through my hair. I rose from the bed, looking for my dress. When I spotted it, I let out a frustrated sigh. It was in tatters; Caleb had ripped it to pieces. There was no way I could wear it again.

When I looked back at him, there was a self-satisfied smirk on his face. Annoyed, I grabbed the dress and threw it at his face.

Of course he caught it easily.

"Very mature," he commented dryly.

"One more word," I warned, shooting him a glare.

He made a show of zipping his lips, and I narrowed my eyes at him. His stance was insolent as he angled his head and raised his brows in challenge.

Well, good. I was ready for a challenge.

"Do you know how much this dress cost?"

When he shrugged carelessly, I wanted to stuff the expensive tattered dress down his throat.

"I'll just buy you a new one."

I closed my eyes and counted to ten. When that didn't work, I started taking deep breaths.

Okay, I mentally praised myself as my temper started to calm down a bit. *Okay.*

Picking up his dress shirt, I put it on and hastily buttoned it closed—what was left of the buttons, anyway. I grabbed his dress pants next and threw them at him. The belt was still around the hoops of his pants, and it made a clunking sound as he caught them in his big, stupid hands.

I wished it would hit him in the face instead.

"Put those on," I demanded. "I'm not going to have a discussion with you when you're naked."

"You've definitely done more than discussing with me when I'm naked," he challenged.

My eyes widened in incredulity. Was he trying to provoke me?

He appeared relaxed, but I knew he was still upset by the gleam in his eyes and the unspoken dare I heard in his tone.

If I let my temper control me, I had a feeling I'd start screaming like an animal and we wouldn't be able to discuss anything.

That, or I might just kill him.

I crossed my arms in front of me, leaned against the wall opposite him, and raised an eyebrow. I wouldn't talk until he put those damned pants on.

He smiled knowingly, never breaking our gaze as he discarded the pants, grabbed his boxers instead, and put those on. When he was done, he just leaned back against the wall again, staring at me.

I stared back. I wasn't going to be the first one to speak.

Damned maturity.

I knew the moment it stopped being a staring game. His eyes lost their spark, replaced by hurt and the unmistakable love he felt for me. I watched him push away from the wall and stalk toward me with purpose.

He stood close, lifting his hand slowly, carefully, as if to caress my face. Suddenly, his green eyes filled with uncertainty, as if he was scared I would reject him, and then his hand dropped to his side.

"I saw my dad at the party," he whispered.

His eyes lowered, and his long lashes cast shadows on his cheeks.

"I didn't know my mom invited him. Why would she? She hates his guts. He had his mistress with him. I think she's younger than I am." Disgust and shame colored his tone.

"He brought her to this house where he raised his kids, where he built a life with my mom. What kind of person would do that?"

His voice was hard, but it broke as he said, "What kind of father would do that?"

I knew his pain, the torture he was feeling inside for a thoughtless, selfish parent he loved. If he hadn't turned away at that moment to lean against the wall beside me, I would have reached out to hug him.

"I was furious," Caleb continued. "He makes me really angry, and my mind gets clouded with hate. I looked for you," he continued, his voice so quiet that I could barely hear him.

We were silent for a moment. A thousand thoughts and

emotions flooded through me, and I didn't know how to articulate them all to him. So I just stayed quiet and waited for him to speak again.

"I knew you'd make it better, Red. You always make things better. But when I found you…I saw you there with him. With Damon. I heard what you were telling him, and it finally made sense why you were acting different tonight."

My eyes lowered, and I saw his hands ball into fists.

"It didn't help that he talks to you like he knows you really well. That he touches you with familiarity. That you allow him to be that close to you, to stand that close to you.

"I know for a fact that I'm the only guy you allow to be that near to you. So please forgive me if I lose my mind when I see you giving him the same liberty. You're mine. I don't want anyone standing close to you that way.

"My mind was already clouded with anger and hate for my dad, and seeing you with Damon, hearing you tell him what was bothering you tonight…I just lost it. He didn't even ask you, Red. You just…told him willingly what I've been begging you to tell me…"

My heart hurt.

"I didn't want to ruin your special day, Caleb," I murmured quietly when he didn't continue. "That's why I didn't tell you."

"I know that, but if you have any problems, I want to be the one you tell them to first. I want to be the one to fix them."

His hand slowly moved beside mine, our pinkie fingers touching. And then he looped his around mine. I turned my head to look up at him.

My heart squeezed as I looked into Caleb's green eyes. He was staring at me like I was the only girl in the world.

"I crave you, and I can't help it. I'm a terrible work in progress. I ask too much from you. I know this. But Red, please don't give up on me yet."

I felt my throat close up, and at last, he reached out and held my face in his hands.

"I'm sorry, baby. Please…forgive me?"

"Okay, Caleb," I choked out. "I'm sorry. I should have told you."

Relief was evident in his face, the tension leaving his body as he relaxed and smiled.

"Can I hold you now? Red? Can I be gentle now?"

He opened his arms, and I stepped into them. He held me tenderly, holding me very close to him.

"I hate it when we fight," he murmured.

"I know. But…"

Gently, he grasped my shoulders and pulled me away from him, studying my face intently.

"But what, Red?"

"Don't do that again. Don't manhandle me like that, dragging me and ordering me around. I don't like it."

He lowered his head in shame. "Did I scare you?"

I pursed my lips for a moment. "No," I replied honestly. "You didn't scare me. I knew you'd never hurt me. Physically, I mean."

His head rose sharply, eyes horrified. "Never! No matter how furious I am, I would never—"

"I know, Caleb. It's okay. I know that. You made me really mad, and you…shocked me. I couldn't believe that you were the same person saying those things to me, behaving that way."

His hands fell to his sides.

"Red. I…" He looked at me helplessly, uncertainly, as if he was scared to touch me again.

"I understand how one person can make you blind with anger so that you can't see reason. I do get it, Caleb. But I don't want you to use your strength to get what you want from me like that."

"I won't. I promise I won't."

Satisfied at the sincerity in his eyes and voice, I nodded. "Okay then."

"I would never hurt you." He leaned toward me and kissed my forehead, my nose, and then my lips. "Wrap your arms around my neck."

He smiled, bending down as he scooped me in his arms. Even with the warning glint in his eyes, I squealed, wrapping my arms around him. He nudged the back door open with his foot, flicked a switch so the light flooded the room, and revealed a screen-covered porch.

I realized that we must be in a cottage on the property. It was a large square room with a magnificent view of the lake. I noted the gray and white lounge chairs facing the wide windows, fishing gear hanging on the walls, a couple of mountain bikes stored to the side, and a mini-fridge beside a rough-looking table.

I was expecting him to sit on one of the lounge chairs, but instead, he opened the porch door and carried me into the open.

"Caleb, let's go back inside. Someone might see us here. I'm not…decent."

His grin was quick and meaningful. "I know. Decent is the last thing on my mind right now."

Heat flooded my cheeks. When he saw my face, he let out a soft laugh. "I bet that's the last thing you're thinking too. Let me guess what's on your mind. Hmm…let's see," he teased mercilessly.

"No," I squeaked. "Don't."

He laughed again. My arms tightened around him as he approached a hammock I hadn't noticed before. Carefully, he settled us in the hammock and began to sway. He relaxed into it, pulling me against him and wrapping his arms around my torso. It felt so peaceful.

I knew the outside world was just a stone's throw away, but snuggling here with Caleb, his strong arms around me and the view of the calm lake and the dark horizon beyond, made me forget about everything else.

"I wish I could just stay here with you," I confessed softly.

He laced our fingers together and kissed my temple. "Then we'll stay here."

"Won't they look for us?"

He shrugged. "I don't care. I'd rather be here with you."

I relaxed against him, but something he'd said earlier was bothering me.

"Caleb?"

"Hmm?"

"I get it, you know."

"What?" he mumbled against my hair.

"About your dad."

I felt him tense, and then he shrugged. I squeezed his hand to let him know it was okay if he didn't want to talk about it. I knew how difficult it was to talk about something that affected you so deeply.

He took a deep breath, lifted my hand to his mouth, and kissed it.

"I know you do," he acknowledged quietly. "He's never going to change. I've accepted it, but that doesn't make it easier."

"You still care."

He didn't answer right away. But when he did, his voice was gruff. "Yeah. I do. I never told anyone that before. I even have a hard time admitting it to myself. Because…it doesn't matter, does it? It's not going to change anything."

I nodded. "It's not going to bring him back or bring back what you had before. And that hurts."

"Yeah. Yeah, exactly. It helps that you get it, Red. I'm glad you're here with me."

"Don't beat yourself up for loving him, Caleb. He's your dad. He was a big part of your life. Nothing's going to change that. They say you choose the people you love. I guess most times that's true, but sometimes, however hard you fight it, there's no escape from it. It's like a lifetime punishment."

I thought about how my mom never stopped loving my dad when she was alive. How I still loved my dad no matter how cruel he was to us, maybe because part of me was still clinging to the happy memories.

"And maybe—even knowing it's a punishment—we still

choose it," I went on. "I don't know. What I know is that the pain you feel right now? Eventually it won't hurt as much because…you learn to live with it. You learn not to let it eat you up or control you." I kissed his cheek. "I'll be here for you, Caleb."

"I love you, Red."

"I love you."

I leaned back against him again, and he gathered me close. I listened to his heartbeat, the sound of lapping waves in the lake, the playful dance of the wind in the trees. Even though the night had turned for the worst, it was ending perfectly.

"Can you stay the night?" he asked.

"Yes."

"Good. I have to go back to Regina on Tuesday, so we have all day tomorrow. I'll take you wherever you like. We can even look at houses. I'll call the real estate agent."

I bit my lip. "I can't. I want to, but Kar needs me. I told Beth to come visit tomorrow so we can all hang out. It's a girl's night."

"Don't worry about it." He kissed my hair. "Can you tell me what happened at the shop? I heard you say there was a fire. Where were you?"

My body tensed. "Kar and I were at the office when we heard shouting at the back," I started. "We went out to check it when we heard a loud explosion."

I heard Caleb take a sharp breath, his arms tightening around me. "Are you all right?"

I nodded. "I'm fine, Caleb. Really. Dylan pulled us out right away. The fire trucks came, the police, paramedics. But no one was hurt, thank God. Someone had seen a group of teenagers come out of the shop just before the explosion. They found an empty can of gasoline that they threw somewhere near the shop. The police have witnesses. It won't be long now until the people who did it are caught."

"I'm just glad you weren't hurt." He sighed deeply. "Or anyone. That's why you were late. I never… You should have called me." He paused. "I can't believe after you went through all that, you still came here. And I-I didn't make it easy for you. I'm so sorry. I hope they catch those bastards," he said heatedly. "Insurance will cover most of the damages, but they're going to lose a lot of business while repairs are being done. They might need help. I'll see what I can do."

My heart fluttered. "Kar will appreciate it."

"Maybe you should go with me to Regina. Work for me."

I froze. He said it so easily, so casually. Suddenly, I felt restless. Moving away from him, I rose and carefully walked close to the water. It was inky dark, with shadows and lights swimming inside it.

I felt Caleb stand behind me. "Red? What's wrong?"

"I don't want your money, Caleb."

"What the hell?"

He grasped my shoulders and turned me to face him.

"I'm not with you because you're rich," I explained, "or because you can give me all these…things."

He blew out a breath, studying me for a few seconds. Then a naughty smile appeared on his gorgeous face. "I know that already. You're with me because I satisfy your every need." His eyes glittered in the moonlight. "I also have the dreamy face and sex-god body to go with it. Why else would you be with me?"

I choked out a laugh.

"What is this really about?" he asked seriously.

I sighed and moved away from him, turning to face the water again. I'd be more comfortable if he wasn't looking at my face while I confessed to him.

"Before I met you…" I began, feeling him stand beside me. He must have felt that I needed space because he didn't reach for my hand like he usually would. "I've been alone for a while. I didn't depend on anyone but myself. You know this already."

He nodded.

"Most of my life, I depended on…other people to provide for me. But when I started working, it made me feel good. I didn't feel helpless anymore, because I knew I didn't have to rely on anyone.

"I love working," I continued. "I love earning my keep. It gives me a sense of independence and purpose. I have goals that I work hard to accomplish, and I don't want to lose that. I want to prove to myself that I can."

"I'm sorry, Red. I didn't think of it that way," he murmured after a moment. He picked up a stone, examining it before throwing it at the water. It skipped across the surface four times before it disappeared. "But why would you accept Damon's job offer and not mine?"

"Because I don't love Damon and—"

"I'm *so* glad to hear that."

"*And*," I continued, laughing softly at the way he prolonged *so*, "he won't take it easy on me if I work for or with him. If I accept your job offer, I feel like I'm…taking from you. And I'm not with you for that. I don't want anything *from* you. I just want you."

When I glanced at him, his head was lowered, fingers pinching the bridge of his nose. He was grinning. When he raised his head and glanced at me, he looked really happy.

He caught his bottom lip between his teeth as he picked up another rock. "I love you," he said. "I get it now. I'm sorry I didn't before." He flung the stone across the water's surface again. This time, it skipped seven times.

Grinning, he turned to face me like a little kid. I grinned back at him, chose the flattest and roundest stone from the ground, and threw it. It skipped ten times.

"What the—!"

The shock on his face was so comical. I started laughing.

"That was ten times!"

"Uh-huh." Smug, I threw another one.

When I looked back at him, I was expecting surprise, but he only looked contemplative.

"When I was a kid," he said quietly, studying my face as if it were the first time he was seeing it. "There was this little girl—"

Suddenly, a blaring horn sounded from the house.

"Caleb, the party…"

"Don't worry about it, Red. Really. They won't even notice us gone. Especially now that my uncle has his shofar out. He likes showing it off when he's pissed drunk."

"What?"

"It's a musical instrument made of animal horn. He said he bought it from magic peoples, but I'm sure he got it on eBay. Anyway, I saw you talking with my mom earlier," he said cautiously. "Was she nice to you?"

I bit my lip. When I didn't respond, he gently tugged a strand of my hair.

"She was…polite."

"Polite," he repeated. I could hear the frown in his tone.

Grabbing my hand, he led me to a spot hidden between jutting rocks and old, tall trees. There was a wide tree trunk at the edge of the water. He sat down before he pulled me beside him.

I didn't want to ruin the moment, but I knew he'd be more upset if I kept what happened earlier from him.

"Your mom wasn't pleased that I wore the same dress as Beatrice-Rose. Apparently she told your mom I knew she was going to wear this dress and—out of the evilness of my black heart—I deliberately wore the same one."

He let out a low, sharp expletive.

"The truth is that Beatrice-Rose saw me and Kar at the store yesterday. I was trying on this dress when Beatrice-Rose came in," I explained. "There's more."

Caleb sighed, lowering his head. He looked tired.

"She was trying to humiliate me at the party earlier. And she succeeded when I dropped my clutch and my things spilled out. Do you remember when you put my things down somewhere, when we were dancing?"

"Yeah, I put them on one of the tables."

"She must have planted it there."

"Planted what?"

"The drugs."

"The what?"

"The tiny plastic bag with white powder in it," I choked out. "It's drugs. I know it. Beatrice-Rose must have put it in my bag when we weren't looking."

He gripped my hand. "The same thing they found in my car?"

I nodded. "That's why she deliberately knocked my purse out of my hands. She wanted your mom to see the drugs in my purse. But Damon picked it up, and he said your mom didn't see it. But..." I froze. "What if she did?"

I reached for his other hand that was curled into a fist, squeezing it in comfort.

"Where's the bag of drugs?" he asked.

"It's in my purse."

"Can you give it to me? I'll send it to the PI. There might be prints. Maybe they'll match the ones they found in my car."

"Okay."

He positioned me so that I was facing him and sitting on his lap with my legs dangling on either side of him. He gripped my thighs.

"Are you all right, Red? She didn't hurt you, did she?"

I rested my chin on his shoulder. "No. I'm fine, Caleb."

"Beatrice-Rose was the one who told me she saw you in the gazebo with Damon. That he had his arms around you. She implied you were cheating on me."

I gritted my teeth.

"Of course I knew she was lying. I never believed her for a second, even if that assho—Damon," he corrected, clearing his throat, "had his arms around you. I knew it wasn't because you were cheating on me." He looked at me sheepishly. "I'm sorry, Red. I can't seem to stop apologizing. I feel like a major ass."

I smiled. "You were, but it's okay. Apologizing helps."

He chuckled. With quick, agile movements, he pulled me close and, without warning, stood up, carrying me. My arms curled around his neck as he walked us back inside the cottage.

"You were absolutely beautiful tonight," he said. "Thank you for putting up with this farce."

"How are we getting back to the party? I can't wear my dress. You ruined it."

He looked at me sheepishly. "I'll hide you inside my jacket?"

"Caleb!" I laughed, but then I remembered the affluent partygoers and the opulent world he lived in, and my stomach dropped.

"You're absolutely wealthy."

His eyes widened at the unexpected comment.

"My mom. Not me," he corrected me again.

"There are a lot of rich people at your party."

He looked contemplative. "I'm definitely not leaving you alone at a party ever again." He laid me down on the bed, stretching out on top of me as he spread my hair over the pillow.

"There are a lot of beautiful women," I added.

His finger traced my cheek, his breath fanning warmly on my skin. "Not as beautiful as you."

"I don't belong in your world, Caleb."

He reached for my hand and kissed it before he placed it on his cheek. He stared into my eyes and whispered, "How can you not belong in my world? You *are* my world."

CHAPTER
thirty-three

Veronica

"You should have seen her do the walk of shame this morning."

I narrowed my eyes at the cheery sadism in Kara's voice. She stood at the counter, stirring a spoon in a fat pitcher of rum and Coke she was mixing…or experimenting with, depending on your point of view.

Lime wedges were scattered on the counter, along with a half-empty bottle of rum and various cans of Coke, three open bags of chips, a bowl of Oreos, a plate of pierogis and sour cream, and french fries that Beth was eyeing with lust.

"I was not doing the walk of shame," I argued, but I felt the heat searing my cheeks. Lowering my face so Kara wouldn't see my blush, I walked to the cupboard and grabbed three glasses.

"Yeah?" Beth finally gave up and fished out one french fry,

then nibbled on it. "I've seen your man, Ver. He's hot. How's he in the wham-bam-thank-you-ma'am department?"

"Well, let me just tell you to bleach the hell out of your counters if she and Caleb spend a night at your place," Kara interjected.

"Kar!"

She winked. "Beth is part of our friendship bubble. She has a right to know."

I face-palmed. Kara wasn't even supposed to know about the...counter incident. It had just slipped out that one time.

Beth rolled her shoulders and fanned her face with her hands. "Holy cow." She shivered. "Wait!" Pitcher in hand, Kara froze just before she poured her concoction into Beth's cup.

"No alcohol for me," Beth explained. "I've sworn off sugary drinks. I'm on a diet."

Kara curled one side of her lips. "Bitch, I just saw you eating cookies."

"Correction: half a cookie. It doesn't count if it's only half."

"And french fries," I added, more than happy to move on to another topic.

"*One* french fry. That doesn't count either."

Kara's eyes suddenly gleamed with mischief as she reached for the bowl of cookies.

Beth quickly grasped the bowl. "What are you doing?"

"You said you're on a diet."

Beth narrowed her eyes. "Really?"

They stared at each other.

"I hate you," Beth growled after a moment, plucking one cookie from the bowl before she released it.

As Kara stepped away with the bowl, Beth broke down and fished out another cookie. "Okay. Last one. Take them evil things away now. Take them far, far away."

Kara threw me an impish grin. "Hey, Ver, I've got some cake in the fridge. Want some?"

"You're such an asshole, Kar." Beth paused for three seconds. "Is it chocolate?"

"Oh, please. Is there any other flavor worthy of my mouth?"

"I'll get it," I offered, taking a sip from my cup before heading to the fridge.

"So, how was the party last night?" Kara asked. "You didn't have to come home this morning."

"I wouldn't have left you last night if—"

Kara waved me away. "I told you I was okay. I'm just really, really grateful nothing happened to my dad and Dylan. If—" Kara's voice broke.

Beth squeezed Kara's hand. I set the box of cake on the counter and placed my hand on Kara's shoulder, offering support.

"I'm fine." Kara sniffled, pulling away from us. I handed her a tissue, and she carefully wiped the mascara under her eyes. "Ver, you know Dad sends the guys home when it's not that busy. He and Dylan usually finish up whatever work's left over. So if they had been at the back bay where the fire started... If they..."

"Stop it, Kar. No one was hurt. Thinking about the what-ifs isn't going to help you or them, and it's not going to change anything. They're fine. That's all that matters."

"Ver is right," Beth agreed.

Kara nodded and took a deep breath. "While Ver here was

sleeping off her sexual adventures, I got a call from Dylan after lunch. The kids who set the shop on fire were caught this morning."

"Right on! Idiots think they can get away." Beth paused. "Wait, who are they?"

"Remember I told you about those skaters who kept slapping my car when Ver and I were leaving the mall? And I threw my milk shake at them?"

"What the hell. Really?" Beth looked furious. "They set fire to your shop because you threw your *milk shake* at them?"

"Here's the kicker: someone paid them to do it."

"Wait, what?" I snapped. Shocked, I gripped Kara's arm.

Kara nodded grimly. "According to the officer, all of them said a *lady* approached them at the mall that day. Paid them five grand to do some damage to the shop when you and I were in the building. They were ordered to do it the next day, which was—*ding-ding-ding*—the day of Caleb's birthday party. Are you smart bitches feeling me here?"

I drew in a sharp breath, my hand falling limply from Kara's arm. A chill raced up my spine, and I shivered. "Beatrice-Rose," I choked out. "Kar, it was Beatrice-Rose."

"I've no doubt she did it. Problem is, the kids said she was wearing a big hat and dark shades, so they can't really give a clear description of her. They described her clothes, though, and it didn't sound like what Beatrice-Rose was wearing that day."

"She's cunning. She could have bought new clothes at the mall."

Beth shook her head. "What in the hell is wrong with this psycho? She needs some honest-to-Jesus bitch-slapping."

"Get in line, sister," Kara said. "Ver, you have to be careful."

I nodded. "I will. You too."

My mind was whirling with so many things, trying to piece together everything that happened since Beatrice-Rose showed up at Caleb's flat. If Beatrice-Rose had paid the skaters to set fire to Kara's shop while we were inside, there was no telling what her limits were. I decided to phone Caleb later to tell him about it.

"Kar, did Cameron drop by last night?" I asked.

A shadow fell over Kara's eyes before she turned away.

"He heard me tell Damon about the fire," I added.

I stared at her back, saw her shrug.

"Ooh, somebody's repressing her feelings," Beth teased. "Need Dr. Phil, Kar?"

"Shut up, Beth, or I'm stabbing you in your mouth."

"Sure. With what?"

"With my fucking powers, that's what. Switch topics now."

Smirking, Beth pulled the box of cake in front of her, her beautiful mismatched eyes widening in childlike joy as she opened it and sniffed.

"Well, at the party," I began as I pulled out plates and utensils, "Beatrice-Rose was wearing the same dress that I had on."

"You gotta be fucking kidding me!" Kara exclaimed.

I shook my head at Kara and set a plate in front of Beth.

"I knew she was up to something when we saw her lurking at the store while we were shopping for your dress," Kara said.

"Yep. She told Caleb's mom that I saw her at the store trying the dress on first and that I knew she was going to wear it to the party—"

"And because you're a big, bad bitch, you wore it too," Kara finished.

Beth paused from cutting the cake. "That bitch needs to be executed!"

I pursed my lips, debating whether to tell them more. I saw their angry faces—these two beautiful girls who had come to mean so much to me. If someone had told me a year ago that I would be sitting in a cozy kitchen having drinks with my two best friends as they listened to my problems, I would have laughed in their face.

"There's more," I added. "Caleb had to take an important business call, so I was by myself for a while. Beatrice-Rose tried to humiliate me in front of people—"

Beth cut a tiny square piece of chocolate cake and laid it carefully on her plate. "You should've phoned me. I would've brought Theo. Without his leash."

"Thanks. At first, she was singing praises about having the legs for ballet and—"

"She can use those legs to crawl the hell out of my sight," Kara interrupted, "because if I see her again, I'm going to make sure she can't walk anymore."

"I'll bring the chainsaw," Beth added. "We'll Hannibal Lecter her." Kara and I stared at Beth, taken aback. "What? Too much? Okay. Sorry."

I told them the rest over cookies, cake, chips, and the rum and Coke that Kara kept pouring. My story was met with indignant growls from Kara and threats of torture from Beth.

Kara reached for her drink. "So, did you make good use of

Caleb's mama's counter last night?" I chucked the roll of paper towels at her. "Ow."

"Actually," I started, blushing again, "let's move to the living room. I have more to tell you."

We settled in Kara's living room, and I relayed what happened after Caleb saw me with Damon in the gazebo. I gave them a censored version of what happened in Caleb's cabin, and there were earsplitting squeals from both of them.

I found that it was getting easier to share things about myself, things I never would have shared with anyone before I met them. This scene might have been a common occurrence to a lot of girls, but not to me. I cherished these moments when I could confide in them and know they wouldn't judge or ridicule me.

"I'm surprised it didn't trigger your…" Kara trailed off, her eyes widening in alarm as she slapped her mouth with her hands. "Sorry! I know you don't like talking about your dad."

"It's okay," I said. There was a hollow feeling in my stomach every time I tried to talk about my dad. It was there now as I worried my lip and thought of how to answer Kara's question.

"I guess if you really think about it, since I was…abused as a child, Caleb's behavior should have been a trigger for me," I said. I paused for a moment, gathering my thoughts. "If anything, I was really mad that he would manhandle me like that. But I… *knew* he wouldn't hurt me."

"How do you know?" Beth asked.

"It's in the eyes. I've seen the look of…cruelty so many times. I've seen the eyes of someone wanting to cause you not just physical pain, but emotional damage. I know even when they're trying to hide it. Like Justin. Beatrice-Rose hides it well, but if you watch closely, it's there.

"Caleb doesn't have that…meanness in him. He never did," I continued. "But if he did, if there was even a remote chance of him hurting me, I don't think I could be with him. I *know* I couldn't be with him," I corrected. "If he lays a hand on someone, it's because they're threatening the people he loves and he needs to protect them. He's not like my dad," I finished after a moment. "And I'm not my mom."

"I believe it," Kara said, hiccupping, her eyes glassy from the alcohol. "I guess it could mean something different to everyone, because to me, it's sexy as fuck when your man goes all caveman for some sexy time."

I let out a soft laugh.

"But, Ver, where's your dad now?" Kara asked. "You don't have to talk about it if you don't want to."

It was irrational, but my heart skipped a beat and that hollow feeling in my stomach intensified. "I'm not sure. I never tried to find out," I replied honestly. "He might even be…dead now. My mom told me he was really sick last time she'd seen him, and that was years ago. He's got liver failure from… He was drinking himself to death even when I was a kid, and he refused treatment."

"I hope he's dead."

"Kar!" Beth exclaimed.

"It's true." Kara turned to Beth, her lips pursed in disgust. "Ver's dad is a useless son of a bitch who"—*hiccup*—"didn't deserve"—*hiccup*—"Ver and her mom."

I nodded. Kara was right, but I didn't voice what I was thinking or hoping. That, yes, I wanted him to be dead too. It made me feel ungrateful and cruel to wish him dead, because no matter how monstrous he was to my mom and me, he was good for a time. We were happy, and he had taken me into his home. But I was also realistic enough to understand that it was better that he was out of my life. I had no reason to expect to see him again.

"What about your biological parents?" Beth asked. "Weren't you curious to find out who they are?"

"Of course I was. Especially when it got really bad at home. I remembered wishing that my biological parents would show up and save us from my dad."

I took a deep breath, recalling the time when I tried to hide from my mom that I was looking for my biological parents. When she found out, she'd cried and said she would help me find them.

"My biological mom was an immigrant. I learned that she got pregnant with me just a few months after she arrived in Canada, but the man who got her pregnant left her. She died right after giving birth to me, and I was told she had no family."

I wish I'd had a chance to meet her, the girl who had given birth to me. I was told she was very young when she died. She must have been terrified—alone and pregnant in a foreign country. She had never been real to me, but thinking about her made me feel sad.

"Wow. All the men in your life were spineless dicks. Caleb has a huge hole to fill." Kara giggled. "God, someone needs to sanitize my mind, because now I'm thinking I just said something really, really dirty. Or am I just really drunk?"

"Too much, Kar. Too much." I laughed, pouring more rum and Coke into my cup.

Still exhausted from last night, I leaned back against the couch, closed my eyes, and drifted into a light sleep. I woke up with a start when I heard Kara and Beth arguing and giggling drunkenly.

"Captain America is boring. Thor looks like he's got a lot of...energy. I want all that yummy energy focused on me," Kara said, wagging a chip at Beth.

"Shut the hell up!" Beth shot back. "Captain America is *not* boring. He's sweet and good and responsible—"

"Otherwise known as boring. He looks like he folds his underwear."

"—and very much disciplined. It makes me wonder what he's like when he loses all that...control."

"Be honest," I chimed in, reaching for my empty cup. I'd filled it with iced tea this time. I realized someone needed to stay sober among us three. Just in case. "You only like Captain America because he reminds you of a sweet guy who has tattoos and whose name starts with a *T*."

"Nope!" Beth pouted. "Besides, this hypothetical sweet guy whose name starts with a *T*...his type is skinny bitches. Like Kara. If I didn't love you already, I'd fucking hate you, you skinny-ass gorgeous bitch. Hand me those cookies, Ver."

"I thought you were on a diet?"

She glared at me. "I'll diet *tomorrow*."

"That's what you said last week," Kara added, grinning impishly.

"It changes every day. Don't I have the right to change my mind?" Beth's glare shifted to Kara. "Is this country under martial law? What's the big deal if a girl isn't skinny? Is being skinny one of the Ten Commandments?" Beth burst out. "Food will never judge me. Food loves me, and I love food." She rose quickly and snatched the brownies from the coffee table.

"You don't know what it's like to have thunder thighs," Beth continued, returning to the couch and glaring at Kara's long, thin legs. "Do you know how difficult it is to get jeans that *don't* make your legs look like fat sausages about to burst from their casings?"

"Or jeans that fit your legs but get stuck halfway up your butt," I added helpfully.

"It's a great thing," Kara interrupted, glaring at us, "that your fat asses fill up the spaces in your jeans. It's a great thing a dress doesn't droop down your chest because you have no tits to hold it up. It's a great thing—"

Beth cut off Kara's speech, continuing enthusiastically as if Kara hadn't spoken. "Or jeans that fit your fat thighs and huge butt perfectly, but hang really loose on the waist."

"Absolutely," I agreed.

"Screw it!" Kara burst out. "You know what? We're all beautiful, badass bitches. Huge tits or no tits, huge ass or flat ass, we rule. We should be proud and loud about our bodies. They're works of art."

"Amen," I agreed.

"Damn right. And if a dumb geek can't see that, that's his loss," Beth added.

"Amen again," I said.

"No matter how sweet or thoughtful he is. And how klutzy

and cute and adorable he is whenever he spills his coffee. Or buttons his shirt wrong or… I'm totally not describing Theo. There are so many guys out there who are like that."

"Sure, Betty," Kara winked.

"Don't call me Betty. Theo calls me Betty Boop." She groaned, rolling her eyes. "Please, make me stop. Make my mouth stop."

"Just keep stuffing it with food," I suggested.

Kara reached for the pitcher of rum and Coke, but when she found it empty, she slumped back in her seat, deflated. "I'm too lazy to make more." She turned to me, scrunching her face pitifully.

I sighed. "I'll make more. Be right back."

Kara smiled at me goofily. "I love you."

"Ver, can you bring some cookies, please? Please? Please? And more chips too," Beth drawled, her eyes half-closed. She was clearly drunk.

"Hey, sugar," Kara teased. "Put on a movie."

"Why do I have to get up? I'm comfortable. You're the one who owns the apartment. I'm a visitor. You should serve me and—"

Shaking my head, I left them to argue. Five minutes later, I could hear the sounds of a movie playing from the living room. Kara drunkenly cheered, "Woop! Woop! Magic Mike, baby. Give Mama some love!"

Laughing, I finished making the rum and Coke. Pitcher in one hand, three bags of chips in the other, and a bag of cookies in the crook of my arm, I proceeded to the living room.

"I'm not getting up again after this…" I trailed off when my phone vibrated on the coffee table. Setting everything on the coffee table, I picked up my phone. It was a text from Caleb.

"Problem?" Kara asked, lifting her head from the couch to look at me.

I frowned. "Caleb says he forgot that he'd set up an appointment with the real estate agent tonight." I checked the time. "And by tonight, I mean right now."

"I thought he said the house hunting wasn't till Friday. And what time is it?" Kara asked.

"That's what he told me this morning," I said. "And it's half past six now. I'm going to call him."

Kara rolled her eyes and turned back to the movie. I glanced at Beth as I dialed Caleb's number. She was already snoring.

"He's not answering. I think he's there already. Probably talking to the agent."

"Well, go. I bet you it's a surprise something. Maybe this house has huge-ass counter space." Kara cackled. "Is he picking you up?"

"He said he's sending a taxi to pick me up—right now," I answered as I texted him Kara's street address to send to the driver.

Kara looked over her shoulder at me, winking. "I think Lockhart has something up his sleeve again."

The taxi dropped me off at the address Caleb had texted. I looked up at the house, admiring it. It was Tudor style with big windows and a wraparound balcony on the second floor. Welcoming warm lights flooded the house inside.

I stood outside for a few moments, smiling. I could see us

living here. Raising a family. Caleb talked about getting a dog. Maybe we'd have a couple of them running in the yard.

I could picture Caleb and me having breakfast on the balcony together, or sitting on the front porch at night talking about our day. An image of a little boy with copper-brown hair and green eyes flitted through my mind, and I felt something squeeze my heart.

"Daydreaming," I muttered to myself, my lips splitting into a goofy smile. I realized I must have drank more of Kar's rum and Coke than I thought.

The porch light flicked on as I stepped up to the front door and rang the doorbell. There was no answer. I looked at the house number again. It was the right address. Maybe they were somewhere in the house where they couldn't hear the doorbell.

I pulled out my phone and dialed Caleb's number. No answer again. I placed my hand on the doorknob and turned. It opened easily.

If Caleb had accidentally given me the wrong address and I was arrested for trespassing, I'd kick his butt to Timbuktu.

For a moment, I hesitated in the doorway. And then I heard something inside the house. Letting out a sigh, I stepped inside.

"Hello?" I called out, my voice echoing.

The house was beautiful inside. There was no furniture, providing an uninterrupted view of the large, open space where I could appreciate the wide windows and modern light fixtures.

"Caleb?" I called out again. Again, there was no answer. Something didn't feel right. Uneasiness suddenly flooded me, some instinct telling me to leave. Before I could even turn around, I felt a presence behind me.

The sound of a gun being cocked froze my blood.

"Turn around," the familiar voice said.

I held my breath, slowly turning around. Beatrice-Rose stood a few feet from me, a smug grin on her bloodred lips.

"Hello, Veronica." She pointed the gun at my head, then lowered it to my heart. "Did you miss me?"

CHAPTER
thirty-four

Caleb

DRIVING AROUND THE AREA CLOSE TO WHERE YOUR FIANCÉE WAS spending her day with her friends wasn't a sign of an obsessed stalker.

Definitely not.

I had already booked a showing with my agent on Friday, but it wouldn't hurt to look at houses where it felt more familiar to Red.

The neighborhood was pretty good, quiet. Well-kept lawns, couples walking their dogs, families having barbecues in their front yard. When a small, pretty girl riding a pink Barbie bike waved at me, I shot her a grin and waved back.

Someday Red and I would have a daughter.

The grin on my face widened when I spotted a *For Sale* sign outside a great stone house. I parked in front of it, climbed out of my car, and just stared. It had those fancy slopes and curves on the roof, two thick chimneys jutting up, and casings on the windows to deter thieves. Good condition, wraparound balcony on the second floor, amazing shade from the trees—

"Cal?"

My grin disappeared as I turned and spotted Beatrice-Rose standing by her car, which she had parked behind mine. She was wearing a tight red dress and red lipstick that made her look older. Or maybe it was the dark circles under her eyes.

"I was in the neighborhood when I thought I saw your car. I'm doing a photo shoot today with a client." She tucked her hair behind her ear, looking unsure.

I should have stayed home today.

She smiled, gesturing at the house. "Your mom told me you're looking to buy a house. Is this the one you want?"

When I didn't answer, she took a step forward, but the look I shot her made her pause.

"Cal, can't we be friends again?"

I opened my car door. "I don't think so."

"Wait!"

"What do you want, Beatrice-Rose?" I said coldly.

"Have coffee with me, Cal. I have some things to say. To apologize for. Please." Her eyes were soft and pleading as they looked at me. "For old times' sake?"

I hesitated, then realized there were things I had to say to her too. And what better time than now? I told her to meet me at the coffee shop down the street.

When I stepped inside, Beatrice-Rose was already seated in one of the booths, watching me as I took the seat across from her.

"I already ordered your favorite. Orange juice and burger and fries," she started, twisting her hands on the table.

"Thanks, but you shouldn't have. This shouldn't take long."

Her face crumpled, her hand closing around the pendant on her neck. Guilt wormed its way into me, but the memory of Red upset last night crushed it.

"Let me get to the point, Beatrice-Rose. I want you to stop."

She blinked slowly. "Stop?"

"Don't insult both of us by pretending you don't know what I'm talking about. I know you. Or I thought I did."

"Of course you know me, Cal! We grew up together. You know everything about me, like I know everything about you. I know Veronica told you so many lies about me. But, Cal, I would never do anything to hurt you. Don't believe—"

"Stop."

"—anything she says."

"Stop," I repeated, hearing the coldness in my voice. "If I hear you say another lie about her, I'll leave now."

"But, Cal—"

I narrowed my eyes at her, and she stopped midsentence. "I want you to leave Veronica alone. I want you to leave *me* alone. Do you think I don't know about the drugs you planted in her purse last night? Did you plant the drugs in my car too?"

"No! Caleb! Please believe me. I didn't! *I didn't!*"

"I don't believe anything you say anymore. I'm telling you now, if you don't stop harassing Veronica and me, I'm going to file a restraining order against you. You've done enough."

Tears started to pour down her face.

"But I need you," she said quietly, brokenly.

I wasn't sure if her tears were real or fake, but the sight of her sitting across from me, her thin shoulders curved forward and her hands covering her face as she cried, made me pity her.

"I need you, Cal."

"I need her," I said simply.

Her hands fell limply to her lap as she looked up at me.

"I need her," I repeated more firmly.

"You don't even know how much I love you. You have no idea, do you?" she asked.

"If you really love me, you'll want me to be happy. And nothing makes me happier than being with Red. Nothing."

She drew in a sharp breath.

"I know you're sick. Ben told me about Paris."

Before I could say anything more, my phone rang. I looked at the screen and cursed. "Excuse me. I'll be right back," I told her, walking outside to take the call from Clooney, the private investigator I hired. "Hello?"

"Caleb, we got him."

"They've arrested Justin?"

"You bet. Bastard's been hiding at his uncle's place in Devil's Lake," he replied.

"The small town south of here?"

"Yep. Apparently, the uncle's old as dirt and never leaves his house. He had no idea what his little nephew had been up to. That's why he hasn't reported Justin."

"How did they find him?"

He scoffed. "Idiot got roaring drunk and vandalized a

resident's property. He's in a holding cell. I'm here now, and if you want to talk to him, I can arrange something with the constable. I go way back with the guy."

"Yeah, I want to talk to him. Be right there."

"Just hurry up before he starts squealing for a lawyer."

Beatrice-Rose was just taking a seat as I went inside. The food she'd ordered was on the table. I stood in front of her, noticing that she looked more composed.

"I'm sorry, but I have to go. Don't worry about this. I'll pay for it," I said, holding my phone tighter in my hand as she shook her head, her eyes filling with tears again.

"Caleb, please. At least stay to finish your meal. I promise I won't bother you anymore after this."

"Hi, guys! How's the food so far?" The server appeared, looking confused about why the food was sitting on the table untouched.

"I'd like to pay for this now, please," I told her.

"Of course. I'll be right back with the swipe machine."

I nodded and sat back in my seat.

"Ben is right. He saw me in Paris. I do need help, Cal. After the last time I saw you, at the parking lot in school, I-I fell apart. I had a nervous breakdown." She paused, watching me.

Was she trying to send me on a guilt trip?

"My mom sent me to Paris. She doesn't want anyone finding out that her only daughter has mental issues. All this time, whenever I go to Paris, I've been...staying at a clinic there. I tried to call you, but you never answered." She reached for her glass of water and sipped. Her hands shook. "My therapist said that I need to solve my issues by talking to the people I've

wronged, to ask for their forgiveness. But he said I'm in denial.
I know that. My head is just too clouded, Cal. I can't...function
when Dad...when Dad is dying. I don't have anyone else. You
know that. I only have you and Benjamin."

The server returned with the pocket-sized credit-card
machine. "I can come back later if you guys need more time."

"No," I replied. "I'll pay now please."

Placing my phone on the table, I pulled out my card and handed
it to her. She ran my card and gave me the machine to put in my
code, but it only beeped. She ran it again, and it beeped again.

"I'm sorry. We were having issues with the machine this
morning. Is it all right if I meet you at the front? I'll take your
payment there."

I nodded and followed her. When I finished paying, I was
surprised to see Beatrice-Rose behind me.

"I understand you don't want to be with me right now, Cal.
She's your rabbit," she murmured quietly. A chill raced up my
spine at the look in her eyes. "She's your rabbit, just like Atlas
was mine."

"What are you talking about?"

She smiled. "Nothing. Just memories. I'll see you soon, Cal."

It wasn't until I was on my way to the station in Devil's Lake
that I realized something about Beatrice-Rose's smile, something
about her voice, disturbed me. But once I saw Clooney at the
station, the thought left my mind.

He was waiting for me outside, having a smoke with an
older officer with a very distinguishable bushy beard and kind,
brown eyes.

"We're holding Justin Dumont in a cell at the back," Constable Penner informed me after he introduced himself. "Kid's looking for trouble. Small town like this, you're bound to know everybody's business. Makes my job easier, if you ask me." He took a long drag of his cigarette before putting it out and throwing it in the trash. "Follow me."

Clooney and I followed Constable Penner inside the small building. "Now I heard this fellow's been staying at his uncle's for a while. I just got back from a vacation in the Philippines with my wife when I got a phone call from Jim. He's the owner of the White Beaver Farm you passed on your way here," the constable explained.

I nodded.

"Anyway, Jim calls me screaming bloody murder. He was going to blow this kid's brains out if I didn't arrest him right that minute. He would have gone and done it if I didn't get there on time. Wake up, son."

Justin was sitting on the floor, his back against the wall and his chin on his chest as he slept like the dead. His blond hair was greasy, his clothes filthy. The sight of him made me more disgusted than angry.

"Son, wake up!"

Justin woke with a start, his limbs twitching as he struggled to open his eyes. "What do you want?" he spat out. When his eyes met mine, they cleared from sleep and filled with hate. "The fuck you doing here, asshole?"

"You have guts, calling me an asshole after you planted those drugs in my car."

Justin got unsteadily to his feet, his dirty hands grabbing the bars of his cell as he pushed his face close to me. "Don't know what the fuck you're talking about."

"I want you to clean up your language now, boy," Constable Penner interrupted. "No one curses in my station."

"I'll say whatever the fuck I want, old man. This bumfucking town is good for nothing. Was just passing through."

"You don't want to insult my town. You're being charged with trespassing, destruction of property, breaking and entering, vandalism, and disturbing the peace. What's wrong with you? Pissing your life away for nothing. Do you know how much time you'll be doing for this, son?"

"I'm not your fucking son."

"And thank the Lord Jesus for that."

"I didn't *do* anything."

"Listen here, punk," Clooney barged in. "We have footage of you sneaking inside Mr. Lockhart's building, down to the basement parking. Sound familiar?"

"I don't know dick about nothing."

"Tell me, where'd you get the drugs?"

At Justin's blank stare, Clooney shook his head mockingly. "Don't make this hard for yourself. They'll put you away for twenty years if you don't cooperate."

Fear lit up Justin's eyes. "You're lying."

"I'm sure they can make it twenty-five. What ya think, Constable Penner?"

Constable Penner stroked his beard. "Easily, I'd say."

"Possession of drugs, theft...and what's this?" Clooney gripped Justin's wrist, whistled softly. "A Piaget watch."

Rage boiled in my blood.

In a lightning-fast movement, Clooney took the watch off and inspected it. "Lookee here. I see an engraving on the back: *To my grandson, Caleb*. Mr. Dumont, this is possession of stolen property. This is worth over five grand, eh? That means longer jail time, for sure. Does this look familiar to you, Mr. Lockhart?" He handed the watch to me.

I looked at Justin. "This is my watch. My grandpa gave it to me before he passed away, you motherfucker."

"I got it from a pawnshop!" Justin backed away, but the holding cell was no bigger than a five-dollar bill. He bumped against the wall behind him. "I didn't steal it from you!"

"How did you get into my apartment?" I demanded. "You better tell me everything. You know the connections my family has, you bastard. I'll put you away for life."

He shook his head, swallowing nervously. "Sh-she gave me the code. Beatrice-Rose. It was her. She paid me to watch your girlfriend."

"*Watch my girlfriend?*"

"I have Beatrice-Rose's text messages. I'll show you everything. It's evidence. I have evidence! It's not my fault!"

"Start talking," I said quietly. The urge to smash his face was getting stronger every second.

"She wanted me to follow your girlfriend while you were spending the night at her place. I told her I saw your girlfriend buying a present, and she told me to steal it."

A present. Red had told me she bought me a present. A key chain, Kara had said.

I realized he was talking about the night when Beatrice-Rose visited my flat while Red was there. The awful night that had started everything—when I took Beatrice-Rose home, thinking she was having a panic attack, and left Red alone in my flat.

"But I didn't steal it. Beatrice-Rose went back for it. She stole it! Said she'd pay me if I scared your girlfriend a little bit."

"Scare her?" I reached through the bars and grabbed his arm, pulling hard. He let out a howl of pain as I slammed him against the bars. "Touch her again, and I'll cut both your arms off," I whispered in his ear, softly enough that only he could hear me.

"He's threatening me! Did you hear that? He said he's going to cut my arms off! He said he's going to cut my arms off! Do something!"

"Didn't hear nothing, son. Calm down now." Constable Penner placed a heavy hand on my shoulder. "Let him go."

"What the fuck did you do to my girl?"

"I'm not telling you anything more! Get him away from me!"

"Son, calm down now," Constable Penner said to me. "Let him go. Don't make me arrest you too."

Before I let Justin go, I slammed him against the bars again.

Constable Penner cleared his throat until Justin looked at him. "I'll make sure you won't rot in prison if you tell us everything," Penner said. "If you don't, I'll try my best to keep you there for thirty years. I'm not kidding. I take my job very seriously."

I didn't know if he was telling the truth about the prison sentence or if it was just a tactic to make this asshole talk, but I certainly wasn't going to stop him.

Justin moved to the corner of the cell, as far away from me as possible. "I didn't do anything. I just pushed her a little, and she fell on the ground. Didn't hurt her or anything."

My hands balled into fists. "You fucker."

Constable Penner nodded. "What happened after that?"

"Beatrice-Rose gave me the code. It's not that hard to sneak into the building. The guards in the building are dumb fucks."

"And the drugs in Mr. Lockhart's car?"

Justin looked down at the floor. "I need some water. I'm thirsty."

"You can drink your spit until you've told us everything we need to know," Clooney said.

"You fucking owe me," Justin yelled as he glared hatefully at me. "You had me suspended from that fucking school, booted off the team, took away my friends. I had to do something to get back at you, didn't I? You spoiled, rich fucker."

"Did Beatrice-Rose ask you to plant the drugs in Mr. Lockhart's car?" Clooney asked.

Justin let out a derisive laugh. "Beatrice-Rose wouldn't hurt a hair on Lockhart's head if it was up to her. She's as obsessed with him as his other bitches. It was my idea to plant drugs in this asshole's car. Damn great idea too. He went to jail, didn't he? Did you have a good time?" he sneered, then chuckled. "You think you're so clever, don't you, rich boy?"

"What about the drugs in Ms. Strafford's purse at the party last night?" Clooney continued.

Justin started hooting with laughter. "That was her idea. Beatrice-Rose is going to kill your bitch. You know that, right? She's fucking insane. Last time I talked to her, she said she'd wipe your girlfriend off the planet. Now let me out. I told you everything."

"You're going to prison. I'll make sure of it," I promised.

Worried and shaken, I wanted to hear Red's voice to reassure myself that she was okay. I'd stand guard outside Kara's apartment before I let anyone hurt her. But when I searched for my phone, it wasn't in my pocket. I ran out to look in my car. No phone. Where the hell was it?

I went back inside the station and asked if I could use their phone, but when I dialed Red's number, there was no answer.

She was fine. Her phone was just probably on silent because she was having a good time with the girls.

But I couldn't stop the warning ringing in my head. Heart knocking against my chest, I called information for Kara's phone number and dialed it.

"What do you mean, where is she?" Kara slurred, her voice rising. "She said you texted her. That you booked an appointment with the real estate agent tonight. She was on her way to meet you. What the hell is going on, Caleb?"

A chill ran up my spine. "Kar, what time did she leave?"

"More than an hour ago. What's going on?"

"I can't explain right now. I have to go."

"Wait! Caleb! What—"

Frantic, I found Clooney and the constable. I gave them the addresses of the three houses Red and I were due to see on Friday and told them to alert the authorities for a possible kidnapping. They might not take action since Red hadn't been missing for more than twenty-four hours, but I knew my mom had connections. I called her quickly. She didn't ask questions. She heard the urgency and fear in my voice, and that was enough for her to do what I asked.

I slid into my car and stepped on the gas. I was speeding, but I didn't care. I needed to get to her.

Hold on, Red. I'm coming.

Halfway to the first address, I stepped on my brakes. Something didn't feel right. Like I was missing something... The car behind me blasted his horn. How did Beatrice-Rose know about the addresses? My mom could have told her. I should have asked if she had.

But I remembered the disturbing look on Beatrice-Rose's face when I saw her outside the house I was looking at earlier today.

I might be wrong, but my gut was telling me to go to that house instead. If something happened to Red... I floored the gas, praying to God I wasn't too late.

CHAPTER
thirty-five

Veronica

Icy fear flooded my veins as I stared at the gun pointed at my heart.

"Not so feisty now, are you?" Beatrice-Rose sneered.

My eyes flicked up to her face. There was a look of wildness there, of insanity.

"Caleb. Oh God, where is he? I swear if you hurt him—"

"Hurt him?" Her upper lip curled as if I'd insulted her. "Hurt *my* Caleb?"

"Where is he?"

"Where is he?" she mimicked, her voice taunting and child-like as she moved closer to me.

I cried out in pain as she slammed the gun into my cheek.

"Hurts, doesn't it? Uh-uh-uh." I prepared to strike, but Beatrice-Rose stepped back, shaking her head and pointing the gun at my head again. "Make another move, and I'll blow your brains out. Red." Feral amusement lit up her eyes. "Red. Get it?" She laughed, and there was madness in it. "You'll earn your name once your brains and blood are splattered on the floor. Red. Red. Red!"

"You're crazy."

She froze, the amusement leaving her face. "What did you say?" Her voice held a warning to tread very carefully.

"Just let me go. Let me go, and I won't tell anyone about this."

Her eyes narrowed. "Do you think I'm stupid? You're never getting out of here."

A fresh wave of terror slid up my spine. Beatrice-Rose was going to kill me.

"Where's Caleb?"

"Don't say his name! You don't deserve him. Move!" she ordered, slamming a door open. The banging noise echoed throughout the empty house. "Down those stairs."

It was pitch-dark, the smell of turpentine and fresh paint hitting my nostrils. She moved behind me, shoving me forward. I grabbed the railing to keep from stumbling, scraping my knuckles against the rough stone walls.

"I said move!"

This was my chance. If she was close enough behind me, I could surprise her, grab her, and push her down the stairs.

But the lights came on suddenly, blinding me. Before I could recover, hands shoved at me mercilessly, and I fell down the stairs with a scream. I was fast enough to shield my head, but I grunted as pain shot up my left leg when I landed hard on it. I realized there were only a few stairs. If there had been more, I would have been hurt far worse.

I could hear her laughing.

In my back pocket, my phone vibrated. I had to find a way to get it without her seeing me. I had to answer it or dial 911, but she was already skipping down the stairs toward me, a triumphant smile on her face.

"Not so pretty now, are you? Maybe I should cut up that face he loves so much before I kill you. Then he wouldn't love it anymore, would he?"

Anger bubbled in my throat, pushing away the fear. I had been helpless before. I knew how fear could numb your limbs and mind so you were trapped, at the mercy of someone evil.

But not this time.

No, not this time. I wouldn't go without a fight. I'd kill her before she killed me.

I could feel my pocketknife biting into my back as I carefully sat up. If Beatrice-Rose came closer, I could jump up and stab her.

Still, I looked around for any additional weapon I could use to defend myself. It was obvious the owners were renovating. Some of the furniture was stacked on the other side of the room. There was drywall everywhere, exposed beams, and tables covered in plastic. There should be tools, maybe on those tables, but they were too far away.

"All my life, I've never been good enough," Beatrice-Rose snarled. "But with Caleb, it's different. He made me feel beautiful, important. I was *enough*. You should have stayed away. He's mine. He's mine, and you stole him from me. But I'll get him back. He always comes back."

"Not this time. Not if you kill me."

"We'll see about that. Daddy killed Atlas, didn't he? Daddy killed Atlas, and I forgave him. And Caleb will forgive me just as I forgave Daddy for killing my pet rabbit. You're Caleb's Atlas. You're his rabbit. Do you see?"

She stood there, aiming the gun at my head, scratching her arm absently until it started to bleed. Her eyes were almost pleading for me to understand.

Keep her talking. Keep her distracted.

When she started pacing back and forth, muttering under her breath, I carefully reached for my phone behind me, pressing the emergency button. When I heard the quiet voice of the operator, I sagged in relief and placed the phone on the floor, hiding it behind me. Now they would hear; now they would come.

"Put the gun down, Beatrice-Rose. Please."

Her eyes seemed cloudy, crazed. "Daddy killed Atlas with a hammer. Did you know that? Because Atlas ruined his shirt. He hurt Daddy's feelings. You hurt Caleb. You hurt him!"

"I understand," I said quickly. "I see what you're trying to say."

She nodded, smiling at me like a proud teacher whose student answered a difficult question.

"But *shh*." She placed her index finger on her lips. "You can't tell. You can't tell, okay?"

I nodded.

"I tried really hard to be a good girl. But Caleb can't see that anymore because you're in my way! You ruined everything, *Red*. You ruined Caleb."

"I'm sorry, Beatrice-Rose."

Slowly, I pulled the pocketknife from my back pocket, unfolded it.

"I was going to give you a few more days with Caleb before I got rid of you, but that moron Justin got himself arrested. I heard Caleb on the phone. He's on his way to the station to see that lowlife now. There's no more time to waste. I have to get rid of you. It was all Justin's fault, all his plan."

Relief flooded through me that Caleb was all right.

She stepped closer, swinging the gun beside her like a toy. My palms were damp with sweat as I gripped the pocketknife.

"Was it his idea to plant drugs in my purse? The drugs in Caleb's car?"

She paused. "I would never do anything to hurt Caleb! That was all Justin's doing! I nearly killed that moron for doing that to my Caleb. And if he hadn't run away, I would have. The drugs in your purse?" She laughed. "That was all me. Not very original, I'll admit, but I wanted Miranda to see! To think that they were your drugs in Caleb's car. Then she'd hate you."

So I was right.

"That cheap key chain you bought for him? I burned it." She snickered. "It's gone. You know how I got into Caleb's apartment, right? He gave me his code. He loves me so much that he gave me the code to his apartment. He trusts me. You, however, couldn't be trusted. You're a fake, a liar."

Her eyes narrowed in anger. "But how the fuck do you get

away with everything? Miranda's even on your side now! How dare she accuse me of lying to her about you? You're really good at hiding your true self. You fooled her. You fooled Caleb."

"You're right. Let me go. Just let me go. I'll talk to Caleb."

"*Liar*," she spat out. "You think I'd believe you? You think I'm stupid?"

"Of course not. You were the one behind the fire at the shop, right? You paid them. You paid those boys."

"Of course. Idiots. What a waste of space. Couldn't even kill you. Couldn't even stop you from coming to his party."

"You nearly killed Kar and her family!"

"I should have told them to burn that slut's house too. I'm going to kill your friend Kara after I kill you."

"*No!*"

With rage in my veins, I leaped up, leaning heavily on my uninjured leg, and slashed at her hand. I lost my balance and fell on the floor with a thud.

She screamed. The gun clattered on the floor and slid under the couch.

"You fucking bitch!" she shrieked, blood dripping from the deep cut.

The gun! I have to get the gun!

Heart racing madly, I crawled on the floor, but the shooting pain in my leg made me cry out in pain. She grinned at me, confident now that I was injured, and went for the gun.

Gritting my teeth, I rose and, with a desperate cry, hobbled and threw myself at her, stabbing her in the back with my knife. I felt the sickening slide of the metal as it buried in her flesh.

She bellowed in pain, spun around, and punched me in the jaw. I staggered back, dazed. My injured foot gave out, and I fell on the floor, hitting the back of my head. Nausea rose in my throat.

"I'm going to kill everyone you love, you fucking bitch!" she screamed.

Swallowing the bile, I got up. The world spun. I blinked away the blurriness and saw Beatrice-Rose crouched on the floor by the couch, the knife obscenely sticking out of her back Her right arm rested on the cushion of the couch to support her, her left hand groping blindly underneath for the gun.

With rage and adrenaline fueling me, I rushed at her, pulling the knife from her back. She shrieked in pain. Without hesitation, I stabbed her hand. I felt the tip of the knife as it wedged itself in the couch. She was trapped.

She howled like an animal, flailing around. When she dragged her free hand from under the couch, I saw the glint of metal. She turned her head and glowered at me with hate in her eyes— just as I grabbed her hand holding the gun.

The deafening sound of a gunshot rang in my ears.

Caleb

Slamming on the brakes, I jumped out of my car and ran toward the house where Beatrice-Rose had seen me earlier. And then I heard the gunshot.

The pungent taste of mind-numbing fear was ripe in my

mouth, shooting through my limbs like ice as I ran to the front door and kicked it open. I shouted for Red, sprinting through empty rooms.

She had to be okay. She had to.

"Red!" I yelled.

From the basement, someone screamed. I raced through the basement door and down the stairs. When I reached the bottom, I froze at the sight in front of me.

Jesus. *Jesus*. Blood soaked Red's hand where she held her arm protectively against her chest. Beatrice-Rose's face was ravaged with loathing as she held the gun to Red's head. Her other hand was stretched behind her, a knife pinning it to the couch.

"I'm going to kill you. Then I'm going to kill everyone you love. Every one of them, you fucking bitch!" Beatrice-Rose shouted at Red.

"Beatrice-Rose," I whispered softly. "Put the gun down."

Her eyes were wide with horror as she turned her head toward me, her arm swinging in my direction. The gun pointed at my chest.

"Caleb! It's not what you think. Veronica tried to kill me—"

Red let out a bloodcurdling scream as she leaped on top of Beatrice-Rose. The gun fell from Beatrice-Rose's hand, landing a few feet away from them. Red twisted Beatrice-Rose's arm and pulled, dislodging the knife, then shoved her to the floor.

Beatrice-Rose screamed in pain as she landed on her back, cradled her bleeding hand in front of her. Red straddled Beatrice-Rose, punching Beatrice-Rose's face with her good hand. Blood gushed from Beatrice-Rose's nose, but Red wasn't done. She kept on pounding, clawing, hitting viciously like a wild animal.

"Jesus. Red." I grabbed Red's waist and dragged her away kicking and screaming. Her arms and legs kept striking, even as Beatrice-Rose lay unconscious on the floor. I turned Red to face me as my arms wrapped around her.

"Red. It's okay. You can stop. It's over. It's over."

When she stopped struggling in my arms, I held her close, tucking her head under my chin.

"Caleb?"

"Right here, baby. I'm right here."

"She had the gun pointed at you... She was going to shoot you... She was... She..."

"Shh. Baby, it's all right. She didn't. She didn't."

Her arms wrapped around me, holding me tight. When I brushed her right arm, she winced. "You're shot!" I exclaimed.

"No. I'm...fine. Just nicked me in the arm."

When her legs gave out, I scooped her up. She rested her head on my shoulder as we heard the sound of sirens.

"You kicked her ass, Red."

"Damn right I did."

I held her tightly. "You scared the hell out of me. I thought..." My throat closed. When I felt her lips on my neck, I buried my face in her hair. "I love you so much."

"I love you, Caleb. I want to go home. Let's go home."

I pressed my forehead against hers and kissed her. "Always."

CHAPTER

Veronica

IT HAD BEEN TWO WEEKS SINCE THE INCIDENT WITH BEATRICE-
Rose, and almost every day after that, I woke up to the feel of
Caleb's fingertips gently caressing my cheek.

"Hi, Red," he said softly. "Good morning."

He was sitting on the edge of the bed, and when he leaned
closer, hovering over me, a lock of his hair fell over his eyes.
"Dreaming of me?"

He propped his hands on the bed, caging my body, and I could
feel the heat radiating from his skin. Green eyes peeked at me
from between the strands of his bronze hair.

I covered my mouth with my uninjured hand, smiling up at him.

He sat back, his lips stretching into an amused smile as he
absently brushed my hair from my eyes.

"I've kissed you so many times in the morning. I already
know what your morning breath smells like."

I groaned, turning my face away from him as he tried to pry my hand from my mouth.

"Caleb!" His name came out unintelligible.

"What was that?" he teased, then let out a deep laugh.

If there was ever a morning person, it was Caleb.

"You have to speak clearly so I can hear you," he added.

Playful Caleb was irresistible. His hands moved to my waist to tickle me, but not before he accidentally brushed my arm. I winced.

He pulled away quickly, his eyes widening in concern. "I'm sorry, Red. Did I hurt you?"

I shook my head, reaching for his hand to pull him back to me.

Caleb had been more attentive than usual after the incident. He kissed my hair, his lips skimming ever so gently down my arm where the bullet had grazed it. Instead of sitting beside me on the bed, he moved to the floor, looking at me with worry.

"I'm just going to sit over here so I don't hurt you again," he said apologetically.

"I'm fine, Caleb. Really."

My sleep-addled mind cleared, and I realized where we were as I took in the unfamiliar room.

He leaned against the dresser behind him, bending his leg and resting his arm on his knee. His green eyes continued to study me. As usual, he had picked up on the change in my mood.

"You didn't say much last night when we got here," he observed.

Here was his family cabin five hours outside town.

"Don't tell me you're missing my mom already. You spent a

week together in Saskatchewan, and now you're best friends?" he teased.

I gave him a big smile. We weren't best friends, but Caleb's mom had been quite apologetic for believing what Beatrice-Rose had told her, and she'd started warming up to me. Caleb had been very happy about that, and so was I.

"I do miss her," I said. "And we would have spent more time together if you weren't so clingy."

"Clingy!" He pouted. "Who's clingy?"

"You wanted to take me to all your meetings so you could keep an eye on me." I rolled my eyes. "Remember?"

I rose from the bed, walking carefully to the en suite bathroom to brush my teeth. Caleb followed me.

He couldn't possibly know what this town meant to me. How it had made me sick to my stomach as we drove past the welcome sign.

He lifted his shirt and scratched his stomach as he leaned against the doorjamb. "Is your leg still bothering you?"

I shook my head, but I didn't look at him. "Not anymore."

He sighed, pushing away from the doorjamb to kiss my shoulder. "I already made pancakes."

He knew me well enough to understand that I needed to be alone to gather my thoughts. He also knew that whatever was bothering me, I would tell him when I was ready. Before Caleb, I was much, much different. I wouldn't have thought of sharing my problems with anyone else.

His lips lingered on my skin as he looked up and met my eyes in the mirror. "I'll meet you in the kitchen, Red."

I smiled at him. "Okay."

Caleb was just placing a plate of eggs and bacon beside a tall stack of pancakes by the time I entered the kitchen. His smile was huge as he stretched his arms out in a grand gesture, showing off the food he had prepared.

"A breakfast for my queen. Should you reward this loyal servant with a kiss?"

I let out a small laugh, kissing him on the cheek.

"Wait. That's it?" He tapped his lips.

I kissed him on the lips.

He shook his head. "But you missed a spot."

Laughing, I playfully pushed him away.

Sitting on one of the stools at the island, I looked around the kitchen. Like the rest of the cabin, it was spacious and had a charming, homey feel to it. Natural light came in through the wide glass windows. Caleb had opened a few to let in the morning breeze, which blew the white curtains and brought in the smell of flowers and grass.

"This looks good, Caleb. Thank you for making breakfast."

He poured tea in the cup he'd placed in front of me. "I want to make breakfast for you every day. Want some eggs?"

My heart melted. I could only nod.

"Pancakes?" He gestured.

I nodded again.

"I made one in a perfect round shape. No, there are two," he said excitedly, like a little boy. "Here, you can have them."

My throat tightened. "I love you," I whispered.

"Red." He kissed my forehead. "I love you."

We ate breakfast together, and he entertained me with ridiculous stories that had happened at his work. I was glad he seemed to really enjoy working.

"Is there a bug on your plate?" Caleb asked.

I startled, realizing I had been drifting in my thoughts. I looked up to discover him watching me, his green eyes patient.

"Caleb, would you like to take a walk with me?"

"Yes," he answered automatically, but then he paused, blinking at me. "Am I in trouble?"

Even with the dark thoughts now clouding my mind, he could still make me laugh. "I don't know. Why don't you tell me what you've done to put you in trouble?"

"Uh-uh." He shook his head, grinning at me adorably. His dimples winked. "I'm not playing this game with you." Then his eyes widened. "Wait." He paused. "Are *you* in trouble?"

I laughed, and it sounded strained even to my ears. Trouble. There was trouble, all right.

"Let's go, Caleb."

"Sure. Let me just get my keys so I can lock up."

"No need," I said offhandedly. "People don't lock their doors around here."

He looked at me curiously, giving me an uncertain smile, but he didn't comment.

Outside, the sky was a clear cerulean blue. It was pleasantly warm, and dew sparkled like diamonds on the trees and grass. There were no paved roads here, just a trail and the forest surrounding us. Birds and crickets sang.

Caleb walked beside me, uncharacteristically silent. His

head was lowered, his thumb and index finger rubbing his bottom lip.

I reached for his hand and laced his fingers with mine. He turned his head to smile at me, his eyes clearing from the thoughts in his mind.

"Where are you taking me?" he asked, angling his head as he tried to read my expression.

"Nowhere special. Just walk with me."

"Anywhere," he said, squeezing my hand. "What..." He paused, and I felt the muscles in his arms tense. "You never told me what happened when you visited...her at the facility."

He'd never asked me about Beatrice-Rose since the incident because he knew I wasn't ready to talk about it. But since I visited her yesterday, I was ready to talk about her.

"I only saw her briefly."

"Why did you even visit her at all?" He sounded confused and frustrated.

I had asked Caleb to visit her with me, but he had refused. He said he wasn't ready yet.

"Ben told me what Beatrice-Rose's dad did to her pet rabbit and how her mom abused her emotionally. Maybe that was what motivated me to visit her at the clinic," I explained. I needed Caleb to understand because I didn't want anger to control him. He was too soft-hearted to let anger fester inside him.

"I felt compassion for what she had gone through with her parents because, like her, I know what it's like to be abused by a parent. God only knows, I might have turned out the same way if my mom hadn't loved me and protected me from an abusive dad. And maybe, just maybe, Beatrice-Rose was seeking forgiveness for what she had done. If not, I just wanted to send the message that if she ever wanted forgiveness, my door wasn't closed to her. That I understand."

"Is that what you told her?"

I nodded, remembering that brief moment of connection and understanding between us when I told Beatrice-Rose this during my visit. "She asked for you," I said.

"I don't know if I can forgive her. If she... If you..." He took a deep breath. "I couldn't bear it if something much, much worse happened to you. If..."

I rubbed his arm. "It's okay, Caleb. I'm safe now."

"If it were up to me, I'd have sent her to prison for what she did to you."

"She's sick, Caleb. She needs help. The clinic is a form of prison too."

He lowered his head so I wouldn't see his eyes, as if he was ashamed by what he had just said. "I know. I think I'm still angry. Once I realized that Beatrice-Rose had you," he continued, his voice deepening, "I don't even remember how I got there. Everything was a blur. When I saw that gun pointed at you, when I saw you bleeding..." He rubbed both his hands over his face.

"Caleb—"

He stopped suddenly and pulled me to him as if he was afraid to let me go. "I will never let anything or anyone hurt you ever again. I can't lose you, Red. I can't bear it. I won't."

I closed my eyes, burying my face in his neck and wrapping

my arms around his torso. My heart constricted from the pain I heard in his voice.

"I won't go anywhere, Caleb," I whispered.

He seemed to calm down, and we continued our walk. I thought we were just walking with no destination in mind, but I realized that my feet were leading me to a particular place.

My heart started to pound when I saw a familiar bend in the road. Somehow, it looked more ominous than I'd remembered. A giant black rock jutted out of the ground onto the side of the road. It used to hold a sign, but the sign was gone now.

My palms began to sweat, and I pulled away from Caleb's grasp, but he held on firmly.

"I'm here, Red. Right here," he promised.

I smiled back at him, nodded, and continued to walk until we stopped in front of what was once my home with my parents. I recoiled at the sight of it, at the ugliness of the decaying house. My mom's garden, always immaculate, was now a home for weeds and garbage. Most of the windows were broken, holes perforated the walls, and the roof was completely gone. Cold now, I wrapped my arms around my torso, my steps faltering.

"Red?"

I swallowed, but my mouth had dried up. My legs felt leaden, every step heavy, but I continued to walk toward the house.

"Stop," Caleb said, alarmed. "What is it?"

I closed my eyes again. Maybe I was dreaming. Maybe I wasn't actually standing in front of my childhood nightmare. For a moment, I let myself drown in the ugly memories.

"Come back to me, baby."

When I opened my eyes again, it was Caleb's face I saw in front of me. His green eyes showed kindness and honesty and, most of all, love.

"Where'd you go?" he asked, cupping my face in his hands so he could look into my eyes. All I wanted was to hide.

"Just…memories."

"Do you want to tell me?"

"They're not good ones."

"I'm okay with that."

I pulled away from him and faced the house again, as if I could will it to disappear.

"I remember…" I looked up, blinking away the tears that threatened to spill. "I remember the feeling of my mom's fingertips when she wiped my tears. The way her voice broke when she told me not to cry. But I couldn't stop crying.

"He had already left us by then. We were forced to move out of our house because she couldn't pay the mortgage. She thought I was crying because we were leaving our house in the country and moving to the city. But it wasn't that.

"I was crying because I felt relieved. I was happy that he wouldn't be able to find us again. That he wouldn't be able to *hurt* us anymore."

"Your dad," Caleb whispered.

"Yes. She had a friend in the city, and we stayed there for a bit until my mom found a job. But she was still waiting for him. Still hoping he'd come back."

"Did he?"

"Yes, but I was in school when he did. I never saw him again.

He found out we were staying at my mom's friend's house, and he broke in. Stole what he could. My mom's friend kicked us out after that.

"After everything my dad had done, my mom stayed faithful to him. She withered away, pining for him. I never understood her." I took a deep breath. "Until I met you."

I faced Caleb. His eyes were intense, full of questions. "I never understood how loving someone can consume every-thing until I met you. You've shown me that, Caleb.

"But what I never understood was how she could still take him back after everything he'd done to her, to me, and I want you to know that I would never stay with someone like my dad."

"I'm not like him."

"I know." I smiled at him, touched his face. "God, I know. I've never met anyone like you, Caleb. Never."

He lowered his head so his cheek rested against mine. I closed my eyes and felt the warmth of his skin, smelled the soap he had used this morning to shower. And the unmistakably wonderful scent that belonged only to Caleb.

"I love you, Caleb."

"I love you more, my Red. I promise no one will hurt you ever again. And remember that you kicked the asses of those who tried to." He tucked a strand of my hair behind my ear, caressed the side of my cheek. When I opened my eyes, he was smiling at me. "My strong, brave girl. You can face anything, and this time, I'm with you. I'm always with you, baby."

I let out a deep breath, holding his hand as I faced the house again. "This was the house where I lived with them, Caleb. With my mom. And dad."

He fell silent. I wanted to look at him, but I felt embarrassed. Ashamed.

"It's ugly as sin," he said after a moment.

A surprising laugh bubbled out of my throat.

"You know what I think about this place?" he asked.

"Why don't you be honest and tell me how you really feel?"

He grinned at me, placing his hands in his front pockets as he started to walk away, whistling.

When he kept going, I frowned at his back. Was he going to just walk away? I guessed he'd shown me what he really thought about the house.

I rolled my eyes and was about to call out to him when he suddenly stopped. He looked down at the ground and bent to pick up something. When he turned around to face me, he was holding a huge rock half the size of a basketball.

"Watch me, Red," he said cheekily, dimples flashing.

He grabbed the rock with both hands, raising his arms up as if to throw a shot.

"And three points for Lockhart! Boom."

The sound of glass breaking felt like freedom as he flung the rock at the house.

I choked out something between a laugh and a cry.

"Phew! I'm still the MVP." His smile was proud as he bent to pick up another rock. "Here. Your turn, Red."

What the hell?

I snatched the rock from his hand, and taking aim, I heaved it as hard as I could. It smashed through a window, and the sound of glass breaking woke something inside me. Something dark and heavy and huge was stirring inside me, straining to let loose. Once I started, I didn't want to stop. The more I threw rocks at that dilapidated house, the lighter I felt. I searched for more rocks and kept throwing them at the house until I was breathing hard. When I finally threw the last one, I felt a form of release so sweet, so light that it brought me peace. It was like a heavy burden had been lifted from my chest.

"That's my girl."

I smiled up at him, dusting off my hands. "Thank you."

"It's just a house, Red. It can't hurt you. Your dad can't either."

I looked at him questioningly.

"I asked Clooney to look for your dad."

"What?"

"I didn't want him bothering you again."

"Caleb…"

"He's dead, Red. A few years ago. Your mom must have known. They had to notify next of kin. He was living on the streets, homeless. Breaking and entering, stealing, dealing and using drugs."

His brows drew together when I remained quiet. My throat had gone dry.

"I told you I won't let anyone hurt you anymore. I had to make sure that after the incident with Beatrice-Rose…" He took a deep breath. "If you're mad at me—"

The breath whooshed out of him as I threw my arms around his neck. I wanted to answer him, to thank him and pepper him with kisses, but if I spoke, the tears would come.

"You're not mad at me?" he asked after a moment.

I shook my head, my arms tightening around him. He couldn't possibly know how much this meant to me. I had been wondering about my dad for so long, afraid that he would come back and hurt me again. Afraid that he *wouldn't*, and that I'd never know what happened to him. Now I did.

"I will always keep you safe."

"Oh God, Caleb," I choked out. "I love you. I love you so much."

He stroked my hair gently, pulling back so he could hold my face in his hands. Leaning closer, he kissed my forehead. "That's what I love to hear from you every day, my Red."

"I'll say it every day."

"I'll make sure you say it." He grinned, kissing me on the lips. "Let's go back. Wanna watch a scary movie?"

I'd learned something new about Caleb. He loved scaring himself.

We walked back to the cabin and settled on the couch in front of the TV. Caleb picked *Evil Dead*, *The Descent*, and *Jeepers Creepers*.

He was adorably loud and hilarious, covering his eyes or staring wide-eyed at the screen during the scariest parts. Not even halfway through the first movie, he grabbed a blanket to cover our faces, his arm wrapped around my waist to glue me to his side.

Every time I screamed, it was because Caleb waited for the movie's silent, suspenseful parts, and once I was completely absorbed in the scene, he growled and poked my ribs to scare the hell out of me. It worked, but I did land a few playful slaps in retaliation.

By the time the first movie ended, his cheeks were flushed, his long and lean body plastered to mine. By the time the *third* movie ended, I jumped up from the couch and threatened to electrocute him in his sleep.

He laughed, scooped me out of the blanket, and dragged me into the kitchen. It seemed like he'd grabbed all the food from the fridge before he dragged me again, this time outside to the garden, where we ate on the blanket he had spread on the grass.

It was a beautiful day.

A very beautiful day with my Caleb.

"Red?" he said softly.

It was hot, with the sun hanging high in the sky. Caleb had removed his shirt to battle the heat, and he'd twisted my hair into some crazy semblance of a ponytail.

We lay side by side on the blanket, staring up at the clouds, but when I turned my head to look at him, he was staring at me. His green eyes looked incredible in the sunlight, his lips pinker than usual. He rolled to his side to face me, his gaze lingering on my mouth. I licked my bottom lip unconsciously.

"I feel married already," he whispered.

When his eyes lifted to mine, my breath caught in my throat. He was so beautiful.

"Should we just elope?" he asked.

"Kar would kill us," I said breathlessly. "She's planning everything."

My mind wandered as I watched his teeth catch his bottom lip.

"Yeah," he agreed. He was smiling. And it was a knowing smile. The bad boy knew what he was doing to me.

"What else do married couples do?" he continued. His voice low now, deeper. His fingertips leisurely skimmed along my arm.

I swallowed. "We should wash these dishes."

His pink tongue peeked out to quickly lick his bottom lip. "No. Something fun."

I squealed as he grabbed my waist and pulled me on top of him.

"Something really, really fun, Red."

"Caleb!" I placed my palms on either side of his body and pulled myself up. "It's…it's daylight!"

"Yeah. I noticed." His green eyes danced with a naughty glint. "Know what else I noticed?"

His chest was warm, his scent intoxicating. His touch drove me insane as his palm stroked the exposed skin on my back, then moved down to my ass and squeezed before his fingertips slowly, slowly made circles along my inner thigh.

"Caleb…"

"I noticed," he began, not stopping his pleasurable touch, "that even in my dreams, I know what you feel like. How you smell, how your eyes light up when you see me. I know you."

His hands gripped my waist, moving me so that I was the one under him now.

"I know that face so well. More than my own. Your moods, what you like and don't like. I'm drawn to you, and I can't stop myself. I don't *want* to. I want to keep knowing everything about you for the rest of my life, Red."

"Oh, Caleb."

"Now *I* want to show you something. Take a walk with me?"

Choked up, I could only nod. He rose and then helped me up.

Caleb was silent as he held my hand while we walked. I didn't know where he was taking me, but I knew I would go anywhere with him.

The sound of water met my ears even before we reached the lake. I knew this place, this forest. I played here all the time when I was a kid and wanted to escape.

How did Caleb know about this place? It was hidden, a secret oasis that only the locals knew about.

I looked at him curiously. Releasing my hand, he walked ahead of me. A wooden bridge stood a few feet above the lake, and Caleb took his time crossing it. When he reached the middle, he stopped. A slow, tender smile appeared on his face as he looked down at a certain spot.

I had no clue why my heart started to pound, except that it all looked so familiar.

He crouched, removing his shoes and folding his long, lean body so he sat on the edge of the bridge, dangling his legs down. His feet disappeared into the water. He looked into the distance and seemed to be lost in a memory.

Butterflies fluttered in my stomach as I sat beside him. And then he turned to look at me. The sun was shining so brightly behind him that for a moment, I couldn't see his face, but I knew.

"Do you remember, Red?"

I did.

I knew him.

Oh God.

"Hey, Batgirl."

A choked sob escaped me, and I covered my mouth with my hands.

"Even when we were kids, I was drawn to you," he whispered, pulling my hands from my mouth so he could kiss my palms.

"It was you," I murmured.

He nodded.

"The boy who gave me the peanut butter sandwich."

"I always had this feeling that I knew you somehow," he said. "But I didn't know why until the tree house. You were standing on the bridge just like you did when we were kids. And I knew. I just knew."

"You...you were my very first friend."

His smile was wide and happy. "And you're my first love."

I looked down into the water and spotted a big rock embedded in the bottom of the lake. Behind the rock were two fishes lazily swishing their tails, protected from the current. They made me think of the boy with the peanut butter sandwich.

"Red?"

My heart was beating wildly against my chest as I looked at him.

"I'd never been sure about anything in my life until you came into it. Thank you for giving me the best gift. The best gift I could ever receive in my entire life is your heart. I will take care of you, protect you, love you for the rest of my life. That's my vow to you, my Red."

Slowly, I pressed my lips to his and let him feel how much he meant to me.

"I thought I wasn't waiting for anyone. But I was. And it's you. It's you, Caleb."

I blinked, and the tears I was holding back fell down my cheeks. He smiled at me, wiping them with his fingers.

"I never thought I would find you, Caleb. Not in this life. But I did. And I want you to know that you are the best thing that ever happened to me. The best thing."

He took a deep breath, his shoulders relaxing as if a huge weight had been lifted off them. "I love you, Red."

He stood up, held his hand to me palm up. "Pancakes?"

As I stared at the face of my beloved, I knew without a doubt that I had found the one who was made for me. I smiled up at him and placed my hand in his.

"Pancakes."

THE END.

Acknowledgments

I was born and raised in the Philippines before we moved to Canada, and drama series are very popular there. I remember five days a week between 6:00 and 9:00 p.m., without fail, I would be in front of the TV with my parents, brother, and sister—sometimes even with my cousins and aunts—watching shows back to back.

I think watching all those shows inspired me to write. I've had these characters in my head for so long that it wasn't a struggle to write about them. Since I started writing, I've written different versions of all the characters in *Chasing Red*, and I realized all those stories were practice and led me to write this book.

To my Wattpad readers—there are so, so many of you to mention. Please know that I wouldn't be where I am without your positivity, your support, and your love. Thank you for the friendship, the endless encouragement, and the fangirling for Caleb and Red. There is no *Chasing Red* without you. I wake up grateful because of you.

Lianne, my twinks. Thank you for all the late-night phone calls and coffee dates as we brainstormed on the next chapter of Red and Caleb's story. We talked so much about them that they feel real to us. You are irreplaceable and I love you.

The amazing Wattpad team, especially Caitlin O'Hanlon—you

are my energy drink. I still remember that first email: it's legit! Ha-ha. Thank you for always taking care of me and replying to my crazy text messages. The sparkle in your eyes always makes me smile. Ashleigh Gardner—how many times you've clearly explained things to me so I can stop panicking. You are an amazing force of nature and I can't thank you enough for everything. Teach me the ways, master! Aron Levitz—I'm very grateful for your hard work and super cool glasses. Nazia Khan—I learned so much from you. I still have the notes you gave me and they will forever be pinned to my corkboard. And to Allen Lau and Ivan Yuen—thank you for creating Wattpad. You didn't give up on your dreams, and because of that, ours came true.

The Sourcebooks team, especially my editor, Cat Clyne. Because of you, *Chasing Red* is a better book. Thank you for your guidance and understanding my vision. You've taught me so much and I'm grateful! You are Wonder Woman. To Laura Costello—you're incredible. I'm so thankful for your valuable suggestions, and I'm glad you love Caleb's taste in scary movies! A very big thank-you to Heather Hall and Diane Dannenfeldt for all your hard work and feedback. Beth Sochacki—I still wear my pin, girl. Thank you so much for helping me promote *Chasing Red* on social media. Dawn Adams—you are a genius and I love the covers so much!

Tatay and Mama—you've worked so hard to raise us and all I want is to make you proud. I love you both so much.

My Adam. When I told you about my dreams and I know they sounded impossible—but you believed them because you believed in me. Thank you for the pancakes. You're my Caleb.

And to God. For making everything possible. For loving me despite all my faults. For never letting me forget what's important. For giving me all the people in my life. For being there always.

love,
Isabelle

About the Author

Isabelle Ronin is a Filipino Canadian writer based in Winnipeg, Manitoba. Her Wattpad story, *Chasing Red*, has garnered more than 150 million reads and was Wattpad's most-read story of 2016. As a result of the story's immense popularity online, several major publishers around the world have acquired the rights to *Chasing Red*.

When she's not writing, Isabelle can be found hanging out in bookstores, cafés, and, whenever possible, the beach. You can follow her and read her stories on Wattpad at wattpad.com/isabelleronin.

ALSO BY ISABELLE RONIN

Chasing Red